Peggy Eaton was bor
She is married and
worked as a librarian

BRIGHTON BELLE

Peggy Eaton

WARNER BOOKS

A *Warner* Book

First published in Great Britain in 1994 by Warner Books
Reprinted 1994, 1995, 1999

A CIP catalogue record for this book
is available from the British Library.

ISBN 0 7515 0690 7

Typeset by M Rules
Printed in England by Clays Ltd, St Ives plc

Warner Books
A Division of
Little, Brown and Company (UK)
Brettenham House
Lancaster Place
London WC2E 7EN

for
Ashley Daniel
and
Elizabeth

Acknowledgements

Books:
Tightrope by Anna Reynolds
Make Your Own Gloves by Gwen Emlyn Jones

Thanks to the Society of Authors for permission to quote from *Fairies* by Rose Fyleman

Also to Myra Turner (a theatrical landlady} and Joan Tate.

1

'Look at her skirt!'

'And her boots. I bet they're her brother's.'

'Poor thing! Perhaps she hasn't got a mother.'

Belle could hear the whispers going round the classroom and clenched her fists under the desk. She hated them! With their nice clothes and polished shoes. One day she'd have pretty things to wear and then they wouldn't be able to feel sorry for her. Anyway, she liked her boots.

Isabel Kelly, Belle for short, was small for her age. A fairy child, all skin and bones, with untidy ginger curls framing her pale face. Her nose was sprinkled with freckles and her mouth pouted delicately, showing pearly-white uneven teeth.

The hands of the clock in the tower passed twelve and the bell rang out to announce the end of morning school.

Belle ran on her skinny bare legs across the playground to wait at the gate for her brother Charlie. Normally they made their separate ways home to dinner, for Charlie, eleven, found his ten-year-old sister Isabel an unexciting companion. Belle openly adored him, and he found it unmanly to have a girl tagging behind. But this morning when they'd parted to go to their classrooms he'd said, 'Wait for me at dinner-time, Belle. I've got a penny for sweets, and there's liquorice strips in Gander's shop.'

'What about coupons?' Belle had enquired.

'Miss Gander promised me,' Charlie said importantly. 'She's kept some under the counter.'

'That's black-market!'

'Who cares. If you don't want any, don't come.'

He sounded as if he didn't care but he knew Belle would be waiting, as much to keep him company as because she wanted the sweet sticky strands of black liquorice he'd promised her. Afterwards Belle always said it was 'meant'. If she hadn't waited for Charlie that day she wouldn't have had a chance to say 'Goodbye'. At least, that was what Father Joe assured her.

She was sitting on the wall admiring her boots when she saw her brother approaching. His hands were deep in his pockets, and the regulation gas-mask trailing over one shoulder on its webbing strap. The only smart thing about him was his boots: new and shiny black, bought at the Co-op last Saturday and not yet broken in. He still hobbled painfully, aware of the hard leather rubbing against his blistered heels. Belle's boots in comparison were scuffed and worn, with broken laces knotted together, and the tongue flapping faster than a gossiping housewife's. Belle was proud of her boots, for she'd inherited them from her brother when he'd got his new ones, and wasn't a bit jealous that there hadn't been enough money to shoe them both. After all, in the Kelly household it was an unspoken law that Charlie, as the eldest and a boy, should always have the first call on the family finances.

They started off home together; not the most direct way along the Ditchling Road, but through a series of backstreets that meant crossing the iron girdered bridge under which the Lewes trains rumbled and steamed. Charlie paused to watch a snaking iron monster below, and rest his feet, while Belle clattered past on the loose slatted boards, happy just to be with him.

Miss Gander's shop was a dark hole behind the station, its dirty window cluttered with cigarette advertisements and sticky jars of stale sweets that nobody wanted. The proprietor, a rigid spinster in black, with an unsightly mole on her cheek from which several coarse hairs protruded, handed over the liquorice to the children just as the first wail of a siren sounded.

'You'd better be getting home,' she said, dropping the penny into the till and closing the drawer with a satisfying thump. 'Your mum will be worried about you.'

'Mum won't worry about me,' said Belle happily. She was busy inspecting the comics on the counter and wishing she could buy one, and not have to wait for someone to pass on their outdated copies. 'Mum never worries when I'm with Charlie.'

'Even so, I can hear planes overhead,' said Miss Gander, listening with her head on one side.

'They sound like ours,' said Charlie, opening the shop door so that the bell jingled. He looked up into the sky hopefully.

'How can you tell?' Belle was proud of his manly knowledge. But he wouldn't tell her, and just instructed her to 'come along home.'

They set off at a merry jog, the black sweets staining their mouths. But the boots slowed Charlie down and soon he was limping badly.

'You go on, Belle,' he said at last. 'I'll take me boots off and hang them round my neck. I'll soon catch up with you.'

'The planes sound awfully close.' Belle was looking up at

3

the sky and her face was white and frightened.

'They're ours I tell you. The engines sound different – I can tell.' He was resting on a garden wall where the iron railings had been sawn off in aid of the war effort. 'Get on with you, Belle, or Mam will tan us both.'

'I'd rather wait for you, Charlie.'

Flushed with the struggle with his boots Charlie turned an angry face at his sister. 'I'll catch up with you, and beat you without these blessed boots. Go on – Goodbye.'

Belle knew better than to argue when he was in that mood. She almost expected him to say, 'I'll tell Mam on you,' like he did when he caught her with her finger in the sugar bowl. She turned away obediently, and muttering 'Goodbye' started for home.

It was uphill and she was soon panting, and could feel the beads of perspiration trickling down her neck and into the collar of her blouse. The drone of the planes seemed nearer and louder, almost overhead, and she didn't care if they were 'theirs' or 'ours', they still frightened her. She reached the bottom of Duke's Road in safety, and didn't dare pause to look back in case there was no sign of Charlie. 'Please God,' she prayed silently, 'let him be right behind me and I'll never lie to Mam again, or laugh when Gran's teeth fall out.'

'Come on in Belle, and shelter.' It was Mrs Jeffreys of the corner shop, afraid of no man, English or German. She was standing in the doorway, arms akimbo, her hair tucked away untidily under her husband's old cloth cap.

'No thank you, Mrs Jeffreys,' Belle panted, arms still going like pistons, afraid that if she stopped she wouldn't be able to start again. 'I have to get home to me dinner before Mam gets worried.'

'Please yourself.' Mrs Jeffreys slammed the door shut with an offended shrug of her well-padded shoulders.

The road was quite empty. Everyone was indoors sheltering from the air-raid. Even the cats, who were usually unconcerned, sensed danger and stayed inside. Belle felt as if she was the only living creature abroad and prayed again for God to get her home safely – or else! She had talked this problem of her prayers over once with Father Joe, and the fat old priest had winked at her conspiratorially before warning her of 'doing deals' with God.

'I'm not doing deals, God,' she prayed defiantly. 'But if you let a bomb get me I'm never going to mass again.'

It was uphill all the way now, and the blood was drumming in her ears so that she couldn't hear anything else. For all she knew the planes had passed over and the all-clear sounded, but she wouldn't stop now until she was safe indoors.

Their battered blue door with its peeling paint stood open. Bess Kelly watched for her children: thin as a rake under the outsize folds of her print overall, and an extra frown of worry on her brow. Her daughter took the last few yards with the speed of a rocket and flung herself at her mother, hoping to be enfolded in the safety of maternal arms.

Bess was relieved at the sight of her daughter. But the frown on her forehead deepened and she grasped the child's arms with her sharp fingers, digging into the delicate flesh, and held her at arm's length. 'Where's Charlie?' she demanded.

'He's right behind, Mam. Let go – you're hurting.'

Mrs Kelly loosened her grip long enough to shade her eyes and peer down the road. 'I can't see him.'

'His boots hurt. He stopped to take them off.'

'You shouldn't have left him. Get along in then, under the stairs with your Granny.'

She pushed Belle down the dingy linoleum-floored

passage which smelt of cats and boiled cabbage – the smell she would always associate with home. From the dim yawning cavity under the stairs protruded two swollen feet clad in carpet slippers, and Belle was glad that Granny Kelly was already in residence. Once Belle had been first, and had surprised a frightened mouse who lived in a hole in a dark corner, and wasn't used to human beings invading his territory. She'd never been scared of mice until that day, but his pink eyes had looked evil in the dim light, and his long silky tail had made her shudder. No sensible mouse would venture out of his hole with Granny Kelly so near.

Now that she was safe Belle felt her fear subsiding. She even grabbed a thick slice of cold bacon pudding from the kitchen table before diving under the stairs to land softly on the cushiony bulk of Granny Kelly.

If Bess Kelly was too thin and busy to be maternal to her offspring, Bridget Kelly made up for it. Old and fat and jolly, with unreliable false teeth, and clothes smelling of camphor and peppermint, she hugged her ginger-haired granddaughter as if she hadn't seen her for years, just as there was a dull thud from somewhere close by that shook the foundations of the house and made the old woman and the little girl clutch each other tightly. Belle buried her face in her Granny's sleeve, and when the shuddering had stopped she peered up into her lined old face.

'What was that?' she whispered.

'It was that Hitler,' said Granny Kelly knowingly. 'He's everywhere with his bombs and things, goose-stepping all over England.'

'I'm scared.'

'Scared of a little man with a moustache? Shame on you, Isabel Kelly. Your brother's not scared, is he? He didn't run home like a frightened rabbit to hide with the women under the stairs.'

'Only because his boots hurt,' explained Belle patiently.

'WHAT HAVE YOU GOT THERE?'

Belle had forgotten the hunk of pudding she was still clutching. Knowing the old woman's fondness for anything soft and chewy she unravelled the savoury roll and carefully picked out the pink meat.

'Which will you have, Gran?' she asked. 'Pudding or bacon?'

'I'll have the pudding, Miss,' and Bridget Kelly helped herself to a cold wedge as if it were a delicious delicacy. 'You young 'uns need the meat to help you grow.'

'Then I'll save half for Charlie,' said Belle, generously dividing the small heap of pink pieces into two. 'I wonder if he's here yet.'

Another thud shook the house, shaking loose plaster from the walls, so that Belle and her Granny coughed on the brick-dust they were breathing in. When the air had cleared a little Granny Kelly said, 'That one was close.'

'I wish Charlie was here,' lamented Belle, dusting the film of plaster from her brother's pile of bacon pieces, and then stopped to listen to the moaning sound that rent the air.

'What's that, Gran?'

'The all-clear. It means Hitler's gone home and I can go back to me chair.' Granny Kelly pushed Belle aside, and heaving her quivering bulk on to all fours backed out of her hide-out into the passage. 'Now where is Bess? What we need is a good cup of tea.'

Bess Kelly's thin frame was still standing in the open doorway where her daughter had left her. She seemed oblivious to the noises of the air-raid that had gone on around her, leaving her apparently unharmed. Seeing her standing there, strong and unyielding, Belle quickly removed her shabby boots and pushed them out of sight. It was an unwritten law in the Kelly household that the children should go bare-foot indoors, apart from the winter when old socks or stockings were allowed. They only had one set of footwear each, so they had to guard them from unnecessary wear and tear and make them last as long as possible.

'Granny wants a cup of tea,' said Belle, approaching her mother hesitantly.

Bess looked down at her daughter but didn't seem to see her: her mind was far away. 'I must go and find Charlie,' she said, and unhooked her coat from the back of the door, pushing her arms down into the baggy sleeves and buttoning it anyhow. 'If your dad comes in before I'm back, tell him I won't be long.'

'Yes Mam,' said Belle in her most grown-up voice, and standing as tall as she was able. Mam was leaving her in charge and she knew this was an important responsibility.

'I want a cup of tea,' wailed Mrs Kelly, watching her daughter-in-law disappearing down the front steps. 'Where's Bess going?'

'To look for Charlie, Gran,' said Belle consolingly. She led the old woman to her chair in the corner of the kitchen. 'I'll make your tea.'

'Well make it good and black. I don't want any of that pale gnat's pee you gave me last time.'

Belle lit the gas under the kettle with a taper from a pot on the table and fetched the big brown teapot from the dresser. She measured two spoonfuls of tea into it, and then a third for luck, before pouring the boiling water from the corroded spout of the battered kettle. Two cups stood on their blue-and-white saucers next to two chipped enamel mugs: one for Belle and the other for Charlie. She filled Charlie's first, as a sort of omen; he would be home in time to drink it before it got cold. But then George Kelly arrived home, and at the sight of her dada she forgot the morning's troubles and clung to him, a child again.

'Hey, what's all this then?' George asked, ruffling the ginger curls. 'Where's your mam?'

Belle explained again about Charlie. While the words poured out her father filled the cups and carried one to his mother. 'Did you hear the bombs?' he asked. 'I was on my way back from the allotments, but I stood up in the bus station. They say Jerry's dropped one on the abattoir, and another just missed the school.'

'The house shook,' Gran said cheerfully. 'But we had bacon pud, didn't we Belle? Under the stairs. This is good tea,' and she smacked her lips and dribbled with appreciation.

'It is that,' agreed George, pouring himself a second cup. 'Make the most of that 'cos I've left my job.'

'Oh Dada, not again,' Belle breathed.

She followed his every movement with love. He was a quiet man dominated by a shrew of a wife; a rough diamond whose best asset was a useful pair of hands.

'I've been there over six weeks and nothing I do is right. I know the job as well as the next man so I don't need to be told what to do. You know I don't like working indoors. Don't look like that, Belle. We won't starve; there's plenty to do on the allotment and I might find more treasures washed up on the shore tomorrow. You can come scavenging with me if you get up early. We've never been short of fresh vegetables or fuel for the grate.'

'Bess won't be happy,' Gran mumbled. 'You're just like your father: money used to slip through his fingers when he had any, which was seldom; and he couldn't keep a job down either.'

Belle looked worried. There'd be trouble when Mam heard: the rent was overdue, and there were bills owing at

Jeffreys' corner shop. When things got to their worst, and Bess began to fear the workhouse he would take any job offered, cash in hand, pay off as many debts as possible and then disappear for fear his employers wanted him permanently. Bess and Belle were aware of his weaknesses, but where Bess became hard and disheartened because it was left to her to make ends meet, Belle just saw her dada, and loved him just the same.

'Look what I've got for you,' said George suddenly, and rummaging in his pockets he pulled out a brown paperbag. He tossed it to his daughter who caught it deftly.

'Biscuits!' Belle told her grandmother triumphantly, more excited than if it had been the world's best chocolates. 'Here Gran,' and she put one into the mottled outstretched hand. Gran Kelly dunked the biscuit expertly, but wasn't so efficient at manoeuvring it to her mouth, and a dribble of brown tea and crumb remained fastened to her chin.

The dingy kitchen began to take on a party atmosphere to stop them worrying about the absent members of the family. Old Mrs Kelly even started to sing an old music-hall song, that had something in the chorus about a bicycle made for two, and she waved her cup about in time to the tune. It was the old woman, whose chair was facing the open door, who alerted George and Belle by dropping the cup, her voice wavering away to silence in the middle of a line.

Belle was just rifling the bag for another biscuit and George was pouring himself a third cup of tea; they turned and looked along the passage towards the front door in the direction that Bridget Kelly was staring. The door was open as Bess had left it, but the street was blotted out by the group of people who were crushing through the opening. There was the fire-watcher and Mr Jeffreys from the shop, a couple of neighbours who usually didn't speak to the Kelly family, Henry Murtell who was in Charlie's class at school and lived next door with his aunt, and one or two complete strangers. But the figure in front, the one who led the strange procession, was the one who held their eyes. It was Bess Kelly, the scarf she'd absently tied over her head slipping sideways, and on her white face an expression they'd never seen before. It wasn't fear, or despair, or even grief, it was an emptiness that was more frightening to Belle and George than any of the other three, for in her arms she carried Charlie, like an offering.

Bess was a thin gaunt woman who probably didn't weigh much more than eight stone, and Charlie was a sturdy eleven-year-old. But like a wild animal Bess had found a superhuman strength to carry her son home.

'Leave him,' the fire-watcher had said when she'd followed her instinct and pushed her way through the crowd. 'There's nothing you can do for him.'

'Get out of my way – he's my son.'

'He's dead, Mrs Kelly,' Mr Jeffreys said gently, trying to guide her away, but she'd dropped to her knees beside the body stretched out on the pavement where the falling masonry had thrown him. But she'd ignored them all. Charlie had been coming home so that's where she would take him: back home with her where he belonged. His reddish hair, so like his sister's, was cradled against her bony chest, and his long legs with scarred knees and stockinged feet dangled lifelessly. One of the strangers was carrying the boots: the shiny new boots that had been the cause of his delay.

'We said we'd see to him,' Mr Jeffreys said, 'but she wouldn't let us near.'

'A doctor?' said George hopefully.

'Too late. They missed the school and the railway, thank God, but they demolished a row of houses nearby. Your

Charlie was sheltering by the wall, and it fell on him when the bomb hit the house.'

Bess was still standing in the doorway and George went to her, his hands held out to relieve her of her burden. 'I'll take him,' he said gently. 'We'll lay him out on the table, and I'll send Belle for Father Joe.'

'No!' Bess's voice was sharp with pain. 'I'll put him in his bed. That's where he belongs.' Ignoring the outstretched arms she plodded up the stairs to the slip-room that Charlie and Belle had shared all their short lives and lay her son's body on the iron bed. No one dared to follow her; there was a certain dignity about the woman who had loved her son more than her husband or her little daughter; almost more than life itself.

'Is there anything we can do George?' someone asked.

'No. We'll be all right. Just leave us.'

They went, slowly and sadly, and someone left the black boots standing side by side on the door-mat. The last to leave was Henry Murtell. The lanky bespectacled boy, with his pale face already showing the first signs of early adolescent acne, had followed the proceedings with an awareness well in advance of his age. Now he followed the others as far as the door, and then turned back to Belle who hadn't moved from her position by the kitchen table. She still held a biscuit in one small hand, and her face was so pinched and white that the freckles stood out on the bridge of her nose.

'Belle.'

Hearing her name seemed to spring her to life. She crushed the biscuit on the table-top and turned on Henry sharply. 'You heard Dada. Leave us alone; we're all right.'

Henry, who was used to obeying Belle, stepped outside, closing the front door carefully behind him. It was only then that Belle was able to summon up enough strength to move, and luckily George was there, with open arms and a

12

heart full of love for his little girl, to try and comfort her.

Belle didn't go for Father Joe, but the priest found out through some invisible grapevine. Later that day his fat black figure was seen climbing the hill, stopping often to fan himself and get his breath back, until he arrived at the Kellys' front door.

The other residents of Duke's Road watched him arrive from behind their lace curtains or through the half-opened front doors. To all but the Kellys he was an alien figure, as foreign as if he had dropped from space. They were all good Church of England families and proud of it; even if they didn't go to St Saviour's Church on Sundays, and only sent the children to Sunday School to give themselves a bit of peace and quiet.

But the Kellys were Catholics, and the fat old Irishman, Father Joe, was their spiritual adviser. They weren't very good Catholics, just as they weren't very good at anything else; in fact George hadn't been inside a church for years and was almost proud of the fact. Although Belle and Charlie had been baptised he hadn't allowed either of them to attend the church school, and had enrolled them instead at the local school where they were not allowed to join in the assembly because of the prayers. They hadn't taken their first communion either, although it was usual around the age of seven. George kept making excuses to the priest and delaying matters. It had now become almost a battle of wills between the two men, and any day now one of them was likely to give way.

Bess went to mass on Saints days, Christmas and Easter; more from habit than anything else. Although old Bridget had been a daily attender she was now too old and frail to venture so far from home, so Father Joe called regularly once a month to administer the sacrament and listen to her rambling confession.

13

Usually the priest was kept waiting on the step while Bess whisked a clean cloth on to the table and inspected the children's necks for water-marks, but today he had been watched for. The door opened silently to admit him as he toiled up the steps, and closed as silently behind him.

He spent a good hour in the small bedroom with Bess and the body of her son, and no one knew what went on behind the closed door

George, for the umpteenth time, tried to explain to his mother what had happened, and at last gave up because her feeble brain didn't seem to be able to grasp the fact that her grandson was dead. She listened carefully each time to George, one hand cupped behind her ear as if she was deaf, which she wasn't, as well as old. Just as he would sigh with relief, thinking that he'd at last got through to her, she would say cheerfully, 'Is Charlie coming down to his tea? He's a growing boy and he missed his dinner.'

Belle, locked out of the bedroom and not needed in the kitchen, roamed about like a lost ghost. When at last the door at the top of the stairs opened and Father Joe began to descend, blotting out the landing light with his huge black figure, he found the child sitting on the bottom step hiding something under her skimpy skirt. He put one hand gently on the top of her head: trying to smooth down the tangled curls, and with the other traced a cross on her forehead.

'It's a sad day, Isabel Kelly,' he said, groaning audibly as he let his bulk down slowly on the step beside her. 'But God will be pleased: he doesn't get many red-haired angels.'

'How do you know?' asked Belle, her blue eyes like saucers in her white face.

'Well now, haven't you looked in your missal recently? The one I gave you on your birthday, with the pictures of the Holy Family and the Stations of the Cross.'

14

'Not lately, Father,' admitted the child.

'Well fetch it now, and we'll look at it together.'

Luckily the missal, together with a cheap rosary, was kept on the kitchen window-sill, and soon they were poring over the pages. Father Joe gave a sigh of relief after they'd inspected all the pictures that depicted angels in white robes, singing, playing musical instruments, or just kneeling in the straw. Most of them had golden hair to match their haloes and harps, and a few were dark; in fact one had almost negroid features. But not one had ginger hair, or the tendency for freckles, like the younger members of the Kelly clan.

'You're right,' said Belle, closing the book carefully.

'What did I tell you, child? Charlie will be the first redhead in the heavenly choir.'

'He'll like that.'

Father Joe was struggling to his feet, glad to see that there was a little more colour in Belle's face. She stood up beside him, still clutching something under her skirt.

'Whatever have you got there?'

'Nothing, Father.' Even as she said the words, an innocent lie born from grief and embarrassment, there was a double thump as two black objects fell to the floor and landed at Belle's feet. She dropped to her knees to gather them up.

'It's a pair of boots,' said Father Joe thoughtfully.

'Yes, Father. They're Charlie's.'

'So I see; and almost new by the look of them. What are you going to do with them? Charlie doesn't need them now you know.'

'No, but he was so proud of them, although they hurt him badly. I wanted to keep them.' For a moment her eyes filled with tears and Father Joe was glad. He'd seen over the years the healing power of tears, and he was hoping that she would cry. The mother upstairs hadn't cried, just sat stony-faced, staring at her dead son while the priest prayed over his body. But just like Bess, Belle bottled up her agony and her eyes were bright as marbles as she looked at the priest.

'Perhaps your mam will let you keep them,' he said doubtfully.

'Not she!' Belle spat out the words as if they hurt. 'She'll make him wear them in his coffin I guess, even if they do hurt him; or she'll sell them to the rag and bone man. She won't give them to me; she won't give me anything,' and Belle fled through the scullery and out of the back door, leaving the priest to see himself out.

The day of the funeral dawned cold and wet, so there were only about twenty mourners in St Anne's Church to attend the funeral mass of Charlie Kelly. Father Joe looked out upon the sparse congregation and wondered again if there was a God, and if so what purpose there was in his treat-ment of the stricken family.

Even old Bridget had made it to the church.

'Get me down my black hat,' she'd commanded, and Belle had handed her the straw hat that had seen better days. 'These shoes are too small,' she complained as she tried to force her feet into her only pair of outdoor shoes.

'No, they're not, Gran. It's your feet: they're swollen.'

Bess and George sat upright in the front pew with Belle between them. They were all in solemn black, even the child, and their white faces were devoid of all expression.

Father Joe was pleased to see that the child's red curls were as unruly as ever, even under the black felt beret that had been forced on to her head. In her hands she carried her missal, and the priest guessed correctly that one of the younger looking angels in the picture of the nativity now had scribbled ginger hair.

An air-raid siren droned plaintively just as he was about to sprinkle the coffin with holy water. But undeterred he carried on, raising his voice to drown the warning as if daring Hitler to do his worst. No blow the Germans could cause this innocent family would hurt them as much as the one they had already sustained, so they might as well carry on as if they were deaf.

A week after the funeral the weather changed. The rain stopped at last, and after a misty start the sun came out and dried the freshly washed gardens. Back doors were left open and cats began to prowl again and scavenge the dustbins.

The sunshine and warmth went to the heads of the housewives in Duke's Road. They beat their mats, polished their windows, and hung out rows of flapping washing in the back gardens. Every house was a hive of industry – all but the Kellys'. There was no washing hanging in their garden or clatter of pots from the kitchen, and the windows and doors were closed firmly against their neighbours who, after their initial sorrow towards the family, had found the tragic death of Charlie an embarrassment.

George was seen plodding off to his allotment in all weathers, a sack over his shoulders to keep off the rain, and his head bowed in resignation. Belle was sent to school as usual, but her hair seemed wilder than ever and her clothes more creased and dirty. She was so quiet that the other children avoided her. All but Henry Murtell, who tried to cheer her up, without success.

Indoors old Bridget had taken to her bed. The funeral had drained the last of her stamina, and her cot was the only place where she felt safe and warm. Bess wasn't any help to any of them. She'd stopped cooking and cleaning and bothering now that Charlie was gone. For eleven years her life had revolved around his like a moth around the warmth of a candle, and now she wandered through the days, her pain so deep she wasn't aware of the suffering around her. The selfishness of grief.

On Saturday she did notice that there was no food in the cupboard and no money in her purse.

'Belle,' she called.

Her daughter's heart lifted expectantly, her need of her mother was so great, but her hopes were soon dashed when Bess handed her a canvas bag.

'Take these down to Jim Hilton and see what he'll give you. You should get seven and six, or even ten shillings. They're almost new. Then bring in a loaf of bread on the way home.'

The bag contained Charlie's boots, still black and shining. Belle carried them to the second-hand clothes shop where she exchanged them for nine shiny shillings. She cried all the way home. Father Joe would have been relieved if he'd seen her, because they were the first tears she'd managed to shed since her brother had died.

2

Belle was sitting under the laburnum tree at the end of the garden reading *The Wind in the Willows*. It was her favourite book and this was the third time she'd read it – although she did skip bits now so that she could read the chapters about Toad. Toad and his adventures were, she thought, by far the most exciting bits in the story, because Toad was rich, lived in a big house, and had a motor-car. Belle couldn't understand why the author had made him such a figure of fun, for in Belle's eyes anyone who was rich should be admired.

She closed the book and sighed. 'When I'm grown up I shall be as rich as Toad,' she told herself. 'I shall have a fur coat and jewels, and a white dress to wear to church.'

The white dress was a very important item on this sunny June day, and the problem of procuring one was at the forefront of her mind. Her father had at last relented and she was to take her first communion at the forthcoming Corpus Christi.

Only yesterday at the weekly communion class Sister Marie Jesu had stared at the squirming assortment of boys and girls in front of her. She was severe, but kind, and everyone was in awe of her.

'Now, I want to go over the arrangements,' she said. 'So listen carefully, because it's going to be the most important day of your lives. The girls will wear white dresses and veils over their heads, and the boys can wear their best Sunday suits. Can everyone manage that?'

'No,' said a girl in the front row. 'My mother says she can't spare the coupons.'

'Are you a Girl Guide?' the nun enquired sympathetically.

'Yes, Sister.'

'Then you can take your first communion in your uniform; and that also applies to any boys who are Scouts. Any more problems?'

Belle wasn't a Guide and she had no idea where she was going to get a suitable dress. There was no point in asking her mother, because Bess these days wasn't interested in anything outside her own grief. The problem of the dress was very worrying. She was the oldest girl in the communion class and stood a head taller than the other children, so she knew she was going to stand out like a sore thumb.

Belle was admiring the picture of the toad on the front cover of her book; he looked very elegant in his motoring coat and goggles. If she were as rich as Toad she would have a silk dress and real flowers in her hair, and be driven to the church in a long red car by a uniformed chauffeur. Lost in her dreams of longing she didn't hear Henry Murtell come out into the neat garden next door. It was only when she heard his tuneless whistle that she put down her book and showed herself. Henry had a tennis ball in one hand and an old frayed racket in the other. He was tall and gangly for his eleven years, and round-shouldered from peering at the world short-sightedly through his wire-rimmed glasses. His hair was dark brown and straight, and he had an annoying habit of continually brushing a lock away from his eyes. His face lit up at the sight of Belle.

'Shall we play tennis?' he asked, indicating the wall dividing the two gardens which they usually used in place of a net. Belle would have liked to play but she didn't have anything that resembled a racket, so she shook her head as if she wasn't interested.

'I'm reading,' she said.

'Do you want to come over?' Henry asked, wondering how he could tempt Belle over the wall on to his side. 'Some of Auntie's early strawberries are ripe enough to pick.'

'Better not, Henry. I don't want to get you into trouble.' Belle disappeared from view. When Henry peered short-sightedly over the wall he saw that she'd resumed her seat on the grass with the book on her lap. 'Why don't you come over here?'

This was the invitation Henry had been waiting for, and with a quick glance over his shoulder to see that Auntie Mabel wasn't watching he clambered over the wall and dropped to the ground at Belle's feet.

Mrs Murtell's garden was a neat show-place, with orderly beds of fruit and vegetables, and a greenhouse full of trailing plants leaning against the back wall of the house. The Kellys' garden was an overgrown wilderness. George loved his allotment and worked it every spare minute he had: partly to feed the family, but more because it got him away from home. Since Charlie's death the atmosphere indoors had become depressing to the point of being unbearable. Both George and Belle spent as much time away from the house as possible, leaving old Bridget shut in her room and Bess shut in with her grief. So the garden had quickly become a wild place, with weeds and dandelions growing where once there had been a flower border. Poppies and grass-heads seeded themselves freely, a home for beetles and grasshoppers, and butterflies danced among the straggling brambles.

Like an overblown wildflower herself Belle grinned at Henry. He was so thin and awkward, his wire spectacles slipping down the bridge of his narrow nose, and the lock of straight dark hair always hanging forward over his eyes. She loved to tease him and see the flush of colour creep up his neck when she said something that embarrassed him – which was often.

'Sit down, Henry,' she commanded, patting the patch of rough turf next to her.

Henry was glad to sit, even if it did crease his trousers. At least he was now out of the view of the house and Auntie Mabel wouldn't spot his whereabouts so easily. She didn't approve of the Kellys. Even before Charlie died she'd tried to keep the children apart.

'They're a poor, ill-mannered family,' she'd told her nephew, 'and not good enough for decent people to mix with.' Somehow this had only made them more attractive to Henry.

He'd liked Charlie. They'd been in the same class at school and had led each other in and out of the same games and troubles. It was usually Charlie who'd been the leader. Many a time Henry had taken the blame for something Charlie had done: whether it was breaking a window or stealing milk from a doorstep, or any one of a hundred mischiefs a couple of healthy boys could get up to.

But if Henry had liked Charlie, he loved Belle. Looking at her now as she sprawled in the grass in front of him, he swallowed nervously, and his heart thumped in his thin chest. She was only a skinny scrap of a child with stick-like legs and dirty bare feet. Her red cotton skirt was torn and barely reached her knees, and her head with its unkempt curls seemed top-heavy on her thin neck. But her pouting red mouth was beautiful, showing a row of slightly uneven teeth, and her eyes were as blue as the June sky and sharp as needles.

'What shall we do?' asked Henry, happy to let Belle take the lead.

'We'll make a daisy chain,' said Belle. She rolled on to her front and began to pick the flowers with the longest stems that grew around them.

Henry was clumsy and broke more flowers than he picked. Belle's fingers were quick and deft and soon she had a chain long enough to wind around her head.

'I'm Queen Isabel,' she said, holding out the flowers to the boy. 'Now you can crown me.'

He placed the coronet on her head, and when he stepped back he saw that she was laughing at him. 'What is it?' he asked, beginning to blush again.

'You look so serious, Henry. Its only a game', and tearing the flowers from her hair she broke them apart and threw them on the ground. When she turned to face him the smile had vanished and she was frowning. He never got used to her sudden change of mood.

'What's the matter, Belle?'

'It's a silly old crown. I hate it, Henry Murtell; it's almost as silly as you.'

'I'm sorry.' Henry wasn't sure what he was apologising for, unless it was for appearing silly in her eyes. 'I thought it was beautiful.'

'You would. Everything's beautiful to you. I want a white dress, not a silly old crown made of flowers.'

'I think you look fine just the way you are.' Henry looked at her as if she were dressed in the finest clothes, and not the old torn cut-down dress that was only fit for the rag-bag.

'I can't wear this to my first communion. All the other

girls will be dressed to kill in the best dresses their mothers can afford, even if they do use up all their coupons. Sister Marie Jesu told us it's the most important day in our lives, and who would wear a torn dress on the most important day of their life?'

'Perhaps if you asked your mother . . .'

'Mam! There's no good talking to her; she doesn't hear anything any more. And Dada's got no money; not even enough to buy an ounce of tobacco. Now if Charlie were here he'd buy Dada a whole tin of tobacco for his pipe, and he'd think of a way to get me a white frock.'

'I'll get you a white frock, Belle.'

The words slipped out before Henry realised what he was committing himself to, but he stood an inch taller as he made the promise.

'Will you, Henry?' She was looking at him sideways from under her long coppery lashes. If she'd been a year or so older, and not so innocent, she would have been accused of flirting. As it was she was looking at Henry properly, for the first time, as Cinderella must have looked at her Fairy Godmother when she was promised a ball-gown.

'I'll get you the most beautiful dress, Belle. I promise,' and at that moment Henry believed that it would be the easiest thing in the world to grant Belle's wish, particularly when she pressed a kiss of gratitude on to his cheek. He would have willingly died for her at that moment.

She was gone, leaving Henry alone with his promise and he was suddenly thrust back into the real world and its problems.

'Henry!' his aunt was calling him.

'Yes, Auntie.'

'Where are you? Come in to your tea at once.'

'Coming.'

He climbed hastily over the wall, brushed his trousers,

24

and walked back to the house, past the neatly trimmed borders and freshly mown patch of grass that Mrs Murtell called her lawn.

The back door stood ajar. He could see Auntie Mabel pottering about in the kitchen. She was a grey woman, always dressed in neutral colours, from her dull complexion and fawn dress, right down to her neat grey stockings and black court shoes. Her hair, which she twisted every night around metal curlers, was trapped under a net that was held tightly in place by knotted elastic. As Henry appeared in the doorway she was just carrying a fat brown teapot from the stove to the table.

'Wipe your shoes, Henry. How many more times do I have to tell you?'

He wiped his feet obediently, and then washed his hands under the cold tap in the scullery without being reminded. Then he took his seat at the kitchen table. On top of a crisp white cloth with a hand-crocheted border were plates of bread and margarine, cut into triangles, a bowl of jam, and a plate of home-made cakes. He waited until his cup and saucer were in their place and then helped himself to bread, spreading it liberally with red jam, which was delicious even if the raspberry pips did taste like sawdust.

'You're very quiet, Henry. Is something the matter?'

'No, Auntie.'

He longed to unburden himself; to tell her about Belle and the white dress. But he couldn't. She would go on and on about 'those useless Kellys, and their wicked Catholic practices', and she'd end up making Henry promise not to have anything to do with them.

Henry was fond of his aunt, and he knew she was fond of him. After all, neither of them had another relation to turn to. Mabel Murtell had been a widow now for over fifteen years, and had cared for her nephew ever since his parents had died in a flu epidemic when he was a baby. She'd had no children of her own and Henry hadn't been a very attractive proposition, but she'd done her duty and never stopped reminding him of the fact. Mabel needed Henry: he was her purpose for getting out of bed in the mornings. She needed him even more than if she'd carried and given birth to him herself. He was her reason for living and she dreaded him growing up and leaving her. He replaced the lover and son she'd never had, and she was fiercely jealous of anyone who might come between them.

But she didn't love him. She didn't love anyone, even herself. She'd just started learning to love her husband, after she'd got over the shock of the marriage bed, when he'd been cruelly taken away from her by death. So the delicate emotion of love had been frozen, unfulfilled. Mabel hadn't travelled beyond the first selfish need of the awakening lover. She could only demand and take; she couldn't give. So poor Henry had quickly learned that life was more comfortable if he obeyed his aunt, admired and thanked her for the way she cared for him and the home, and stopped expecting and hoping for warmth and affection.

Now he watched her across the tea-table as he slowly masticated his food, wondering if somewhere in her massive mahogany wardrobe she might have hidden a white dress he could borrow. But he couldn't imagine that, even in her youth, she would have worn such a thing. Brown, grey, or even navy blue, but never white.

'More tea, Henry?'

'No thank you, Auntie.'

'Another cake?'

'I've had enough.'

'Have another one. I made them specially for you. I know how much you like my home-made cakes.'

'No, really. I'm quite full up.'

He felt guilty when she bit her thin lips in disappointment. He knew she made the cakes for her own pleasure, not his, to bind him to her with sweetmeats, and other gifts he had no use for. So she could revel in his refusals, and say 'After all I've done for you'.

'Well, if you've finished I'd better clear away.' As she spoke she was pouring the tea-leaves back into the pot to be emptied around the rose bushes. Nothing went to waste in Mabel Murtell's kitchen.

'I'll do it,' said Henry, leaping to his feet and wondering how she always managed to make him feel so guilty.

'No you won't. Last time I let you near my china you chipped one of my best cups. Men and boys are useless in the kitchen; your uncle was just the same.'

'I'll get my homework out then . . .'

'I'll need half the table.' Mrs Murtell emptied the dirty crocks into the sink, and Henry marvelled again at how she managed to make so much noise and not break anything. 'Mrs Heather gave me a bag of clothes she'd turned out and they're all washed and dried. But I need room on the table to iron on before I take them down to Hiltons. I might get a couple of pounds on them if Jim's feeling generous.'

Henry spread his school-books out on the end of the table in the space his aunt allotted him, and watched as she balanced the flat irons over the gas ring to heat and unrolled the singed ironing blanket. The handles of the irons became so hot that she had to use a padded holder before she could pick them up, but even so she spat on the underside to test the heat and her spit sizzled reassuringly.

His teacher had set the class an essay to write and Henry sat biting the end of his pencil dreamily. It was to be entitled 'A day in the life of . . .' and he had to choose an animal to write about, imagining that he was that animal. He'd chosen a red squirrel because he'd seen pictures of them in his nature-study book, and the rusty colour of their soft coats and their sharp enquiring faces had reminded him of Belle.

He wrote carefully 'A day in the life of a squirrel' at the top of the page, and then underneath, 'I woke up early, before all the other squirrels, and had a breakfast of nuts.' Then he stopped because he'd run out of ideas. He wished he'd chosen a different subject: a lion or a tiger; even a dog would have had more potential than his chosen animal. A dog could have adventures: nosing in people's dustbins and being taken for interesting walks. But it was too late now. He'd already started, and teacher would be bound to notice if he tore a page out of his exercise book.

The table jumped on its uneven legs as Mrs Murtell slapped another iron down on to a wrinkled garment. The hot surface sizzled on a damp hem and a curl of steam floated skywards.

'Some of these things are too old and worn even for the rag and bone man,' Mrs Murtell muttered. 'But there was a cotton dress that might do me a turn, and there's a grey flannel shirt that should fit you. It only needs the collar turned.'

'Thank you, Auntie.'

'What do you think of this?' There was amusement in her voice and Henry looked up in surprise; it took a lot to amuse Auntie Mabel. She'd picked up a garment from the pile and was holding it against her shoulders, where it hung in limp folds down to the black toes of her shoes.

'What is it? A wedding dress?'

'Don't be silly. It's a nightgown. It's so old-fashioned it must have belonged to Mrs Heather's old mother. Look, it's all made by hand; you can see the tiny stitches. It must have been lovely when it was new.'

It was the funniest nightgown Henry had ever seen; not

that he'd seen many. Auntie Mabel wore plain pink stock-inet, and in the winter, flannelette. This garment was like a white cotton tent reaching from neck to feet, with long full sleeves finishing at the wearer's wrists. In its day it must have been handsome, but now the material had worn thin and was darned in places. The frill around the neck and cuffs was still undamaged, though, and the tiny rows of tucks and inserts of lace around the body still made it a feminine and attractive garment.

'It's pretty,' said Henry admiringly. 'Are you going to wear it?'

'Get along with you, Henry Murtell. It's so old it would most likely fall to pieces if I turned over in the night.' Nevertheless she looked pleased at his words. 'I might get a few pennies for the lace, but the rest is only good for dish-cloths. I'll put it in the rag-bag with these old shirts and look at it again later.' She picked up an armful of discarded clothing, and together with the nightie bundled it into an old pillowcase hanging behind the back door. 'What are you mooning for?'

Henry jumped. 'I was thinking about my essay, Auntie,' he lied. Actually he'd been thinking about Belle and her first communion. She needed a dress and he'd promised to get her one. Although a nightgown wasn't a dress the garment his aunt had spoken of so slightingly was white, and with a bit of imagination could have potential. A tuck here and a safety pin there could make all the difference. He decided there and then to remove the nightgown from the rag-bag as soon as he had the opportunity. He wasn't going to steal it because he was well aware that his aunt kept tabs on everything that came into the house. He would just bor-row it for Belle to wear, and then return it, hoping that it wouldn't be missed in the meantime.

'Pardon?' Auntie Mabel had been talking to him and he

hadn't heard a word, so occupied had his thoughts been with Belle and the all-important dress.

'I asked if you wanted your cocoa yet. What's the matter with you, boy? You get dreamier every day.'

'Sorry, but I was thinking about my essay. If I don't finish it Miss Roelich will keep me in after school on Monday.'

'It doesn't look as if you've got far.' Mrs Murtell sniffed as she saw the nearly blank page in front of her nephew.

'I like to think it out first; then when I get to writing it comes easier.'

'Think! Think! Thinking's all you ever do, Henry Murtell. You'd better get your own cocoa while I lock up. And don't take too long about it.'

'No, Auntie.'

Henry bent over the page and pretended to write, but really he was trying to hide the grin of satisfaction that he knew was stamped on his face. As soon as his aunt had disappeared, her shoes clumping noisily along the uncarpeted passage, he leapt to his feet. It didn't take a minute to rifle through the rags in the pillowcase until he found the coveted garment, roll the white cotton up as small as possible, and stuff the bundle into his shirt-front. It did make rather a bump, but when Mrs Murtell returned he was standing at the stove with his back to her, waiting for the saucepan of milk and water to boil.

After that it was easy. There were the breakfast things to arrange, the bottles to rinse for the milkman, the cat to wake up and put out. A hundred little jobs his aunt had to perform before she went to her bed; and they all took her mind off of Henry. In fact, as he crossed to the door after washing his cup, hoping she wouldn't notice the tell-tale bulge, she thrust his school-books into his arms so that they covered his chest.

He said goodnight and carried his prize upstairs to his

bedroom, not daring to inspect it until he heard his aunt's footfalls pass the door. A few seconds later he heard a slam that told him she was safely ensconced for the night. Then he pulled out the nightgown and hung it on the door of his wardrobe. It dangled like a headless ghost, moving slowly and provocatively in the slight draught from the door.

He undressed quickly and leapt into his narrow iron bed, leaning his head back against his folded arms and staring at the gown, trying to imagine Belle inside it. Her thin body would barely make an imprint on the white cotton, she was still as flat in the chest as a boy. But he could imagine how her thin neck would swan out of the collar of lace that framed her delicate face, and the way her tangled red curls would fall in an untidy knot on to her shoulders.

She would look beautiful, he decided, as he sleepily removed his glasses, disappointed that now all he could see was a white blur. He soon fell asleep however, with the vision of Belle still to the forefront of his mind.

The next day was Saturday and Henry was up and about early. Mr Jeffreys would be expecting him promptly at nine to deliver the boxes of groceries he'd packed ready the night before. Henry hated the big heavy bicycle he had to ride, the cardboard boxes balanced on the front making the machine top-heavy. He hoped there weren't any eggs in the deliveries because if he cracked so much as one they deducted it from his wages. With eggs so scarce they were as valuable as gold-dust.

Often he was late and received a reprimand from his employer, but this morning he was there just as the shop door was being unlocked, and the cardboard sign turned around to indicate that the grocer's was open for business.

'You're early, Henry,' Mr Jeffreys said, surprised to see him so prompt and looking so bright. 'That boy must be turning over a new leaf,' he remarked to his wife after he'd seen the lad off with his load.

Henry whistled tunelessly as he peddled along. He was happy and excited: not because he was enjoying his work, but because he was counting the minutes until he could see Belle and show her the gown. He was finished by half past ten, with two shiny shillings in his pocket. One he would have to give to Mrs Murtell, but the other he would keep for ribbon or cotton, or any other materials Belle might need to transform the nightgown into a pretty dress.

If his aunt had been out he would have rushed next door immediately, and knocked loudly, not being able to contain himself. But Mrs Murtell was kneeling in the doorway with a brass rag in her hand and her sleeves rolled up to the elbows. He stepped over her, and after putting her shilling on the kitchen table went out into the garden and peered over the wall. The garden next door seemed to be deserted, and the back of the house also had a blank appearance. It was a warm June morning but all the doors and windows were closed as if the house was empty.

Henry was disappointed. He prowled about all morning, getting under his aunt's feet, until she shouted at him in exasperation. 'For heaven's sake Henry, can't you find something useful to do? The vegetable patch needs weeding.' Henry jumped at the idea. Surely Belle would see him from the window and eventually appear, and he would be on the spot and have a good excuse to speak to her.

But fate wasn't on Henry's side that day. There was still no sign of life next door by the time he was called in to his dinner. It was steak and kidney pudding with peas and mashed potatoes, usually his favourite, but today his mind was on other things and he had no appetite.

'What's the matter?' Auntie Mabel asked as he pushed

the food around on his plate. 'You sickening for some-thing?'

'No. I'm not hungry, that's all.'

'After all the time it took me to cook, and now you turn your nose up at good food.'

'I'm not turning my nose up. I'm just not very hungry. Can I get down?'

'You won't get anything else until tea-time, and then it'll only be bread and jam.'

'I don't mind, Auntie.'

He headed for the back door but Mrs Murtell stopped him abruptly with a quick 'Where are you off to now?'

'I was going to finish the weeding.'

'That'll have to wait.' She indicated two brown paper carrier bags standing by the door. 'I haven't had time to go down to Jim Hilton's shop, so you can go for me. Tell him I want two pounds at least. I'll have to give Mrs Heather half even if some of it is only rags.'

'Do I have to?'

'Yes, you do. What's the matter with you today, boy? You look as if you've lost a shilling and only found six-pence.'

There was no use arguing with Auntie Mabel when she was in one of her moods, so Henry picked up the bags by their string handles and set off.

He trudged down Duke's Road, alert for any sign of a member of the Kelly family, and turned into Ditchling Road. The bags of clothes were heavy but luckily it was all downhill. A bus passed carrying shoppers down to the town, but Henry wasn't going to waste money on luxuries and he tramped on.

The steeple of St Peter's Church was his signpost. It reared its graceful spire above the terraced rows of shops and houses, a focal point for the dwellers in this seaside town of Brighton. Before Henry reached the sombre grey of its walls he was side-tracked. From the Level, a stretch of open grassland bordered with walks and tall trees, he was hailed by a howling gang of boys kicking an old ball about.

'Come and play, Henry.'

'Can't.'

'Why not?'

'I'm on an errand.' He held up the lighter of the two bags. 'I've got to take these to Jim.'

'Take 'em later. Football's more important.'

Henry agreed, but he was frightened of angering his aunt. 'She'll flay me alive if I find the shop shut. I daren't risk it.'

'Cowardy cuts. Scared of his old auntie,' and losing interest in Henry the boys resumed their game.

Henry dived into the crowded market. It was out of his way but he liked the smell of ripe fruit and the crowds of busy shoppers. Even the stalls reeking of fish and fly-blown meat were intoxicating to his uneducated palate.

But best of all, at the end of the market was Marshall's Row where the smithy stood. Henry loved to watch the blacksmith hammering the horseshoes into shape until the sparks flew like coloured stars, while the horse stood patiently, the sweat glistening on its sleek haunches as it tossed its huge head contentedly waiting to offer its hoof for a new shoe.

Henry could have stood there all afternoon, he often did, but after a few minutes he turned away and pushed through the crowd into the London Road. The first turning led into a back-alley, and soon he was standing in front of the window of Jim Hilton's second-hand clothes shop.

3

Jim Hilton was the biggest rogue in Brighton; he was also one of the richest. He always dressed in the same clothes: in an aged pin-striped suit and frayed plimsolls, with a muffler round his scrawny neck, and a trilby tipped over one eye to hide the shrapnel scar he'd sustained in the war. His pockets were always stuffed with crumpled notes and loose coins which were the profits he made on second-hand clothes.

His shop made a suitable background for his tight-fisted dealing. Like a cross between Fagin and Scrooge he padded around his domain, treating buyers and sellers alike to a disdainful stare from his sharp eyes that didn't miss a trick. He knew all the games the public would try to get the better of him: from the woman with the hard luck story right down to the schoolboy trying to sell a ragged coat stolen from the school cloak-room.

Behind the dirty windows his stock hung in rows. Moth-eaten fur coats and tippets, curly astrakhan capes and heavy uniform jackets rubbed shoulders with dated cocktail dresses threaded with beads and more homely cotton frocks and blouses. Heaped in corners were shirts and underwear in all varieties of grey, and broken shoes, and

35

boots with their tongues hanging out panted from lidless cardboard boxes.

Henry and Jim Hilton knew each other well and mutual warfare flared periodically between them. Henry liked to poke around in the shop looking for bargains in dark corners. Once he'd found a smart jacket that he thought his aunt would like and asked if he could take it home for her to try on. Although she hadn't liked the colour she'd found a ten shilling note in the pocket and insisted that as finders were keepers she would keep the note, although she did send Henry back with the garment. Without thinking, Henry had told Jim about the money and Jim said that as the jacket still belonged to him the ten shillings did as well. An unpleasant scene developed, and although Mrs Murtell had eventually given in Jim didn't trust 'those thieving Murtells', as he called them. As to Henry, he still held hopes of finding a fortune in the second-hand shop, although the owner tried to follow him around while he was on the premises.

Henry had to put down one of the carrier bags in order to open the door. A bell somewhere overhead jangled a cracked note. Jim looked up from where he was sitting cross-legged on a bench behind the counter, just like some old-fashioned tailor. Spread in front of him was a garment made of maroon velvet, and with a huge pair of scissors he was busy snipping the stitches of a seam.

'Hello, Mr Hilton,' Henry said nervously. He deposited one of his bags carefully on the only empty space on the counter.

'Why, if it isn't young Mr Murtell,' said Jim sarcastically, peering at the boy from under the brim of his hat. 'Found any ten shilling notes lately?'

Henry coloured; he wished Mr Hilton would stop harping back to that unfortunate incident.

'Auntie sent me,' he said as he placed the second bag beside the first. 'She wants a fair price. Two pounds at least.'

'I'm a poor man, Henry,' said Jim dolefully, scratching his neck under the muffler with one dirty finger. 'Your aunt drives a hard bargain.'

'It's good stuff,' said Henry. 'It came from Mrs Heather.'

'Mrs Heather eh? Old but quality – like this,' and he held out the velvet.

'What is it, Mr Hilton?' Henry asked.

'A smoking-jacket. What the gentleman used to wear in the old days. The ladies would retire to the drawing-room to drink tea while the men smoked their pipes. That's why it's called a smoking-jacket.'

'Why are you cutting it up?'

Jim looked from the scissors to the open seam, grinned, and then winked at Henry conspiratorially. 'I just checks that nothing's slipped through the lining. You never know with gentlemen; careless they are. Once I found a gold sovereign. That's twenty shillings, Henry.'

'What did you do with it?' Henry's eyes were round as brandy balls; he'd never owned more than half a crown in his life.

'I gave it back of course. They don't call me Honest Jim for nothing.'

Henry wanted to believe him, but the way he was peering sideways as he greedily felt in the secret corners of the jacket made him fear that it was all a lie. Auntie Mabel always called him a mean old skinflint who would steal a shawl from his own grandmother if he got the chance. He didn't argue because he wanted to get a good price for his aunt so that she would be pleased with him. He carefully lifted a neatly folded blouse from the nearest bag, saying, 'Shall I show you what I've got, Mr Hilton?'

'Leave it boy; I'll do it.'

With a speed and agility that surprised Henry he pulled the bags nearer to him and rummaged amongst the carefully packed layers. Henry wondered what Auntie Mabel would say if she saw the rough treatment, after the hours she'd spent the previous night pressing and folding.

Seeing Jim so occupied he walked around the counter bravely and pulled his sleeve to get attention. 'How's Queenie?' he asked.

'Fine, Henry. Three boys and three girls she had this time. I let her keep two: one of each. I drowned the rest.'

'Can I see them?'

'Of course. She likes visitors.'

'Where is she? Out the back?'

Jim nodded, and Henry crossed to a door behind the counter covered by a torn chenille curtain. As he walked through into Jim's living-room the smell of sour milk, cat urine, and cabbage water hit him. It was even more unpleasant than the dusty mothball odour of old clothes, but Henry's nose was hardened to smells. Jim Hilton's shop wouldn't have been the same without its own unsavoury smell, just as the open market wouldn't have felt right without the reek of fish.

Queenie, Jim's tabby cat, stared at Henry from the depths of her bed, which was the base of an old cardboard suitcase padded with rags and newspaper. Two striped kittens with identical orange eyes suckled noisily, keeping a watchful eye on Henry at the same time. He dropped on to his haunches to watch the cats. The mother soon decided her babies had had their fill and batted them away gently with her paws. They mewed plaintively until Henry started to pet them, and then they rolled about on the dirty bedding, waving their tiny feet in the air and thrashing their banded tails about fiercely.

Henry was charmed and on impulse called out to Jim, 'Mr Hilton, can I have one of Queenie's babies?'

Jim grunted to show that he'd heard the boy, and then asked, 'What about your auntie? I didn't think she liked cats.'

'Auntie Mabel loves cats,' said Henry indignantly. 'We've got one already.'

'Then you'd better not take home another. They'd fight. Queenie rears her kittens to be fighters.'

Henry's face fell. Of course Jim was right: his aunt would be cross if he arrived home with another mouth to feed tucked in his jacket. He didn't really want one anyway; he'd just been thrilled by their antics, and the longing to have something of his own to care for had got the better of him.

'I expect you're right,' he said, losing interest, and looked around for something else to investigate.

Jim's living quarters were an extension of the shop. The floor was piled with unsorted rags and boxes of old hats and shoes, handbags and belts, and all the other second-hand accessories that would raise a few pennies. The kittens forgotten, Henry began to rake through the nearest container to see what treasures he could unearth. His sudden silence worried Jim, who didn't trust anybody, especially boys.

'What are you doing in there, Henry?' he called out sharply.

There was no immediate answer, and he was just about to investigate when Henry's small dark head appeared round the curtain. In his hands he held a pair of shoes. They were ladies' evening sandals, probably dating from the twenties, when the flappers liked to tango in their short skirts, their toes tapping in time to the music. They had once been silver, although a lot of the surface had worn off with use showing bald canvas underneath. But there was still a pattern of crystal chips decorating the dainty instep and minute pearls and pieces of mirror stitched across the toes.

'Put those down,' Jim said. 'I've told you before not to play with the stock.'

'I'm not playing. I want to buy them.'

'You want to buy them? A pair of ladies dancing shoes!'

Jim threw back his head until his hat nearly dropped off, and laughed until he caught his breath and it turned into a cough.

'How much are they?'

'Henry Murtell, you'll be the death of me. What do you want them for?'

'Auntie's going to a tea-dance: she asked me to look out for some shoes for her. How much are they?'

'Five shillings to you; and that's cheap at the price.'

'I've only got one shilling,' admitted Henry.

He'd lied about the tea-dance and he guessed Jim knew he was lying. As soon as he saw the pretty shoes he'd thought of Belle. He'd got her a dress, or something as good as, but he hadn't thought about her feet. As far as he knew she only had Charlie's old cast-offs, but she could hardly wear those with a communion dress. She'd look a proper clown clumping into the church in laced-up black boots. The silver shoes were the prettiest footwear he'd ever seen. He longed to have them to give as a gift to Belle, and see her face light up with delight as he handed them to her.

'Well you can put them back if you've only got one shilling,' Jim was saying. 'I'm not giving them away. If your auntie wants them that badly she'd better come and see me herself.'

Henry turned away to return to Jim's inner sanctum but he got tangled up in the curtain hanging over the door. While he was extricating himself from the muffling folds he

40

heard the cracked clanging of the bell. From the sound of a man's voice he guessed Jim had a customer. He didn't hear the first exchange of words but he suddenly heard a rough voice say, 'You'd better hand over the cash old man or I'll string you up. Come on now, I'm not fooling.'

'I'm a poor man,' Jim answered. He didn't sound terribly frightened.

'You're an old miser we all know that. Where do you keep it – the money?'

'In the back room.' Jim answered calmly. 'There's a wooden box on the dresser.'

'Go and get it.'

'I've told you where it is. If you want it that badly you must go and get it yourself.'

'If you're telling me lies . . .'

'Do I look like a liar?' There was a pause as if the two men were summing each other up. Then: 'If you want the money that badly you'll have to take my word for it. Take the risk and see if it's worth it.'

Henry held his breath hoping the folds of the chenille curtain were hiding him from view. He was very frightened, particularly when he heard heavy footfalls crossing the floor in his direction. A dark shape blotted out the light as the thief elbowed his way to the opening. As a foot clad in a workman's boot appeared on the threshold Henry acted impulsively. He didn't have time to think, he just put out his own leg and tripped the intruder up. The noise of the man's fall woke the kittens, who fled from their mother's side to hide in the darkest corner of the room. Apart from their faint cries all was silent. Henry and Jim looked at the sprawled figure blocking the doorway.

'Have I killed him?' Henry asked at last. Proud of his action, but terrified that the answer might be 'Yes.'

Jim approached the body and stabbed it with the toe of

his plimsoll. 'No. He's just out for the count. Look, he's stirring already.'

Henry looked and saw the man move slightly. 'Shall I go and fetch someone, Mr Hilton?' he asked quickly, ready to run if given the instructions.

'No.' Jim, unconcerned, was scratching his scalp under the brim of the trilby. 'When he comes round he'll be glad just to get away.'

'Are you sure?'

Before Jim could answer the man groaned, shook his head and opened his eyes. His face was an unhealthy purple colour and his eyes small and evil: he was like a rat caught in a trap.

'What happened?' he asked automatically, looking from Jim to Henry, whom he'd never seen before.

'You were trying to rob me,' Jim said, 'but this young David here put a stop to your tricks.' He placed a hand proudly on Henry's shoulder.

Suddenly the thief seemed to gather his wits and remember what he was doing before he blacked out. With a roar like a demented lion he scrambled to his feet, and swaying slightly, launched himself at the shopkeeper. Jim seemed to anticipate the action, and with an equally quick movement he brought out his tailor's scissors from behind his back. They looked huge and dangerous as he held them like a weapon, the light shining on the sharp blades.

'We'll have none of that, unless you want me to rip you up the front. Just get out of my shop before I smell blood or I swear I'll hang for you.'

The intruder didn't take long to make up his mind. With an oath he crossed to the door. Once in the street he took to his heels as if he feared Jim was right behind him snipping away with his scissors.

'He won't be back in a hurry,' Jim said calmly, as if

42

dealing with rogues was all in a day's work. 'Thanks Henry.'

'You were wonderful,' said the boy, unwrapping himself from the curtain now that the danger was past. 'Why did you call me David?'

'Have you never heard of David and Goliath? What do they fill your heads with at school these days? David was a poor shepherd boy and Goliath was a giant, but David felled him with a stone from his catapult; which goes to show that the weak can inherit the earth. David used his brains just like you did.'

Henry was proud of the comparison. 'We frightened him, didn't we?' he said.

'Yes, we did. He'll think twice before he tries his tricks again.' Jim was busy straightening his hat and adjusting his muffler. 'I'm closing up now so you'd better be running along.'

'What shall I tell Auntie?' Henry was hopping from one foot to the other.

'What about?'

'Mrs Heather's things.' He indicated the two now empty carrier bags and the jumble of garments still spread out on the counter.

Jim grunted. He felt in his pocket, bringing out a handful of loose change, from which he extracted four half crowns which he held out to the boy. Henry shook his head.

'She said two pounds, Mr Hilton.'

'Two pounds!' Jim considered. 'Your aunt drives a hard bargain. One pound ten shillings – not a penny more.'

Henry stood his ground. 'I think she'd be pleased with one pound fifteen.'

'Done,' said Jim promptly, and handed over a screwed up note and two more coins. 'You've done well. You've got a good business head on your shoulders. When you leave school I might give you a job.' Henry grinned, delighted with the praise. 'You can have one of Queenie's kittens if you want. Pick one now.'

He propelled Henry back towards the other room. The boy stumbled over something in the doorway, and when he bent down to pick it up Jim saw it was one of the silver shoes. Henry had dropped it during the skirmish.

'If it's all the same with you Mr Hilton, I think you were right. Auntie Mabel might be cross if I take home another cat without asking her first.' He paused in order to pluck up courage to continue. 'If you want to give me something, I'd like these shoes.'

Jim looked from the worn sandals to the boy's beseeching eyes and considered. 'For your aunt? Eh?'

'Yes.' Henry coloured slightly at the lie.

'All right. Take them quickly before I change my mind. No wonder I'm such a poor man; always being taken advantage of. He pushed Henry out of the door into the street, and shot the bolt inside with a rasp of metal.

Henry couldn't believe his good fortune. He'd done it! Not only had he got Belle a dress but he'd got shoes to match. Now all he had to do was find out where she was hiding herself so that he could give her the presents. He had no doubt that she would be delighted with the gifts because in his eyes they had now assumed the quality of the most expensive fashion house. When Belle took her first communion she was going to be the most splendidly attired girl in the church.

Clasping the shoes to his thin chest he gave out a whoop of glee, and like something demented danced a jig along the pavement. Soon he calmed down and started the long climb towards home. He had to see Belle before the day was out or he would burst.

He was panting by the time he reached Duke's Road but he refused to slow his pace. When he saw a figure sitting on the top of the Kellys' front steps he broke into a run. It was Belle, dressed in her ragged red skirt, her bare legs crossed elfin-fashion and her tangled hair falling forward over her face. She was eating something out of a tin; concentrating on getting her spoon into all the bottom corners.

He wanted to yell to attract her attention, but she looked up anyhow and he swallowed nervously at the expression on her face. She looked so sad and small huddled there in the doorway that he wanted to do something, anything, to make her smile and take the coldness out of her blue eyes.

She would smile when she saw the presents he had no doubt. The tin empty, the last morsels scraped, she suddenly hurled the empty can into the road, where it just missed Henry and rolled downhill clattering against the curb. She did see him then, but her face didn't change, just a fleeting glimpse of recognition passed across her features.

Henry was just about to join her, to drop the pretty shoes into her lap and tell her about the dress, when he heard a knocking noise. It was Mrs Murtell rapping on the front-room window and gesturing him to come indoors at once. He had to obey or she would nag at him for the rest of the day. Using a mixture of sign language and facial expression he directed Belle to join him in the garden later, as he had something exciting to tell her. Without smiling she nodded and got to her feet, and with a swirl of her torn skirts ran into the house, shutting the door with a bad-tempered slam.

Auntie Mabel was waiting for him and she didn't seem too pleased either, although her face softened a little when he handed her the money.

'Here's sixpence,' she said, holding out a small silver coin. 'Take it quickly before I change my mind.'

'Are you going out?' he asked automatically. She was slipping her arms into a loose navy coat with a moth-eaten fur collar. The sight of it made Henry itch and perspire.

45

'Just down to Mrs Heather's to give her her due. I won't be long, only about half an hour, so don't get up to any mischief.'

'No Auntie.'

Henry had to turn his face away to hide his delighted expression. Mrs Heather was housebound and loved a gossip. She would insist on his aunt stopping for a cup of tea so that she could hear all the news. He knew from experience that he would be alone for at least an hour, perhaps even more. Plenty long enough for him to join Belle, who he hoped had interpreted his message correctly.

There was an awkward moment when Mrs Murtell came back for her gloves and almost caught Henry retrieving the sandals from behind the umbrella stand in the hall. Although she looked a little puzzled, she accepted his explanation that he was trying to find a lost marble.

At last she'd finally gone and Henry breathed a sigh of relief. It only took a few minutes for him to collect the things together, and then he was in the garden, peering over the wall at the spot under the laburnum tree where they usually met.

There was no sign of Belle and the back of the house was as usual closed and blank. His disappointment was hard to bear. He tried to tell himself that her father had needed her, or even Mrs Kelly had come out of her coma and demanded her daughter's attention. But he couldn't really believe these excuses. Probably she just hadn't intended coming.

He wondered how long he should wait, and was just about to turn away, when he heard a sound in the bushes. It sounded like something in distress: a cat maybe. When it came again he was almost sure that it was someone crying softly, and trying to stifle the sounds. As soon as he'd identified the direction he spotted a flash of red between the leaves, that looked like a girl's skirt. Then he knew it was

Belle, hiding from him. He knew she wouldn't come out if he called, she was too stubborn for that, so he clambered over the wall and parted the bushes, disclosing the child huddled on the ground with tear-stained cheeks and swollen eyes.

'What's the matter, Belle?' he asked softly. 'You can tell me.'

'Go away,' she said angrily. 'Leave me alone.'

'Not until you tell me why you're crying.' Henry was surprised at how firm his voice sounded. Belle was usually the strong one, and he just followed and did what he was told. 'Has something happened? Is it your mother?'

Another tear slid down her cheek. Henry was glad that he had a fairly clean handkerchief in his trouser pocket to pass to her. She took it silently and blew her nose.

'Dada's never hit anyone before,' she said at last.

Henry looked at her in surprise. Mr Kelly was the most unaggressive man he knew; he couldn't imagine him hitting anyone.

'He hit your mother?'

'No.' She turned her heart-shaped face towards him and with a graceful gesture pushed her hair away so that he could see the discoloured mark staining her cheek. 'Dada hit me.'

'He did that?' Henry put out his hand and touched the bruise gently, as if he could spirit it away. She flinched at the light pressure of his fingers. 'Why?'

'They were arguing – Mam and Dada. He said she was no wife any more and he'd had enough.' She paused and swallowed with emotion. 'He said he was going . . .'

'Where?'

Henry knew Belle wasn't always honest, he'd caught her out lots of times, but although he wanted to believe this was just one of her stories he knew inside that this time she

47

was telling him the truth. The bruise was enough to back up her words.

'He said he'd go to Maud.'

'Maud?'

'Maud Carter. He said she knows how to treat a man and Mam doesn't. He said Mam's driven him to it and she only has herself to blame. I heard him.'

'But Belle, Maud Carter's an awful woman. Auntie Mabel says she's wicked.'

'I know. Mam said she was evil and Dada would be going into a den of vice.'

'What does that mean?'

'I don't know, but it sounds horrible.'

They stared at each other glumly and Henry didn't know how to comfort her. Grown-ups acted so strangely at times; even Auntie Mabel was known to act out of character. At least Belle had stopped crying. Henry suddenly remembered why he'd asked her to meet him.

'I've got something for you.' he said excitedly pushing the bundle of white material into her hands.

'What is it?'

'It's a dress: a white dress. You know I promised to get you one for your first communion.'

'Oh, Henry!' He could see by her face that it had been worth all the trouble he'd taken. He watched as she unrolled the nightgown, and then stood up to hold it against herself. 'It's a bit big,' she said, her face clouding.

'Try it on,' Henry instructed. 'I won't look, I promise. I'll turn my back.'

He could hear her rustling about on the grass and longed to peep. It didn't take more than a minute for her to slip out of her skimpy clothing and slip the dress on. It slid down her thin body to the ground. When Henry was ordered to turn round he saw the folds of loose material around her

48

bare feet, and a frill of lace at the cuffs completely hid her hands. Her face was woebegone.

'I can't wear this: I'd look like a freak. It's much too big. It looks like that thing they dressed Charlie in for his funeral.' Tears welled in her blue eyes again and began to run down her cheeks.

'It's not that bad,' said Henry doubtfully. 'It just needs altering. Wait a minute.'

He searched in his pockets and amongst the string and screwed up bits of paper found his prize possession: a rusty pen-knife with one remaining blade.

'What are you going to do?' Belle asked breathlessly as he approached her with the open knife in his hand. For a moment she was frightened, he had such a determined expression on his face. But it was only her friend, Henry. He wouldn't hurt anybody; least of all her.

'I can make it fit. It's easy.'

He pierced the material with his blade just below her knee, at a point where there was a band of lace, and then, gritting his teeth, tore the material quickly. He did the same thing to the sleeves. Belle stood there in a white smock looking down at herself doubtfully.

'It feels funny,' she said. 'It still doesn't fit. It's too loose.'

But Henry hadn't finished; he was busy ripping up the surplus material. He used a strip of cotton to tie around her waist as a sash, and rolled up the sleeves to disguise the frayed edges. Then he stood back to inspect his handiwork.

'You look grand,' he said proudly.

'Do I?' Belle was beginning to smile again. 'But what about a veil. I must have a veil to cover my hair; all the other girls will have one. And shoes – I can't go into church bare-foot.'

The next few minutes were the proudest of Henry's young life. A band of lace he'd cut out of the skirt was folded carefully and spread over her shining hair, where it hung to her shoulders framing her face and white neck. Then, like Cinderella's fairy godmother, he produced the silver sandals and held them out to her.

Never had Belle seen such pretty shoes. She took them in her hands and held them as if they were made of the most fragile porcelain. She didn't notice the worn soles or the frayed canvas. All she saw was the silver and glass, and the milky pearls. She laughed then in delight, and to Henry that meant it had all been worthwhile. He blessed the intruder in Jim's shop, because without him the shoes would have remained unattainable.

'Aren't you going to try them on?' he asked, because Belle was happily trying to see her reflection in one of the minute pieces of glass. 'Fairy mirrors' she called them.

Of course, like the gown, they were much too big. They'd been made for a woman, not a little girl. Belle looked disappointed, but Henry refused to give up. He quickly stuffed the toes with pieces of torn-up cotton and used a safety pin to replace a broken buckle.

'Now try them.'

Belle carefully slid her feet into the sandals and wriggled her toes to make sure the fit was now right. Then she stood up gingerly, trying to balance on the unusually high heels. She walked about, stumbling at first, but soon she gained confidence and ran to Henry laughing, and threw her arms around his neck in one of her spontaneous gestures.

'Thank you. Thank you,' she said.

They swayed together under the laburnum tree like two young ponies in a meadow. When she kissed him it was almost too much. Henry was the happiest boy in Brighton, but he did wonder afterwards why, at that moment, he thought of Belle's father and the mystery of why he wanted to go to Maud Carter.

4

In the street backing on to Duke's Road stood a public house called the Black Mill. It was named after a tarred windmill that used to stand in the vicinity, and was pulled down early in the century. Nobody missed the mill, although it had ground the wheat for one of the first baker's shops in the town. Beer was more important than bread at that time.

The pub was snugly tucked in between a row of houses which had been built from the bricks of the demolished building, so the story was told. Some of the residents remembered the days when the windmill had been only one of many towering over the town, their huge fan-like sails turning slowly in the wind as the heavy machinery inside crushed the grain.

Arthur Booker was the publican, and he was a popular man. A small squat figure with a red face and thinning hair, he was a jovial fellow, and everybody's friend. He never refused a drink to a thirsty customer even if it meant putting it on the slate. If all the money owed to him was paid back in one day he would have suddenly found himself a rich man.

But Arthur's brain didn't work like that. He saw good in

51

everybody, was a sucker for a hard-luck story, and had never wanted riches for himself. Of course it soon got around that he was a soft touch, so the public bar of the Black Mill was the regular meeting-place for Brighton's down-and-outs.

Those who'd emigrated from the north to make their fortunes, and couldn't find a roof to cover their heads, were soon bedded down in one of the warren of poky rooms on the top floor of Arthur's pub. Some stayed a night and disappeared the next day without even a word of thanks; others stayed a week or more, and, if Arthur was lucky, did odd jobs for their keep. The one who'd stayed longest was a woman called Maud Carter.

Maud had come down last summer on the train from the London slums. She'd planned to spend a day by the sea: strolling along the pier and drinking in the sea-front bars. She'd no money, only her return ticket, but she knew how to wangle a drink or a free meal out of people she met. She'd met a man that day on the promenade who'd treated her to a day of luxury. In the evening they'd ended up at the Black Mill, where he ditched her while she'd been answering a call of nature.

It had happened before and wasn't unexpected; it took more than that to get Maud Carter down. Anyway, she still had her return train ticket. She never did use it. She'd ended up on an iron cot in one of Arthur's rooms, and when she woke the following morning and sniffed the sea air and smelled the bacon frying downstairs she decided to stay. She'd been there ever since.

Maud was a striking woman in more ways than one. Nearly six feet tall and strong as an Amazon, she towered over Arthur when she stood beside him in the bar. She was well built too, with fully developed breasts and hips, and a narrow waist. The weight her legs and feet had to carry for so many years had taken their toll, and she suffered from varicose veins and dropped arches. She didn't walk far if she could help it because of this condition, but when she did her large feet waddled under her weight, splayed like a duck's.

On the credit side she had long black wavy hair like a gypsy, brown eyes, and smooth unlined skin the colour of honey. Nobody knew how old she was, but most guessed correctly that she was the wrong side of forty. Actually she was forty-six but hadn't bothered about birthdays since she was a girl. She was a woman and proud of it. People could take her as they found her; age had nothing to do with it.

Men usually found her attractive, and this was because she always looked happy and had a smile on her face, even when she was getting over one of her drinking sprees, or when her legs and feet were playing up.

Arthur found her an asset to the Black Mill and blessed the day when she'd turned up on his doorstep. Although she didn't officially work for him, she more than paid for her room by helping behind the bar two or three times a week. Her raucous laugh and gay wit soon endeared her to the rough locals who found they didn't have to tone down their crude humour in front of her. She enjoyed a rude story as much as any of them.

That's where George Kelly first met her. He wasn't a drinking man as such, although he did enjoy a glass of port with his mother on special occasions. The reason he'd gone into the Black Mill in the first place was to take shelter when he heard an air-raid siren. It was nearer than climbing the hill to his home, and he'd spent a hard morning digging on his allotment and was feeling thirsty.

It was a dull misty day, and although it was early the lights were on – the regulation black-out was in place. Stepping from the bleak outdoors into the cosy bright bar was comforting, particularly as there was little cheer at home now that Charlie was dead. He'd ordered a beer and carried it to a nearby table where a couple of men he knew slightly were sitting. The beer tasted rank and watery, but he was soon accepted and began to enjoy the unusual company.

'You're not a regular,' Ted, one of his companions, said in a friendly fashion, offering George a cigarette from a squashed packet. He took it and accepted the light. The world seemed to take on a happier glow.

'I like a beer,' he admitted. 'Specially when I'm in good company.'

'You can say that again,' Bill, the other man, said. 'Arthur keeps a good house and we're always welcome.'

The publican, who was passing at that moment, with a dirty apron tied around the place where once he'd had a waist, grinned and wiped a nearby table sloppily. He knew about the Kelly family and their tragedy, and stopped in his work to sympathise with George.

'How's that little girl of yours, Mr Kelly?' he asked.

'A comfort,' said George sadly. 'A comfort.'

'I'm sure,' said Ted, whose wife couldn't have children. 'You're lucky, George. You may have lost a son but you've still got a daughter.'

George nodded. He wasn't used to attention but he felt the genuine kindness behind their enquiries.

'And the wife?' asked Arthur. 'How's she bearing up?'

Before George had time to answer he heard a loud laugh and the clatter of feet. The opening of the doorway behind the bar was almost blocked by the figure of a woman. It was Maud Carter, whom George had heard stories about but never met. Some said she was a thief or a prostitute, or both, and her reputation was such that when her name was bandied about with a man's, his wife, if he had one, knew there was trouble ahead.

Maud that day was in a particularly benevolent mood. She'd turned over a new leaf the night before, which she did periodically, and hadn't drunk more than half a pint all evening. Because of this she'd woken up with a clear head, and an appetite for the kippers Arthur often cooked for breakfast. After that she'd combed her hair, dressed herself in her best dress of electric blue, and decided that she owed her host a few hours' work.

She entered the public bar with a crate of bottles on her shoulder. Many a man had struggled and groaned at the weight, but Maud took it in her stride. She slammed it down noisily on the counter, making the glasses sing tunelessly, wiped her hands on her wide hips and beamed at the three men sitting in the corner. Maud liked everybody, but she had a particular fondness for men. A new man was a challenge and she'd never seen George in the Black Mill before.

'Another half, Maud,' Ted called out, draining his glass. 'How about you two?'

Bill refused, but George, feeling daring, accepted. He was mildly titillated by Maud as she carried their drinks across the room. Her hips swayed provocatively under the thin material and he didn't notice her ungainly walk. She put the tray down with a thump; George noticed she'd poured one for herself.

'I'm on the waggon,' she said cheerily. 'This one's just to wet my whistle.' She picked up the glass and drank a third of the beer in large gulps. The heady foam stayed on her upper lip, making her look like a side-show freak, until she wiped it away with the back of her hand.

Bill started to tell a story about a woman he'd known once, before he met his wife of course; describing her physical attractions in detail, and using his hands to illustrate her perfections. George felt embarrassed: he wasn't used to this sort of talk, particularly in front of a woman. When he glanced at Maud to see how she was taking it he saw she was grinning broadly, and seemed to be enjoying every revelation.

He was almost sorry when closing time came. He couldn't remember when he'd enjoyed himself so much. As he walked along the Ditchling Road with Ted, who lived in the same direction, he asked about Maud Carter. He knew that she'd been partly responsible for the good time he'd had.

Ted told him how she'd arrived at the Black Mill and been taken in by Arthur. Then he said, 'She's one of the best, is Maud, and I should know.'

'How do you mean?' George was really interested.

'Well, she knows how to make a man feel good.'

'In what way?' Suddenly George suspected what Ted was getting at in his roundabout way. 'You don't mean . . .?'

'Yes, I do mean . . .' Ted left the rest of the sentence for George to imagine. He tucked his thumbs into his lapels and whistled jauntily.

That gave George something to think about: after all Ted was a married man, like him. He'd never felt the need to stray from the nest; he'd married Bess when she was seventeen and he was only two years older. Old Bridget had brought him up strictly, to fear God, and he'd never thought about breaking his marriage vows. Bess and George had enjoyed a good sex life and had been quite content until the fatal air-raid.

The bomb that had been responsible for killing his son had gone a long way to killing his marriage. At first he made allowances. In his rough way he'd tried to comfort Bess, but she'd turned her stony face away at his kind words, and shook off his gentle arm when he tried to embrace her.

They still shared the same bed but the gap between them seemed to get wider as the weeks went by. Bess would be in bed before he'd finished locking up for the night, and when he joined her she'd be curled up with her face to the wall, and her even breathing gave a pretence of sleep. He knew he had to give her time: after all Charlie was her adored first-born. But he'd been his son as well, and how much time did she need?

After his visit to the Black Mill and his meeting with Maud Carter he felt brave and decided to try again. For the first time his eyes seemed to be opened to his surroundings, and he couldn't help noticing how unkempt his home had become. He went into the scullery to fill the kettle, thinking he'd make Bess and his mother a cup of tea, and found the sink full of dirty crocks and the drain choked with scraps and tea-leaves.

It took him half an hour to clear the mess of days, but he persevered. Then he carried a cup upstairs to his mother who now rarely bothered to leave her bed. The window was shut and the room stifling, and the smell of old, unwashed flesh was overpowering. George frowned: he'd really have to do something about his mother. This state of affairs had gone on long enough.

'Here you are, Mother,' he said. 'I've brought you a nice cup of tea.'

Old Bridget had been dozing uncomfortably, dreaming about her childhood in Ireland. She opened one eye in surprise and chomped her toothless gums at her son. Her false teeth were safely floating in a dusty glass of water by the bed. With shaking hands she grasped the cup and drank greedily. George watched her sadly.

'How are you feeling today?' he asked.

'Oh, poorly . . . poorly. But don't you worry, son. I'll be dead soon.'

'Don't talk like that. You'll be back on your feet in no time, Mother. We need your help.'

'I'm no help to anyone.' She screwed up her wrinkled face and managed to squeeze out a tear. 'Nobody needs me any more.'

'That's where you're wrong.' He sat down on a chair by the side of the bed and took her hand. It felt like a scrawny chicken's claw between his palms. 'I need your help,' he said earnestly. 'This business with Bess has gone on long enough.'

'What business?'

'Mourning over Charlie.'

'Charlie?' The old woman sat up with a start. 'Where is he? He hasn't been in to see me lately.'

George sighed. It was no good, he had to accept the fact that his mother was going senile.

'Don't you remember the air-raid, Mother? Charlie's dead.'

'Is he?' Bridget looked confused and fixed her mind on something she could understand. 'Where's the biscuits?'

'I don't think there are any.'

'Don't be silly. I always have biscuits with my cup of tea. Tell Charlie to bring them up.'

He left her then: there probably wasn't bread in the house, let alone biscuits.

That night he lay next to Bess, thinking deeply. She slept beside him like a child: undemanding, in a world of her own. Once, in the early hours, he ventured to put an arm around her, but she groaned in her sleep and rolled away from him. The picture of Maud Carter came into his mind: the earth mother, all breasts and goodwill, doing favours for men like Ted. But a clear picture was beyond his powers of imagination. In the early hours he drifted into a restless slumber until the sunlight woke him to another day. He felt edgy and depressed, and suddenly wanted Bess urgently, as he had when they were first married.

He pushed himself up on to his hands so that he could see her sleeping face. Even in repose the lines showed deeply between her brows and she was grinding her teeth softly. Her thin back was warm and he could feel the sharp knobs outlining her spine as he traced it with his fingers; a preliminary he used to use before lovemaking long ago.

'Bess!' he whispered pleadingly. 'Are you awake?' There was no answer so he tried again. 'I love you, Bess. Turn over and look at me.'

She heard him then and her eyes flew open. They were hard eyes now where once they'd been soft and girlish. He bent to kiss her: to drive away the hurt and show her that he understood. As his face approached her lips drew back from her teeth in a snarl, like a cornered wild animal. Her eyes seemed full of hatred.

'Don't touch me,' she spat. His hand which had started to encircle her breast drew back. He could only watch with mounting despair as she threw back the covers, pulled a faded dressing-gown over her nightclothes and ran from the room.

Rage filled him. How dare she! What had he done to be treated so? He clambered from the bed and followed her on his bare feet. He knew where she was going: to the slip-room at the top of the stairs that Charlie had shared with Belle. He stood in the doorway in his flannel pyjamas, a laughable figure with his ruffled hair and wild eyes. In the corner, Belle, woken by the intrusion, peered at her parents over the patchwork quilt that covered her. She was frightened by the way they didn't seem aware of her presence. This was the grown-up world she didn't understand. Her mother was sitting on Charlie's empty bed, her wispy hair hanging over her face, rocking to and fro in silent misery.

'Bess,' George said in a voice Belle had never heard before. 'This nonsense has got to stop.'

Then Bess spoke: a tired trickle of sound like the sighing of the wind in the trees. 'Nonsense! So that's all Charlie's death means to you . . . nonsense.'

'I didn't mean that, and you know it. Charlie was my son just as much as yours, and I miss him too. But you should be thinking of the living not the dead. I need you, Bess. Come back to bed.'

'Is that all you can think about? – bed.' Her voice was rising in a passion, as if her tongue, suddenly let loose, was unable to control the words that tumbled out. 'It was going to bed with you that conceived Charlie, and now he's gone and I can only feel pain. Being a mother is pain from start to finish. I don't know how I can bear it.' She grasped the pillow that had belonged to her son and cradled it on her lap as if it were her baby; and all the time her eyes were filled with bitter unshed tears.

'I know, lass.' George felt helpless, defeated, faced with such agony. 'Just come back to bed and I'll help you forget it.'

'Bed!' Suddenly Bess was screaming. 'Is that all you think about? I'll never share your bed again, George Kelly. I'll sleep here, where I can be near to Charlie,' and she stretched her thin body along the narrow cot.

George took a step towards her, comic in his crumpled nightclothes, and then stopped as if overcome by the helplessness of the situation. 'I can't take any more, Bess,' he said. 'I've had enough. You're no wife to me any more. It would serve you right if I went to . . .' His voice faltered.

Bess turned her bitter face to him. 'Who'd want you, George?' she said. 'Who would you go to?'

'Maud Carter,' he said, as if the idea had only just come to him. 'You don't know how to treat a man, and she does.'

The fatal words seemed to echo round the room; neither George nor Bess were aware of Belle creeping from her corner. They'd forgotten all about their daughter, so absorbed were they in their own concerns.

'Dada, stop,' she said, walking forward across the strip of threadbare carpet on her bare feet, dressed only in her night-shift, her eyes still puffy with sleep and her flaming hair tangled. 'Mam,' she beseeched the figure on the bed. 'Make him stop. I'm scared.'

The eyes of both parents turned to stare at her as if they were seeing her for the first time. She wished for their sake that she could become Charlie, so that they would look at her with joy. 'Dada,' she said again in the little girl voice he couldn't usually resist, but as she reached for his hand his face was suffused with anger. He tried to push her from him, and when she clung, slapped her across the cheek with the palm of his hand.

He'd never hit her before and was mortified at allowing himself to do such a thing. Belle cowered away from him, her hand to her face, and her huge eyes staring at the father she loved, proving to be no more than a fallen idol.

There was nothing to do, nothing to say. George walked out of the room, dressed, and out of the house to his allotment where at least he felt at peace. He might just as well have walked out of their lives as well. The passions that were released that day could never be forgotten.

He soon felt better and settled down to some steady digging. With his spade he filled a sack with potatoes; smooth and uniform in shape, with the earth still clinging to their dun-coloured skins. Then with a fork he began to break up the soil, grunting with the exertion. He thought he'd successfully blocked out his troubles but his mind couldn't have been completely on the task in hand, because as he lunged the prongs into the earth, he didn't notice a piece of

brick protruding from the ground. The fork hit the hard
object and slid off sideways into his working boot, through
the leather and pierced the side of his foot.

With an oath George dropped the fork to inspect the
damage. Although the wound hurt and his sock was oozing
blood he was more bothered about the state of his boot. It
would cost nothing for his foot to heal, but he hadn't the
price of another pair of boots, new or second-hand. He
decided to call it a day and packed up his belongings,
shouldering the heavy sack and limping badly.

He could have reached home directly along the Ditchling
Road, there were no air-raids that day to delay him, but he
found himself instinctively taking the turning that led him
past the Black Mill. It was the middle of the afternoon so of
course the pub was closed, but there was a side door leading into a yard where kegs and cases were stored waiting to
be lowered through a trapdoor into the rat-infested cellar.
The door was open and Maud Carter was sunning herself
on the step, a bowl of shucked peas standing on the ground
beside her from which she was eating as if the taste were
delicious.

George stopped in the shade of a tree, ostensibly to shift
the sack to his other shoulder. Sitting down, Maud didn't
appear so ungainly. He couldn't help noticing the way the
bodice of her flowered dress gaped between the buttons
across her ample chest. Her tanned legs with their cord-
like veins were stretched out in front of her, and her skirt
rucked up so that her knees were bare and he could see the
wide pale expanse of thigh in the shadowy folds. He felt an
unusual prickle of excitement which spread between his
loins when she looked up lazily and smiled at him.

'If you eat all the peas there won't be any left for the pot,'
he said.

'They're nicer fresh, and uncooked. Better than the dried

or tinned kind. With a few 'taters and a bit of meat they make a tasty meal.'

'I'll give you some spuds if you want,' said George. He dropped his load to the ground and filled an enamel pail for her before she could answer.

'Thanks,' she said with the same slow smile. 'What's the matter with your foot?'

George had forgotten his injury. He looked down, in the direction of Maud's gaze, and saw the dried blood caking the holes in his leather boot.

'I did it with a fork. Wasn't looking where I was digging.'

'It looks nasty. You should get it seen to. Does it hurt you?'

'A bit.' George had forgotten the pain that caused him to limp, but now it began again as a dull throb. 'I'll clean it up when I get home.'

'If you come upstairs I'll do it for you.'

It was an invitation and George should have known better, but he was under her blowzy spell and seemed to have no will of his own. He followed her through the kitchen quarters, where she deposited what was left of the bowl of peas on the table, and then along a dark passage and up a winding stair. They passed no one. The pub seemed deserted, and George breathed a sigh of relief when Maud stopped at a door. The lintel was low and she had to stoop to pass through, but she did it automatically.

He expected the room to be as casual and untidy as its owner, so he was surprised at the sparseness of the attic he found himself in. It was a small space under the eaves, with brownish walls that had once been yellow. There was a marble-topped wash-stand with a bowl and jug patterned with flowers, a packing-case she used in place of a dressing-table with her celluloid-backed brush and hand-mirror carefully arranged, and in the corner a high bed covered with a white quilt.

The window overlooked the gardens of Duke's Road. He crossed to the window which was open at the bottom and leaned out.

'We're almost neighbours,' he said. 'I live over there.'

'I know. I've seen you in the garden.'

He didn't know why this remark embarrassed him; after all she had every right to look out of her window, and he had nothing to feel guilty about.

While he did what she instructed she was busy pouring water into the bowl, and finding clean rags and a brown bottle of iodine. Her touch was firm but gentle, and when she'd washed away the dried blood the wound didn't look so bad.

'You'll live,' she said with a smile, and finished with a dressing of clean cloth. 'What do you want now?'

There was no use pretending he didn't know what she meant. Her large fleshy body that gave off a soft odour of perspiration, her wide red mouth and steady gaze; her very proximity was a revelation to the tormented man. He put out his hand and ran his finger down between the upper curve of her breasts. To help him gain access she languidly undid the buttons and shrugged off the top half. Her breasts were so large that, once free, they hung almost to her waist: smooth and honey-coloured like the rest of her, with rosy tips like freshly picked raspberries. With a groan he buried his face in her, and she enveloped him in her strong arms and crooned to him as if he were a baby.

'Poor boy,' she whispered softly. 'Poor old boy. Is that all you want then? Maud's here – you're safe with Maud.'

He knew that he was: safe and happy. She didn't seem to mind that she was doing all the giving, and he was taking, and giving nothing in return. That would come later, they both knew. For the present his need was to be comforted by her mother figure, to feel her flesh against his cheek, and smell her womanhood. He loved and trusted her then, as a newborn baby loves and trusts the mother who gave birth to it.

It was late afternoon before he left the Black Mill, and the first person he met outside was Father Joe. The old priest was surprised to see George but he was careful not to show it. He stood there, smiling a greeting, the brim of his black hat shading his face.

'I didn't know you were a drinking man, George.'

'I'm not, Father.'

They surveyed each other silently, until George felt he had to give an explanation. 'I've been visiting.'

'Oh, yes. And who has had the pleasure of your company? Not Mr Booker: I passed him in the town. So it must be Miss Carter.'

'Yes, Father.' Caught out, George tried unsuccessfully to tear his eyes away from the old man's penetrating gaze.

'No doubt we shall see you at confession then?'

'Yes, Father.'

The priest tapped his teeth with his fingernail thoughtfully. 'What a blessing Miss Carter is to me, George. Her visitors usually turn up in the confessional. If not before, then soon after.'

If George had been a younger man he might have blushed. As it was he shuffled his feet in discomfort, anxious to get away. But Joe wasn't going to let him off the hook so lightly. 'Are you coming to mass on Sunday then: to see Isabel take her first communion? It's going to be a grand day.'

George had forgotten all about the special occasion, so he blustered emphatically to cover his oversight. 'Of course I'm coming. I promised Belle. You won't keep me away.'

'Good man,' said the priest and continued on his way, his round figure slowly disappearing from sight.

George relaxed, pleased that he'd been reminded of the forthcoming event. He'd hurt Belle enough; but he'd try and make it up to her by being present on her big day.

The weather was kind to them. The sun shone, but it was not too hot, and there was a cooling breeze coming in from the sea. It stirred the white skirts of the seven girls, and ruffled the hair of the four boys as they waited with the nun to process through the church to the altar rail. The girls wore new dresses, even if they were made out of parachute silk. Their heads were demurely covered, and in their hands they carried posies of flowers. They entered the church with an escort of devoted parents to lead the way.

Because Belle was the eldest, and alone, she'd positioned herself last in the line. All eyes seemed to be turned to her as she walked proudly, her head high. She was certainly the prettiest of the communicants, even if the square of lace on her head was ragged, and her dress so obviously a cut down night-gown.

When she'd looked at her reflection before leaving the house she'd seen the outline of her baggy navy-blue knickers through the thin cloth. Not having any others to change into she'd compromised by not wearing any at all, but even on a hot June day the church felt cool and draughty. The silver shoes kept slipping and tripping her up so that she limped slightly, like her father had after his accident with the garden fork.

George's heart turned upside-down when he saw her. She looked so pretty and innocent in her dreadful dress, although she looked proud and carried herself like a queen.

Suddenly on impulse he got up from his pew, crossed himself hurriedly, and pushed his way to his daughter's side. He wasn't going to let her be the only child without an escort on this important day. She lifted up her heart-shaped face and smiled at him, and he could still see the fading mark on her cheek where he'd struck her. But her face was all alight and shining with joy and showed that she'd forgiven him.

Side by side they approached the altar and Father Joe, whose face beamed as radiantly as theirs.

5

The alarm clock exploded with an earsplitting sound. It was spring; an April morning in 1944. George stretched and silenced the clock; he felt sleepy and contented. The light soon chased away the cobwebs and he pushed back the covers and swung his legs over the edge of the bed.

It was a Monday morning, and as he dressed himself in his working clothes he could hear the clatter of plates downstairs in the kitchen. One of the women had beaten him to it, and he guessed correctly that it was his daughter.

Belle had been up and about since six. Today was a very special day for her, and the excitement had given her a sleepless night and taken away her appetite. Even so she knew her father would want a good breakfast, so the kettle was steaming busily to make the tea, and on the table there was toast, marmalade and porridge. The kitchen looked different: it was still shabby because everything was so old and worn, but at least George had given the walls a coat of gay yellow paint, and everything was clean and put away in its proper place. There was even a jam-jar full of primroses standing on the window-sill, and Belle looked as fresh and smart as the flowers.

Four years had passed and she was now fourteen.

Although her wide blue eyes gave her the innocent appearance of a child her body had almost developed into the shape of the woman she would soon become. That woman was going to be a beauty without a doubt. She was tall for her age, with long slender legs which today were covered by their first pair of silk stockings. Her narrow back was straight, and her waist tiny, so that her small breasts looked more voluptuous than they really were. She was wearing a grey pleated skirt and a blouse that matched her eyes, and her curls were tamed by an army of pins into a knot on the nape of her neck from which tendrils escaped to tickle her white skin. As she worked busily she had to stop on occasion to push the curly red strands away from her face.

George stopped in the doorway to admire her. She pretended not to see him and spun a little on the heel of her shoe to show off the pleats in her skirt. In one hand she held a butter-knife and George jumped forward to take it from her.

'I'll do that,' he said. 'You'll spoil your things with grease.'

She pouted her lips at him and smiled. 'No I won't. I'm careful; not like Gran.'

'Where is she?' George looked around. 'I thought she was going to do the honours this morning.'

'She was still asleep, so I left her. If she's not down by the time the tea's brewed I'll take her up a cup.'

'Well, put an apron on over your new clothes: you don't want to spoil them. Isn't there one of your mother's around somewhere?'

'I'm all right.' Belle shrugged and began to pour the tea. Her hand shook slightly under the weight of the heavy pot but she didn't spill a drop. Today, in her stockings, with her matching grey jacket waiting to slip on and perhaps a smear of the Woolworth's lipstick she kept hidden in her pocket, she was going to start her first job. She felt grown-up, important, and she wanted to be a credit to her Dada who'd saved up so carefully for the money to buy her the new outfit. She wasn't going to let him down.

'I'll take you down to Jim Hilton's,' Henry had said. 'He's got some really good dresses and things. It'll save you money and coupons.'

'No, thank you,' Belle had answered quickly. 'Dada's promised to buy me everything new. I'm never going to wear other people's cast-offs again.'

'But you'll be helping the war effort.'

'Bother the war effort.'

Henry had left school the year before and, as promised, Jim had offered him an apprenticeship in his business. Auntie Mabel was disappointed.

'I thought I'd brought you up for better things than selling second-hand clothes,' she'd said.

'But I like Mr Hilton,' Henry insisted, 'and I like the shop. I want to work there.'

'I'm sure Mr Jeffreys would give you a job; after all, you used to be his delivery boy. You'd look smart in one of those white overalls, and they'd teach you to slice bacon on that new machine. Think of all the extras you might be given to bring home for the larder. Not black market, I wouldn't want you to have anything to do with that, but they must have leftovers. All open and above-board, a token of your hard work.'

Henry had been adamant. 'I like Jim and I like the shop,' he insisted. 'That's where I'm going to work.'

Since the day when Jim had nearly been robbed and he'd called Henry David, Henry'd wanted to protect the old man, and was quite happy at the prospect of throwing in his lot with him.

Henry didn't spend all his time in the shop. Often he was

70

sent out with a barrow to knock on doors and buy up people's unwanted clothing. At first he found this frightening, particularly when an argument ensued over the value of some rag, but under Jim's tuition he soon learnt to haggle, and even enjoyed it. After all he had the upper hand, and a pocket full of silver coins to tempt the public to raid their attics and wardrobes if they wanted a fair price.

Back at the shop he learnt to sort and price the clothing, looking for holes and tears and feeling for treasures that might have inadvertently slipped through the linings. Jim was quite pleased with him and gave him an old cap to wear, which he cocked over one eye proudly, and with his first pair of long trousers and black plimsolls made him look like a miniature version of his employer.

His wages were a pound a week and his dinner, which was either a bowl of watery soup or a hunk of bread and cheese. He gave his aunt fifteen shillings for his keep, and saved one of the two remaining half-crowns in a tin box under his bed. He was the proudest boy in Duke's Road, and went off to work every morning on his old push-bike as cocky as a sparrow.

Belle, like his aunt, thought the job was demeaning, although neither of them refused the treats he bought them. The cut-price fruit from the open market was always a luxury, as was the cheapest seat at the Duke of York's Cinema. Henry loved westerns, having not yet outgrown his boyhood passion for horses and guns, but Belle liked films with a strong romantic appeal, where the heroine either lives happily ever after or dies in the last reel, in the hero's arms. Usually if there was a choice Belle won and Henry was quite happy to escort her, even if he found it not to his taste. After all, if the main picture was one he considered sloppy, there was always the B feature after the Pathe News, which was usually something short but packed with action.

But however hard he tried, Belle refused to accept gifts of second-hand clothing, however good they were. She'd never forgotten an episode after her first communion when she'd heard two of the other girls giggling together, and heard them refer to her as a 'scarecrow'. Although it was nearly four years ago it still felt like yesterday.

At least nobody could call her a scarecrow today. Belle took a bite out of her toast and a blob of margarine dropped on to her plate, just missing her lap. Remembering her father's advice she crossed to the dresser, and pulling out one of the drawers found an apron that had belonged to her mother. She shook out the folds and tied it neatly around her waist to protect her skirt, and then resumed her seat at the table to finish her breakfast. The apron made her think about her mother.

'When are you going to visit Mam?' she asked.

George was busy stirring sugar into his cup. 'I don't know,' he admitted sadly. 'Saturday perhaps, if I can fit it in. Or Sunday, after morning mass, if Father Joe can spare me.'

Father Joe had offered George the job of caretaker at St Anne's when it had become vacant. At first he hadn't been keen to accept the post, thinking there might be strings attached, but the priest had taken him aside and assured him that it was purely a business arrangement, and George's relationship with the Almighty and his attendance at service was optional.

His duties were to open the church, stoke the boilers, and supervise the team of ladies who cleaned and arranged flowers on a rota basis. Extras, like emptying the offertory boxes, cleaning windows and delivering magazines, were a profitable private arrangement, and George was very happy with his position. He still had plenty of time left to 'dig for victory' on his allotment, and even managed to sell extra vegetables to the priest's housekeeper for a fair price. All in all Joe and George were well satisfied with their new relationship of employer and employee. In fact George was becoming quite a regular attender at mass these days, and had even surprised himself by feeling the need for confession.

Today was a Monday, always a busy time at the church. He had to bundle up the vestments and deliver them to the laundry, and then put away the missals and hymn-books that would have been left higgledy-piggledy after the last mass on Sunday.

'You didn't go to see Mam last week,' said Belle, trying not to sound accusing.

George put down his cup carefully. He wiped his moustache on the back of his hand to give himself time to think before replying. 'I know, lass. But it takes a good half hour to get there on the train and then there's the price of the ticket. Often when I do go she doesn't know me.'

'I thought perhaps I could go now I'll be working, Dada. I'll be able to afford the fare out of my wages.'

George smiled. This was going to be her first day at Lena Watkins's glove factory, and her wages were to be one pound five shillings for a full five-day week. Twenty-five shillings sounded like a fortune, but she would soon learn just how far it would go when she had to keep herself in stockings, underwear, and all the other things he knew females wanted.

'We'll see,' he said. 'Perhaps later on.'

'But I haven't seen Mam for months; not since they moved her from the hospital.'

'I know, Belle, just be patient.' Belle's chin was jutting in an ominously petulant way and George had to think quickly. He knew only too well how stubborn and argumentative his daughter could be on occasion. 'I'll have a

73

word with the doctor next time I go and see what he says.' He pushed his cup across the table. 'Pour me another cup, will you.'

Belle did as she was bid and decided not to pursue the conversation. She knew she was on difficult ground when discussing her mother, and the memory of that day last year when it all started was still painful to her.

Bess had continued to go downhill slowly over the years since the death of her son. She'd retreated into a world of her own, where none of her family had been able to follow her however hard they tried. At first it had just been the memory of Charlie that had been the centre of her concentration, as if by keeping the image of him in her mind's eye, she was at the same time keeping part of him alive.

She slept in his room and refused to let anyone else touch the few things that had belonged to him. She would rock herself to and fro on his cot at night, humming to herself the nursery rhymes and lullabies she'd sung to him during his babyhood.

Belle, on her narrow bed in the far corner of the room, she would ignore. Frightened of the frail, ghost-like figure her mother had become, Belle would pass sleepless nights under the covers. At last one night she had appeared like a fairy creature herself in the doorway of her grandmother's room, clutching a blanket around her shoulders, her eyes huge with fear in the moonlight. The old woman, whose own brain had only a fragile hold on reality, had been moved by the sight of the child. She remembered the days, long past, when she'd comforted her own children's fears; humped her fat body to the side of the bed and held out her arms. No mention was made of the change in the sleeping arrangements, but the following day George moved Belle's bed into her grandmother's room. It had remained there ever since.

After that Bess was rarely seen. Only as a spirit who roamed the house when everyone was out, picking at crumbs from the pantry, or searching the drawers and cupboards for some missing object. At last even her memories of Charlie seemed to lose importance, and her reason for existing was forgotten. This state of affairs couldn't have gone on indefinitely but no one even noticed when she withdrew her presence altogether. She'd been gone for several days when a policeman appeared on the doorstep late one evening, leading by the hand a wild, partially clothed figure, with mad eyes and trembling hands. George didn't recognise his own wife.

He'd felt guilty and tried to make amends. He'd washed and spoon-fed her and put her to bed, but she made no response to his overtures. In the morning he had no alternative but to call in the doctor. When an ambulance was called and Bess was removed, unresisting, to the nearest hospital, he felt guilty because his only feeling was one of relief. He knew he'd stopped loving his wife a long time before, and life became somewhat more pleasant when they'd got used to her absence.

Belle went to visit her mother every day. She'd meet George after school, and together they'd walk through the town and up the long steep hill to the big grey building overlooking the downs. At first the child found it rather daunting but she soon got used to it.

Mrs Kelly's bed was in a long side-ward painted a dingy shade of green. There were plenty of windows but most of them overlooked a quadrangle, and all you could see was row upon row of dustbins and the windows of the wards in the next block. From the end window you could just see the sea in the distance, but as that was where the Staff Sisters' desk was positioned it brought no pleasure to the patients.

Belle had never been inside a hospital before and the first

75

thing that struck her was how noisy it was. It was a ward specially designed for mental and nervous disorders, so the only women occupying the beds in the daytime were patients who were heavily sedated for their own good, or going through a period of sleep therapy. All the patients were dressed in their night clothes with dressing-gowns over the top. The clothes in which they'd been admitted were safely locked away, to prevent them discharging themselves and walking out into the street. It was that, or keep the ward locked, which was a Victorian procedure the authorities frowned upon.

In the centre of the ward was a long table where the patients sat, making baskets or knitting, or any other occupational activity that was provided. They chatted noisily like a flock of birds as they worked, and the air was heavy with the smoke from a thousand cigarettes.

The nurses had tried hard to encourage Bess to join the other women but so far had been unsuccessful. They found her always in the same place, sitting in an upright chair beside her bed, facing the wall. She wore a wool dressing-gown the hospital had loaned, and a pair of blue felt slippers left behind by a previous patient. Her hair had been cut to her ears in a ragged fashion, as the nurse who admitted her couldn't get a comb through the unkempt tangle. She neither moved nor spoke, being led about the ward like some imbecile child, potted and spoon-fed at regular intervals. The staff were quite fond of her because she gave no trouble. Not like some of the women who were always complaining, arguing, or fighting.

So nobody was prepared for the day when Bess suddenly came out of the coma she'd been in for so long. Two of the patients, a woman called Lily, who couldn't read or write, and an old fat woman called Dot, were talking about their husbands.

'Bert hasn't been near me since I've been in here,' Lily complained. 'I know he's got the kids to look after, but you'd think his mother would give a hand at looking after them.'

'He sounds like a good bloke,' Dot said. 'After all, he could have put them in a home.'

'I suppose so.' Lily thought for a moment and then asked, 'What about your old man, Dot? I haven't seen you get any visitors. Hasn't your husband been to visit you?'

'He can't,' said Dot bluntly. 'I'm a widow. Charlie's dead.'

Lily looked at her friend anticipating a good gossip, but before Dot could elaborate an unusual movement caught their eye from the direction of Bess Kelly's chair. The thin gaunt figure was struggling to her feet, the first spontaneous reaction she had taken to her surroundings since she'd been admitted to the hospital. So surprised were her fellow patients, and the staff, that they watched fascinated to see what was going to happen next.

Steadying herself on the back of the chair she stared at Dot, her eyes faintly shot with blood. Then she opened cracked lips and her voice croaked, 'Charlie's dead?' in a vague wondering tone. Then louder, her vocal cords growing stronger, 'Charlie's dead!' and then with an awesome shriek as if she'd at last accepted the truth, 'Charlie's dead . . .!'

The nurse in charge of the ward, a young girl, still fairly inexperienced, came to life and stepped forward, but Bess was too quick for her. With a cry that sounded more feral than human she dodged the nurses restraining hand, and fled down the length of the ward gathering speed as she ran, and losing one of her slippers on the way. Without stopping she ran straight through the clear glass window behind the Staff Nurses' desk, and disappeared from view.

No one could guess whether this had been her intention,

a sort of dramatic suicide attempt, or whether she tripped and fell headlong through the pane. It all happened so quickly that when questioned afterwards everyone came up with a different version of events. If it was oblivion her disordered mind was after, she failed, because although horribly lacerated about the face and head, the height from the window was not a great one. She was still alive and breathing when help reached her.

For the second time a policeman turned up on the doorstep of George Kelly's house. This time with news of the accident, and the information that Bessie had already been transferred, for her own safety, to a security wing of the nearest asylum. She'd remained there ever since and there had not been any noticed, or reported, change in her condition.

George went to visit his wife when he had the money for the fare. He was horrified by what he saw, so he always discouraged Belle from going with him. If Bess didn't recognise him, how could he expect her to recognise her own daughter, who was rapidly changing from a child to a young woman? He found the visits painful and it was only conscience that kept him going at all. He saw no resemblance in the blank scarred face that stared at him across the bare visitors' enclosure to the pretty young woman he'd married.

The only positive thing that came out of the removal of Bess from their lives was the change it had on old Bridget. As Bess seemed to lose her senses Bridget slowly regained hers. Old she might be, and fat, but it was the sedentary life that she'd been leading that had been her downfall. One day hunger pangs had carried her from her bed to the scullery, where she shuffled about on her swollen feet muttering to herself. Obviously displeased by what met her eyes she remembered her own housekeeping days. When

Belle and George arrived home at the end of the day they found a potato pie in the oven, and Gran bent over the sink washing dishes. From then on things continued to get better. Because of her age and size there were many things that were outside her capabilities, but she could cook, sew, and even do some of the cleaning that no one had bothered about for months. She became an inspiration to George and Belle and they were soon doing their bit as well; not as a duty, but because they enjoyed living in a well-run house.

Often the old lady was up before them, because she took cat-naps when she was alone so didn't need a full night's sleep. This April morning they'd beaten her to it because she'd forgotten Belle was starting work.

'You should have woken me,' she grumbled as she gulped the cup of strong tea Belle put in front of her. 'I like to be first in me kitchen, before you mess it up.'

Belle grinned: amused by her use of the word 'me', as if the kitchen belonged exclusively to her. 'Don't worry, Gran,' she said. 'We'll soon be gone and leave you in peace.'

'I'll be going to the allotment when I've locked up the church,' George said. 'What do you want for the pot? I've some young carrots, and the spring greens look good.'

'I thought I'd make a stew for tonight,' Bridget pondered. 'There's none of the meat left; it was such a small joint we finished it yesterday. But with lentils and suet dumplings it should be filling.'

'Lovely, Ma,' said George. 'I'll pull some onions as well to give it flavour.'

Bridget dipped a finger of cold toast into her teacup and sucked on it happily. Belle pushed back her chair and saw her grandmother staring at her.

'What's the matter, Gran?' she asked, smoothing down her skirt. 'Don't I look all right?'

'You look a picture, lass. But why do you pull your hair

back tight like that? You're too young to wear it so severe.'

Belle touched the rows of pins doubtfully and looked at her father. 'I wanted to look grown-up. What do you think, Dada?'

'You're young and pretty,' he said. 'Wear it loose, or tied back with a ribbon.'

'I haven't got a ribbon.'

'There's one on my dressing-table,' Bridget said. 'I found it when I was clearing out a drawer yesterday. It's blue and will match your blouse.'

'Thanks, Gran,' said Belle, giving her a quick hug. 'I'll go and get it.'

The ribbon certainly made a difference, Belle decided, viewing herself in the glass. It kept her unruly curls in order and brought out the colour of her eyes. Her father was waiting for her when she stepped out on to the landing.

'That's better,' he said. 'I thought you'd like this, for luck.' He pinned a small silver brooch in the shape of a cat on the lapel of her jacket. 'It belongs to your mother, but I'm sure she'd want you to have it.'

Clutching her cheap black handbag Belle paused at the bottom of the front steps, looking for twitching curtains. She wanted the neighbours to see the new Belle. Never again was she going to be the poorly dressed little girl wearing her brother's boots. She'd hated feeling that everybody despised or felt sorry for her. It was annoying that Duke's Road was quite deserted, and there was no sign of life in any of the houses. She hadn't walked more than a few yards when she heard a bicycle bell and someone calling her name.

It was only Henry Murtell on his rusty machine, with his working cap pulled tightly down over his ears, and his glasses catching the sunlight. He slowed down with a screech of brakes and free-wheeled along beside her.

'You're out early,' he said, not being able to keep the admiration out of his voice at the sight of Belle in her new clothes. 'Where are you going?'

'To work,' Belle said proudly. 'At Lena Watkins's glove factory. It's my first day.'

'Do you think you'll like it?'

'Of course. I don't expect they'll let me do anything very important today, but I'm going to work hard so that they give me the best jobs. I'll be making gloves for famous people soon.'

'I'm sure you will.'

At the bottom of the hill Belle expected Henry to leave her. He would have to turn left to reach Jim's shop in the town centre, whereas her destination was a row of business premises further up the Ditchling Road. To her surprise he turned to the right and scooted along beside her.

'I have to go to the home-bake shop first,' he explained, showing her a half-crown Jim had given him. 'I have to get two Cornish pasties for our lunch. If I get them on my way to work, and wrap them in my scarf, they stay hot.'

Belle's mouth watered: she knew the shop on the Preston Road. Many a time she'd stopped outside, her face to the glass, smelling the savory and fruity smells that wafted in the air. Once Dada had bought her an apple pie, all to herself, and she still remembered the taste of the crisp sugary top, and the way the pastry melted in her mouth.

Seeing the expression on her face Henry said, 'If you want to come, I'll buy you a pie.'

'I can't. There isn't time. I mustn't be late on my first day.'

'You won't be. Sit on the cross-bar and it won't take five minutes extra.'

'And spoil my skirt? You must be joking!' but Belle's

voice had softened with yearning. 'I'll run by the side. You know how fast I can run, Henry.'

It was all downhill and they reached the shop in no time at all. Belle's heart sank at the sight of the early morning queue of shoppers. Business was always brisk first thing in the morning, when the pies were fresh and hot from the huge ovens that roared continually at the back.

'Don't worry,' Henry said reassuringly. 'There's always a queue, but it moves fast because everybody's in a hurry. What would you like? Meat and potato – cheese and onion?'

'I'd love a fruit pie, with sugar on the top.'

'Apple or rhubarb?'

'Rhubarb. Can I have one that's well done; where the sugar's all brown and bubbling?'

Henry paid for his Cornish pasties, and bought Belle her rhubarb tart that was so well cooked it was burnt around the edges. His were parcelled up to take to work but Belle insisted on eating hers straight away. Her eyes were sparkling as she swallowed the last mouthful, licking the crumbs from her fingers greedily. Then she noticed the big wooden clock hanging over the counter, and grabbed Henry's arm.

'Look at the time! I'm going to be late.' It was eight minutes to the half hour and she wouldn't get there on time however much she hurried. Standing in the queue and eating the pie had taken longer than she thought. She turned her blue eyes on Henry, and he saw they were full of a mixture of tragedy and despair. He guessed the implication. 'I'll never make it,' she whispered.

'Yes you will. Climb on the cross-bar.'

'But it's out of your way. I'll make you late as well.'

'It doesn't matter. Mr Hilton won't care how late I am as long as the pasties are still hot.'

The cross-bar was useless so in the end Belle had to ruck up her skirt and climb up behind him. It was still after the half-hour before they arrived at the destination. The factory was situated on an upper floor, over an empty warehouse. It comprised two large workrooms, a front office, and the inner sanctum where the owner, Lena Watkins, reigned supreme.

Belle half fell from the pillion on to the pavement and brushed down her clothes. 'Do I look all right?' she asked.

Henry studied her critically. 'You've lost your ribbons,' he said.

Belle put her hand up to her head, and felt the loose tumbling curls that she'd tried so hard to tame. She ran her fingers through her hair knowing that it was useless asking Henry if he had a comb to lend her, let alone a grip. Her skirt was creased and there was a grease mark on it where it had brushed against the unprotected chain, and there was no way in which she would be able to hide the ladder in her new stockings.

'It'll have to do,' she muttered tearfully. 'Thanks Henry.' She ran up the stairs and pushed open the door that had OFFICE painted on its glass panel in black and gold lettering.

A woman was working busily at a desk in the middle of the room. She was typing on a large upright machine, her fingers brisk on the noisy keys. As Belle entered breathlessly she looked up and regarded the girl kindly. She had a friendly face and Belle relaxed slightly.

'I'm Isabel Kelly,' Belle said. 'I'm sorry I'm late.'

6

Belle stood on the strip of carpet inside the inner door and looked at Lena Watkins. The proprietor of the factory wasn't at all what she'd expected, nor were her surroundings.

The outer office had been sparse and businesslike, but this small room, heated by a gas fire even on this spring day, gave an exotic feeling of opulence. It measured not much more than twenty square feet, but into this small space was crammed the usual contents of a normal drawing-room: an armchair covered in shiny leather and a drop-leaf table, a row of book-shelves, and a two-seater settee covered in chintz printed with an overblown and gaudy design of flowers. The walls were hung with embossed paper: brown and green, reminiscent of William Morris. The small window was swathed in lace and fringed looped green velvet.

In the corner a large brass cage stood on an occasional table. A frayed grey parrot with solemn beady eyes peered through the confining bars in a bored fashion.

Lena Watkins was standing by the cage making comforting hissing noises at the bird, and trying to feed it with peanuts. A pile of empty shells was scattered around her feet on the carpet, and also a few rejected nuts and grapes. These were pushed back through the bars spitefully, by a clawed foot. The parrot's name was Warlock, which was apt, as he seemed to ooze evil through every tattered feather. Warlock hated everybody and everybody hated him; with the exception of his owner, Lena Watkins, who adored him for some reason unknown to the staff.

Mrs Watkins turned to Belle a sharp little face with a long hooked nose that resembled a beak. Her greying hair was carefully set in Marcel waves, as shiny and rigid as corrugated iron. Her dress of pale violet crêpe floated about her tiny birdlike figure, the frilled neck and sleeves as feathery and ruffled as her pet's plumage. Her eyes, small, black and piercing, stared at Belle from over the gold-rimmed half-moon glasses that had slipped and settled halfway down her nose.

'So you are Isabel Kelly,' she said with a snort that sounded to Belle a mixture of laughter and disbelief.

Belle found her cheeks growing hot and shuffled her feet unhappily, all too aware of the ladder in her stocking.

'Yes, madam.'

Lena Watkins pushed the glasses up a notch or two, the better to study her new employee, and then let them slide back into their usual position. 'You will call me Mrs Watkins like everybody else,' she said.

'Yes, madam – I mean Mrs Watkins.'

'And it's best for you to understand at the very beginning that the three things I won't tolerate from my staff are: rudeness, untidiness, and unpunctuality.'

'Yes, Mrs Watkins,' answered Belle, automatically putting a hand up to her hair. She guessed her employer was referring to the escaped curls and the missing ribbon. She knew she was late and wasn't sure if she should apologise as this would only bring it to Mrs Watkins's notice. She didn't think she'd been rude – yet. But there was still plenty of time for that.

'Why were you late?' Lena Watkins inserted a thin finger through the bars of the cage to scratch Warlock's head. With a little shriek of rage he bit it. She withdrew quickly, inspecting the bead of blood, and then dabbed the place with a fragile square of lace that she kept in her pocket for this purpose. Belle was surprised that any blood could issue from a finger that looked more bone than flesh.

'My little sister's ill. I had to go for the doctor.' The lie came easily although Belle felt guilty. She'd never seen the harm of little white lies, or even bigger darker ones, if they got her out of trouble. But she'd promised herself, now that she was a working grown-up woman, to tell the truth. She'd broken that promise within a few hours of making it so she might as well continue with the falsehood, to make it sound plausible. 'She was took bad in the night, Mrs Watkins. With terrible pains in her belly. I've been up all night with her.' Belle looked down sadly, contemplating her bitten fingernails, and waited to see what effect her story had made.

'Stomach, not belly,' Lena corrected. 'Perhaps you shouldn't have come in at all if your sister's so ill. Perhaps you'd like to go back home now?' The words were kind but not the voice. Belle guessed that Mrs Watkins didn't completely believe her, particularly when she added, 'How old is your sister, and what's her name?'

'She's four years old, and her name's Dorothy,' Belle answered glibly. She rather enjoyed the opportunity to invent an imaginary sister. In her mind's eye she saw a frail little figure stretched on a bed and writhing in agony, with herself in a white cap and apron adorned with a red cross, administering beef tea.

'You'd better run along home, Miss Kelly,' Lena Watkins said, brushing the crumbs of nutshell from her palms as if dismissing Belle before she'd even started work.

Belle knew she'd gone too far. The story had only been an excuse for being late; she'd been looking forward to her first day at work, and how could she explain her early return to Gran and Dada?

'Oh, no, Mrs Watkins!' she said quickly 'I'm sure she'll be all right when the doctor gives her some medicine; and my Gran's at home with her.'

Lena Watkins gave another of her little snorts, that could mean satisfaction or disbelief. 'Well, now you are here we mustn't waste any more time. Your first duty every morning is to clean out Warlock's cage,' and she indicated the parrot. Belle looked at the horrible bird and opened her mouth to argue but her employer butted in before she could make a sound. She seemed to have read Belle's thoughts. 'If you think it's beneath you, Miss Kelly, you can pick up your things and leave now. A good employee is obedient whatever task they might be set, and they tackle it cheerfully and without question. You'll find the things in that cardboard box in the corner.'

'Yes, Mrs Watkins.'

Belle carried the box to the table and spread newspaper on the polished surface, before scraping the bottom of the cage clean and spreading fresh sand and grit. All the while she was aware of the evil eye of Warlock watching for an opportunity to peck her, and the critical eyes of Mrs Watkins. When she'd finished Mrs Watkins actually smiled at her as if she'd passed some kind of initiation test.

'Good girl,' she said. 'Now, if you go outside, Miss Binns will want to see how good you are with your needle,' and she turned away as if in dismissal.

Miss Binns, known to her colleagues as Joyce, was the typist who Belle had first seen on arrival. She was a capable woman in her thirties and was Lena Watkins's right-hand person. Nothing was allowed to happen in the factory that she didn't know about, and her main aim in life seemed to be to protect her employer from worry and stress. She always dressed in the same fashion: almost a uniform of navy-blue skirt and cardigan, and a crisp white blouse that resembled a man's shirt. She always sported a tie, changing its colour with her mood and the seasons. Today, to denote spring, it was striped green and yellow. On her large feet she wore sensible brogues and hand-knitted stockings, and her brown hair was wound in earphones each side of her head. If her appearance was solid and masculine, her voice was pleasantly modulated, and her eyes gentle and kind.

'Now that wasn't too bad, was it?' she asked as Belle left Mrs Watkins's room and approached the desk for instructions.

'She made me clean out the parrot's cage,' Belle said woefully. 'She said I have to do it every morning.'

'Don't worry, you'll get used to it. It's always the job of the new girl, and Warlock isn't so bad. He enjoys frightening people, just like his mistress, but he wouldn't really harm you.' Belle looked doubtful, but Miss Binns's words seemed reassuring. 'If you follow me, I'll take you to the workroom to meet the other girls. They're all about your age. The older ones have either left to have babies or do war work. Don't look so worried, we're not going to eat you.'

Belle followed her through a door at the end of the room. She stood nervously behind Miss Binns, surveying the long table in the centre of the room around which sat six young women, all working away busily. The room itself was full of light because the walls were painted white, and the long uncurtained windows gave a panoramic view across the roofs of the houses, showing the distant blue sea and far horizon. It was such a bright room that they didn't need artificial light to do their close sewing, but the regulation blackout blinds were rolled above each window as a reminder that there was still a war on.

Six pairs of eyes looked up from their work to stare at Belle, and the owner of a pair of hazel eyes that held hers for a trifle longer than necessary and then winked in a conspiratorial fashion particularly interested her.

'Now girls,' said Joyce Binns, 'this is Miss Kelly.'

She introduced all the workers to Belle who found it impossible to remember any of the names, apart from 'hazel eyes' who was introduced as Miss Smart. A piece of soft fabric was handed to her, a needle and a length of thread, and she was instructed to cut the material in two and practise stab-stitching. She was so nervous that she felt her hands were all thumbs, and even had difficulty in threading the needle. But then Miss Smart, of the hazel eyes, grinned at her across the table and put her at her ease. Stab-stitching she found was similar in appearance to a running-stitch, but the needle had to go in and out every time in a separate motion. At first her stitches were too large, but at the third attempt Miss Binns nodded her approval and told her to try a Streatley stitch, which she found easier as it was more like oversewing.

When the wall clock struck half past ten Miss Binns rang a hand bell and everybody stopped work. The girls started chattering and stretching, and a plump girl with spots informed Belle that this was the fifteen-minute morning break when tea was available.

Belle had her first chance to look around and noticed some large framed photographs of film-stars hanging on a nearby wall. She was busy studying a glamorous picture of Vivien Leigh when Miss Smart came across to join her.

'Hello,' she said, her smile as merry as her hazel eyes. 'My name's Flora – what's yours?'

'Isabel, but everybody shortens it to Belle.'

89

'It's only old Watkins who insists on calling everybody "Miss", so watch it when she's around. Miss Binns likes us to call her Joyce, and the fat girl sitting next to you is Betty.'

It sounded a more friendly arrangement, but Belle was still admiring the photographs. 'Isn't she beautiful?' she sighed over a picture of Anna Neagle who was wearing an evening dress and elbow-length gloves. 'I wish I could dress like that.'

'Don't we all.' Flora perched on the edge of a table and swung bare legs that were streaked orange with imitation stocking make-up. 'Those gloves she's wearing were made here.'

'Really!' Belle hadn't noticed that all the stars were wearing gloves. 'Did you help make them?'

'Don't be silly. Before my time. I'm sixteen and I've only been working here a year; before that I was making lampshades. Joyce made the pair Patricia Roc's wearing; if you ask her about it you'll be in her good books for ever. Let's go and get our tea.'

Belle followed her new friend through an archway into another room that seemed to be multi-purpose. At one end was a butler-sink and a small stove where the tea was brewed, but the other end was used for packing and storing materials.

A tall cabinet stood against the wall, its narrow compartments labelled with the types of leather it contained. Belle recognised pigskin and goatskin, but Flora had to explain that lamb-mocha was from an Arabian sheep, and doeskin is from deer or antelope and was very expensive. An elderly man in a brown workman's overall was busy stretching skins on a side-bench. When the girls appeared he manned the teapot, and poured the thick brown liquid sloppily into a row of chipped china cups. Belle noticed that each girl dropped a penny into a jam-jar before taking their drink. She'd brought no money so stepped back in embarrassment.

'It's all right,' Flora whispered. 'I'll pay for you this time; but you have to bring your own sugar and a mug with your name on. Take that blue china one now, it belonged to a girl who left last week.'

The cup had the name Pam painted on it in red nail varnish. It was slightly cracked, but the tea was hot and strong, just as she liked it. When the bell rang again she felt part of the team as the girls paraded back to the workroom.

The rest of the morning was spent practising embroidery stitches. Belle had thought she could only do chain-stitch, but with a bit of encouragement from Joyce Binns she found that she had a natural flair for French knots and feather-stitch. She loved the feel of the coloured silks and the way they slipped so easily through the fabric. Betty was busy sewing sequins on to the back of a black velvet evening-glove. Belle watched in anticipation of the time when she would be trusted to perform such tasks.

At one o'clock the factory closed down for one hour. Quickly the girls packed their work away, snatched up their coats, and hurried away in all directions. The only ones left in the workroom were Belle and Flora, and the man in the packing department. He was pointedly rattling his keys as if he were waiting to lock up.

'Come on,' Flora hissed in Belle's ear. 'Follow me.'

The two girls walked through the now deserted front office and down the stairs. The warm sun hit them as they reached the street and Belle turned her face gratefully: she wasn't used to spending so long indoors.

Flora ran across the road and perched on a crumbling wall opposite. She was a blowzy girl with heavy lids over her hazel eyes, and a head of rich brown hair as smooth as a nut. She wore it tucked away inside a snood, threaded through with a pink ribbon and tied in a bow over one ear. Her full lips were made even fuller by a generous application of bright red lipstick, and her cheeks were too rosy to be natural.

'Most of the girls live nearby and go home to dinner,' she explained patiently. 'I come all the way from Portslade and it takes over half an hour on the bus, so I usually bring a sandwich. But I didn't have time for any breakfast this morning so I ate it on the way in. Have you brought anything to eat?' she finished hopefully.

'No,' Belle admitted. 'I didn't think to. I didn't even know we stopped work at dinner-time.'

'It doesn't matter,' said Flora cheerfully. 'I'll get the boys to get us some chips.'

While Belle was still wondering who 'the boys' were, they arrived from a neighbouring saw-mill. They were big fellows not much older than Flora, in working clothes and heavy boots. Their hair and skin was encrusted with wood-shavings, and their hands were rough and blistered. Flora introduced them as Benjie, Sam, and Sydney. It was unusual to find young men who were not serving in the forces, but Belle soon found out that Benjie was blind in one eye, Sam failed his medical because of fallen arches, and Sydney was obviously not quite right in the head.

With whoops of delight they greeted the girls. They were only too pleased to pool their resources and send Sydney off to the nearest fish and chip shop. Belle was handed a parcel of chips wrapped in soiled newspaper.

'They're hot,' she said, peering between the greasy folds.

'I've put on plenty of salt and vinegar,' Sydney said. 'I hope you like it.'

'Oh yes,' Belle said greedily. 'Even if it does make my tongue sore.'

'There was only enough money to buy one piece of fish,'

he explained. 'We'll pass it round and have a bite each.'

The fish was delicious and they all got a large bite. The cheerfulness of her companions, and their generosity, won Belle's heart. She couldn't remember when she'd enjoyed a meal more.

The boys had to leave early as they only had a forty-minute break. Benjie kissed Flora sloppily on the mouth, Sam swung her off her feet in an energetic bear-hug, and Sydney slapped her boldly on the bottom. Then they raced off down the road, playing tag like a trio of schoolboys. Flora stretched herself lazily along the top of the wall, soaking up the sunshine. Belle sat down beside her.

'I like your friends,' Belle said. Flora grunted in agreement. 'Is one of them your boyfriend?'

'What do you mean?'

'Well, you know: do you like one of them better than the rest?'

'I like them all.'

'I know.' Belle persisted. 'But do you go out with one of them alone – as a couple?'

Flora half opened her hazel eyes and turned her head to look at Belle. 'I go out with all of them. Benjie's mother is an invalid, so he can only take me out at weekends when his dad's home. Sam works in a pub at weekends so he's only free in the week. But Sydney's free all the time so he takes me out when the others can't.'

It took Belle a few minutes to take this in and sort it out in her mind. Then she asked, 'Do you let them do anything?'

'Do you mean, do I let them kiss me? Of course I do. They give me a good time and I have to reward them.'

Belle was fairly streetwise, but the mysteries of what happened between the sexes in private had so far only been gleaned verbally and she was still rather mixed up. But she had to ask the question that was bothering her: the answer might open the door to the information she craved. 'Do you let them do anything else?'

'Sometimes. After all, they expect it. Benjie's not very good because he's still tied to his mother's apron strings, and Sam is rather nervous about it all. But Sydney's pretty good.'

Belle found this hard to believe and was inclined to think that Flora was teasing her. 'But Sydney's a bit simple isn't he?' she said, trying to put it kindly. 'I mean, he's nice, but he didn't seem very bright to me.'

'What's that got to do with it?' Flora sat up impatiently and began to massage her bare arms, flexing her muscles like an athlete getting ready for a race. 'He's a man, isn't he? And being a bit slow makes him a better lover. He's not shy or inhibited like the others, so he performs better.'

Belle looked at her companion, her eyes round with amazement. 'Are you going to marry him then?' she enquired. In the world she knew and lived in, the sort of relationship Flora was having should, by rights, lead to the altar, even if she had jumped the gun in the eyes of the Church. Flora started to laugh and Belle wondered what she'd said that was so funny.

'I'm not going to marry anyone for years and years,' Flora said firmly. 'Not until I'm at least twenty. I intend to have a good time first. Have you got a lover?'

Belle thought of Henry. If Flora had asked if she'd got a boyfriend she might have answered in the affirmative; after all, Henry might just pass muster in that category. But Henry Murtell in the role of a lover was outside the scope of even her vivid imagination.

'No,' she admitted, and tossed her head proudly. 'I'm a bit particular about things like that. I don't know how you can bear to let someone like Sydney near you, let alone touch you.'

Flora jumped off the wall and smoothed down her skirt. 'I didn't think you were going to turn out a prude with hoity-toity ideas. I thought we could be friends; but if you think you're so posh I was mistaken. Come on, let's get back inside. There's Enid and Betty back already and we musn't be late.'

Belle felt uncomfortable and wanted to make amends. After all, Flora had put herself out to be friendly towards her, and what she did in her spare time was her own business. The older girl strode ahead and Belle had to run to keep up with her.

'I didn't mean to upset you,' she said shyly. 'It's just that I haven't had any real experience of boys. I'm not posh, really I'm not.'

'You'd better not be,' said Flora grimly, 'or you won't get on with the rest of us. We're plain working girls and proud of it, so remember that if you want to be one of us.'

'I will, Flora,' said Belle quickly.

They joined the other girls hurrying up the stairs and on their way back to the workroom had to pass Mrs Watkins's door.

Belle still viewed it with morbid feelings of dread, as the parrot Warlock lived and waited there for her daily ministrations.

The door was partly open and Belle could hear voices inside, as if her employer had company. She couldn't resist peeping as she hurried past. Lena Watkins was reclining gracefully on the settee facing the door. The man in the brown overall who'd been in charge of the morning tea and the keys was sitting beside her. They were drinking coffee, by the aromatic smell, out of delicate china cups not much larger than the ones they used at home to hold the one boiled egg they were allowed each week. It wasn't this that astonished Belle: it was the intimate way they were sitting,

95

a bit too close for employer and employee, and the man's brown-clad arm was actually resting around Lena Watkins's thin shoulders. Belle couldn't help slowing down to get a better look in case her eyes had been deceiving her.

'Come on,' Flora hissed, pulling her arm. 'Don't let them see you.'

Belle obediently turned away, her mind in a whirl. After Flora's disclosures, and then seeing Mrs Watkins in what seemed to be a delicate situation, she began to wonder if the glove factory was a cover for a den of vice.

As they separated to take their seats for the afternoon session Flora said softly, 'Don't say a word Belle, about what you saw just now, or you'll only put your foot in it. I'll tell you when we break for tea.'

The disclosure was quite disappointing when Flora enlightened her. The two girls stood apart with their cups, and Flora explained that the man in the brown overall was actually Mr Watkins, their employer's husband.

Because Belle looked so interested Flora told her the full story. It had been handed down through the workers who had known Lena Watkins from the day she'd opened the factory for business. She was first known as Lena Brown, and had worked as a young seamstress in one of the sea-front hotels; repairing and turning linen, and watching over the laundry for split seams and missing buttons. Albert was a porter: a quiet introverted sort of man, with no interest in the bustle of hotel life, no particular ambition, but a careful head for money. It didn't take Lena long to find out about his Post Office savings book in which he'd accumulated a tidy sum.

Lena was ambitious, not for riches exactly but for enough wealth to get her out of her lowly position in the hotel where she was at everybody's beck and call and her work repetitive and unappreciated. She wanted to give the orders, not take them, and she saw Albert and his savings account as a step in the right direction.

Albert was flattered: Lena was the first woman to show any interest in him. When he found out that she was learning the art of making gloves from a book she'd borrowed from the library, and she suggested that they go into business together, he was quick to agree. The arrangement was that he would provide the money for the materials, do the packing and delivering – to begin with they only anticipated local trade – and Lena would produce the product.

She did more than that. When a famous actress was appearing at the Theatre Royal, Lena waited outside the stage door on the first night with a box of samples. Her cheek, and the quality of her work, paid off. She came away with an order for half a dozen pairs of elbow-length gloves, and a dozen pairs of mixed day gloves to match the actress's different outfits. Lena stayed up all night for a week, and after Albert delivered the completed order and came back with requests to supply other members of the company, Lena had to think about employing a couple of girls to help her out.

The factory, as they called it, was Albert's idea. They started with one room behind a church, but it was dark and out of the way, and as their number of clients grew they had to look for larger premises.

On the anniversary of their first order Lena married Albert at the local Registry Office. It was her idea. Left to himself Albert would have been quite happy to plod along in Lena's wake, stretching skins, packing boxes, and delivering orders to their growing number of customers. But Lena needed a husband to give respectability to the venture, and Mrs Lena Watkins sounded better than Miss Lena Brown. She also guessed that Albert would never give her any trouble. He didn't smoke or drink and he wasn't likely to flirt with any of the girls she employed. So she married him.

Instead of a honeymoon they took over the rooms above the warehouse, furnished it with the tools of their trade, and never looked back. Soon they not only had a team of girls who were employed full-time, but also a growing band of outworkers who were glad to earn a little extra cash doing simple sewing from home. There was also one lady who came in on a casual basis to work the sewing-machine that had pride of place in the workroom. Everyone else was warned not to touch it. Lena knew she'd made it when she was made a member of the 'London Guild of Glovers' and hung their framed certificate in a prominent place for visitors to admire.

How much of this story was fact and how much fiction Belle had no idea, but it gave her plenty to think about. When Mrs Watkins appeared in the workroom to inspect the day's work she saw her in a new light; even her frilly violet dress and rimmed glasses seemed attractive. Belle was ambitious, and finding that her employer had come from a poor background made her believe that there was hope, that she could also improve her lot if she worked hard. Of course Mrs Watkins had Albert and the only person Belle had was Henry. She couldn't imagine him being much help.

'You've worked very well, Miss Kelly,' Mrs Watkins said when she came to inspect Belle's handiwork. 'Your stitching is very neat for a beginner, and the fourchette you've inserted looks quite professional.'

'Thank you, Mrs Watkins.'

'You learn quickly as well. Keep up the good work.'

'I will.'

Belle positively glowed with the unexpected praise.

She'd made some mistakes that day and she intended to learn by them. To start with, tomorrow she would be on time, and she wouldn't shirk the task of cleaning out the parrot's cage. She would bring her own sandwiches, china cup and tea money, and of course she would have to do something about her fly-away hair.

She studied a studio portrait of Patricia Roc wearing a pair of Lena Watkins gloves. The film star's hair was swept up on to the top of her head and secured by combs. A row of cork-screw curls was arranged across her forehead, and the soft curling ends were piled loosely on the crown of her head. If Belle cut her hair short at the front, and back-combed the top, she might be able to secure the rest with hair-grips, even if Gran and Dada thought it too old for her.

'Did you enjoy your first day with us, Miss Kelly?' Mrs Watkins had come up beside her as she was putting on her jacket.

'Yes, thank you, Mrs Watkins.'

'We'll see you tomorrow then – and don't be late.'

'No, Mrs Watkins.'

Belle walked with Flora as far as the bus-stop and then broke into a run: not because she was late, but because she'd been shut up all day and felt exhilarated by her freedom. It didn't matter now about her laddered stocking or her tumbled hair; she was on her way home and suddenly the shabby house in Duke's Road seemed very welcome. Her hand was on the door-knob when she heard a voice hailing her. It was Henry, cycling up the road towards her, standing high on the pedals to keep himself moving. He looked young and grubby after a day spent pushing Jim's barrow around the town. His shirt-tail was dangling and his cap was folded and thrust into his belt; Belle felt ashamed of him.

Flora might be satisfied with rough boys like Sydney and

Sam, and Mrs Watkins might be content with her Albert, but Belle had set her heart on better things. She wanted someone like the leading men in the romantic films she enjoyed. Someone who would appreciate her and who she would be proud to be seen with. Not a spotty boy with glasses on a rusty bike.

Although Henry continued to call her name she pretended not to hear him. She turned the handle and disappeared into the house, slamming the door firmly behind her.

7

'Are you going out with Henry tonight?'

'I suppose so.' Belle frowned over her sewing. She didn't like chatting when she was trying to concentrate, and the neat, even stitches she was so proud of were the result of painstaking care.

'Where's he taking you – the pictures?'

'That's where we usually go on a Friday night. It's the only time he's got any money: pay day.'

'Benjie's the same,' admitted Flora. 'But he is generous, I grant you that.'

The spear point needle pierced the soft chamois leather and Belle pulled the waxed thread through smoothly. Around them the other girls were working silently. The glove she was working on was part of an order for a Lady Patterson, who lived in a tall Regency villa in one of the squares bordering the sea-front in neighbouring Hove. Belle was the only girl Mrs Watkins trusted with this work. After two years she'd surpassed even Joyce Binns in the quality of her handwork. Joyce wasn't jealous. She was quite happy spending more time typing out accounts; and she was learning short-hand at evening classes and liked the opportunity to practise. Flora was working on the linings. It was simpler work, and as she wasn't as skilled as her friend she didn't mind doing the simpler jobs.

In the two years she'd worked at the glove factory Belle had changed considerably. Gone was the childish innocence she'd worn as a protective cloak on that April day in 1944 when the two girls had met and made friends. Belle was now sixteen, and if anything looked older than her years. Her face was thinner and she seemed to have developed even more freckles.

She hated the smattering of brown pigments that marred her white skin and had tried every method she knew to get rid of them. She'd dabbed them with an infusion of elderflowers, and castor-oil and lemon juice, a treatment she'd read about in a newspaper. Next she'd experimented with a lotion bought from a chemist's shop that cost almost a week's wages. All to no avail. In desperation she'd turned to an old wives remedy recommended by Gran: bathing her skin with dew as the sun rose, and at the same time whispering an incantation. Gran said it couldn't fail because it was magic. Perhaps she'd memorised it incorrectly, or missed something vital out, because afterwards the freckles were as unsightly as ever. Some people seemed to find them attractive and Belle could never understand why.

Her blue eyes were if anything larger, and looked at the world with wonder and excitement. Belle was convinced that life had something incredible waiting for her just around the corner, and she was frightened of missing it. But the thing people noticed about her first was her glorious hair. It hung to her shoulders like an amber and gold mist with bronze highlights that caught the sun. The curls were still loose and untamed and she staunchly refused to cut it as fashion decreed, or to pin it back tightly as Mrs Watkins instructed.

There were a lot of things about Isabel Kelly that Lena

Watkins disapproved of, and she'd tried over the past two years to change the girl, unsuccessfully. When Belle had started coming to work without stockings she'd taken her aside and explained that bare legs were unladylike and gave men the wrong ideas. Belle had stared at her employer innocently, and then dropped her eyes so that Mrs Watkins wouldn't see the pleased curl of her lips.

'I'm sorry, Mrs Watkins,' she'd answered over-politely. 'I laddered my good pair on a packing-case Mr Watkins left in the passage. I didn't have any money to buy a new pair.'

'But you were only paid on Friday, Miss Kelly, and I gave you a bonus for the work I let you take home.'

'My Dada had to visit Mam in hospital. He hadn't got the fare so I had to give him enough to buy the train ticket. And my Gran's on a special diet because her blood's bad. She has to have liver every week, and fresh fruit every day.'

'Is your father out of work again?'

'Yes, Mrs Watkins. He fell out with Father Joe because of his drinking.'

Mrs Watkins looked at Belle in surprise. 'Your father's taken to drink?' she asked, her sympathy immediately aroused.

'Oh, no, Mrs Watkins!' Belle said emphatically, as if such a thing was impossible. 'I meant Father Joe.'

'How terrible,' said Lena Watkins. She knew nothing about Catholics, but had always believed that priests of all denominations were immune to the sins of the flesh.

Of course it was just one of Belle's white lies, and she didn't dare look at her employer in case she guessed. The first suggestion was the truth: that George Kelly these days did like a drop of the hard stuff; and on occasion had been found the worse for drink. Belle was ashamed. In her young eyes her Dada was still the finest person in the world and nobody was going to know about his lapses if she had anything to do with it. Father Joe was a different matter; he was a priest, and if he couldn't stand up for himself he had God to do it for him.

Another bone of contention between Mrs Watkins and Belle was the wearing of the overall. To improve the appearance of the girls they had been supplied with overalls and instructed to wear them while they were working. They were made of army surplus material because it was cheap; it was also the only fabric available.

Both Belle and Flora hated the shapeless garments and their colour of dull browny yellow. The coarse cotton material hung stiffly no matter how many times they washed it, and the collars and cuffs rubbed sore marks on their tender flesh. They'd tried everything to get rid of the offending garments: from stuffing them behind the packing-table to deliberately spilling tea and indelible ink down the fronts. But Mrs Watkins seemed to have an unlimited supply of patience and overalls, and as fast as they disappeared to the laundry or dustbin, fresh ones seemed to spring up overnight, like mushrooms. The girls had no choice but to put them on.

Today Flora was wearing hers tightly belted to show off her shape, and the skirt was hitched up above her knees. Belle's was hanging over the back of her chair, ready to put on if her employer appeared suddenly.

The bell rang for dinner and the other girls quickly departed leaving Flora and Belle alone. Belle started to fold up her work, and when she looked up found Flora staring at her. 'What is it?' she asked, thinking that her friend had some problem she wanted to talk about. 'Are you feeling all right?'

'I've been waiting all morning to tell you something.' She wouldn't meet Belle's eyes, and this showed that whatever was on her mind was important. 'I couldn't talk in front of the other girls. You know how nosey they are.'

Belle did know. 'Well, they've all gone now,' she said. 'So what is it?'

Flora still wouldn't look at Belle. She was usually so unembarrassed and gregarious that Belle was surprised. At last Flora said, 'I'm getting married – to Benjie.'

'But are you old enough?'

Belle knew that Flora had been going out with the one-eyed boy from the saw-mill more regularly than with Sam or Sydney. Even so the news was unexpected; Flora wasn't that much older than she was.

'I'm eighteen.' Flora jutted out her chin aggressively, as if she were waiting for Belle to argue. 'And my mum and dad say I can – so there.'

'Well then Flora, that's fine. Congratulations.' Belle didn't know what else to say, because her friend didn't look as happy as she should after imparting such exciting news. In fact Belle suspected that the girl was near to tears. Anything that could so affect Flora must be devastating as she usually shook off trouble easily, and Belle had never seen her cry. On impulse she put her arm around the girl and asked, 'What's the matter Flora? Don't you want to marry him?'

'Oh yes, of course I do. I always knew I'd marry Benjie one day – but not like this.' Belle waited without saying anything. Flora managed to compose herself, and when she spoke again her voice was almost a whisper as if she expected Mrs Watkins could hear her. 'I'm going to have a baby,' she said at last.

'Oh Flora, you are silly; why didn't you tell me before? But why is it so awful? Benjie's kind and he'll make you a good husband; and he'll be a good father to the baby. Lots of girls are pregnant on their wedding day – you won't be the first. So cheer up and tell me why you're so unhappy?'

'Because Benjie's not the father.'

'Oh!' Belle saw the dilemma and didn't know what to say. She was broad-minded but, even so, she was slightly shocked by the revelation. 'Is it . . .?'

'Sydney's? Yes.'

Now Belle was shocked. Not because her friend was pregnant, but because she couldn't understand how she could bear Sydney, with his drooling mouth and unfocused eyes, near her; let alone touch her in the way she must have allowed.

'Does he know?'

'Who?'

'Benjie. Does he know the baby isn't his?'

'Of course not!' Flora was regaining her usual air of care-lessness now that the burden was off her chest. 'And you're not going to tell him, Isabel Kelly. It's just between you and me.'

'Of course I won't tell him; what do you take me for? It's just – it doesn't seem fair somehow.'

'Fair!' Flora's eyes flashed. 'It's not fair on me either. It's bad enough having a baby I don't want, but I'm not going to be shamed by not having a husband. Anyway, he could have got me into trouble, he knows that. He hasn't bothered to check dates or anything so he's never likely to find out.'

'I suppose not.'

'Sh!'

A rattle of keys heralded Mr Watkins's approach, and they quickly put away their work and their overalls. He became quite surly if they kept him waiting when he wanted to lock up.

Today however it was his wife, Lena, carrying the keys. She was dressed to go out in a black cloth coat and a stylish hat with a feather, which Belle suspected could have been shed or stolen from Warlock's rump. Like a shadow her husband hovered behind. He also had changed his brown overall for an overcoat and bowler hat. Belle had never seen him dressed in anything but his working clothes and she had to put a hand over her mouth to suppress a giggle.

'I'm glad I've caught you both,' Mrs Watkins said. She was smiling so they guessed she wanted them to do something for her. 'Mr Watkins has to go up to town on important business. He has to collect samples for that new order, and deliver some goods personally. We believe the personal touch brings in customers.' She indicated Mr Watkins who was still hovering silently in the background. 'I am going to accompany him to the station, so I want you, Miss Smart,' and she nodded to Flora, 'to lock the door and have charge of the keys.'

Flora looked surprised at the responsibility. She took the keys and muttered a 'Yes, Mrs Watkins,' in her employers direction. Belle was just about to move in the direction of the door when Mrs Watkins stopped her with a quick gesture.

'I have a job for you also, Miss Kelly,' she said. 'Mrs Bishop, who lives in Dyke Road, telephoned me this morning. She wants someone to visit her this afternoon to take measurements for gloves to match her new winter coat. Here is the address, and some money for your bus fare.' She handed Belle a brown envelope. 'Remember to take a pattern book, and a gloving tape to get the size right. If she wants motoring gloves I would suggest rabbit. Tell her we have some good Chinchilla and Beveren pelts, which are especially warm and smart with a fleecy lining. If they're just for walking out she might prefer mittens. They're quicker and easier to make if she's in a hurry.'

'Yes, Mrs Watkins.'

'And do remember to be polite, and call her madam.'

'Of course, Mrs Watkins.'

'And tidy your hair before you go, Miss Kelly, and wash

your face. You know I don't approve of my young ladies wearing lipstick. It gives the wrong impression.'

'Yes, Mrs Watkins,' Belle said to her employer's back as Lena Watkins turned on her heel and ushered her husband down the stairs.

The girls watched from the window until the two figures had disappeared in the direction of the station. Then Flora did a war-dance around the workroom, rattling the bunch of keys like castanets. She grabbed Belle's arm and tried to make her join in, but Belle laughingly freed herself.

'You'll make yourself dizzy,' she said. 'You shouldn't leap about like that in your condition.'

'You're as bad as my mum,' Flora said with a sigh. But she did stop prancing about, and surveyed her figure in the glass window-pane. 'I don't show yet, do I? I mean, nobody would guess I'm having a baby, would they?'

'No. Don't worry. I'll soon tell you when the time comes.'

Belle had finished gathering her things together, and Flora waved to her as she set off on her errand. She walked down the road gaily, swinging her bag; glad to be away from the confines of the factory. It was September but she was still wearing a summery dress of green cotton, patterned with tiny clusters of daisies. Her shoes were also summery: white, with an ankle strap and wedge heel. They gave her extra height, and made her ankles and legs seem slimmer than they already were. Because the mornings were cooler now she wore a short swing-back coat in fawn, with the collar turned up under her curly hair. Her mother's brooch, the silver cat, was pinned to the lapel; it had become a sort of good-luck charm and she always tried to remember to wear it.

A man working on a nearby roof whistled his appreciation and Belle grinned with pleasure. She knew she was pretty, and was glad when strangers found her so as well. If

Flora had been with her they would probably have whistled back. As it was she pulled back her shoulders, like the fashion models in her favourite magazine, and tossed her head proudly. The red curls bounced on her shoulders as if they had a life of their own.

The bus was crowded with afternoon shoppers and Belle was pleased to push her way off when they reached the Clock Tower. This memorial to Queen Victoria's Diamond Jubilee of 1887 was in the very centre of the town; and Dyke Road, where Mrs Bishop lived, was one of the turnings that led from it up a steep hill in the direction of Devil's Dyke.

Belle started off bravely but she was soon breathless. She passed the old Norman church of St Nicholas, and then began to look for the house numbers. They started with single, even numbers, and the address Mrs Watkins had given her was in the hundreds. She stepped out gamely but it still took her three-quarters of an hour before she was standing outside Mrs Bishop's house. It was a large building overlooking a school playing-field, with a wall separating it from the pavement and a sort of gravelled drive leading up to the front door. A white Austin motor car was parked directly outside, with shining bumpers and polished bodywork.

Belle stepped around the car to admire the façade of the house, and she couldn't help comparing it with her home in Duke's Road. This was just the sort of house she would like to live in, with its large bay windows and fresh paintwork. There was even the glimpse of a conservatory at the side. She particularly liked the brightly polished brass front door furniture, in the shape of a lion's head, with the open mouth and sharp teeth holding the knocker. Deep in her own thoughts she didn't hear the crunch of feet crossing the gravel, and jumped when a man's voice said at her elbow, 'Can I help you? You look as if you've lost your way.'

Belle came down to earth with a bump. It was a young man wearing a loose raincoat and trilby hat who was leaning on the bonnet of the car, and watching her with a half-smile on his lips.

'I don't think I'm lost,' Belle said, searching for the address she'd stuffed somewhere in her pocket. 'Is this number 144, where Mrs Bishop lives?'

'I hope so.'

Belle noticed what a pleasant, educated voice the young man had, and the slightly amused quirk of his lip. For some reason this annoyed her.

'What do you mean, you hope so?' she said a little too quickly. 'It either is or it isn't.'

'My! My! What a fiery temper you have. I suppose it goes with that hair. All I meant was Mrs Bishop is my mother, and she hasn't told me we're moving.'

'So you live here too?'

'Yes. Do you like it?' He turned to look at the house critically. 'It's a bit large, but it's very comfortable. They tried to make Mother take evacuees during the war, but she managed to lie her way out of it.'

'Is that your mother's too?' Belle asked, indicating the car.

'No. This belongs to me.' He patted the bonnet possessively. 'Trouble is getting petrol and spare parts. I'd take you for a spin but I need a new tyre. By the way, my name's Joseph – Joseph Bishop.'

He held out one hand for her to shake and with the other doffed his hat. Belle was immediately mesmerised by his blond hair and clear grey eyes. Compared to Henry, and Flora's friends, he was quite the most handsome man she'd ever seen.

'Isabel Kelly,' she said, introducing herself nervously.

Joseph held her hand a little longer than seemed necessary. 'Isabel! What a pretty name.'

110

'I'm usually called Belle.'

'And are you a friend of my mother's, Isabel Kelly? She's a great collector of pretty faces. I think she's trying to marry me off.'

'No,' Belle admitted, feeling her face growing red. 'I'm from Lena Watkins's glove factory – to collect your mother's order.'

When Joseph had taken in this admission he burst out laughing. 'What a joke,' he said. 'So you're one of our factory slaves and I thought you were a lady, at least.'

'I am a lady,' said Belle indignantly. 'And you shouldn't laugh: that shows you're not a gentleman.'

'You're quite right, Belle. Please forgive me. I'm sorry if I upset you.' He looked so serious that she warmed to him again. 'But with your looks you're wasted in a factory. You should be in the films; you're better looking than a lot of the stars you see on the screen.'

'Don't be silly.' Although Belle knew he was teasing her she couldn't help liking it. She was reluctant to put an end to their conversation, but she'd been sent to see Mrs Bishop, not her son. 'Shall I knock on the door?' she asked.

'No need. I'll take you in. We don't keep a servant any more; they were all called up at the beginning of the war. There's just a char-lady who slops around with a bucket and mop. She won't answer the door because she's deaf, so if I don't take you in to Mother you'll probably find yourself on the doorstep all afternoon.'

He stepped in front of her and turned the handle, swinging the door inwards, before giving Belle a mocking bow. She took this as an invitation to enter and stepped forwards eagerly.

She found herself in a hall, which was at least three times the size of the largest room in Duke's Road. The carpet under her feet was the softest she'd ever stood on: the pile deep, and of a rich shade of mahogany and blue. Against the wall stood a long antique bench with the seat padded with cushions hand-stitched in coloured wool-work, and a tall grandfather clock that was ticking away noisily, its heavy brass pendulum swinging rhythmically. The only clock Belle had seen before that was as magnificent was in the Royal Pavilion itself. Over her head hung a chandelier, its crystals moving slightly in the draught they'd created from the front door. The light caught the cut glass and reflected strings of coloured lights across the embossed wallpaper.

Belle was so busy looking around that she forgot what she was there for. Mrs Bishop's son had to remind her.

'Mother's in the music room.' he said cheerfully. 'I can hear her playing the piano. It's that door on the right. Do you want me to come in with you?'

Belle shook herself. 'No, of course not, Mr Bishop.' She crossed to the door he'd indicated and put her hand on the handle. Then she paused and looked back over her shoulder. 'Should I knock?' she asked.

'I should. Mother's of the old school and she appreciates good manners.' Belle blushed again: was he insinuating that she didn't know the proper way to behave? 'Don't worry,' he said as she tapped on the door, 'she won't bite.'

At the second knock the tinkling notes of the music stopped and a woman's voice bade her enter.

She found herself in a room the magnificence of which surpassed the grandeur of the hall. A noble lofty room, with french windows leading out into a well-ordered flower garden, where late roses still climbed and bloomed around the trellised walls. Deep comfortable chairs that begged you to sit on them, and a low table casually strewn with women's magazines. Pictures of Pre-Raphaelite women, sombrely looking into the distance with sad eyes, which Belle, in her

112

innocence, thought were paintings of Bishop relatives. In pride of place, in the centre of the room, stood the grand piano.

Mrs Bishop was still sitting at the keyboard although her hands were still. She looked up as Belle entered and smiled. Belle couldn't help smiling back because she looked so friendly.

'Do you like Chopin?' Mrs Bishop asked.

'Pardon?'

'I asked, do you like Chopin? You looked as if you enjoyed the music I was playing.'

'Oh, yes. It was pretty. I liked the twiddly bits: they reminded me of a shower of rain.'

'What a good description.' Mrs Bishop got up from the stool. She was a handsome woman in her late forties, with prematurely white hair softly curling around her plump white face, which was carefully made up in the latest fashion. She was wearing a dress of floral crêpe, with long sleeves and a draped panel of material around the hips. 'I heard Joseph's voice. Are you a friend of his?'

'No, madam. I met your son outside and he showed me the way in. I'm Miss Kelly; Mrs Watkins sent me about the gloves.'

For a moment the older woman's face looked blank and then she broke into a smile. 'Yes, of course. How silly of me to forget. You're the girl from the factory.'

'Yes, madam.'

'You must be thirsty coming all this way across town to keep a lazy old woman happy. Would you like some tea, or is it too early?' Before Belle could answer she added, 'Or perhaps a lemonade?'

'Thank you. A lemonade would be lovely.'

Mrs Bishop crossed the room to a drinks table standing by the french windows and busied herself with the bottles and glasses. 'I make it myself, you know. If you like it I'll give you the recipe.'

Belle sipped from the glass she was handed. The lemonade wasn't as sweet as the commercial kind she was used to: there was a pleasant minty tang to it that was clean and refreshing. 'It's lovely,' she said.

'Well then, don't forget to let me write out the ingredients for you before you leave. Now we must get down to business as I mustn't be late for my hairdressing appointment. Have you brought the samples?'

The next hour was taken up with discussing the different patterns and styles, measuring, and sorting through the pelts and linings. Mrs Bishop seemed to know exactly what she wanted, although she listened carefully as Belle explained and recommended certain furs that would give good service for everyday wear. In the end, to their mutual satisfaction, she chose a pair of fur-lined, fur-backed gloves, with the palms made of black leather. The backs were to be made of silver-fox rabbit fur. The main part of the lining was to be of white fur, but the sides of the silver-fox skins were to be used for the inside of the cuffs as edging. She also ordered a pair of buttoned gloves in chamois leather, and some black gauntlets stitched in grey for her son.

'I shall give them to him as an extra Christmas present,' she said in a pleased voice. 'They will be excellent for motoring, don't you think so, Miss Kelly?'

'Yes, madam,' Belle assured her. 'I'll make sure you get them in plenty of time.'

'Good girl.' Mrs Bishop watched as Belle packed her things away, and then stood waiting to be dismissed. 'Thank you for coming all this way at the whim of an old lady. I will telephone Mrs Watkins tomorrow to tell her how pleased I am.'

'Thank you, madam.'

Belle turned to the door, but Mrs Bishop suddenly called her back. 'Just a minute, my dear.' She picked up a purse from a side-table, and extracted two silvery coins which she held out to Belle. 'I'd like you to have these for all the trouble you've taken. Buy yourself something nice on the way home.'

'I mustn't,' said Belle. 'It's very kind of you, but I don't think Mrs Watkins would want me to.' Even so she looked at the two half-crowns longingly. Her weekly wage was still only one pound five shillings, and the extra would come in very useful.

Mrs Bishop pressed the two coins firmly into her palm. 'There's no need for Mrs Watkins to know, my dear. If you don't tell her, I won't.'

She was dismissed and once again found herself in the hall. She looked around, hoping and half expecting Joseph Bishop to be waiting to show her out. But there was no one in sight and the only sound came from the ticking of the clock. Her nerves were still on edge because of the responsibilities of the afternoon, and to her the heavy pendulum seemed to be beating out the order 'GO HOME', 'GO HOME', 'GO HOME'.

With a sigh Belle turned the handle and opened the front door. The sky had clouded over and the warmth had gone out of the day. She shivered in her summery dress, and buttoned her jacket up to her chin before walking along the drive to the pavement. She stopped, turned, and had a last look at the house. It was even more attractive at a distance, with the white car still parked in front of the steps.

She thought again of her favourite childhood story: *The Wind in the Willows*, and Toad in his motoring goggles parping on his horn. Her dreams of one day living in a house like Toad Hall, and having a car and fine things had never really changed. She loved Dada and Gran, but she felt the time would come when she would have to leave Duke's Road and her family behind, and stride out bravely into the future. Meeting Mrs Bishop, and seeing her fine house and handsome son had only increased her restlessness.

She turned away and began to walk along the road towards the bus-stop. Traffic bowled past, and from the playing-fields opposite she could hear the shrieks of school-girls playing netball. Life was back to normal; it would never change; girls of her class would never escape the sort of life they'd been born to. The Toads would go on living in the big houses; but she was only a Mole, and would have to spend her life in the river bank unless she was strong enough to break loose.

She kicked a stone out of her path, and then saw the scratch the sharp edge had made on the toe of her shoe. Everything was going wrong and she felt tears pricking her eyes. Isabel Kelly, she told herself firmly, pull yourself together and stop wallowing in self-pity, or you'll miss the golden opportunities even if they do arrive. She pulled back her shoulders and tossed her curls, lengthening her stride, but before she had a chance to get far she heard someone calling her name.

She stopped, recognising the voice, and turned to face Joseph Bishop. He was running along the pavement towards her waving a piece of paper wildly in the air. He'd taken off his hat and overcoat, but he looked casual and smart in the sportscoat and flannels he was wearing. Belle's heart leapt: he was so blond and handsome, and his eyes were so clear and grey. She knew she could easily fall in love with this man who was everything that Henry Murtell wasn't.

He came to a halt in front of her. She could see by his expression that he liked her and was admiring her appear-ance. She dropped her eyes, hoping he couldn't read her thoughts, and waited, aware of the thudding of her heart.

The silence between them seemed endless, and then he said abruptly, 'Mother sent me after you with this recipe for lemonade.' He turned on his heel and retraced his steps, leaving Belle standing forlornly with the piece of paper clutched in her hand.

8

April is the kindest month for the residents of Brighton: enough visitors staying over from the Easter holidays to make it lively, but not enough to take over the town, as they do in July and August. The sun was shining, and people basked in the warmth on benches lining the promenade. One brave soul was wading knee-deep in the cold water, although he still wore a jacket with the collar turned up.

Even the war, now long over, couldn't dampen the spirit of the town, living in the very stones of this seaside watering place. Most of the barbed wire and sand-bags had been removed from the beaches, to be replaced by tarry ropes and freshly painted boats moored high above the water-line.

Stretching out to sea like a pair of elongated grasshoppers stood the two piers. Workmen crawled like flies along the rusty iron scaffolding, renovating the ugly structures in readiness for the season ahead. The tide was out, and in a deserted corner, away from the gaze of passers-by, two young women sat with a little boy enjoying the sunshine.

Flora had unbuttoned the top of her blouse and rolled up her sleeves, in the hope of getting an early tan. Her skirt was as usual hitched up above her knees showing an expanse of plump white thigh, the blue veins prominent from carrying the extra weight of pregnancy. The child, a toddler named Peter, was sitting bow-legged on the pebbles, scrabbling amongst the stones with his fat fingers.

'Pity there isn't any sand,' Flora remarked lazily. 'He wanted to bring his bucket and spade and make sandcastles. That's the trouble with Brighton beach: all stones.'

'Don't put it into your mouth, darling.' Belle prized open the child's fingers and extracted the pebble that he was putting too close to his lips. She was wearing a blue dirndl skirt, with a white drawstring blouse embroidered with red poppies. Around her shoulders she'd draped a matching cardigan to protect her skin which still freckled far too easily.

Flora rummaged in her handbag and brought out a crumpled silvery packet containing some squares of chocolate. 'Here love,' she said to her son. 'Chocolate. Tastes better than pebbles.'

Peter held out his hands greedily, but his mother waited for him to open his mouth and then popped the sweetmeat inside. A beam of delight crossed his baby face, and he immediately spat out the chocolate into the palm of his hand to investigate it.

'Leave him,' said Flora, as Belle started to take it from him. 'If you take it away he'll scream blue murder. I'd rather have peace and quiet, and clean him up when we get back home.'

Belle laughed. They both watched as the child started to run his sticky brown fingers through his blond curls. Flora produced a squashed packet of Du Maurier cigarettes and offered one to Belle. They had to make a shelter from their bodies to keep the match alight long enough to light their cigarettes, and then puff madly to keep the tips glowing. Belle coughed. She didn't really enjoy smoking and only did it to keep her friend company.

All the girls at work smoked, because it was considered

grown-up to ape their favourite film stars' habits. Anyone who didn't was labelled old-fashioned. Belle compromised by keeping the smoke in her mouth and blowing it out in quick puffs, instead of swallowing it deep into her lungs. Flora was busy trying to blow smoke-rings, but she wasn't very successful. A silence fell among the trio. Belle was occupied watching a grey and white seagull perched like a figure-head on a nearby groyne.

'Penny for them,' Flora said.

'What?' Belle jumped as if her thoughts were miles away. 'Oh, sorry. I was watching that gull. Don't you think it looks like Warlock?'

Flora thought of their employer's grey parrot and grinned. 'More like Mrs Watkins herself,' she said with a wicked laugh. Belle joined in the laughter. Flora was right: the beady eyes and hooked beak certainly bore a marked resemblance to Lena Watkins.

'I was also thinking how lucky you are, Flora.'

'Me? Lucky?' Flora turned to stare at Belle, and there was genuine surprise in her expression. 'Whatever are you talking about?'

'Well, you've got Peter.' They both turned to watch the grubby child who was happily crawling on all fours away from them across the beach towards the foamy edge of the ocean.

'I think he's the most beautiful child, and I do so envy you. And you've got Benjie.'

'Oh yes, you can say that again,' Flora said with a cynical snort. 'I've certainly got Benjie.'

'He's been good to you, hasn't he? And if he hadn't married you it would have been so different.'

'In what way?'

'Harder. I mean it's not easy being an unmarried mother these days. Things could have been awful for you.'

'I know. I suppose I am lucky.' Flora leant back and blew out an almost perfect smoke-ring. 'No one knows about Peter's real father except Mum and Dad, and they'd be too ashamed to say anything. They were pleased that Benjie wanted to make an honest woman of me. And you Belle . . . you're the only other person who knows the truth. You'd never let on, would you?' Flora's hazel eyes had suddenly filled with fear and Belle hastily assured her.

'Of course I wouldn't. You know me better than that.'

Flora let out a sigh of relief and stubbed out the glowing end of her cigarette. 'I know you must think me wicked, deceiving Benjie and all that. But you weren't in my shoes, and as you say it has turned out well. The only thing is . . .'

Belle waited, and when Flora didn't go on she asked 'What's the matter? You can tell me. We're friends, aren't we?'

Flora turned to her a woebegone face. She was usually so cheerful, but now she hastily rubbed her cheek with the back of her hand, as if to brush away a tear. When she spoke her voice held an unusually hard note which gave emphasis to her words. 'I'm bored.'

Belle tried not to burst out laughing. She'd imagined some tragedy, like a life-threatening illness, or the landlord giving them notice. To be bored seemed tame in comparison.

'Is that all?' she said. 'At least you're not stuck in the factory all day like I am. You just take your work home with you and do it in your own time. I'm still at Mrs Watkins's beck and call every day. Sometimes I even have to clean Warlock out although I'm not the new girl any more. I hate that bird. But she insists that he's fond of me, and the others are frightened of him. One day I shall probably lose my temper and wring his neck.' She wrung her hands together in a strangling gesture and laughed, hoping to cheer Flora up.

121

'It's not that!' There really were tears now in Flora's eyes. 'It's not life I'm bored with – it's Benjie.'

'In what way?'

'He's so predictable. He gets up at half past six every morning, summer and winter, never a minute later or earlier. And every night at exactly ten o'clock he stretches and says "Bed time, Flo. Let's go up the wooden stairs to Bedfordshire." On Fridays he always expects fish and chips for his dinner. One day I gave him sausage and mash for a change; he was so cross he wouldn't speak to me for the rest of the day. His clothes have to be ironed in the same way, even his working shirts, and then they have to be put away in exactly the same place. But the worst thing of all is when we're in bed . . .' Flora paused dramatically, took a deep breath and then carried on. 'He'll only make love to me if he can go on top.'

Belle didn't know what to say. Flora's life didn't seem too bad to her. She'd been brought up with the idea that every girl's ideal was a husband, good or bad, who would take the worries off of his wife's shoulders. If your man turned out to be a good one you were lucky, and if you'd chosen a bad one you only had yourself to blame. If you couldn't change him you had to put up with the consequences. Also Flora had a beautiful baby to love and care for, and Belle envied her that. As to the revelation about their sex life: as Belle, at eighteen, was still a virgin, she didn't feel knowledgeable enough to comment. After a pause Flora carried on with her story.

'Do you know, I get so desperate sometimes that I do bad things.'

'What sort of things?'

'I steal things from the counter at Woolworths. Pretty things that Benjie can't afford to buy me. I stole this.' She pulled a lacy handkerchief from her belt and waved it recklessly in Belle's face. 'Benjie would say that a plain one is cheaper and more serviceable. And one night when he was working late and Peter was fast asleep I left the house and went to the pub on the corner. Just for a quick drink and a bit of life. I was home before he was, so he never knew.'

'I suppose there was no harm done,' Belle said. 'But I shouldn't make a habit of it or he's bound to find out.'

'Don't say that, Belle.' Flora looked quite distraught at the thought. 'Because I met someone there: a man. His name's Brian and I think I love him.'

'Oh, Flora!'

'Don't say "Oh Flora!" like that. I tell you I can't help myself. What do you think I should do?'

Belle thought quickly. She knew she had to be careful what sort of advice she gave, and with her inexperience she didn't feel capable of advising a married woman who was older than herself. Even if it was Flora.

At last she said, 'Why don't you have another baby?'

'A baby! You must be mad, Isabel Kelly. I've already got one. It was having Peter that got me into this mess in the first place.'

'I said another baby. With Benjie as the real father this time. It might make all the difference.'

'You don't know what you're talking about. You don't understand.' Flora spoke angrily and jumped to her feet, shaking out her skirt. 'I'm going to buy some shrimps for tea. Will you look after Peter?'

Belle nodded; there was nothing she liked better than caring for the pretty child, and pretending he belonged to her. 'I'll meet you later at the bandstand.'

Flora was already halfway up the beach, slipping and sliding over the pebbles, the wind whipping her skirts up into the air and exposing her bare legs. Belle guessed the purchase of shrimps was only an excuse; Flora just wanted to get away on her own for a while and think things out. She probably regretted already disclosing to her friend the intimate details of her married life.

Belle gazed dreamily out at the far horizon. She wasn't going to trust her heart to anybody. Oh, no! It was going to be different for her. She was going to wait until the right man came along and then let him sweep her off her feet. Of course he would have to be rich and handsome and shower her with presents and fine clothes.

She saw herself visiting Mrs Watkins's establishment and ordering the best gloves that money could buy. How the girls would stare, and how envious they would be over her good fortune. Of course there was always the possibility that the right man wouldn't find her, but she thought that was unlikely. But if she was left on the shelf, a phrase the girls used when talking about Joyce Binns, well then she would have to accept it. She would become a career girl instead, and learn to be the best glover in Brighton. One day she would have a rival factory, and perhaps a department store as well. With the sort of dreams only the young dare have Belle couldn't see the pitfalls along the path, or the difficulties that would probably dog her grand plans. No: for Isabel Kelly everything was going to be plain sailing. Her future was rosy and secure.

A cry brought her down to earth with a bump. It was Peter. He'd tried to pull himself on to his feet, something that he still found difficult, and had over-balanced, falling into a puddle of water and banging his head on a rock. Instead of trying to right himself he chose to stay sprawled on his back, and screamed his rage for everyone to hear.

Belle rushed to rescue him. She picked him up and hugged him to her own body for comfort, and made crooning noises in an effort to quiet him. He stopped crying in surprise: he wasn't used to so much attention. Usually when he hurt himself his mother was too occupied with her own concerns to notice. He stared at Belle, his solemn baby eyes round with wonder, and sucked on his plump fists. Belle tidied him up as best she could, although he was still wet and streaked with chocolate.

'Come on, lovey,' she said in her most cheerful tones, 'let's go find Mummy.'

With the child cradled awkwardly astride her hip Belle struggled across the pebbles towards the promenade. The weight of Peter bore her down and she had to go slowly for fear of dropping him. Where the beach met the Tarmac there was a raised curb, and as she tried to step over it carrying her burden she slipped and thought that she was going to fall. In fact she would have fallen if a passer-by hadn't come quickly to her rescue. A young man in a blue blazer was strolling past, and seeing her predicament put out a strong arm to steady her.

'Thanks,' she said, looking down at Peter to see that he hadn't been frightened by the jolt. 'That was kind of you.'

'It's a pleasure to help a pretty girl in distress. If you're going my way I could carry him for you.'

The man's voice was pleasant and strangely familiar. 'I'm only going as far as the bandstand,' Belle said.

'That's the way I'm heading.'

He took the child from her awkwardly, in a way that showed he wasn't used to children. She rubbed her weary arms and turned to smile her thanks, and found herself looking into a pair of clear grey eyes. The young man was staring at her in a curious fashion and she suddenly felt embarrassed. They walked along the promenade side by side; Belle tried to think of something to say.

'Are you sure he's not too heavy?' It was a silly remark but she couldn't think of anything better.

'Not at all.' Their fair heads were close together; the boy's

125

curled, but the man's short and smooth.

'There's a De Marco's kiosk over there,' the young man said, slowing his pace. 'Do you think he'd like an ice-cream?'

'I'm sure he would – and his name's Peter.'

Three ice-creams were purchased, and as Belle reached out her hand to take one the man held it out of her reach, teasingly.

'I have a silly feeling that I've met you before,' he said. 'You can have your ice when you've told me your name.'

'Isabel,' she said, 'Isabel Kelly; but my friends call me Belle.'

'Miss Kelly, of course!' He beamed delightedly and gave her the cornet. 'The girl from the glove factory.' Then Belle recognised him: Joseph Bishop of course, with the Austin motor car, and the mother who played Chopin on the piano. 'I've never forgotten you although it must be two years ago at least. Every time I walk behind a girl with red hair I think it's you, and then I'm disappointed when I find out it isn't.'

Belle knew he was only joking, but even so she'd had the same experience herself. For several weeks after her visit to Mrs Bishop's house she'd looked at every young blond man she'd passed in the street, imagining that one day she would meet Joseph again. She'd even hoped Mrs Watkins would send her back to the house in Dyke Road with the parcel of finished gloves. But Mr Watkins had delivered them himself, and gradually her memories of Joseph had faded.

Peter, who was no respecter of persons, pushed his ice-cream up into Joseph's face. It left a white blob on the end of his nose which made Belle giggle. When she pointed it out he licked it off with the tip of his tongue, and pulled a funny face to make Peter laugh.

126

'He's a fine little fellow, isn't he? What's his name again?'

'Peter.'

'Is he yours?'

'No,' Belle said, a little too emphatically. 'I'm looking after him for a friend.'

'Good.'

'Why do you say that?'

Joseph seemed to think carefully before replying. 'Because you're too young and pretty to be tied to a child. It's different for a man. I've sewn my wild oats and had a good time. Now I'm ready to settle down.'

'Do you mean you're getting married?'

'I don't know yet. Perhaps – perhaps not. Only time will tell.'

Belle didn't know whether to be disappointed or pleased by this information. If he was trying to tell her that he was engaged to be married, then the sooner she forgot about him the better. She only knew that when she'd first met him at his mother's house she'd been instantly attracted. In the language of the romantic novels she liked to read, he'd pulled at her heart strings. And now, seeing him again after two years, he still had the power to captivate her emotions. She guessed that his remark about marriage didn't refer to her at all, although he had admitted that he found her pretty.

She looked at him sideways from under her long sandy lashes, and tried to read the expression on his handsome face. But he was still concentrating on Peter. They were approaching the bandstand now, where Flora would be waiting, and then they would say goodbye. She might never see him again.

She had to think of something to say, fast. 'Are you going to the May Day fair, on the Level?'

He turned quizzical eyes on her. 'I shouldn't think so. I

don't agree with the proletariat enjoying themselves.'

Belle felt as if someone had thrown a bucket of cold water over her. She knew that the word proletariat referred to the poor, to which she and her family belonged, but it was cruel of him to be so demeaning.

'I suppose you think you're too good for us, just because you come from a better home. But I think you miss out on a lot of good things in life,' she said firmly, as if daring him to argue. 'I think the fair sounds exciting. It's the first one they've been allowed to hold since peace was declared. There's going to be swing-boats and side-shows, as well as dancing after dark.'

'Belle,' Joseph said, looking at her seriously. 'Will you promise me one thing?' Her heart leapt. She waited breathlessly, hoping he was going to say that he'd changed his mind, and wanted her to promise to go to the fair with him. Instead he said, 'Promise me not to ride on the big-dipper. I've heard it's dangerous.'

'I shall ride on anything I've a mind to, Joseph Bishop,' she answered, 'and I don't have to ask your permission first. And I'll take Peter now; his mum will be waiting.'

Joseph passed the child over silently, and Belle turned to go.

'Belle!'

'What is it?' She waited, hoping for some kind word, showing that he might miss her and hope to see her again.

'I wondered – that is . . .' He seemed to have difficulty getting out the words and she longed to prompt him. 'Do you still work for Lena Watkins?'

'Yes.'

'Have you ever thought of changing your job?'

The question was so unexpected that she could only reply, 'Leave the glove factory? No; why should I?'

'It's like this. Now the war's ended Mother can't get staff.

The girls who used to be happy in domestic service only left to get married, but now they seem to want to be career women. It all started in the nineteen fourteen war and steadily got worse. I thought you might be looking for a change, and would consider coming to work for us. You'd have your own room if you lived in, and Mother's generous about wages and time off. What do you say?'

Belle was so angry that she didn't trust herself to speak immediately. She clutched Peter to her as a sort of defence against this young man and his outlandish idea. She'd been harbouring dreams of romance, and all he wanted her for was as a sort of glorified scullery-maid. She'd show him what she was made of: that Isabel Kelly was built of sterner stuff than he imagined. When she finally turned to him her face was composed, but he should have been warned by the sudden flush of colour to her cheeks, and the cold glint of steel in her blue eyes.

'Thank you for your offer, Mr Bishop,' she said. 'I wouldn't insult your mother by expecting her to employ a factory girl, even if she does have ideas above her station.' The sarcasm in her voice was obvious, and was not lost on Joseph. 'If I ever need a job your house would be the last place I would choose to work. Even the proletariat, as you label us, have feelings.'

'I didn't mean it like that, Belle. Listen . . .'

'I'm sure you did mean it, Mr Bishop; and I won't listen to you any more.'

'Won't you call me Joseph?' He'd changed his tune now that he knew he'd upset her, and was anxious to make amends, so that they could part on a friendly basis. For some reason that he couldn't fathom this was important to him.

'No. I shall call you Mr Bishop,' and she bobbed a sarcastic curtsey. She was graceful, even with the child on her

129

hip. 'And I'd rather you called me Miss Kelly. Now I must join my friend; after all you wouldn't want anyone you know seeing you talking to the lower orders.'

'Please listen, Belle. Don't be silly . . .'

His voice was almost pleading but Belle was so angry she wouldn't listen. If she hadn't been carrying Peter she would have clapped her hands over her ears. As it was she just wanted to get away from Joseph Bishop as quickly as she could, and try to forget the events of the afternoon. She turned quickly on her heel and walked away without even saying goodbye; although Peter whimpered in her arms, and stretched out his hand towards the man who'd given him the ice-cream.

Flora was waiting, as arranged, in front of the empty bandstand. She looked sulky and restless.

'Where have you been?' she asked crossly. 'I've been waiting for you for ages.'

'I met someone I used to know,' Belle said, handing the child over. 'Did you get the shrimps?'

'They've sold out. Benjie will be cross; he'll have to have spam for tea instead.'

'I'm sorry Peter's so grubby,' Belle said, trying to rub the blobs of dried ice-cream from the child's clothing.

'Let him be.' Flora pulled away. 'I've got to hurry before the shops shut.'

The girls parted, each with plenty to think about.

Joseph Bishop was uppermost in Belle's mind. She still felt angry, but underneath the anger was hidden a sadness. She'd been so pleased to see him again; but now they'd parted on a disagreement which she saw no way of remedying. She knew she was proud; but he really was unreasonable to think that she would be prepared to lower herself to work for his mother. But perhaps it was she who was being unreasonable, to think that he might look at her in any other way. She wanted him to fall in love with her, and didn't see how that could be. Life was so unfair.

Gran was expecting her home at six o'clock, and she'd been promised kippers and apple pie for tea. But when she turned the door-handle her watch told her that it was only three thirty. She was early enough to give a hand with the pastry. Dada would most likely still be at work on his allotment so she might as well make herself useful.

The house was quiet; the sort of quietness that gives you the shivers, even if it's your own home and you've lived there all your life. Belle threw her cardigan in the direction of a chair in the passage. It was a bad aim, and hit the edge to slide on to the floor. She left it there and walked into the kitchen.

The pie was ready prepared on the table, waiting to go into the oven. The vegetables were peeled and steeping in a bowl of water, and Gran was fast asleep in her chair. Like a cat she'd pulled it into the sunlight, and the warm rays fell on her wrinkled skin and wispy hair. She looked old and worn out, and a sudden affection made Belle drop a light kiss on her head as she passed. Poor Gran, with her swollen legs and thinning blood. Wearing herself out trying to keep the home together, when by rights they should be caring for her, and letting her pass her last days in peace.

There was a pile of ironed clothes on the dresser: Dada's shirts and her blouses all ready to be put away. She picked them up on her way upstairs; at least she could save Gran a climb.

The tiny landing was dark, although the doors were left ajar to keep the bedrooms aired. Belle had returned long ago to her bed in the slip-room that she'd once shared with her brother, leaving Gran in peace.

Charlie's bed was still there behind the door, but her

memories were more of her mother, sobbing and railing there after his tragic death. Belle would never forget the bitter words exchanged between her parents that night when she'd huddled fearfully under the covers in her own corner, not understanding grown-ups and their strange ways. She knew now that the battle had had something to do with sex: that great mystery between men and women that was supposed to bring pleasure, but more likely brought pain if Flora was to be believed.

She put away her own clothes and then carried her father's shirts along the passage to his room. The door stood ajar, and her hand was on the knob when she heard a movement inside. Gran was downstairs and Dada was usually working on his allotment at this time of the day. She pushed the door open with her foot, ready to shoo the intruder downstairs, for she guessed it was the family cat who was always on the look-out for a place where he could sleep undisturbed.

Dada was stretched out on the bed. Belle could see his back, his slightly ridiculous bare legs, and his crumpled shirt-tail. But he wasn't alone. A vast mountain of flesh heaved in his embrace, with loose breasts hanging free from the petticoat that was the only garment covering the pale body, and the long wavy black hair tangled on the pillow. Belle recognised the creature. She'd seen her before standing straddle-legged in the doorway of the Black Mill public house. It was Maud Carter, whose reputation hadn't improved over the years.

The couple on the bed must have heard Belle's quick intake of breath, for they rolled apart quickly. At the sight of his daughter George tried to cover himself. Maud, the queen of immodesty, didn't bother. She just looked casually in Belle's direction, as if it was the most normal thing in the world for her to be found in a bed other than her own;

which to her it probably was. She reached for a bottle standing on the bedside table, missed, and sent it flying. It rolled across the floor, its foaming brown contents leaving a trail, to land at Belle's feet, splashing the white surface of her shoes.

'Father!'

She'd never called him 'Father' before. It had always been 'My Da', or 'Dada'. Her voice was also that of a stranger. A woman's voice, not a child's. A feeling of sorrow drowned George because he knew that their easy relationship, which had meant so much to them both, was now changed. She would never be his little girl again.

He scrambled from the untidy bed, and reached for his trousers which were lying in a heap on the floor. The first leg was easy, but then, in his haste, he tripped and sprawled on the ground at Belle's feet. His knees landed in the puddle of brown ale from the dropped bottle.

'You're drunk!' Her voice accused him of the crime which was the least of the two evils. She ignored the woman on the bed as if she were beneath contempt.

'Only a little,' George admitted. He struggled to his feet and held himself upright on the door-post. 'Come outside and let me explain.'

'Explain! What is there to explain, Father? You bring that slut with you, and entertain her in the bed you shared with my mother. How could you!'

'I'm sorry, Belle.'

He groped his way past her, buttoning his trousers with fumbling fingers. The two women heard his uneven footsteps on the stairs. Then Belle turned to the woman who'd just climbed out of her parents' bed. She'd heard about Maud Carter and knew her by sight, but this was the first occasion when they'd been at close quarters.

Maud didn't look the slightest bit embarrassed as she

stood on the cold linoleum, pushing her heavy mane of hair away from her face. She slowly adjusted her petticoat before stepping into her bright gipsy-style dress. She walked across the room towards Belle, almost graceful on her large flat feet.

'I'll be off then,' she said to Belle, in what was a surprisingly friendly voice. 'Don't be too hard on him.'

Belle controlled her own voice with difficulty. 'Get out of our house and leave my father alone,' she said. There was almost a note of desperation in her voice.

'I'm going.' There was kindness and understanding in her rough tones. 'He's only a man, you know. And he misses your mother.'

'So do I! So do I!'

Belle couldn't help the words escaping in a half-sob as Maud passed her. When she was at last alone, she flung herself down on the tumbled bed, that still smelled of sweat and passion, and cried as if her heart would break.

9

It was May Day morning. When Belle opened her eyes the view from her bedroom window was obscured by a sea of mist. But within half an hour the breeze had blown it away, the sun had broken through, and it was a glorious spring morning. Belle had prayed for good weather because today, for the first time, she was going to visit her mother in the sanatorium.

She hadn't seen Bess for a long time – not since she'd been transferred from the local hospital after the horrific accident with the pane of glass. George had discouraged her every time she'd brought up the idea of visiting. He'd feared that the terrible injuries to his wife's face would frighten a girl of Belle's tender years. At first he'd visited as frequently as he could afford, although the train fare was a drain on the family resources. But as time went by and there didn't seem to be any marked improvement in her condition, he made excuses and stopped visiting regularly, even when he could afford it.

Today's visit had been instigated by Belle herself.

'I'm going to visit Mam,' she'd told George. 'I've got a day off work.'

'I don't think you should,' George looked worried.

'Why not? She's my mother.'

'Sometimes she doesn't recognise people. I don't want you to be upset.'

'Don't you? You should have thought of that before.'

George looked uncomfortable: he knew Belle was referring to finding him with Maud Carter. 'You listen to me, my girl. I don't want you to go, but I doubt if you'll take any notice of me.'

'I'm sorry.' Belle lowered her eyes. 'I'm going, and I need some money for the fare.'

'What about your wages?'

'I've nothing left. I needed stockings and things.'

'Well, there's no use coming to me.'

Since finding her father in bed with Maud Carter their relationship had changed drastically. Belle had grown up overnight. Instead of loving George without question, she was now well aware of the frail human being living in her parent's body, with all its weaknesses and shortcomings. She felt the need to protect him, and refused to listen to the gossip about his drinking. She was quick to come to his support in public and squash any rumours that reached her ears, whether they were true or false.

These days she didn't ask his advice, or tell him where she was going, or why. She kept her own council and relied on her own instincts. So she didn't ask George if she could visit her mother; she told him she was going.

The problem was raising the money for the fare. In the old days when she was in difficulties she turned to Henry Murtell: so she did so again. Henry never seemed to mind being used. It was always happening to him, and he was pleased, especially when Belle needed him.

She waylaid him on the way home from work one day, and didn't beat about the bush. That wasn't her way; she believed in the direct approach.

'Mrs Watkins has given us all a day off work,' she said. 'I thought I'd go and see my mother.'

'What does your dad say?' Henry looked serious, he knew about Belle's mother being detained in some sort of asylum.

'He doesn't want me to go.'

'I'm not surprised. He probably doesn't think it's the right place for a young girl.'

'I've told him I'm going anyway. I thought you'd help me.'

'In what way?'

'Keep me company.'

Henry's face brightened. Belle didn't often seem to want his company these days.

'You'll have to get the day off,' Belle told him. 'Mrs Watkins is giving us extra time to celebrate the first of May; but it's not a public holiday.'

'Mr Hilton won't mind,' Henry assured her. 'He owes me some time off anyway. Auntie Mabel is more likely to object because she's waiting for me to plant her seed potatoes. They've already sprouted.'

'Don't tell her then,' Belle said quickly. 'Now, how are we going to get there? How much money have you got?'

'Only about five shillings.' Henry wasn't going to tell Belle about the tin box under his bed which was now nearly full of half-crowns. He must have over twenty pounds saved now, and if she knew about it she would be sure to beg him to spend some on her. The money was for his future, and as he was hoping this would include Belle, she'd get her share one day. 'Can you ride a bike?'

'Yes,' Belle said optimistically, thinking back down the years to her dead brother, Charlie. As children they'd taken turns rattling around the streets on an old bone-shaker their father had brought home from the scrap-heap. How many knocks and falls and bloody knees they'd suffered; but what fun they'd had. Belle hadn't been on a bicycle since, but they did say it was something you never forgot. So she said confidently, 'Of course I can.'

Neither of them knew where Henry was going to procure a machine for Belle, but he had plenty of contacts. He wasn't going to let the chance of a day out with Belle slip through his fingers.

True to his word, when she ran out into the street on that May morning, two bicycles were leaning against the garden wall. The old machine Henry rode every day to work and beside it a ladies' equivalent: a 'sit up and beg' type that had gone out of fashion years before. It might be out of date but it was sturdy and looked reliable. Henry was busy polishing the bodywork with his pocket handkerchief.

'It's got a basket, a bell, and the brakes work. I've tested them,' he said proudly, as if these were unnecessary extras. 'If the saddle's too high, just tell me.'

'It's fine,' Belle said impatiently, tossing her cardigan and handbag into the capacious basket. 'Don't fuss. I haven't forgotten how to ride a bicycle; it'll just take me a while to get used to it.'

After a wobbly start she was soon guiding it in a straight line along the road. At first it seemed to have a life of its own, and like a frisky mare tried to zig-zag into the path of the on-coming traffic and tip her off into the gutter. But Belle persisted and soon she was in control. By the time they'd left the houses behind and the long green curve of the Sussex Downs loomed ahead, she was beginning to enjoy herself.

They rode two abreast, with Henry on the outside to protect Belle from any passing traffic. She was wearing a dress of yellow cotton, with puff sleeves and a full skirt. A wide white belt encircled her narrow waist. She was becoming increasingly proficient with her needle, and had made the dress herself from a cheap remnant bought for a few shillings in a spring sale. Her hair hung loose and streamed out behind her in the breeze. There was no one today to order her to pin it back or tie it down. She looked very young and innocent; more fourteen than eighteen years old. It was true that, although she had the body of a woman, her mind was still in some ways childlike: unawakened to the desire of the opposite sex.

Henry had grown from a plain spotty boy into a gangling young man. His face was long and pale, and he wore his short dark hair neatly parted and slicked down with water. He was wearing grey trousers secured by bicycle clips, and a knitted pullover over his white open-necked shirt. He still gazed at the world short-sightedly through wire-framed glasses, which he was always removing nervously to polish. He gave the impression of being a nice, clean, uninteresting young man, which was, at nineteen, exactly what he was.

A strange excitement gripped Belle. To get away from the town into the countryside was stimulating in itself, so used was she to Tarmac, buses, and rows of houses. To see fields on either side, and trees in their early finery, reminded her that she was young, at one with nature, and the pulse of life beat strongly in her veins.

Henry had chosen their route to avoid the main roads filled with busy traffic. He'd worked out that it would take them nearly two hours to reach the sanatorium, which was situated on the outskirts of a country town. At first they behaved like two young animals racing along the deserted roads, seeing who could pedal fastest; and singing silly songs to pass the time.

After the first hour Belle began to flag.

'My legs and arms are beginning to ache,' she complained.

'It shouldn't be far now,' Henry reassured her.

'Can't we slow down?'

Henry slackened the pace and noticed a worried frown on Belle's face. 'What's the matter?'

'I'm a bit scared,' she admitted. 'I don't know what I'm going to find when we get there. Mam's very ill, and I think Dada was trying to warn me. Thank you for coming with me.'

The first excitement was evaporating and a trickle of fear was taking its place, bringing a chill to the sunshine which had first felt so warm, and slowing down the speed she revolved the pedals. She was glad Henry was with her. His lanky body bent almost double over the handlebars beside her made her feel safe and not quite so alone.

Lately, loneliness had been the worst of her emotions. Flora seemed sunk in gloom these days, brooding over the boredom of her married life. She didn't come to Belle now asking for guidance, knowing that ultimately any decisions she made must be her own.

George was living in a world of lust and booze. When he occasionally surfaced, he had to acknowledge what was happening to him. Instead of pulling himself together it was easier to forget, and who better to help him to oblivion than Maud Carter and the bottles she obtained for him at the Black Mill. He watched his daughter growing away from him through an alcoholic mist. It was sad but inevitable, and he didn't know what to do about it.

Gran was friendly, but she slept most of the day now when she wasn't working. She was too old to be bothered with the sort of trouble a teenage granddaughter might have. Even Father Joe, watching Belle pass St Anne's Church, shook his head in dismay. Instead of going to mass with a bowed head and a rosary between her fingers, she was dangling a cheap handbag and tossing her proud head mockingly in the direction of the presbytery.

So Henry was her salvation; her buffer against the dragging isolation of loneliness. She used him shamelessly, as she had always done.

'Are you tired?' Henry had slowed down to enable Belle to catch up with him 'We could take a rest if you want.'

Belle nodded. They were approaching a wood, which although bordered by a fence, had several broken spaces where the public had forced their way into the shelter of the shady trees. Henry guided his bicycle through a convenient gap and Belle followed him, glad to dismount and lean her machine against the nearest tree. A strange excitement gripped Henry. He'd had no experience with girls: in fact he'd never been particularly interested. Belle was just Belle: the girl next door who he'd always adored from a distance. But suddenly, today, he saw her in a new light. She wasn't a little girl any more: he was aware that she was a woman – and a lovely one at that.

They were hidden from the road in a sort of glade. Among the long grass tall bluebells stirred in the breeze. Belle immediately dropped to her knees among the flowers and began to pick the pale green stems with their heavy violet blue heads. Henry watched her from a distance. He was mesmerised by the pretty girl in the yellow dress, with her head like a flame, and her arms full of flowers. The world outside seemed to fade. They were like two people shipwrecked. Henry took a deep breath to control the rapid beating of his heart.

'Don't pick too many,' he said. 'They'll die before you get them home.'

Belle paused in her picking and sat back on her heels gracefully. 'I'm not taking them home. They're for Mother.'

She spoke the words childishly. Henry was reminded of how she'd once picked daisies and threaded them into a chain to make a fairy crown. She placed the bluebells beside her on the grass; their heads were already beginning to droop as if deprived of moisture. Belle drooped herself as if she was suddenly overcome by weariness. When Henry asked if she was ready to continue she yawned and shook her head. 'We'll take ten minutes' rest then,' Henry said, looking at his watch.

Belle flung herself back on the grass, and stretched her slim body languidly. She'd never appeared so attractive to Henry and he couldn't take his eyes from her, and the way the thin cotton material covered her womanly shape, revealing the gentle slope of her hips and breast. Her face with its dusting of freckles was heart-shaped, and the long sandy lashes veiled her eyes so that he couldn't guess what she was thinking.

He knew she wasn't asleep because her fingers were playing amongst the grass stems as if feeling for hidden treasure. He sat down beside her and leaned his back against a tree stump, trying to control the sudden desire to kiss her. There was something provocative about her pouting lips with the stain of red make-up still around the edges, and the tips of her small white teeth just showing.

Henry leant forward slightly and looked down into Belle's face. Her eyes flew open and stared up at him, as blue as the sky over their heads. She knew immediately what he wanted, and why. It wouldn't be the first time he'd kissed her. They'd exchanged childish kisses in the past: his had always been serious and demanding, whereas hers were gay and carefree. But Henry was a man now and she'd never been kissed by a man before. She didn't know what she wanted but her body was demanding something.

Joseph Bishop had woken some need in her but Henry would have to fulfil it.

She smiled as Henry's lips brushed her cheek. The innocent gesture ignited a spark. She took his face between her hands and guided his lips on to hers. He was trembling so that he half-fell across her body, and his glasses slipped off into the grass. Through a mist he saw her writhing body, and his manhood flared into maturity so that he had to master her. She was like a yellow butterfly and he had to pin her down.

His struggle for mastery was soon over and she lay beneath him, patient and waiting, her face flushed by his kisses. She'd dreamt of this moment many times, not daring to believe that it would be anything but a dream. His hands were cool and tender, and when they touched her intimate places she was set on fire by a sudden yearning. She wanted him to be rough with her, to make her break and bleed, to feel like a woman. She wanted to be used. By the time Henry came she was bored. He was too gentle, too considerate, and she remembered Flora's complaint that when Benjie made love to her he would only go on top.

Henry rolled off and fumbled blindly in the grass for his spectacles, and Belle turned on her side away from him. She was angry; not with Henry but with herself. She didn't want him to see the tears in her eyes, or realise how disappointed she was. After all, he'd seemed satisfied, moaning and groaning on top of her, and whispering words of love into her ear. How gentle he'd been as he tried not to hurt her. All the things she hadn't wanted.

She'd dreamt of her first sexual experience being something she'd remember all her life. After all she was young and beautiful and that was the time for passion. She thought of her father, and hoped it had been beautiful between him and her mother when she and Charlie had been conceived. Then her mind turned to Maud Carter and she shuddered. She saw the heavy blue-veined breasts, and her father's shrunken legs under his flapping shirt-tail, and vowed that when she was past the bloom of youth she'd give up that sort of thing. By today's experience it wouldn't be a hard thing to give up, because after the first heady excitement, she hadn't really enjoyed it.

Belle sat up quickly and pulled the skirt of her dress down over her knees in a childishly demure gesture. Henry was sitting beside her, his clothes now so tightly buttoned that for a moment she wondered if the thing that had happened between them was just a dream. Then as she moved she felt a soreness between her legs, and knew that she was wide awake and would never be a virgin again. She felt soiled, disgusted that she'd allowed Henry to do such a thing to her. She was no better than Maud, and Henry was worse than her father.

She looked almost angrily at her companion, wishing that she could wave a magic wand and make him disappear, to be replaced by the blond figure of Joseph Bishop. If she'd lost her virginity to him things would have been different. Flora was right: sex was boring with the wrong man, so what a good thing it was that she had no intention of marrying Henry. She tried to push what had happened out of her mind so that she could concentrate on what lay ahead.

Silently they wheeled their machines out into the road and mounted. They had to continue their passage in a stately procession as the path was too narrow to ride side by side. Henry rode in front with Belle a few yards behind. The sky had clouded over and Belle had to surreptitiously wipe away something wet from her cheek. She thought it was a raindrop; it couldn't be a tear because she had nothing to cry about.

144

The sanatorium was easy to find as there were plenty of road signs to direct them. Within the half-hour they turned into the gates and dismounted, to stare in disbelief at the building in front of them. The hospital Bess had been in, in Brighton, had been a businesslike structure: old-fashioned, but clean and full of life. The only thing Belle hadn't cared for was the clinging smell of disinfectant, and the slippery surface of the floors. This was a sanatorium in name but had all the looks of a Gothic mansion about it – straight out of a horror film or the stories of Edgar Allan Poe.

It was long and low, with windows covered by shutters. Belle wondered if there were bars behind the shutters to keep the inmates prisoner. The outside walls were painted the shade of green vomit, and the bare stems of ancient ivy crawled up the walls and held the building in a stranglehold. In keeping with its grim exterior, a bank of storm clouds backed the turreted roof and tall chimneys. Rank grass grew on the lawn, and the flower-beds contained a few late daffodils, brown and wind-blown. Not a tree broke the grim landscape.

Belle turned a tragic face to Henry, and said, 'Are you sure this is the place?'

'I'm afraid so. Perhaps it will be better inside.'

Belle doubted it. The day that had started so well was fast becoming a disaster. Nothing good could exist in a building like the one in front of them. It was a house for the dead, not the living. She longed to say that she'd changed her mind; that she didn't want to see her mother; that it was all a mistake. She wanted to get back on her bicycle and ride away, back into the warmth and sunshine, where the bluebells were nodding their stately heads.

It was too late. The flowers they'd picked and forgotten would now be crushed and faded on the ground, and the first drops of rain were falling. She had no alternative but to follow Henry up the drive, and wait beside him as he followed the instructions on the front door: to ring the bell and wait.

The person who opened the door to them was forbidding to say the least. Tall and square in a starched white uniform, all creases and corners. By the cropped grey hair and hint of a moustache on the upper lip, Belle thought it was a male nurse, until she spotted the ribbed stockings and flat shoes so like those worn by Joyce Binns, and realised that it was undoubtably a woman.

'I've come to see Mrs Kelly,' Belle said. 'I'm her daughter.'

Briskly they were ushered inside and the door closed as if to stop a mass exodus of patients. The entry hall was surprisingly inviting. There was a waiting-room with shabby but comfortable chairs, and well-thumbed magazines on a low table. The reception nurse busied herself behind a desk in the corner, and began leafing through the contents of a large metal file.

At last she found what she was looking for, and read out questioningly, 'Elizabeth Mary Kelly?'

'That's right.' It seemed funny to hear Bessie's full name read out by this severe-looking woman.

'Victoria ward. It's not visiting time so I'll have to ask Sister's permission. It may not be convenient.'

They waited while a call was put through. Belle tried to listen to the drift of the one-sided conversation, but she could only pick out the odd word. The nurse spoke softly, her body half turned away as if she didn't want them to hear what she was saying. Occasionally she would glance over her shoulder in Belle and Henry's direction. They wondered what she was saying about them. At last she put the receiver back on its rest and turned to them with a smile, as if they'd passed some test.

'You can visit your mother for fifteen minutes. If you go along that passage,' she pointed through an inner door, 'you'll find a staircase at the far end. Victoria ward is on the floor above. You'll find all the doors are clearly marked.'

They got up from the chairs in which they'd been resting, but the nurse stopped them before they reached the door. She was looking at Henry accusingly. 'Are you Elizabeth Kelly's son?'

'No,' Henry admitted.

'Are you a member of the family?'

'No. I'm a neighbour.'

'Only relatives are allowed to visit patients. It's a very strict rule.'

'But we've cycled all the way from Brighton.' The words burst out in anger before Belle could stop them. She needed Henry beside her before she faced the woman she felt was almost a stranger. She hated to admit it but she was afraid to go through the door into an alien world, on her own. 'Henry's a close friend of our family. Mother knows him well. I know she'll be pleased to see him.'

'I'm sorry,' the nurse said almost kindly. 'But I don't make the rules you know. Your friend must wait for you here.'

'But . . .' Belle wanted to argue, but she knew that she wasn't going to win. The other woman had the power of the authorities behind her. She could just as easily change her mind and refuse Belle admission if she felt like it.

Henry put his hand on Belle's arm reassuringly. 'You'll be all right,' he said calmly. 'It'll be better for you to visit your mother on your own. I'll sit down here and look at a magazine. I promise I won't go away.'

He made everything sound so ordinary that Belle calmed down slightly. It was after all only Mam she was going to see. Nothing terrible was going to happen. But as she passed through the door it swung to behind her with a final slam, and the passage in front looked dim and deserted.

Her heels made a tapping sound on the uncarpeted floor, and the noise seemed to echo around her. At every door she passed she imagined faces peering at her through the glazed panels, and far away she heard a muffled scream that was quickly silenced.

She was nearing the staircase when she first had the feeling that she wasn't alone. Her foot was on the bottom step when a hand came down on her shoulder and made her jump and spin round, her heart racing; only to let out a sigh of relief when she saw a man's friendly face smiling into hers. He was about forty, with dark curly hair and a fringe of beard. Over his check shirt and navy-blue trousers he wore a short white coat, open at the front, with a monogram on the breast pocket. Around his neck hung a stethoscope. He looked like any one of the doctors she'd seen stalking the wards of the general hospital.

'I'm sorry, did I frighten you? Where are you going?'

'To visit my mother in Victoria ward.'

'I know all the patients. What is your mother's name, my dear?'

She didn't like the smooth way he called her 'My dear', but she supposed it was all right as he was so much older than she was, and also a member of an honourable profession. So she said, 'Elizabeth Mary Kelly.'

'Oh, Elizabeth Mary! And you're her daughter? I'd never have guessed.'

'So you know my mother?'

'I'm her doctor, my dear. Doctor Nelson.'

Then Belle saw the name embroidered on the pocket of his white coat. What good luck to meet her mother's doctor so soon, and on such a friendly basis.

'Then will you tell me how she is? My father comes to see

her sometimes, but he doesn't tell me very much.'

'She's coming along very nicely. In fact, I'm discharging her soon.'

Belle looked at him in surprise, her expression a mixture of happiness and dismay. 'You mean she'll be coming home?'

'Whenever you want. You can take her back with you today.'

'I can't do that! There are things to sort out. I came here on a bicycle and I've got no money.' A series of pictures passed slowly before Belle's eyes, of Mam on the pillion of her bicycle, followed by their arrival back at Duke's Road, surprising her father entertaining Maud Carter. 'It's impossible, Doctor Nelson,' she said. 'Mother's been away from us for such a long time; there are things we have to do first. And my father would have to be warned.'

'Don't you want her home?'

Belle wished she hadn't used the word warned; she was giving Doctor Nelson quite the wrong impression. If only Henry were beside her: he'd know what to say.

'Of course I want her home,' she said at last. 'It's a bit of a surprise, that's all. A nice one of course.'

Doctor Nelson's hand was on her arm again, pulling her from the stairs and back into the dim passage. 'Perhaps we'd better go and ask her if she wants to go home.'

'The nurse told me she's in Victoria ward. She said it's up these stairs.' Belle looked up the curving staircase which was brighter than the passage Doctor Nelson was trying to usher her along.

'She must have made a mistake; your mother is down here.'

He gave her no option but to follow. His hand on her arm was cold and felt like an iron clamp. She was too frightened to remonstrate and walked beside him blindly. After all, he

149

was a doctor, and he knew her mother. Although she didn't like him there was no reason to distrust him as well.

At the end of the passage was a pair of double doors, with round windows in the upper panels, like port-holes. Without slowing his stride Doctor Nelson pushed the doors apart with his shoulder and pulled Belle through behind him. A blast of noise, smell and movement hit her like a tangible force.

They were in a long ward, and the walls were lined with iron beds which were all empty. The occupants, all men, were roaming the vast centre space like caged animals, occasionally emitting a shrill laugh, cry, or hoarse cough. They were dressed in an assortment of clothes. Some wore baggy flannel pyjamas under trailing dressing-gowns, and others were dressed in day clothes that hung in badly fitted layers from their shoulders. It looked just as if, on rising, they'd grabbed the first pair of trousers or shirt they could lay their hands on and forced their bodies in no matter what size they, or the garment, happened to be.

A frail old man caught her eye from a corner of the room. He was wearing long woollen underpants and a vest, and his white hair hung almost to his shoulders. He badly needed a haircut and a shave. When he saw Belle looking at him he threw back his head, his toothless mouth dropped open, and he laughed in a humourless fashion.

'Look what I've brought you,' shouted Doctor Nelson, dragging Belle into the middle of the room. 'Something you haven't seen for a long time.'

'Where did you get her from?' an ugly man with a patch over one eye asked. 'Tell us where you found her, so we can go and get one.'

The other men joined in the laughter. They stopped their prowling and circled Belle, studying her with interest from all angles, as if she were a prize exhibit in a show-ring. She almost felt sorry for the pathetic picture they made. But she was uneasy at the same time, and turned to her bearded companion who was still holding her arm far too tightly.

'You told me you'd take me to see my mother, Doctor Nelson,' she said. 'Where is she?'

A man standing in front of her let out a laugh that ended in a rattling cough. A glob of spittle from his wet mouth landed on the ground at her feet, just missing her shoe. She felt sick; the smell of sweat, unwashed male bodies and urine made her stomach heave. The man wiped his mouth on his sleeve before saying, 'Oh! It's Doctor Nelson today is it Willie? And you've been stealing the doctor's coat from the staff-room, have you? You'd better put it back before Sister finds out.' Belle opened her eyes wide and backed away. How stupid she'd been. The man beside her wasn't a doctor; he was just a sick man with a twisted mind who'd told her lies. She wondered how she could possibly have been taken in.

The one-eyed man continued in conversational tones, 'Yesterday he turned his collar round the wrong way and called himself Father. He's quite harmless; don't look so frightened. We call him Barmy Bill. It's only when he gets his hand on a knife and says he's Sweeney Todd that you've got anything to worry about.'

The group of men seemed to be advancing on her and Belle looked around frantically for a nurse, or a real doctor. Anyone who was in charge and would come and rescue her.

'I had a girl like you once,' a voice whispered in her ear. 'I was in the navy at the time and we'd put in at a foreign port. The girls were hungry for us, and we made them dance I can tell you.'

Belle felt a hand on her skirt and shuddered; and when a sharp finger prodded her from behind, as if testing a joint of meat, she opened her mouth to scream.

'What's going on in here?'

The men froze as if they were playing a childish game of statues, and slowly turned to the doorway. A woman had entered: an Amazon in a navy blue uniform, with a frilly cap perched on top of her iron-grey hair. Belle let out a sigh of relief as her tormentors broke away with pretended concern.

'I'm Sister Williams, and I'm in charge of this ward,' the woman said to Belle. 'Perhaps you'd better come into my office and tell me just what you're doing here.'

10

Sister Williams turned out to be an Angel rather than an Amazon. She propelled Belle into her private office at the end of the ward and immediately made a pot of tea on a small gas-ring in the corner. As she poured it from a brown pot and added milk and sugar, she smiled at Belle in a friendly fashion.

'Now, tell me what my naughty boys have been up to?' she demanded, beaming over the rim of her cup. When she'd heard the story she let out a guffaw of laughter and had to put the cup back on its saucer to avoid spilling it. 'Oh, dear!' she said at last, wiping her eyes on a large handkerchief. 'What will that Willie get up to next?'

'It was very frightening,' Belle insisted. She was certainly feeling better but still had a feeling of outrage. 'He said he was Doctor Nelson, and he was roaming the passages.'

'What do you think we should do – lock them in? This is a hospital, not a prison.' The smile had gone from her face and Belle suddenly felt that Sister Williams had more compassion for her disturbed patients than she had for the visitors they tormented. But then her face softened again. 'I'm sorry you were upset but it was only a bit of fun on their part. Willie should have been an actor; he's always stealing clothes so that he can dress up. Once he pinched my uniform, cap and all, rolled his trouser legs up and tried to take in a group of probationary nurses. That was before he grew a beard of course.' They had to exchange a smile at this story. Then Sister Williams said, 'You tell me you've come to visit Mrs Kelly?'

'Yes. She's in Victoria ward.'

'Then I'd better take you myself; to make sure you find it this time. Are you on your own?'

'No. I have a friend with me. They made him stay in the waiting-room because he's not a relative.'

'Is he your fiancé?' Belle looked up sharply. 'I mean, are you engaged to him?'

Belle thought quickly. Perhaps if she said yes, Sister Williams might think that made Henry a member of the Kelly family and would go and fetch him.

'We're getting engaged very shortly,' she said, feeling her cheeks go hot at the deliberate lie.

'I'm pleased to hear it. A pretty girl like you needs a young man to look after her.' She got out of her chair and Belle followed her to the door. 'I'll take you upstairs and then I'll go and tell your young man why you've been delayed. Perhaps he'd like a cup of tea as well.'

Outside Victoria ward a plump little nurse, who introduced herself as Sally, was waiting. She laughed when Sister Williams explained why Belle had been such a long time and then opened the door of a small side room and ushered Belle inside. It was just a bare little room, with no pictures on the walls, or any sign of ornamentation to soften the stark simplicity. Linoleum covered the floor, smelling of polish, and only the simple furnishings of a table and two upright chairs in the centre.

'Now my dear,' Nurse Sally said jovially. 'I thought it

would be better if you saw your mother in here. Relax and make yourself comfortable; I won't be long.'

Left alone Belle felt her nervousness returning. What changes would the last few years have wrought on her mother? Would they recognise each other? She wandered around the small room aimlessly. There was nothing to look at or read; even the window only gave a gloomy view of the now rain-swept grounds. They were going to have an unpleasant ride back to Brighton by the look of it, and she'd only brought a cardigan. Misery swept over her. She wished whole-heartedly that she could be spirited a hundred miles away.

At the scrape of the door opening Belle turned slowly, glad that she was standing close to the wall and so had something solid to support her. Nurse Sally's arms were around a tiny figure that shuffled uncertainly into the room.

'That's not my mother!' something screamed in Belle's head. Mam had been thin and bony even when she was young; and the hard life she'd led and her own highly strung disposition hadn't helped her to put on flesh. But she had been strong and upright, with an acid tongue when talking to her young daughter. Only with Charlie, and occasionally George, had a softness crept into her voice, and her touch become gentle.

The creature before Belle was a very different woman. So old and bent, she must be seventy at least, whereas Bessie could barely have reached her half century. Wrapped about with clothes that reached to her ankles, all that could be seen of her was a shrunken head from which wisps of pale hair hung. Two dark eyes, the whites veined with red, stared fixedly at Belle, the only thing about her that seemed alive.

But it wasn't this that made Belle step back in horror. It was the criss-cross of old scars that covered her face, pulling

155

the right eye askew and dragging the thin lips into a pitiable sneer. George had told his daughter about the accident when it happened, but he'd played down the severity of his wife's injuries. Belle had almost forgotten the incident until now, when she was faced so cruelly by the terrible appearance of her own mother.

Nurse Sally led the pathetic bundle to one of the chairs and helped Bess to sit down. Belle wondered what strange garment her mother was wearing, but didn't like to ask. It looked like a grey army blanket that enveloped her from her neck downwards, with folds holding her arms crossed upon her chest and covering her hands. Belle could see that it was held in place by several webbing straps and buckles. The finished object looked like a cross between an Egyptian mummy and pictures she'd seen of biblical swaddling clothes.

'There, dear,' said Nurse Sally, patting Bessie's shoulder affectionately. 'Look who's come to see you! Aren't you a lucky girl to get such a nice surprise?' Her voice was soft and cooing as if she were talking to a baby, but Belle guessed she was only trying to be kind. 'She can still talk, you know, when she wants to,' she informed Belle before turning back to her patient. 'Aren't you going to say hello to your daughter, Mrs Kelly?'

Bess didn't speak and Belle didn't blame her. If she was in her position, tied and cosseted and deprived of all dignity in this horrible place, she wouldn't have spoken either; even if she was able.

'She's just feeling stubborn,' Nurse Sally continued. 'Sometimes she can be very difficult, but we try to make allowances. I don't expect she got much sleep last night. Night Sister reported that the woman in the next bed was crying for hours. Why don't you say something to her?' She smiled encouragingly at Belle. 'I'll stay over here by the door. You can pretend I'm not here.'

She took up her position in front of the only exit; like a prison warder. One side of Belle wanted her to go, so that she could run to Mam and fling her arms about her poor tormented body. But another part of her wanted the uniformed presence in the room, protecting her from the unknown.

The silence was almost unbearable. While Belle was still searching for words a buzzer sounded somewhere outside and Nurse Sally suddenly jumped into activity; as if someone had actually pressed a button on her back and brought her to life like a mechanical toy.

'That's the alarm bell,' she said, looking from Belle to her patient. 'I'm not supposed to leave you alone together, but if you promise not to upset her I think it will be all right. Now, I'll only be a few minutes. Can you manage?'

'I think so,' Belle said; relieved and scared at the same time.

'She'll be fine,' Nurse Sally assured her, the door already open. 'As long as you don't touch her. That's not allowed you know. Visitors mustn't touch the patients for any reason whatsoever.'

Belle wanted to ask why she couldn't touch her own mother. It sounded as if she were made of some delicate porcelain and would break easily; but then her fragility was evident. The door had closed behind the nurse and they were alone. Mother and daughter stared at each other across the room. Bess rocked slightly backwards and forwards on the uncomfortable upright chair and Belle stood helplessly watching her. She must say something to break the ice, before the nurse came back and it was too late.

'Hello, Mam.' Bess didn't stop her gentle rocking, but her sharp eyes moved so Belle knew she could hear her. 'I'm sorry I haven't been before.'

And then Bess spoke for the first time. Her voice was a

157

croak, as if she didn't use it often or her throat were sore.

'Belle,' she said softly.

'Yes Mam, it's me. How are you?'

'Not too bad, but the time goes so slowly. How are things at home?'

'We're managing; but we miss you.'

'And your Dada – and Gran?'

'They're fine. Gran does a lot of the housework now; and the cooking. But I help her all I can.'

'You've grown, Belle. You're quite a lady.'

'Am I?' Belle smiled, pleased with the compliment. Bessie's voice was growing stronger and she sounded more as Belle remembered.

'Just like I was at your age: only prettier. Did you bring me anything?'

'No. I'm sorry, Mam, I didn't think. If there's anything you need, just tell me and I'll bring it next time.' Belle suddenly remembered when they'd stopped to rest in the wood. 'I did pick you some bluebells . . .' her face dropped. 'But I lost them on the way.'

'It doesn't matter.' Bess sighed as if she would have liked the flowers but wasn't a bit surprised that her daughter had lost them. It was just like old times. If Bess had been too pleased Belle wouldn't have trusted her; but now the old relationship had been reformed, of Belle never quite pleasing her mother.

'I'm sorry, Mam,' she said 'I'll bring you some flowers next time.'

'Don't put yourself out.'

The effort of keeping up a conversation was making Bess agitated, and the rocking was getting faster. Suddenly her whole body seemed to be gripped in a seizure, and because she had nothing to grip with, her bound body slithered helplessly from the chair. It happened too quickly for Belle to prevent it. Although she'd been instructed not to touch her mother, common humanity would have made her help if she'd had warning.

The immobile figure was so small and pathetic in its binding of grey blanket, the straps so tight they restricted movement. The tiny face criss-crossed by scars looked up at Belle pleadingly. Her soft heart was moved to compassion.

'Help me,' Bess begged.

Belle moved towards the door. 'I'll fetch the nurse.'

'Help me, Belle . . .'

How could anyone refuse such a request, and after all, what harm was there? Belle leant over the still form, put her arms around the bound shoulders and tried to lift Bess back into the chair. Although she was so small, her mother was a dead weight and unable to help herself. As fast as she thought she'd succeeded in her task, the body would slide back again into its original position.

'It's no good,' Belle said at last. 'I'll have to fetch help.'

'If you could just undo the buckles I could help myself,' Bess said matter-of-factly. 'I only wear it to keep me warm. You can do it up again as soon as I'm in the chair.'

'I don't know if I should,' Belle said doubtfully. 'You know what the nurse said.'

'That's just a ruling; but nobody sticks to it. Anyway, she won't know, will she?'

'All right,' Belle said, moved by the pleading eyes and her own feelings of pity. She fell to her knees beside the recumbent form. 'Keep still now.'

To reach the buckles, she had to roll her mother over like a badly wrapped parcel. Her fingers were deft and she soon managed to loose the straps and unwind the blanketing from the motionless form. Bess lay immobile as her daughter freed her; only her eyes following every movement, and smiling encouragement.

The figure revealed under the wrappings was so pathetic that Belle wanted to cry. A tiny bag of bones covered by a linen shift, as plain as a shroud. Wrists and fingers like dry twigs, bruised with the pressure of the straps. There was no colour in the transparent flesh; no blood could flow under that paper-white skin. Bess was as helpless as a baby and Belle was moved to the very centre of her being. She placed her strong young hands under the withered armpits and gently lifted Bess to her feet. They stood together, with their arms around each other, as if they were going to break into a parody of dance. Belle could feel fetid breath on her face. She felt dizzy: mesmerised by the other's eyes. She wanted to turn her head away so that she couldn't see the terrible features but she was too frightened to move. This wasn't her mother. This was some evil spirit who'd taken over her mother's body, or was she, Belle, in the clutch of a nightmare? That must be it: the whole day was taking on the aspect of a nightmare. Any moment now she'd wake up. She closed her eyes briefly and then opened them again, but the horribly scarred face was still only a few inches from her own.

'Come on,' she said. 'I'll help you into your chair.'

But Bess didn't move, and suddenly the shrivelled arms were holding her in a vice-like grip. The face so close to her own had become that of a stranger.

'Why did you let Charlie die?' Bess spat the words into Belle's face. Foam and spittle ran from the corner of her misshapen mouth.

'I didn't, Mam.' A feeling of fear engulfed Belle. 'It was an accident, you know that. I loved Charlie.'

'Then why did you let him die? Why didn't you die instead of Charlie?'

The words came out on a shrill cry. Too late Belle realised why Nurse Sally had instructed her so firmly not to touch her patient. The garment she'd released her from was a form of strait-jacket, and the woman so confined was mad. Belle could see the madness now in the rolling eyes, and the strength in the wasted muscles that gripped her arms.

'Let me go, Mam,' she begged helplessly, struggling in the manic clutches. But she knew it was no use. Bess might be frail, but the obsession in her tormented brain gave her unusual strength. She seemed anxious to destroy the daughter whose only fault lay in surviving the air-raid that had killed her brother. Belle struggled but she couldn't shake herself free. She opened her mouth to scream. The scream was in her head but try as she could it was trapped there. She could make no sound and no one would come to her assistance. She must have managed some sort of noise and the drumming in her ears muffled it, because within seconds the door burst open, as if the system was geared to rescuing visitors in distress.

The room seemed to be full of struggling figures, and the sharp fingers that had found Belle's windpipe slowly released their pressure. She rubbed her throat carefully and swallowed, feeling arms around her leading her to a chair. Belle's face was hidden in her hands. Perhaps it was as well that she didn't watch as the freshly hobbled figure shuffled through the door without a glance in her direction.

'I did warn you,' Nurse Sally said, waving an admonishing finger under Belle's nose, as if she were reprimanding a delinquent child. 'None of them can be trusted.'

'She looked so harmless.' Belle wiped away a tear from her cheek. She wasn't going to cry now. Perhaps later, when she was alone, she would be able to give in to the relief of tears.

'Harmless!' The nurse laughed, but there was little humour in the sound. 'The first thing we're taught is never to turn our backs; but most of us learn the hard way.'

Belle shuddered. She still couldn't digest the fact that her own mother had tried to kill her, and but for the grace of God might have succeeded.

'Thank you for coming to my rescue,' she said gratefully.

'Don't thank me,' Nurse Sally said. 'It was your friend who got here first; although he had no business to.'

Only then did Belle realise that the person standing behind her with the comforting hand on her shaking shoulder wasn't a hospital official. It was Henry, who she'd left waiting for her in reception a lifetime ago. He grinned ruefully.

'Sorry,' he said. 'You were such a long time, I got worried. I followed the nurse up here after she brought me the tea. I'm glad I did, because I heard you scream and got here in time.'

'Oh, Henry!' was all Belle could find to say, but she gripped his hand thankfully. She wasn't ashamed now of the tears that were streaming freely down her cheeks. Nurse Sally took the hint and left them alone.

'I have to go and check on my other patients. I'll be back directly.' She left the room, closing the door gently behind her. Henry saw Belle rummaging through her pockets and handed her a handkerchief. She mopped her eyes gratefully. 'She wanted to kill me,' she said between sobs. 'My own mother wanted to kill me because I wasn't Charlie.'

'Try not to think about it.' Henry's calm voice did a lot to restore her self-control. 'She's a sick woman and didn't know what she was doing. Are you feeling better now?'

'I think so; but I want to go home.'

'Come on then,' said Henry, taking the hint.

He led the way and Belle followed obediently. When they were half-way down the stairs she started to run as if she couldn't reach the front door quickly enough. Henry had to put a spurt on to keep up with her. The nurse at reception looked up in surprise as they sprinted past her desk without slowing down. It was only when they were well past the front door that Belle stopped and bent over double, taking in great gulps of fresh air.

'I've got a stitch,' she explained. Then she stretched and turned a sad face to Henry. 'Father tried to warn me but I wouldn't listen. I had to see for myself.'

'Are you satisfied?'

'I suppose so.' She looked up at the grim building. 'At least I know now that Mam will never come home again.'

'Come away, Belle,' Henry said gently, leading the way back to where they'd left their bicycles. 'At least it's stopped raining and most of the way home is downhill.'

But the spirit had gone out of the day and they seemed to have nothing to say to each other. They rode side by side, Belle deep in her own thoughts and Henry not wanting to intrude. Occasionally he glanced at his companion with a protective expression on his face, and slowed his pace so that she wouldn't get too tired.

Belle looked composed but her brain was in a turmoil. How could she ever forget the look on her mother's face, or the feel of those bony, clutching fingers around her throat? She pedalled blindly, not looking where she was going, not seeing the road ahead or the passing scenery. If it hadn't been for Henry she might have missed the road completely and toppled headlong into a ditch.

Mam had tried to kill her! Mam had wanted her dead! It wasn't her fault that Charlie had died; it could just as easily have been her sheltering under the wall when the bomb fell. Or it could have been both of them. Belle's face felt cold and wet; she let go one of the handlebars to rub it dry with the palm of her hand.

'Watch out!' Henry ordered.

Belle came to her senses and smiled a watery smile as she

straightened up her machine. Even if she had been through a bad time it wouldn't help to cause an accident.

'Feeling better?'

'Yes, thanks.'

Henry grinned, pleased that the colour had come back into her cheeks.

They'd been on the road for about half an hour when Belle looked around as if noticing the passing scenery for the first time. 'Where are we?' she asked. 'I don't remember passing that little church.'

'We didn't. We're going home a different way. It's quicker and I know the route. I used to come this way with the Scouts. There used to be a little tea-shop further on; I thought you might like a rest. I've got five shillings in my pocket so I'll treat you.' Belle was grateful. The traumatic events of the day had drained her and a rest would be more than welcome. She wanted to put off the time when she would be on her own. Perhaps the nightmare would return and she'd never escape the mad stare in her mother's eyes, or the sight of the scarred and palid face.

When they reached the tea-shop they found a rustic cottage, with a garden full of white tables and chairs, and borders of spring flowers. The earlier rain had driven everyone indoors, but there were more chairs and tables set out in the front parlour. A cosy little body, the shape of a cottage loaf, was offering them warm home-made scones straight from the oven. The delicious smell of baking wafted from the kitchen and reminded Belle how hungry she was. She had no money of her own so she shook her head.

'Go on,' Henry encouraged, pulling out his two half-crowns. 'We've got nothing else to spend it on.'

Belle was just biting into her second scone spread with strawberry jam when she noticed that Henry had stopped eating and was staring at her across the table. His eyes behind the thick lenses of his glasses had a strange expression, but she couldn't read what he was thinking. She wiped her mouth daintily, thinking that she might have accidentally smeared her face with jam.

'Thank you, Henry. That was lovely. I didn't realise how hungry I was. Shall we go now?'

'In a minute.' He was often serious, but she'd never heard him sound quite so solemn before. 'I have to talk to you.'

'What about?' Belle looked around, wondering if there was a mirror somewhere where she could tidy her hair. She must look a mess. There was probably a lavatory outside, hidden behind a hedge, and containing only the basics. 'I'm going outside to look for the lavatory,' she said, starting to get out of her chair. 'Can you lend me a comb?'

'Please, Belle . . .' There was such desperation in his voice that she sat down again. 'I must talk to you.'

'Well?' He was silent and she felt impatient with him. 'Look, Henry,' she said. 'I'm sorry today's been a disaster, but it wasn't my fault. You wanted to come with me and I'm grateful, but I'd like to forget what happened if that's all right with you.'

'Do you mean what happened at the hospital, or this morning in the bluebell wood?'

Belle had the grace to blush before replying. 'Both,' she said. She meant it. She wanted more than anything to put back the clock. She didn't want to be grown up if it brought with it all the pain and confusion she'd suffered that day.

'If that's what you want.' Henry was looking everywhere but at Belle. He took off his glasses and polished the lenses carefully. 'I just want to know if what you told that Sister is true.'

'What Sister? What am I supposed to have told her? Come to the point.' Belle spoke angrily. Why couldn't he leave her alone?

165

'That we're getting engaged.'

'That we're getting what!' Belle was struck dumb and couldn't continue, so Henry had no option but to go on.

'Sister Williams, I think her name was. When she brought me a cup of tea she offered her congratulations. Of course I didn't know what she was talking about, and then she said you'd told her we were getting engaged.'

'Oh, that!' Belle wanted to laugh. Henry was so gullible he'd believe anything said to him. Surely he hadn't taken Sister Williams seriously?

'I just want to be sure that you meant it.'

'Of course I didn't mean it. Don't look like that.' She couldn't bear the way his face had dropped as if she'd actually hit him. 'You know the ruling was that only relatives could visit patients. I said we were getting engaged because I hoped they'd let you come in with me.'

'So it was only a joke?'

'Not a joke. Of course not; I wouldn't joke about a thing like that. It was just a little white lie that wasn't going to hurt anybody.' But it had hurt Henry, she could see that. 'Anyway, I'm far too young to talk about getting engaged, or married.' She got up from the table hurriedly as if needing to escape and ran from the room, forgetting to ask again for the loan of a comb, and leaving Henry to settle the bill.

The lavatories were hidden behind a hedge of privet as she'd guessed, and there was a little wash-basin and a mirror as well as a rather primitive toilet. She bathed her face and studied her reflection in the glass. Henry was a good friend and she felt only a little bit guilty about the way she'd made use of him. But gratitude wasn't enough.

She wasn't going to end up like Flora: in a loveless marriage of convenience, with no money and no future. Isabel Kelly was made for better things. She had all the time in the world and could afford to wait – but not too long. The idea of marriage to Henry, and probably a lifetime living in the Murtell household and becoming a grey ghost like his Auntie Mabel, filled her with panic. No, she would wait for someone like Joseph Bishop, who would provide her with a motor car instead of a bicycle and a home like his mother lived in; with an antique clock in the hall and a music room with a grand piano.

By the time she rejoined Henry she was feeling a bit better. She would never forget the horror of the day. She'd lived a lifetime in a few hours. When she'd left Duke's Road that morning she'd still been a child, and she was returning to it a woman, in more ways than one. He was waiting for her at the gate holding two bicycles. He waited for her to mount first and lead the way. The sun was breaking through again, drying the wet landscape, and turning the trees and grass verges sparkling green.

All too soon the grey roofs of the town could be seen below. It was like a town in a fairy-tale, with the spires of the churches towering into the sky, and the blue sea on the horizon making a colourful backdrop. They free-wheeled down Ditchling Road and were soon home, propping their machines against the garden wall. Belle retrieved her cardigan and bag from the wicker basket.

'Thanks,' she called over her shoulder as she ran up the front steps to her own front door.

Henry didn't reply. He seemed to be too busy examining the machines for wear and tear, so she closed the door without even saying goodbye.

Gran was in the kitchen; the radio was on and she could hear her tuneless humming to danceband music. She was rocking in her chair, her old eyes half-closed. Belle was reminded of her mother rocking backwards and forwards, the movement generating her hatred of her daughter.

I mustn't think about that, Belle told herself firmly, and,

seeing a loaf on the table beside an open tin of treacle, spread herself a thick sandwich and carried it upstairs to her room. The sticky sweetness was comforting, and she licked the last drops from her fingers as the twilight gathered outside her window and hundreds of tiny flies hovered, denoting good weather for the following day.

She flung open the casement and leaned out. In the stillness of the evening faint music reached her ears; not the music from a radio, but a rhythmic jangle, gay and tantalising. The sort of music that accompanies a carousel. Of course it was the sound of the May Day fair from the Level, getting into its stride to coax the public out of their houses for a last turn on the merry-go-round, or throw at the coconuts, before they packed up and trailed off to the next town.

What better way to finish the day than a visit to the fair. The lights, colours and music would soon drive away the memories she wanted to forget. Who knows, she might even win a piece of jewellery at a hoop-la stall. Once, when she was younger, she'd won a silver locket. The stone was only a piece of glass and the chain had broken the same day, but she still kept it in a drawer of her dressing-table with her mother's brooch, until she had a proper velvet-lined box to keep them in.

She pulled on a warm jumper over her thin dress and let herself out into the darkening street. It only took her five minutes, running all the way down the hill to the coloured oasis of music and merriment opposite the Open Market.

The fair was in full swing, with excited shrieks coming from the big-dipper, and gipsies calling their wares. In the pocket of her skirt she clutched a crumpled ten-shilling note she'd stolen from the box at the bottom of her father's wardrobe. With the confused state he lived in these days he'd probably not even miss it, and if he did he wouldn't be able to prove she'd taken it. Anyway, she'd put it back on payday if she remembered.

She had a ride on a swing-boat, pulling the rope with her strong arms to make it swing higher. Then she bought a cone of lemonade powder from a sweet vendor, and dipped her fingers into the golden crystals until her hands and tongue were stained a bright colour. The rest of her money, in silver and copper coins, rattled in her pocket. She stood still, looking around at every coloured stall, trying to decide what to spend her money on next.

In front of her was a trestle-table with jars of goldfish. For sixpence you were given three rings to try your luck. If your ring fell exactly over a jar the goldfish would be yours. At that moment the one thing Belle wanted most in the world was to win a goldfish – more for the pleasure of winning than the prize itself.

She passed over her money and threw her rings, but her aim was poor and she felt for another coin. Before she could pass it over a jar containing a wriggling fish was pushed into her hands. A familiar voice said, 'You're late. I've been searching for you everywhere. I knew I had to wait for you before I had a ride on the big-dipper.'

Joseph Bishop was standing at her side, a pleased smile on his face. He'd been waiting for her all evening and was beginning to wonder if she was really coming.

11

Enid Bishop was feeling pleased with life in general, and herself in particular. It was her birthday; she was fifty years old, and was convinced that she could pass for at least five years younger.

She studied her reflection in the dressing-table mirror, and smiled her satisfaction as she fastened the tiny clusters of diamond chips into the lobes of her ears. Her make-up was perfected to an art-form, and her thick white hair was permed regularly by the best hairdresser in the town and waved softly around her face. Life was perfect. She saw no reason why it shouldn't continue in the same way indefinitely.

Enid had been a widow now for nearly twenty years, her husband, Jasper, having conveniently dropped dead from a heart attack in his hotel in a foreign country, while on a business trip. She counted herself lucky: if he'd been taken ill at home she might have been expected to nurse him, and she hated anything messy. Out of sight, out of mind, was her motto. Enid soon forgot him.

But she was grateful, because he'd left her and Joseph very well off indeed. She could easily afford to continue the pleasant, lazy, existence she'd grown used to. Beautyparlours, hairdressers, visiting friends and throwing little informal dinner-parties. Afternoon tea in the lounge of the Grand Hotel once a week, served by handsome young waiters in black and white, and serenaded by the music from a Palm Court Orchestra.

Joseph, their son, was well provided for as well. He need never take a job unless he felt inclined, although Enid was in charge of his inheritance. She had been slightly worried when he was invalided out of the air force due to a weak chest and nerves, but it had all worked out very well. He was better at home with his mother where she could keep an eye on him. He'd looked terribly handsome in his uniform, and she kept a photograph of him in a heavy silver frame on the drawing-room mantlepiece, where visitors couldn't fail to notice it. No one need ever know that he'd never been up in an aeroplane in his life, let alone flown one.

Joseph was the apple of her motherly eye and her main reason for living. Her spare moments were happily occupied choosing a suitable wife for him. So far she'd turned away all applicants for this enviable position.

Beatrice Farmer, the horsy girl who'd just left Roedean, was far too bossy. Joseph had taken her out a couple of times, but Enid had breathed a sigh of relief when she eventually sank back into obscurity, to be replaced by Caroline David. Now Caroline was Enid's best friend Margaret David's daughter. She was a well-brought-up girl who wouldn't say boo to a goose. Completely dominated by a strong mother, she was already moulded to perfection into the sort of girl Enid was looking for as a daughter-in-law. Caroline didn't ride, play golf, or talk too much; in fact she hardly spoke at all. Just a nod of the head, or a soft 'please' or 'thank you' when spoken to. Her only interests seemed to be reading novels, playing the violin, and kittens – a perfect combination for a girl destined to be paired with Enid Bishop's son.

Enid enjoyed reading novels herself; in fact she sometimes consumed three or four a week, and there were usually two or three new ones beside her bed in case she had a sleepless night. The violin would be a perfect accompaniment to Enid's piano-playing, and with a bit of practice they should be able to perform duets at the musical evenings Enid was planning. As for the kittens: they would be easily replaced by babies when the time came. The advent of grandchildren was the ambition of Enid Bishop's middle years.

But today was her birthday and Joseph had promised his mother a surprise. Whatever it was would be delightful as Joey was very good at unexpected surprises, knowing exactly what she would want, and what was likely to give the most satisfaction.

At the bottom end of the scale it might be an exotic plant for the conservatory, or an annual subscription to Boot's Booklovers' Library. Either would be welcome. Or if he was feeling really generous it might be a ring or brooch for her jewel-case, or the pedigree puppy she coveted. She fancied a lap-dog to keep her company when Joseph was out. A poodle or a Pekinese would be nice. Something that she could carry about with her and wouldn't need more exercise than the garden would provide. Now that she had Alice living in the house she was quite keen on a dog. After all, part of Alice's duties could be to let the puppy out night and morning, and see to the disagreeable tasks like bathing and grooming. She'd been told that even animals who were confined to their homes still picked up fleas and other things in their coats, and needed regular attention.

Alice Battey was the new maid and had only lived with them for a few days. Young, and not very bright, she was already proving her worth. Plain as a suet pudding and about as docile, she was at least clean and learnt her job quickly, although she was inclined to drop things if too much was expected of her. With the daily woman to do the rough work and Alice sleeping in the attic, Enid now felt she had a staff again, like in the old days, and she enjoyed keeping them in order and bossing them about. Not that she was unkind. She could afford to be generous to the right people, and she'd found through experience that only the right people would stay for long under her roof.

She finished her toilet and carefully placed a net over her hair in case it was windy outside. As it was a special occasion she'd decided to have afternoon tea in the garden. It would make a change and it really was a beautiful day. July was proving to be a glorious month this year.

The full-length glass showed her ample figure to its best advantage. Her powder-blue crêpe dress still fitted perfectly, although she'd put on a few pounds around the hips since she'd bought it in the spring. She tucked a minute handkerchief into her belt and left the room and pattered down the stairs in her court shoes which Alice polished every morning.

First she must see that everything was prepared in the kitchen. She'd ordered scones served with jam and cream because they were Joseph's favourite; but she still wasn't too sure of the new maid's cooking skills. The toast on her breakfast tray had been burnt on Alice's first morning, and if she'd suggested anything in a foreign language, however simple, the girl had looked positively vacant.

Enid looked with satisfaction at the figure bustling between the trolley and the oven, the young face flushed with heat. What she lacked in experience she certainly made up for in enthusiasm.

'That looks very nice, Alice,' she said, surveying the

plates laid out with food. 'The scones have risen beautifully and I see you've made cucumber sandwiches. My son
will be pleased: they're his favourite.'

'Yes, Mrs Bishop,' said Alice dutifully. 'You told me.'

'I thought we'd use the second-best china as we're having it in the garden. You can't be too careful, and it's so
easy to have an accident. Has the cake arrived from Forfar's
safely?' Alice opened the larder door to show off the blue
and white iced confection that exactly matched the colour of
Enid's dress. She'd fancied candles, but fifty might have
looked a bit ostentatious. 'Good girl,' she said vaguely, and
turned back to the trolley. 'I'll push the trolley and you can
follow with the tray. You can bring the cake out to us later.
I'll save you a slice to have with your night-time drink.'

They made an odd procession: Mrs Bishop in the lead
pushing the laden trolley over the bumpy path so that the
sandwiches and scones leapt off the plates. Alice followed,
picking her way carefully with the tray of china, and biting
her lip in concentration. At the bottom of the garden was a
horse-chestnut tree with shady branches, under which was
arranged two striped deck-chairs.

'I'll just put the trolley in the shade,' Enid said, 'and you
can put the tray down on the garden table.'

'Yes, Mrs Bishop,' Alice said.

'And mind you don't break anything.' Enid sank into the
nearest chair and fanned herself energetically.

'Thank you, Alice. I think I'll stay here and wait for Mr
Bishop. You can tell him where I am when he gets home.
Then you can make the tea and bring out the cake.'

Alice nodded with relief, pleased that she hadn't
dropped anything so far that afternoon. Enid leaned back
and closed her eyes; she found the hot weather rather trying. She would take a little nap until Joey arrived with his
surprise, and then she would be fresh and ready to enjoy it.

She was so lucky to be fifty, in the best of health, and have a son like Joseph.

Something tickling her cheek aroused her. Without opening her eyes she brushed at it with the back of her hand, thinking it was a fly or insect. It came again and she slapped at it irritably, now wide awake and slightly aggrieved.

Joseph was sitting in the other chair, regarding her intently, with a pleased smile on his handsome face. He was wearing white slacks and a short-sleeved fawn shirt, its open neck showing the mist of fair hairs on his chest. A lock of blond hair was falling forward over his tanned forehead, and he slicked it back casually.

'Hello, darling,' Enid said sleepily, stretching out one hand towards her son.

'Are we having a party?' He avoided her touch and helped himself to a sandwich, biting into it with strong even teeth.

'Of course. It's my birthday. I hope you haven't forgotten.'

'You wouldn't let me, would you? Don't worry: I remembered your surprise.'

Enid looked at him excitedly. He was such a perfect son and it was such a perfect day. He got to his feet slowly and stood in front of her, his hands feeling in his pockets. Then he held them over her head, dangling two boxes just out of reach, one from each hand. They were both jeweller's boxes: she recognised the gold trademark embossed on the leather. One was long and flat, the other small and square. Enid giggled excitedly and stretched out greedy fingers.

'Two surprises, Joseph! You spoil me.'

'Not so fast, Mother,' he said teasingly, moving them out of her reach. 'This one is your present,' and he dropped the long box into her lap. It contained a single row of pearls, small but perfect, and she knew how much they must have cost him. But he could afford it, she told herself. Although most of Jasper's fortune was safely under her control, Joseph had a good allowance and was sensible with money.

'It's beautiful, darling,' she said contentedly, and reached her hands out again.

'This one isn't for you,' Joseph said, turning over the square box on his palm. 'This one is the surprise.'

He was deliberately tormenting her and she knew it. So she waited, smiling in anticipation as he lifted the lid and held it open for her to see the contents. On a bed of white satin two rings lay side by side: a cluster of diamonds in a Victorian setting and next to it a wide band of plain gold.

'But Joseph,' Enid said wonderingly. 'That's a wedding ring.'

'I know,' Joseph chuckled. 'That's the surprise.'

There was a silence as if Enid was trying to take in what Joseph was trying to tell her. Then she laughed, before saying, 'Darling, what a funny way you have of telling me things. I suppose you've proposed to Caroline at long last, and she's accepted you?'

'Not Caroline.'

After a pause, 'Beatrice?'

'No.'

'Who then? I hope it's someone I know.'

'Yes. Well, sort of. You met her once a long time ago.' The smile had dropped from Enid's face, as if she was trying to brace herself for the worst. She had nothing to say; all she could do was wait. 'It's Isabel Kelly.'

'Who?'

If Enid Bishop hadn't been so well brought up she would have spat the words out.

'Isabel Kelly.' Joseph repeated the name. 'She came here once to take an order for some gloves. I remember you remarking afterwards what a charming girl she was. You really seemed to like her. But I more than like Belle. I love her, and I'm going to marry her.'

Enid half closed her eyes while she registered this information. Then she opened them again and stared at her son as if he'd suddenly gone mad. 'Not the girl from Mrs Watkins's factory?'

'Yes.'

Enid let out a long sign of relief. 'Now I know you're joking. You mustn't frighten me like that, Joey. And on my birthday too.'

'It's not a joke, Mother. Belle's in the house now. I told her to stay there while I broke the news to you. She'll be here any minute, so I hope you're going to welcome her into the family. Here she comes now.'

Joseph was looking back towards the house, a tender smile on his face, and Enid had no option but to follow his eyes.

Through a haze of sunlight and emotion she saw a slim figure approaching down the garden path. A childlike figure in a white dress, with a mane of red hair blowing around bare shoulders in a most unfashionable way. Enid had to admit that the girl was pretty, and if this was what had turned Joseph's head there was still hope. But the white dress was so obviously home-made. Even for a sun-dress the neckline was cut far too low so that half the wearer's full breasts could be easily seen. She was also wearing too much make-up for the middle of the afternoon, and the orange lipstick was completely the wrong shade to wear with that hair. The heels of her white shoes were high, and instead of making her sway from the hips and look like a model, as she hoped, she tottered on them slightly as if her feet hurt. She looked nervous as she reached them and put out her hand to Enid. Although her nails were carefully varnished they were obviously bitten, and the skin of her palms was rough, and needed a good softening cream to improve their texture.

Enid shook the proffered hand briefly and struggled to her feet. This wasn't easy as the deck-chair was low and deep and Joseph didn't help her as he usually did; his eyes were too full of the red-haired girl to notice. They seemed to be waiting to hear what Enid was going to say. Was she going to voice her disapproval, or put her pride in her pocket and congratulate them?

They didn't have the chance to find out. At that moment they all heard a crash from the direction of the house, followed by a startled cry. Alice, as instructed by her mistress, had been carefully carrying the birthday cake and had tripped on the uneven path, dropping the cake on to the crazy-paving where it broke into pieces, shedding lumps of blue and white icing and wedges of butter sponge into a nearby flower-bed. Alice stood there, helplessly, looking at the debris, and then with another shrill cry turned and ran back into the kitchen mopping her face on the hem of her apron.

Belle started to go to the maid's assistance, but Enid Bishop stepped in front of her, one hand to her forehead in a rather melodramatic gesture.

'Leave her,' she said. 'She really must learn to be less clumsy, and the cake's ruined anyway. I've suddenly developed the most terrible migraine and must go and lie down. It's probably the sun, and I'll be better in a dark room. I'm sure you understand, my dear.' She tried to smile, but it was a travesty of her usual expression. With head bowed she walked slowly back to the house, making a show of stepping over the broken pieces of cake.

Joseph reached out and took one of Belle's hands in his and drew her close to him. He was a head taller than her, and she had to tip her head back to look into his grey eyes.

'That's over. Are you feeling better now?'

'Not really. She doesn't like me. She doesn't think I'm good enough for you.'

'Don't be such a goose. It was just a bit of a shock and I handled it badly. She may not look it but she's pretty tough, and once she gets used to the idea she'll take it in her stride. You'll see.'

'I hope so.'

'Now, I want you to start wearing the ring so everyone knows you belong to me.'

He opened the square box again and took out the cluster of diamonds. Although it was a warm day Belle's little hand felt cold. He caressed her fingers gently before slipping the ring on to her third finger. The sunlight caught the stones and made them fire with rainbow-coloured brilliance.

Joseph placed one hand under her chin and tipped her head back so that he could kiss her on the lips; and then, with a groan, he pulled her to him in a close embrace. She could feel his heart beating through his shirt and the first stirring of love welled in her. She'd always liked and admired him, but more for the things he could give her than anything else: she wanted to love him, so that she needn't feel guilty. She returned his kisses with the sort of passion he'd only dreamt about, and when he reluctantly pushed her away his eyes were still soft with love. 'Later, darling,' he said gently. 'When we're alone. But now I must go in and see that Mother is all right. She's had time to get used to the idea that I'm not her little boy any more; and, knowing her, she's probably planning another campaign. She'll compromise in the end, unless I'm very much mistaken, but I have to handle things so that she doesn't lose her pride.'

'I'll come with you.' Feeling as she did, Belle couldn't bear to be separated from her loved one for even a few minutes.

'No. You stay here. I can handle her best on my own. Tuck into the food if you're hungry. Alice has prepared enough for an army and nobody else seems to want it.' He looked at the plate of sandwiches: the edges of the triangles were already beginning to curl; and the bowl of cream which had been whisked into peaks was now all soft and runny.

Joseph knew exactly where to find his mother. He'd seen the way her bedroom curtains had closed five minutes after she'd re-entered the house. He could hear sobbing coming from the direction of the kitchen as he passed through the hall. It was Alice Battey in full flow, mourning her mistress's squashed cake and broken china. He wanted to commiserate with her, but thought he'd wait until she'd calmed down.

'Women!' he said to himself despairingly: one crying in the kitchen and the other sulking upstairs. At least Belle didn't seem to be a hysterical female. He felt quite proud of the way she'd faced his mother in the garden.

Before he went upstairs he made a detour into the dining-room where there was a well-stocked cocktail cabinet. Not that they were heavy drinkers, but it was only polite to have something to offer guests. His mother liked a stiff sherry on special occasions so he filled two glasses. He drank one down at a gulp to steady his nerves, and then filled it up again to the brim. That should do the trick, he thought as he carried the drinks upstairs.

The bedroom door was tightly closed and there was no sound from within, although he stood outside and listened for a few minutes. At least the silence meant that she wasn't crying. He tapped on the door softly, and then louder, impatient at the unreasonableness of the opposite sex. Still no sound: so he turned the handle quietly and pushed the door open.

180

The room was in semi-darkness as she always liked it when she had a real, or imaginary, migraine. He could just see the outline of her body stretched on the bed, facing the wall. Under the bedside table he could see her shoes neatly arranged, with the shoe-trees already in place. She was very particular about this and Joseph took it as a good sign: the shock she'd sustained over his news hadn't made her deviate from her usual routine. He placed her drink within reach and sipped from his own glass.

'Mother,' he said. 'I want to talk to you.'

'Later, Joey. I have a bad head.'

'I'm sorry, Mother, but it won't keep.'

He crossed to the window and pulled back one of the curtains, the wooden rings rattling like castanets in the quiet room. Then he heard the sighing of the bedsprings as his mother turned over. He could see Belle at the bottom of the garden. She'd slipped off her shoes to rest her feet, and was sitting in one of the deck-chairs swinging her legs in the air. She held a sandwich in each hand and was taking alternate bites. He wanted her so badly that it gave him added strength to turn to the bed and get it over.

'I just want to tell you how much I love Belle. I intend to marry her as soon as possible, and I expect you to welcome her into this house and treat her like one of the family.'

'I shall do no such thing. I think you've taken leave of your senses.'

'But I thought you liked her, Mother.'

'So I did. She was pleasant and polite; and you can't say that about a lot of working girls these days – but that doesn't mean I want you to marry her.'

'Just give her a chance.' Joseph was ashamed of the begging note that had crept into his voice: like a little boy pleading for an extra sweet. 'When she's living here, and you get to know her, I know you'll change your mind.'

'Living here!' Enid Bishop forgot her headache and sat up quickly, pulling a frilly pillow into the small of her back, and stretching her short silk-clad legs in front of her. She was too bothered to be aware that her hair-net had slipped and was dangling foolishly over one ear. 'You're not bringing her to live here.'

'Only for a few weeks until we're married. She lives at the moment in a terrible house in Duke's Road, with a sluttish grandmother and a drunken father. It's almost a slum. I want to get her away as soon as possible.' Joseph finished his drink slowly, trying to assess the effect his words were having on his mother. 'I thought you'd enjoy taking her around and helping her choose clothes and things. She knows what she wants but isn't very experienced. You'd be able to show her the ropes.'

Enid sighed again. An hour ago she'd been so happy: without a worry in the world. But now her birthday had been ruined and she was expected to invite a factory girl into her own home and introduce her to her friends as her prospective daughter-in-law.

'All right,' she said at last. Joseph looked at her in surprise. He'd expected it to take longer to talk her round. 'I'll tell Alice to prepare the small spare room. But only until you're married, mind.'

'Of course.'

'And where are you planning to live then?'

'We rather fancied one of the squares in Hove. There are some lovely Regency properties coming on to the market, and I want Belle to have the best.'

'And who's paying for the best?'

'What do you mean?'

'Who is paying for the Regency love-nest in the most expensive part of town?'

'Well, I thought . . .' Joseph paused, and looked down at

the perfectly whitened toes of his shoes. 'I thought Father's money . . .'

Enid leant back against her pillows and let out a hoot of laughter. It wasn't very ladylike but she couldn't contain herself. She hadn't won, but she'd beaten him in the first round, and he knew it. The cockiness had gone out of his face and he had the grace to look sheepish.

'Your father's money was left to me,' she said, 'and well you know it. He trusted me to bring you up in a style becoming to his son, and I've always tried to be generous. In fact, I think you will agree, you've wanted for nothing. When I die, and I certainly hope it won't be for a long time, you will inherit it all. I've invested carefully over the years with your future in mind. In the meantime you have a substantial allowance, and that will continue whatever you do; but it certainly won't run to expensive houses. Of course, if I approved of your choice of a wife, things might be very different.'

'All right; don't go on.' Joseph turned back to the window. 'If you feel like that I won't take a penny. We'll find a little place to rent and, if necessary, I'll get a job. I must be able to do something. Belle won't mind; what she hasn't had she won't miss. And she's agreed to marry me because she loves me, not because of any fortune she might imagine I have.'

'I hope so, dear boy,' Enid said softly. 'I do hope so.'

At the window Joseph was drawing encouragement from the sight of Belle, skirt tucked up to catch the last of the sun and half a jammy scone wedged in her hungry mouth. She saw him at the window and waved gaily. He gave a thumbs-up sign and she took this to mean that all had gone well.

She felt as Enid had felt earlier: completely content with her lot. After years of struggle she was never going to want for anything, ever again. She was going to be a lady, and didn't intend returning to the role of the submissive factory girl.

The plates were empty, apart from a curled sandwich that the wasps were feeding on, and a couple of scones that were slightly over-done. Belle lay back in her chair and patted her full stomach contentedly; running her hands over the unusually rounded contour. Safely inside, protected by her body, curled the outline of her child: the baby conceived in the bluebell wood nearly three months before. The knowledge of its existence, which she alone was aware of, made her feel powerful now that she had a ring safely on her finger. All she had to do was insist on an early wedding date, so that the birth would look like a premature one. Henry's child would be safely born into the world with a legal father and a secure future.

Belle had no doubt that she was carrying a male child in her womb. She couldn't say why she was so sure, but it was probably something to do with Flora's little boy, Peter, and the maternal feelings he invoked when she held him in her arms. She'd had no experience of girl children.

When she'd first discovered that she was pregnant she'd been filled with dismay and disbelief. That the first and only encounter with sex could result in a baby seemed unfair. Even in the poor area in which she lived, unmarried women were frowned upon and treated as outcasts. Their offspring were whispered about and called names, and were expected to go to the bad. A wedding ring was the only safe way out for a girl in her condition. Henry would marry her no doubt, if she told him. He would leap at the opportunity, and she would be doomed to a lifetime of drudgery and be old before she had a chance to enjoy being young.

But now there was Joseph. He'd taken her out several

times since they'd met at the fair, although she hadn't allowed any liberties. They'd eaten at a restaurant, strange food which she didn't recognise but had to admit tasted wonderful, and she'd been for rides in his motor car. If she played her cards right she'd known she could make him fall in love with her. After all, Flora had done it, and Belle considered herself cleverer than her friend. When she got around to it, it was so easy. Now she had the longed-for engagement ring on her finger and the promise of a wedding to follow, soon – it had to be soon.

'Penny for them?' she looked up and found Joseph standing beside her, his eyes full of emotion.

'I was thinking how much I love you, and how lucky I am,' she said, getting to her feet and kissing him lightly on the cheek. 'Is you mother all right? What did she say?'

'She's fine,' said Joseph, taking Belle into his arms. 'And she's very happy for us, and delighted about our engagement.' When he returned her kiss he seemed to have something on his mind, and a slight shiver of doubt crept up Belle's spine.

12

'Will you look at that then!'

'Who does she think she is: Lady Muck?'

Two sunburnt faces peered over the edge of a roof at a young woman passing along the street below. It wasn't that she was a particularly beautiful woman, some people might have found her red hair and high heels positively common, but it was the way she walked: with her head high, and the seductive swaying of her hips that made the men look twice. Even the lowly task of pram-pushing, which might have consigned another woman to the realms of a house-wife and mother, only seemed to add to her charm. The black baby-carriage was large and expensive, shining with chrome, and sprung high on large wheels so that it was comfortable and easy to push.

Belle was a proud mother, and dressed herself up with care for the daily constitutional. Today she was wearing a coat of olive-green cloth, cut in long panels in the latest fashion so that the bottom of the skirt swirled out like a bell, and the tight waist accentuated the curve of her breasts. Her hair was twisted into a fashionable knot on top of her head and secured by tortoiseshell combs and a black satin bow; but true to form a few tendrils had escaped the hairdresser's skill and blew around her cheeks as they had in the old days. Her gloves were soft kid, made to measure by the staff at Lena Watkins's, and around her neck she wore a narrow collar of white fur.

One of the watchers on the roof whistled and Belle smiled. She might look like the lady she wanted to emulate but inside the smart exterior still lived the wild young girl full of passion and dreams. She glanced up at the roof and winked, and this drove the workmen to delighted cheers, which followed her stately progress until she'd disappeared around the corner and out of sight.

The child, Lucy, had been asleep, rocked by the motion of her carriage. She woke with a start when her mother tipped the pram over a high kerb, scraping the bumpers on the concrete edging, and let out an indignant cry. Belle inspected the pram for damage. In fact she seemed more concerned about the expensive baby-carriage than she was for the welfare of the child inside.

Motherhood had been a bit of a disappointment to Belle. She'd lived through six months of excitement and anticipation, commencing with the wedding at the Brighton Registry Office. They'd decided to dispense with a church wedding. Belle, who hadn't been to mass for ages had met Father Joe in the street.

'I hear you're getting wed, Isabel Kelly,' he said.

'Yes, Father.'

'And when are you bringing your intended round to meet me?'

'Joseph's not a Catholic, Father.'

'Oh! That's sad. But I still have to meet him if you want to be married at St Anne's.'

'We're getting married at the Registry Office.'

Father Joe frowned. 'What's the rush, child?'

Belle didn't know how to explain, so she just said. 'It's

what Joseph wants, Father. I must go now: I'm late,' and she hurried away. Unfortunately Father Joe knew Belle only too well. Her restless nature was an open book to him and he was bound to advise her against a hasty marriage, even if he guessed the chief cause.

Joseph was a Protestant, but not very devout, so neither of them saw the necessity for the church's blessing on their union, although Belle felt a bride's natural wish to wear a long white dress and sweep down the aisle to organ music, with a following of bridesmaids.

George Kelly gave his permission, but apart from that showed little interest in the proceedings. He supposed he'd miss his daughter, but Gran was still there to do the household tasks, and Maud Carter still kept him company when he felt the need, so he had no reason to stand in Belle's way. The day she left the house in Duke's Road for the last time, he pressed a five-pound note into her palm from the box in the bottom of his wardrobe, and returned to reading his newspaper.

Enid Bishop did her duty, but that was all. She welcomed Belle into her house for the weeks preceding the ceremony, took her on trips to the shops to choose clothes, and even footed some of the bills. But there was coldness in her forced smile, and a disapproving hardness in her voice when she spoke to her son's fiancée, that showed Belle how much she was disapproved of.

Joseph continued to show his adoration and fell in with her every whim, so Belle stopped trying to be friendly and win Mrs Bishop over, and just took every day in her stride. She was looking forward to the day when Joseph would carry her away to an establishment as luxurious as his mother's, and Belle would reign at last as mistress of her own home.

The wedding was low key. If Belle had been superstitious she might have taken the grey August day, with its threat of rain, as an omen for her own future. But she refused to be discouraged. She was a radiant bride, in a blue two-piece that matched her sparkling eyes, and a hat made of hundreds of tiny silver and blue feathers, that nestled like a bird on the top of her coppery head. Her hands were full of cream rosebuds, and when Joseph slipped the wide gold band on to her finger to join the cluster of diamonds, her heart was full of love for him.

They didn't have a reception; Mrs Bishop took them out to dinner instead. They went to her favourite resort: the Grand Hotel, and watched the rough grey sea from the window of a private room overlooking the promenade. They ate prawn cocktail and caviare boats followed by Dover sole, washed down by champagne. While they were waiting for the coffee to arrive Belle excused herself and went in search of the ladies' room.

'Doesn't Belle look happy?' Joseph said to his mother.

'Yes, dear. And she seems to have put on weight. She was a skinny little thing when I first saw her.'

'It just shows how contented she is.'

When Belle returned to the table Joseph laughingly repeated his mother's words. Belle gave a secret little smile but didn't take offence. If Enid suspected the reason for the weight gain she didn't say anything. Belle wasn't going to enlighten her.

They had a short honeymoon in London, a place Belle had never been to before. They stayed at a hotel in Mayfair and had most of their meals sent up to their room. Joseph wanted his bride to himself and Belle still found restaurants and waiters rather daunting.

He took her for a sightseeing tour to places she'd only heard of, Buckingham Palace and the Tower of London among them. Knowing very little about world events or social history she found ancient monuments boring and preferred shopping in the West End. Joseph's purse, patience and generosity seemed bottomless. When they returned to Brighton on the train from Victoria the luggage-rack over their first-class seats was full of bags from expensive fashion houses, containing the pick of their summer collections.

Her first disappointment was the home Joseph had prepared for her. It was in Hove, just, and consisted of two floors of a Victorian property standing near a main road. Joseph didn't tell her that he'd only rented the maisonette, and she didn't understand why he didn't evict the undesirable people living in the basement. The furnishings were new rather than antique, which was what Belle wanted, but the whole place had been decorated. Belle chose the colours and the wallpapers, so the finished decor of dove-grey and pink was feminine, and quite delightful to her uneducated eyes.

They also had a maid. Alice Battey had befriended Belle during her stay in the Dyke Road house and had come to her in tears.

'I don't know whatever I'm going to do when you go,' she mourned. 'I shall miss you so much. Mrs Bishop makes me so nervous I'm always dropping things.'

'I know, Alice, she had the same effect on me.' Belle looked sympathetic.

'I wondered if I could come with you. You know, as part of your marriage settlement.'

'Perhaps if Joseph asked . . .'

'Oh, do you think he would? I'd work for lower wages if only you'd give me a home and a job.'

Joseph had been doubtful if they could afford a maid, even at a reduced salary. He was already overspending his allowance and running up debts trying to keep his wife happy. He hoped, prayed, and lived for the day when his mother would come to her senses and give him a fair portion of his father's estate. He wasn't aware of the depths of Enid's displeasure, nor her suspicions about his wife's condition on her wedding day. She played a waiting game, holding the purse-strings and watching her Joey get more and more into debt, with an all-knowing smile on her plump face.

Losing the services of Alice Battey, and to a rival establishment, had infuriated her. She vowed, there and then, that not a penny extra would go to her son and his wife while she was alive. Joey had brought it on his own shoulders and he had to learn by his mistakes, without her motherly shoulder to rely on.

The birth of Lucy, eighteen months ago, had been a traumatic experience for Belle. She'd been so convinced that the baby was going to be a boy that the birth of a daughter came as a shock. She soon found out that she wasn't a natural mother, either in the act of giving birth or in caring for her offspring.

Joseph, wanting the best for his wife, had booked her into a private ward at the maternity hospital. Having no previous knowledge of childbirth he easily accepted that a premature baby was a natural event, even when it was perfectly formed and a good weight.

Belle was still slim, and although her figure was dainty but full-busted, she had the small waist and narrow hips of a boy. She was in labour for nearly two days in the strange clinical environment of a hospital. The staff were kind, but busy with an influx of deliveries. It was only due to Belle's status as a private patient that made them put up with the attention she demanded as her labour progressed.

Belle wasn't usually an attention seeker, but she wasn't prepared for the pain and humiliation. She missed Joseph dreadfully, and he only appeared at visiting times to mutter words of encouragement. Then he vanished again to leave her in tears of loneliness and despair.

The baby was finally born in the early hours of the morning, when everyone was at their lowest ebb, and Belle had begun to pray for death to put an end to her torture. The last pain tore her in two. When the terror ebbed away and peace crept over her bruised body she thought she had already died, and was at last happy. The white uniformed nurse at her bedside was an intrusion; she had difficulty focusing her brain on the words that were being said.

'It's all over, Mrs Bishop. Would you like to hold your baby?'

She was a child again in her narrow bed in Duke's Road, sick with some childish ailment. Mam would be safely downstairs preparing the dinner, and Dada would come in at any minute to cheer her up and bring her a treat. She tried to twist around in the bed to watch for him, but there was only a nurse standing in the doorway holding a white bundle in her arms.

'Where's Dada?' Belle whispered through parched lips.

'Who, dear?' The nurse came closer and held out the bundle for Belle's inspection. 'It's a little girl, Mrs Bishop. You've got a lovely little daughter. Would you like to hold her?'

The bundle was placed in Belle's arms and the shawl pulled away. Everything fell into place; she knew where she was, and what she was doing there. Her baby, her little son, whom she'd married Joseph to protect. And then the words the nurse had spoken penetrated her brain: 'It's a little girl, Mrs Bishop.'

She looked down, almost in indignation, at the usurper of her motherhood. An understanding filled her of how her own mother felt when she had to divide her love between a son and a daughter; and the son had received it all, uncon-ditionally.

The baby in her arms was so ugly. Long and thin with hardly any flesh on its bones, not chubby and soft as Belle had imagined. Its face was purple rather than pink and wrinkled like a monkey, with wisps of dark hair on its bony scalp which was still spattered with blood. Frantically she investigated to make sure that the nurse hadn't made a mis-take over the sex of the child. There was no mistake.

Then the ugly little thing let out a wail as if it sensed its mother's displeasure; it opened its eyes still sticky with mucus, and looked at Belle. She saw, without a doubt, that it was indeed Henry's child: the thin face and large nose were duplicates in miniature of the father. Even the way she peered upwards as if, at only a few minutes old, she was destined to be short-sighted and need spectacles, and the wispy hair grew in the same way from a peak over the eyes. No one would ever doubt who had fathered this child, and the only good thing about it was that Joseph and Henry had never met.

And then Joseph arrived. The worried frown that had creased his forehead for the last forty-eight hours was gone. He looked delighted at the sight of Belle sitting up and looking so pretty in a frilly lace bed-jacket, with ribbons in her hair. He failed to notice the dark circles under her blue eyes, or the disappointment in her voice. His arms were full of hot-house flowers, freesias and lilies, that made the small room smell like a funeral parlour.

'I hope you feel up to it,' he said. 'But mother's outside. I insisted on her coming with me to view her first grand-child.'

Enid Bishop swept past him into the room, laden with duty presents. A bottle of perfume for the mother and a matinée coat for the baby. She leant over the cot and made her inspection. Her expression didn't change at what she saw; it only confirmed her suspicions.

'I hope you're pleased, Joseph,' was all she said.

'I think she's a little wonder,' Joseph answered, his eyes still on the baby.

'I agree with you,' Enid said with a bitter smile. 'I've never seen a premature baby so perfectly formed, even down to fingernails and a full head of hair.'

The sarcasm was lost on her son, but Belle was aware of the meaning behind every word. Her mother-in-law knew Belle's carefully kept secret, and her hatred of her daughter-in-law was now evident. Added to it was dislike of the child she had to acknowledge as her granddaughter.

'I mustn't upset her,' Belle told herself firmly when at last she was alone again. 'She could make life very difficult for me.'

Then it came to choosing a suitable name.

'We could call her Enid, after her grandmother,' Joseph said thoughtfully.

'No,' Belle said firmly. 'If she's to be named after a grandparent she should be called Elizabeth, after my mother.'

'How about Rose, or Louisa? Something pretty and feminine.'

In the end they'd settled on Lucy. Belle just hoped the child would grow up to favour the name. All to no avail. From an ugly, wailing baby Lucy had developed into a plain fractious toddler, who stared at her mother from the depths of her perambulator on that September afternoon, almost accusingly. Sometimes Belle almost imagined that Lucy was aware of her parenthood, and was only waiting to learn to talk before denouncing her own mother.

Belle's attention was so concentrated on the child that she nearly missed her own front door. She made a sudden swing to the left, tipping the pram and its contents sideways. As a matter of habit she glanced down into the basement area. As usual, Mike Walker, the elder of the two brothers who lived there, was pottering about among the old crates and boxes stacked almost to shoulder-height.

The place was a disgrace and something should be done about it. She'd told Joseph many times that the Walker brothers were lowering the tones of the neighbourhood, but he'd shrugged it off saying that he couldn't do anything. Belle had designs on the basement. It would make an ideal nursery, as there were two good-sized rooms as well as a kitchen. Nicely furnished and decorated, Lucy would be very comfortable down there. It was far enough away from her parents' living-quarters for them not to be disturbed when she cried.

Mike Walker looked up and grinned. He was a handsome man, broad and muscular, with the rugged complexion of someone who spent most of his days in the open air. His brown hair was curly and windswept. Mrs Bishop again, he thought. Swirling her skirts as if she was better than the rest of them. He knew all about women like her: brought up in the gutter and no better than she should be. A little bit of money gone to her head. Now her husband – he was a real gentleman and no mistake, but lately he'd been looking worried. Mike, ever curious about his neighbours, wondered what could be wrong. Money, he decided, didn't always bring happiness, it was often more trouble than it was worth. When you had it you worried about what to do with it, and when you hadn't got any you worried about the lack of it. And yet there was something more than her physical appearance that attracted him to Isabel Bishop. He liked the bold glance of her blue eyes, and the way she dropped them modestly when she knew she was being watched. She must be a difficult creature to be married to: all passion and excitement. Life certainly wouldn't be dull. He envied the man who'd beaten him to it and carried the redhead off before he'd got to know her. He sighed at his loss. He couldn't imagine falling in love with another woman since he'd set eyes on Mrs Bishop.

With a last swirl of her skirts Belle opened the front door. 'That awful man,' she thought, as Mike's eyes followed her impudently. The way he always positioned himself, directly below, made her fear that he had a good view up her skirt. And yet a part of her liked it. He was handsome, even if his clothes were rough and his hands dirty; a bit like the boys from the saw-mill so long ago. If she hadn't married Joseph she might have been happy married to a man like Mike Walker – although she suspected he would keep a stronger hold on her emotions than her husband did. Perhaps her nature would find this satisfying. She suspected they could both be passionate and fiery; at least she'd never get the chance to be bored.

Alice bustled out of the shadows to greet them, a big smile on her face. Lucy gave a chuckle and clapped her little hands together. Only Alice could get any sign of pleasure from the child, but then, they understood each other. They were both destined to be plain and unattractive, so they looked below the surface to see the hidden gifts they both held. They both had great capabilities for love, they both had sharp brains when they cared to use them, and they were honest and faithful. Alice wriggled her fingers in Lucy's direction to make her laugh.

'You're late, Mrs Belle,' she said reprovingly. 'I had baby's tea ready ten minutes ago. Boiled eggs and soldiers, my precious.' She lifted Lucy out of her pram and gave her a hefty kiss on the cheek.

Belle unbuttoned her coat and threw it down on the hall chair. 'I went window shopping,' she said, patting her hair into place in front of the mirror.

'Lucy needs new things for the winter, Mrs Belle,' Alice said. 'She's growing that fast.' When the two women had first joined forces the problem had arisen as to what Alice should call her employer. At first it had been Mrs Bishop, but Belle hated the formality of being called the same name as her mother-in-law. She tried not to think too much about that lady. Isabel or Belle sounded too familiar, but Mrs Belle at least showed the difference in their status and suited them both. So Mrs Belle it had remained.

'I'll ask Mr Bishop for some money,' Belle promised. 'I need a new coat, and the shops are just beginning to get their winter stock in.'

'I'll feed Lucy,' Alice said, 'and then I'll make tea for you and Mr Bishop.'

'Is Joseph at home? I thought he said he'd be late.'

'He came in nearly an hour ago, and shut himself in the dining-room. I didn't disturb him as I thought he may have letters to write. I can boil more eggs and make toast if you want.'

'No, Alice; just tea, and perhaps biscuits.'

She watched the maid carry Lucy into the kitchen and then opened the dining-room door quietly. Joseph was sitting at the long table, bent studiously over a pile of papers spread out before him. Behind him in the window his enormous roll-top desk was open, its contents untidy as if he'd been searching for something.

'Hello, darling,' she said. 'You're home early. Is something the matter?'

'What?' He looked up as if his attention had been miles away, a frown creasing his forehead. 'Oh, it's you, Belle. Nothing for you to worry your pretty little head about.'

Temporarily reassured, Belle took her place beside him. He quickly stacked the papers into a neat pile as if he didn't want her to see them and carried them to his desk, rolling the lid down with a final click.

'You look tired,' Belle said. 'Come and sit down. Alice is making the tea, and Lucy is with her so we won't be disturbed. I want to talk to you.' Joseph resumed his seat, and she reached across and took his hand, a gesture she used when she wanted something. 'I need some money for a winter wardrobe. I saw a really smart coat in Western Road this afternoon – and Lucy needs shoes.'

'How much do you need?'

Belle mentioned a figure and the frown between his eyes deepened. 'I'll give you the money for Lucy's shoes but you'll have to wait for the coat.'

'Oh, darling, don't be mean.' Belle pouted prettily; she was so used now to having every whim satisfied. 'You don't want a dowdy wife, do you?'

'Of course not, Belle.' He poured himself a sherry from the decanter on the table, as if he'd already forgotten that the tea would be arriving any minute. 'I'm just a bit short of ready cash at the moment. There are a lot of bills I'd forgotten to settle. You've no idea how things mount up.'

'You could give me an open cheque – or we could open an account.'

'No good. Sorry, Belle. Perhaps you could make last year's coat last a bit longer.'

'I hope you're not serious?' One look at her husband's face and she knew he was: deadly serious. She was immediately contrite and anxious to make amends. She'd been living as if every day was Christmas and money grew on trees. 'Oh, Joseph, I'm sorry. What can we do? Your mother . . .'

'No!' She was startled by the emphasis he put on the one word. 'I have to go up to London tomorrow to see my father's solicitor. I've just telephoned and made an appoint-

198

ment. He may be able to suggest a loophole, so that I can get my fair share of the old man's money.'

'I didn't know, Joseph. I'm sorry. I really didn't understand.' She thought of all the gifts he'd bought her; all the clothes and furs she'd ordered without counting the cost. Even the bills she ran up with the dressmaker and hairdresser would have mounted to more than a year's salary when she'd worked at the glove factory. Joseph got up, drained his glass, and stared out of the window moodily.

'Is there anything I can do to help?' she said to his back, praying that he'd turn around and take her in his arms.

'What can you do?' he said with a bitter laugh. 'You're only good at spending money.'

'Don't talk to me like that.' She was almost in tears. She wanted to take him in her arms and tell him she loved him more than all the money he'd spent on her. That she didn't care if they were poor and she couldn't have a new coat. That she loved him anyway. 'There must be something I can do.'

'Yes there is.' He turned to her slowly and there was a curious smile on his lips, but there was no amusement in his grey eyes as he looked at her. 'There is something you could try.'

'Tell me.' She was too eager, too anxious to please. 'I'll do anything you say.'

'You could agree to have another baby.'

That was the last thing she'd expected. She couldn't understand how a new baby would help their finances. Surely another mouth to feed would only put an extra drain on them. Anyway, she didn't want any more children, she'd made that plain. Lucy had been a disappointment, and the memory of the prolonged labour still gave her nightmares.

'How would that help?' she asked, trying to hide her distaste at the idea.

199

'I can't ask mother for any more money because she's made her feelings clear, and I said we could manage without her help. But she's keen on grandchildren. Unfortunately she doesn't seem to have taken to Lucy. It's not your fault but she certainly isn't an attractive child. If we had a son that really might bring mother round. She'd want to spoil and provide for him, and that would help us.' He saw the doubt in Belle's eyes and finished lamely. 'Well, it's worth a try.'

'Joseph, you know we talked about having more children, and we both agreed that one was enough. Lucy's bound to improve as she grows older, and you know what an awful time I had giving birth to her. I don't think I could go through that again. I've only just got my figure back.'

'I know.' Joseph wouldn't meet her eyes. 'But you said you wanted to help, and it's the only certain way I can think of to get mother to part with any of father's money.'

'But you said you're going to see his solicitor tomorrow.'

'I know; but I'm not very hopeful. Well, what do you say?'

What could she say? She loved him and she wanted to help; but underneath her concern was a feeling that her love was mixed up with selfishness. She'd got used to the good things in life and she didn't want to give them up. Joseph had opened that door for her, but he was her husband and she had to obey him. Was he asking such a high price, if in return she could continue living in comfort and with a good lifestyle?

'I'll do whatever you say, Joseph,' she said, regretting every word as soon as it was spoken. 'As long as we can still afford Alice. She's so good with babies. You know how Lucy adores her; and I'm useless.'

He took her in his arms then and kissed her tenderly. She was pleased to see that the worried frown was gone; he looked happier and more optimistic. Perhaps tomorrow the solicitor would have good news and she could escape the terrors of another pregnancy.

At least Joseph didn't rush her. He left her alone that night, with the excuse of needing a good night's sleep before starting out on the long drive to town. Belle, playing the dutiful wife, promised to rise early and see him off. She spent most of the night worrying about the future and didn't fall asleep until the small hours. So she overslept and it was past nine when she woke up. She was still rubbing her eyes as she wandered into the kitchen, pulling on a housecoat over her night-gown.

Alice was going about her morning tasks, singing merrily. Lucy, strapped in her high-chair, was chewing on a rusk. Her brown hair was fine and straight, combed flat against her skull like a boy's, not a wave or a curl to soften her features. She looked at her mother as if she were a stranger, dropped her rusk on the floor and began to wail.

'Leave it,' Alice instructed, as Belle bent to pick it up. 'She did it deliberately. She got out of her cot the wrong side this morning.' The words were cross, but the cooing tone she always used to the child belied the reprimand. Lucy could do no wrong in Alice's devoted eyes.

'I want to get Mr Bishop his breakfast,' Belle said, looking around helplessly. 'But it looks like I'm too late.'

'He was up at seven, Mrs Belle. He said he wasn't hungry but I made him have toast and fruit. He couldn't drive all that way on an empty stomach. He left at least half an hour ago, and said to tell you that he'd be back about six this evening.'

'Thank you.' Belle took the coffee cup Alice was holding out, and sipped the sweet drink after adding extra sugar from the bowl. She stared out of the window at the grey September day outside.

201

'Can I get you anything else, Mrs Belle? Cereal, toast, or there's some bacon if you fancy it.'

'I'm not hungry, Alice. If you see to Lucy I'll go and get dressed. I'll take her for a walk in the park after lunch. It'll pass the time.'

The day seemed to drag and Belle couldn't settle to anything. She tried to help Alice with the dishes but only seemed to get in the way, and when she lifted Lucy from her chair to bath her the child went stiff and screamed until Alice rescued her.

The walk in the park was quite successful as Lucy slept all the time in her pram. When they returned home Alice took over again, while Belle pattered about arranging fresh flowers and throwing out the dead ones.

There was chicken for dinner with fresh vegetables. Belle instructed Alice to keep it hot as she wanted to eat with Joseph. Seven o'clock passed and he still hadn't returned. Belle paced the floor impatiently, wondering what had happened to him. Would his news be good or bad? She'd know by the expression on his face as soon as he entered the room. Every passing car or slamming door made her run to the window; but eight o'clock came and Joseph still hadn't returned.

Alice came in at nine to try to put her mind at rest. He could have been held up in a traffic jam, stopped for a meal; a thousand unimportant things could have happened to delay him. Any moment now he would walk through the front door.

'You go to bed Alice, and I'll wait up . . .' Belle stopped in mid-sentence and froze. The front-door bell was ringing urgently: a single peel demanding instant attention.

'I'll go,' Alice said, and half-ran out of the room.

Belle let out a sigh of relief. It was Joseph at last: he'd forgotten his key. He'd never done that before, but there was a first time for everything. She glanced in the mirror over the fireplace and saw a pale face and smudged eyes looking back at her. She pinched her cheeks between finger and thumb to give them a bit of colour. Joseph wouldn't want to find her looking exhausted; particularly if his news was bad and he planned to use tonight to forward his ambition for fatherhood.

Alice appeared in the doorway, a strange expression on her face.

'If it's Mr Bishop, Alice, see if you can reheat the dinner; or make an omelette and a salad.'

'It's not Mr Bishop,' Alice said, her voice so low it only just reached Belle's ears. 'It's a policeman.'

'A policeman! What does a policeman want at this time of night? Tell him my husband isn't at home and to come back in the morning.'

'It's you he's asking for, Mrs Belle.' Alice stepped aside and a man in a dark uniform entered the room and gave instructions for her to go and make tea for her employer. He was young, with hair as fair as Joseph's, and he looked kindly. He stood there awkwardly, just inside the door, and Belle wanted to shout 'Tell me what you've come for and then go away. Don't just stand there looking sorry for me.'

Instead she said, 'I'm Mrs Bishop. I hope it's important calling on me so late.'

'I'm afraid I have bad news. Would you like to sit down?' He pulled a chair out from under the table. She sat down on the edge of the seat and could feel the wood cutting into her legs through her skirt. 'Your husband, Joseph Bishop, has been involved in an accident.'

'What sort of an accident?' Why couldn't she feel anything? Only impatience at the time he was taking to tell his story.

'With a train.'

203

'A train!' She wanted to laugh. Joseph had no reason to be anywhere near a train. 'I think you'll find there's some mistake. My husband drove to town in his car.'

'There's no mistake, Mrs Bishop.' She looked so calm the policeman thought she could take the rest of his news. 'His car was carefully parked half a mile away, but his body was found on the Victoria line. He'd been hit by a Brighton train, and I'm afraid it was no accident.'

Belle felt her head swimming. The only thing she could feel was relief – at least now she wouldn't have to try to get pregnant.

13

Alice had lit the dining-room fire but Belle still felt cold. She didn't think she'd ever feel warm again. The leaping flames were comforting and she leant nearer, huddled in her thickest dressing-gown, with no make-up on her face and her hair still in a tangle. She tried to see pictures in the fire as she had when she was a child, but all she could see was Joseph's face, with that worried furrow of a frown between the eyes.

Tears started again at the memory and she wiped her face on her sleeve. She hadn't stopped crying for days and didn't think she ever would. Joseph was dead, and now she knew just how much she'd loved him. Her love, when he was alive, had been tinged with gratitude, and sometimes she wondered if she'd really loved him at all. But now it was too late; he'd gone forever, and she knew the pain she felt was caused by real feelings of affection, not sentiment or other selfish motives.

They'd buried him two days ago. Or what they'd managed to scrape off the track was buried in the hilly cemetery overlooking the town, in the same grave as his father. The plot had been reserved for Enid, but there was plenty of room for all three of them. There weren't many mourners.

A couple of distant cousins had turned up, and an old friend of the family whose name was forgotten; and Belle and Enid of course.

Mother and wife faced each other across the open grave, like two gladiators fighting over the same Christian. Their united grief only seemed to fan their mutual hatred, and in their sorrow each blamed the other for Joseph's death. Belle blamed Enid for not supporting her son's choice of a wife, although underneath she knew she was guilty with her childish extravagances. Enid just blamed the red-haired girl for making her Joey so unhappy that he'd felt the need to end his own life.

The coroner had decided that Joseph Bishop had in fact taken his own life while his mind was temporarily unhinged. They'd produced a medical report about his nervous condition which had first been noticed while he was in the RAF, and had resulted in his being invalided out of the service. The London solicitor spoke about his money worries and the debts which had accumulated since his marriage. Enid Bishop, when asked, had said that she'd refused to hand over any more of her late husband's money as her son had proved himself to be irresponsible, and his wife a spendthrift. The final verdict of suicide was decided when a passer-by reported seeing Joseph walking along the track, waiting until a train was approaching and then calmly lying down across the line. It had all happened so fast that nobody could save him, and the driver of the train hadn't seen the body until it was too late to brake. Condolences were offered to his grieving widow and the case was closed.

Belle bent to put more coal on the fire and blot out Joseph's face that had been glowing sadly at her from the embers. The wail of a child echoed from somewhere upstairs.

Lucy again! Would she never stop complaining? – as if she sensed the unhappiness in the house and wanted to add her tears to her mother's. The cry came again and Belle rose to her feet. Where was Alice? Then Belle felt guilty: after all Alice had a lot to do running the house, answering the door, sending away unwelcome callers, and amusing a miserable child as well. She pulled the edges of her dressing-gown together and shook her hair out of her eyes before trudging upstairs to the nursery.

Lucy was standing up in her cot. Her plain face was blotched with tears, and the starched frill around the neck of her night-gown gave her the startled appearance of a clown. She stared at her mother in surprise but stopped crying, although her mouth remained open like a landed fish gasping for air.

Belle picked her up and held her close; although the thin body failed to rouse her maternal instincts it did make her feel pity: that this child had come into the world unwanted and unloved. She wiped the little face and dropped a kiss upon the top of its head. She hadn't prayed for years, there seemed no point now that she didn't go to mass, but she prayed then silently to anyone who might be listening to help her not to fail Lucy, if it wasn't too much to ask.

'Come on,' she said. 'Let's go and find Alice.'

She carried the child out on to the landing. They were halfway down the stairs when the front door was pushed wide and Alice Battey ran in, a bottle in each hand, and her face white. She stopped sharply at the sight of her mistress and looked back over her shoulder as if somebody was chasing her.

'Whatever is the matter?' Belle asked.

'She's here, Mrs Belle, coming down the road. I just went out to get an extra bottle from the milkman and saw her with my own eyes.'

'Calm down Alice, and put those bottles down before you drop them.' Belle waited while she did as she was told. 'Now, who did you see coming down the road?'

Alice gulped before answering. 'Mrs Bishop. All in black; and such a terrible look on her face. I was frightened.'

Belle felt frightened as well. Joseph's mother coming here, and without an invitation. Belle hadn't seen her since the funeral and the last thing she'd expected was a visit from her mother-in-law.

'Take Lucy into the kitchen,' she said quickly, handing the child over. 'And do try to keep her quiet. I'll go up and dress and you can ask Mrs Bishop to wait for me in the dining-room.'

'No need.' Enid Bishop was already standing inside the doorway. Alice had forgotten to close the door in her haste. Dressed in a black coat and hat, she'd aged at least ten years since her son's death. Her eyes were sharp as flints as she stared at Belle, and her mouth was a thin red gash in her pale face. 'I said, no need,' she repeated as Belle turned to go back up the stairs. 'I don't expect you to change your habits for me. Nearly ten o'clock and still in your night-clothes. And the child as well. But then I suppose that's how you're used to entertaining visitors.'

Belle felt a rush of anger. She put out her hand to support herself on the banister rail. She must stay calm and not lose her temper. Her mother-in-law was still suffering from grief and didn't know what she was saying.

'Will you come in and sit down?' she said, keeping her voice low. 'Alice will make you some tea.'

'I'll not drink anything in this house.' Enid swept past her into the room and looked around critically. She ran a finger along the surface of a table as if expecting to find dust. 'I've been thinking things over and I've come to a decision.'

'What sort of decision? Don't you think you should wait

208

a bit before making any decisions – at least until you feel better?'

Mrs Bishop drew herself up to her full height. 'I feel as well as I ever shall after you killed my son.'

'Please!' Belle put out a hand as if to ward the other off. 'You don't know what you're saying. I didn't kill Joseph – I loved him.'

'Loved him!' Enid let out a laugh that held no humour. 'If that's the result of your loving someone, I pity the person you hate.'

'Stop it!'

The sight of Belle standing before her with her head bowed, her hands covering her ears, seemed to touch something in Enid Bishop and bring her back to her senses. She sat down suddenly on the nearest chair, and crossed her hands stiffly on her lap before speaking.

'I'm sorry, I shouldn't have said that. Joseph made a mistake in marrying you, but he's dead now and nothing either of us can do will bring him back. He loved you and the child, and I have to do the right thing. He wanted money to spend on you both and I refused him when he was alive. I'm not going to change my mind now that he's dead.'

'I'm not asking for anything . . .'

'Be quiet and let me finish. I know that child, Lucy, isn't his. Don't imagine I didn't guess you were already pregnant when you married my son; and he was so gullible he didn't recognise a full-term baby when he saw one. But you can't pull the wool over my eyes. That baby is no more a Bishop than you are.'

'So what are you going to do about it?' The words were spirited and there was a flash of the old Belle as she tossed her red curls defiantly.

'Nothing. There's nothing I can do now. I just want you to know that all you'll get out of me is the same allowance

I gave Joseph. It will keep you and the child off the streets which is where you both belong. I'm not giving you a penny more.'

They stared at each other across the room and then Belle slowly walked to the door and pulled it open; the tail of her dressing-gown trailed on the ground behind her like a train.

'Mrs Bishop,' she said regally, 'I want you to leave my house now, and I don't want ever to see you again. I don't care what you think about me, or whether or not you believe I loved Joseph. But the one thing I don't want is your charity. You can keep your money because I don't want any of it. I'll pay off Joseph's debts, and I'll keep Lucy and myself somehow. I'm not afraid to work, you know. I've done it before and I can do it again, which is more than you can say about yourself.'

'Don't talk to me like that, my girl . . .'

'I'll talk to you anyhow I like. This is my house now, and I've asked you to leave. Alice . . .' Alice must have been hovering outside, because she appeared in the doorway almost before Belle had called her name. 'Alice, Mrs Bishop is leaving now and she won't be coming back.'

Enid rose from her chair; only her tightly clasped hands and white knuckles showing her feelings. Without saying another word she swept from the room, her dark clothes floating around her like the black feathers of a crow. The glance she gave Belle as she passed was one of pure hatred.

Belle didn't move until she heard the final slam of the front door and Alice's footsteps returning to the kitchen. Then a sob broke from her throat and she put her hands up to cover her face. She thought she'd cried enough and there were no tears left in her; but the tears she shed now weren't tears of sorrow for Joseph or for herself, they were tears of pain at the blows life had dealt her. She was crying for her mother and for Charlie, and for Dada who she missed, and when exhaustion made her stop she felt washed clean. It was an invigorating feeling, similar to when she'd come out of the confessional as a child, knowing she'd been given a fresh start.

Wiping her face on the sleeve of her gown she looked around her as if she were seeing things for the first time. The chairs and table were exactly the same, as was Joseph's desk standing in the window, but the sun had broken through and the polished surfaces shone cheerfully. The grey and pink curtains at the window that she'd chosen so carefully looked gay, and Belle's spirits lifted optimistically.

Things weren't so bad. She still had a house and the furnishings, and a wardrobe full of lovely clothes. She could always sell things or rent out rooms; any number of money-making schemes flashed through Belle's mind, some so ridiculous that she wanted to laugh. But at least she was back on top: the old Belle; recognising her faults and shortcomings, acknowledging the mistakes she'd made, but not letting them get her down.

She caught a glimpse of herself in the mirror and was mortified at what she saw. Her eyes red with weeping and her heart-shaped face white as paper; the only colour was the sprinkling of freckles which still dogged her. Her hair was greasy and unwashed so that the beautiful coppery lustre was dimmed, and even her blue eyes had lost their sparkle. If Joseph could see her now he'd be ashamed at how she'd let herself go.

With new energy she ran up the stairs, throwing off her dressing-gown as she ran. In the kitchen Alice looked at Lucy and they both grinned. Everything was going to be all right: the mistress of the house was back on form and they'd soon return to normal.

It took Belle an hour to rejuvenate herself. Just the act of washing her hair and soaking herself in hot scented water acted like a tonic. She longed to put on a gay dress, something bright and silky, but that didn't seem appropriate with her husband so recently in his grave.

But she wouldn't wear black. That was the colour for old people, like Enid Bishop, and she saw again the crow-like figure flapping past. In the end she chose a navy-blue skirt and a crisp white blouse, and with high-heeled shoes and her hair tied back with a ribbon she felt she could face the world again.

First she had to find out the worst. Exactly how she stood financially, and to discover that she'd have to go through Joseph's desk. It wasn't locked, but it had been his private place and she'd never rolled back the lid without his permission. But now, without pausing for thought, she opened it up and surveyed the heaps of papers he'd pushed away so carelessly on that fatal day when she'd so selfishly asked for money for a new coat. They were exactly as he'd left them.

Belle picked the pile up and carried it to the table, spreading the sheets out in front of her. There were bills and receipts, bank statements and cheque counterfoils, as well as account books, the pages covered with her husband's spidery handwriting. He'd obviously tried to keep things in order, but they'd long ago got out of control. It seemed that right from the start of their marriage he'd been spending more money than he could afford. Belle wasn't very good with figures, but with a paper and pencil she made lists and added up columns. After a difficult couple of hours she came to the sad conclusion that between them they'd run up debts amounting to nearly a thousand pounds.

The amount staggered her, but with her new-found optimism she refused to be downhearted. After all, she still had the house and some good pieces of jewellery. As a last resort she could always sell up and start again in a rented flat. The challenge might be good for her. It was then that she found the rent book and her spirits plummeted.

The house had been her lifeline; her insurance against destitution. Joseph had always talked as if he'd bought and paid for it outright; but now, before her eyes, was the proof that he'd lied. Her home was only rented and already the payments were several weeks in arrears.

She remembered with embarrassment how she'd tried to persuade him to evict the two men living in the basement so that she could convert it into a nursery for Lucy. How could he? Mike Walker was also a tenant. She was in no position to evict anyone.

Perhaps she'd been too hasty with her mother-in-law. If she'd thrown herself on the woman's mercy she could have at least retained an allowance, and perhaps Mrs Bishop might have become more generous in time. No! Belle admonished herself firmly. There was no way she was going to be beholden to that woman. She racked her brains. There must be a way, if only she could find it. So deep was she in her thoughts that she didn't hear the tap on the door, and when at last Alice entered without permission Belle looked up in surprise.

'What is it? I'm busy. I don't want to be disturbed.'

'I know, Mrs Belle, but this has just come for you. It was delivered by hand and I thought it might be important.'

Alice was holding out an envelope and Belle took it, half afraid that it might contain another bill or creditor's demand. It wasn't a circular: the envelope was of too good a quality for that. Her full name was printed in bold letters across the front.

She dismissed Alice. When the door was closed and she was alone again she took a deep breath and slit it open with Joseph's ivory paper-knife. The envelope contained two pieces of paper: one a cheque, the other a letter. The signature at the bottom of each was 'Enid Bishop'. She read ...

Dear Isabel,

I don't like you, but after our meeting this morning I have to admire you. You acted with haste refusing Joseph's allowance and ordering me so rudely from my son's house. I won't forget that. But I know that Joseph wouldn't want me to leave you penniless, so in the language of the streets where you were brought up, I am 'buying you off'. Enclosed is a cheque. It will be the last money you will ever get from me so I hope you'll use it wisely. Please put your pride in your pocket, as I have done and accept it, then we need never see each other again.

It was signed by her mother-in-law and the cheque was for a substantial sum. Not a fortune, but at least enough to clear most of the debts Belle had been so worried about.

The piece of paper fluttered to the floor and she bent down to pick it up. It was made out for a thousand pounds. Belle had never held so much money in her hands before. Her first reaction was to tear it up or at least return it with a curt note, but then she came to her senses. If she kept it she could pay most of the outstanding bills. Although it wouldn't put money in her pocket at least it would leave her free to start again. She had Lucy and Alice to consider, so perhaps she would accept it after all. She needn't even acknowledge the gift if she didn't want to. By the tone of the letter Mrs Bishop wasn't expecting any thanks; although a brief note would be polite. Yes, she decided, she'd take the money for Lucy's sake. She folded the valuable slip of paper and put it away safely in her purse.

Now: what had she to sell? She looked around the room

and spotted on the mantelpiece a pair of Staffordshire figures that had been given them as a wedding present. They might bring in a pound or two and the gaudy colours had always offended her taste. She carried them to the table and placed them beside a crystal rose-bowl and a silver tankard. Also the ivory paper-knife which was certainly an antique.

Then she prowled through the other rooms looking for things of worth. Soon she had quite a mound of saleable objects: the sort of things she'd seen in the windows of antique shops in the Lanes. Alice and Lucy looked at her in astonishment when she raided the kitchen and carried away the best china tea-set and a pair of heavy brass scales. Her happy smile of assurance stopped them asking questions.

Next she tried the bedrooms, but apart from some old lace found them comparatively unproductive. She ended up in front of the pair of matching walnut wardrobes in the main bedroom. This was going to be painful Belle knew, as the expensive clothes Joseph had bought for his pretty bride were dear to her. She'd miss them more than jewels or household effects.

Someone was whistling a gay tune outside the window and she was glad to delay the job she'd set herself. She crossed the room to see who it was.

The bedroom was at the front of the house facing the street, and down below in the cluttered basement Mike Walker and his brother were busily moving things around. As she watched, the elder of the two men grabbed the end of an old chest-of-drawers and dragged it roughly towards the steps. It was a huge, old-fashioned piece of furniture, but Mike was so strong he could almost lift it without help. His shirt-sleeves were rolled up and the muscles on his forearms rippled under the tanned skin.

Why, he's really good-looking, Belle thought. She'd

215

never properly looked at him before, but even so, was surprised she hadn't noticed what a handsome man he was for all his rough clothes. Something stirred inside her, and she was quite shocked that she could feel like this so soon after burying Joseph. But she was still young, wasn't she? She could still find the opposite sex attractive even if they were out of bounds. But she was the widow of a gentleman, and Mike Walker was most definitely a member of the working classes who Mrs Bishop had taught her to despise.

Mike called to his brother to help him, and together the two men carried the chest up the steps and loaded it into a waiting van. So they dealt in furniture, Belle mused. That might come in useful if she ever needed to sell bigger things, so perhaps she would cultivate the brothers. They might also be able to advise her on how to go about selling the bits and pieces she'd already sorted out. But she must be careful not to get too involved or they might start getting ideas. She hadn't forgotten the impudent glances Mike always gave her when she went in and out of the house; he had a way of looking that made her feel that he knew exactly how she looked in her underclothes. It always made her feel uncomfortable and excited at the same time.

Belle moved quickly back to the wardrobes and flung the doors open. She fingered the silks and velvets of the dresses and the pure woollen fabrics of the coats and suits. Some of the newest garments hadn't been worn more than two or three times. There was even a full-length evening dress that she'd had made specially, and had only worn once. It was made of midnight-blue velvet, with rows of diamante edging the neckline and shoulder-straps..

Was she ever likely to wear any of them again? She took out the garments one by one, tenderly caressing the soft materials as if she were saying a personal farewell. In the end she had to compromise: the day clothes were hung back on the runners, after all she still needed to look smart and keep up her newly found morale, but the evening clothes and the fur stole Joseph had given her last Christmas were discarded on the bed.

Next Belle turned to Joseph's wardrobe. She thought it would be easy as he'd never need his clothes again. It turned out to be more painful than she'd expected. There was the suit he'd worn on their wedding day, and his favourite sports jacket and made-to-measure slacks. His trilby hats and the corduroy cap he wore for casual walks, together with the rows of hand-made shoes, all brought back memories of their owner. Swallowing her tears she emptied the wardrobe, and before she could change her mind called for Alice.

'Whatever are you up to, Mrs Belle?' Alice stood in the doorway, the expression on her face showing her puzzlement at Belle's behaviour. The new colour in her employer's cheeks, and the sparkle in her eyes, assured the girl that Belle hadn't gone out of her mind, and whatever she was up to was going to benefit them all.

'Have we any cardboard boxes or suitcases?' Belle asked, indicating the piles of clothing. 'Enough to take this lot.'

'There are some cases in the loft. I saw them piled in a corner when I took the workman up there to inspect the loose slates. And I kept the boxes that Rimmingtons delivered the nursery ware in.'

'Go and fetch them now, and then you can help me.' Belle was soon busy folding garments. When Alice returned they packed the cases and boxes to the tops and tied the lids down firmly with string. 'Now help me get them down the stairs, and then get me a taxi. I have got to go out on business. I shouldn't be more than an hour, but if Lucy wakes up before I get back you can take her for a walk.'

Alice nodded speechlessly but she followed Belle without a word. When the taxi arrived the driver helped them load up.

Down in the basement Mike Walker looked up with interest and watched the slender silk-clad legs of the widow upstairs trot past. Now what was she up to? he asked himself, and whistled the air from *The Merry Widow* under his breath. That one was worth watching; particularly now she was on her own.

Belle gave the driver instructions and leant back in her seat. She knew exactly where she was going. She may not know the best place to sell silver and glass, but she knew who might give her a good price for second-hand clothes. Jim Hilton's emporium of course, just off the London Road, and if she was lucky her childhood friend, Henry Murtell, might still be employed there.

For some reason the taxi driver didn't take a direct route. Perhaps he was trying to avoid a build-up of traffic in the centre of the town, or perhaps he thought a tour through the poorer districts of Brighton would be a short cut. Without asking Belle found herself being driven along Ditchling Road, a part of the town she hadn't had cause to visit since her marriage. Everything looked dirtier and drearier than she remembered. When she spotted the Black Mill pub it looked deserted, and there were boards covering windows.

As they approached the bottom of Duke's Road Belle had a sudden desire to see the house where she'd been born. To open the door and see Gran rocking in her chair and Dada in his working clothes. But she wasn't brave enough. She instructed the driver to carry on down the hill towards Jim Hilton's shop, although for some reason tears were prickling her eyes and there was a lump in her throat.

14

'Come on now, old man.' Henry put his hands under Jim Hilton's armpits and lifted him into a sitting position. 'Open your mouth and try not to dribble.' He inserted the spout of the feeding-cup into Jim's mouth and held the handle patiently while he drank. 'Enough?'

'Thanks, Henry.'

Jim held up his face to be wiped and Henry gently dabbed the drops of tea from the unshaven chin. He'd grown fond of the second-hand-clothes dealer over the last few years, and they treated each other more like father and son than employer and employee. After all, Henry couldn't remember his own father, so it was nice to have someone to put in his place.

Their affection had grown slowly, beginning on the day when the scruffy little boy had helped to foil the robber. When he left school Henry had accepted a job in the shop, and had never regretted throwing in his lot with Jim. They'd both found the partnership satisfying. Henry proved to be a quick learner and he soon knew the clothing business like the back of his hand, and could haggle over the price of a garment like an expert. He even managed to clean the old man up, and the shop now gleamed with fresh paint, and the smell of soap and disinfectant had replaced the unsavoury smells that used to discourage clients.

The clothes hanging on the rails were still second-hand, but the quality of goods was better and nothing like the rags Jim used to deal in. Behind the shining windows the interior of the shop looked pleasing to the eye. Henry had even acquired some old dummies and dressed them to show off the best of his stock. A male figure wearing a black evening suit and top hat stood next to a female in pink taffeta with a feather boa around its shoulders, for all the world as if they were just off to an evening at the opera.

Henry put down the feeding-cup and started tidying things up. The torn chenille curtain over the inner door had been replaced by a folding screen for when the old man needed privacy, but most of the time it was left leaning against the wall so that he could see into the shop and watch what was going on.

Six months earlier he'd sustained a stroke. It had struck him out of the blue, rendering him speechless and partially paralysed. Slowly he'd managed to regain some speech; although his words were slurred and Henry was the only person who could understand him. He'd stood by Jim devotedly; visiting him in hospital and keeping the business running.

But now a place had been found for him in a nursing home and Jim was getting ready to go, although reluctant to hand over the reins to a stranger. But young Henry Murtell wasn't a stranger, and the old man had been delighted when he'd offered his hard-earned savings to take over the business. He'd even offered to take over the care of Jim's tabby cat, Queenie, who was getting old now but still produced two litters of kittens a year. There was nothing either of them had overlooked. The business Jim had started years before, with a rag and bone man's barrow and a few pence in his tattered pocket, had grown beyond his expectations. Henry had done more than his bit, so Jim was happy to leave it in his capable hands.

Jim was struggling to say something and Henry bent closer to interpret the slurred sounds. The huddled figure was pathetic, wrapped in a large dressing-gown, a muffler still around his scraggy neck and the same old trilby on his balding head.

'What did you say, Mr Hilton?'

'Sign – sign.' Jim pointed towards the door with a trembling finger.

'The man's coming to paint it tomorrow,' Henry said reassuringly. 'I've drawn a picture; do you want to see it?' Jim nodded his head and Henry produced a piece of paper from his pocket and held it out. 'There,' he said. 'HILTON & MURTELL, right across the front window in black letters edged in gold leaf. What do you think?' Jim mumbled something and Henry bent closer. 'And son?' Jim nodded vigorously. '& SON. All right Mr Hilton, if that's what you want. HILTON, MURTELL & SON.'

Tired out, Jim dozed in his chair and Henry returned to the shop. Even when there were no customers there was always plenty to do. He put an overall on over his shirt and trousers before he started the job of polishing and dusting the counter area. Gone were the days when he'd come to work in frayed plimsolls and a cloth-cap; he was now most particular about his dress. His shirts were always crisp and spotless and his trousers creased carefully. His black shoes were so highly polished that he could see his face in them. Although he was nearly six feet tall and had outgrown his teenage acne, he was still thin and round-shouldered. The lock of spiky brown hair still hung over his forehead, however much he tried to slick it back. His eyesight hadn't improved either, and the glass in his spectacles was thicker, if anything.

He peered at the clock on the wall. It was half an hour to closing time and he just had time to re-arrange some shirts in the window before locking up for the night. Mr Hilton would be all right because a neighbour had a key and came in regularly to check on him.

Henry was on his hands and knees behind the glass pane when the taxi drew up outside. It couldn't be a customer for him. Only rich people could afford to ride around in taxis and they would buy from outfitters in the centre of the town, not from a second-hand shop in a backstreet, however smart.

The passenger door opened briskly. A slender leg and a dainty foot in a high-heeled shoe appeared, followed by the rest of a very feminine figure in a smart navy-blue coat trimmed with white. The driver left the wheel to help unload a pile of boxes on to the pavement. It was only when the woman dismissed the car with a wave of the hand, and grasping a case in either hand turned towards him, that he saw the loosely piled red curls haloing a heart-shaped face and recognised Belle.

Their eyes met through the glass, and it took each of them a few moments to recognise the change in the other's appearance.

Belle was the first to break the ice. She grinned, and the years rolled away and Henry saw again the girl he'd loved so devotedly under the smartly dressed woman standing in front of him. He mouthed her name through the window, and she laughed. He looked so like an ugly codfish with his mouth opening and closing silently. Then he had the door open and was hurrying to help her, taking the cases from her hands and scurrying backwards and forwards, carrying in the boxes from where the taxi driver had dumped them. He was so pleased and excited at the unexpected surprise that he had to keep taking off his glasses, in a well-remembered gesture, to polish the lenses.

'Oh, Belle,' he said at last. 'I am pleased to see you. You look so smart: a proper lady.'

'Thank you. You haven't changed at all; just grown taller.'

She could see he was pleased for all his grown-up appearance. His hands were trembling and he couldn't take his eyes off her. Belle hadn't thought about Henry for ages, but now face to face with him she felt a rush of affection. He was so steady, so safe. If she'd married him instead of Joseph she would have been loved and cared for, and by the look of him he was doing quite well.

She wanted to tell him what a bad time she was having and ask him if he still loved her. She would tell him about his daughter Lucy, and how she looked just like him. How proud and surprised he'd be. But something stopped her and she said instead, 'I've brought these things I want to sell.' She indicated the boxes. 'I thought I'd give you the first offer.' That sounded good, she decided, as if she was doing him a favour.

'Well, I don't know.' Henry glanced over his shoulder at the old man in the inner room. He was fast asleep and snoring gently with his mouth wide open. 'I've been doing more buying than selling lately, and in this business you mustn't get overstocked.' Belle's heart sank. Her disappointment must have shown in her face, because he added quickly, 'But I'll have a look if you need the money.'

Need the money indeed! How dare he! She'd show him who he was dealing with. 'I didn't say anything about needing money,' she said proudly. 'I came to you first because I thought I owed you a favour.'

'Oh,' She was delighted to see his expression change, as if he knew she'd put him in his place. 'Perhaps if I have a look . . .'

Between them they unpacked and spread the garments around the shop.

Henry marvelled. 'I've never seen such quality,' he said, fingering the sleeve of a jacket.

'This is what they call style, Henry,' Belle said proudly.

'I don't get much call for style,' he said doubtfully. 'It's not what my customers are used to.'

'Then now's your chance to educate them.'

'I don't know. I may have difficulty selling them.'

But Belle was like a little girl at a party, playing charades, as she pulled out dresses, hats and trousers, and showed off their quality.

'Look at this,' she cried, holding up a striped blazer. 'Joseph bought this to go boating; and these are his cricket flannels.'

'Won't he be needing them?'

Belle stood frozen to the spot, clutching the garments to her chest. Now was not the time to tell him that her husband was dead, and she was selling his things because she needed the money. He'd feel sorry for her and probably give her a better price than she'd expected; and ask if there was anything else he could do to help. There would be pity in his eyes and she couldn't stand that. Anything might happen if she started to cry again, and she could already feel the tell-tale pricking behind the eyes.

'He's sprained a muscle and has to rest,' she lied. 'He'll buy new outfits when he's better.'

'And your evening dress, Belle? Is he so bad he won't be taking you out?'

'No. This one's last year's.' The lies tumbled out easily just as they had years before when she'd tried to cover up her misbehaviour from Mam. 'I've ordered new. Green velvet with a lace yoke. I'm waiting for the dressmaker to complete the alterations.'

But Henry wasn't interested in what she was saying, he was too busy fingering the midnight-blue gown with its glittering straps, as if he'd never before seen anything so lovely.

'You must look like a queen when you're wearing this,' he said softly. 'Almost as lovely as you did in your white communion dress. Do you remember?'

'That was a long time ago. We were only kids. Did your auntie ever find out?'

'No.' Henry laughed. 'She searched the house for it, and decided in the end she'd thrown it out by mistake. I was going to put it back, but by the time we'd finished cutting it up it wasn't recognisable.' He went behind the counter and began folding up the garments again. 'How much were you hoping to get for them?'

'I don't know much about these things.'

Belle looked down demurely at her hands. The skin was now soft and white, but although the nails were painted a delicate shade of pink they were still bitten. She put them behind her back in a childish gesture, as if she wanted to hide them from him.

'Didn't your husband give you any instructions?'

'No, he left it up to me. How about a hundred – pounds not guineas?'

'A hundred pounds!'

'Is that too much?'

'Probably not, but it's more than I can give you. You'd better take them to somebody else. Or you could advertise them.'

Henry was a soft touch where Belle was concerned, but however much she needed a hundred pounds, and he could see by her eyes that she was desperate, he hadn't got it to give her.

'How much can you give me?'

225

Henry opened the till and counted the notes, flicking through them expertly with a wet finger. 'I can't make it more than fifty.' She looked so disappointed that he added quickly, 'guineas.'

'Done,' Belle said cheerfully, and watched as he counted out the five-pound notes and then added two small pound ones and a ten shilling. 'Thanks.' She rolled the money up carefully and put it away in her bag.

Now she'd got what she'd come for she was anxious to leave. Henry could see how her mind was working and tried to think of something to say to keep her in the shop a while longer. 'I thought I'd see you at the funeral.'

'Funeral! What funeral?'

'Your Gran's.' Her face was a blank, and he wished he could have taken the words back and led up to the subject tactfully. 'Didn't you know?'

'When did she die?'

'Back in the spring. I went to the funeral with Auntie Mabel. Not to the church, of course, as we're not Catholics and you know how Auntie is about that sort of thing, but we went to the cemetery to show our respects.'

'Oh, Henry!' Her face was tragic. 'I didn't know or I'd have been there.'

'I thought your father would have told you.'

'No.' Belle looked ashamed. 'I haven't been in contact with him since I got married. I know it's my fault: I should have asked him to visit but I didn't think he'd feel comfortable.' She saw the expression on Henry's face and ended angrily. 'You don't understand.'

'I think I do,' Henry said softly. 'None of us were good enough for you.'

'Don't say that!'

'Why not? It's the truth and you know it. You should have seen your father at the funeral: he looked a broken man. He kept looking around in a bewildered way as if he was searching for someone amongst the mourners.'

'Me?' Belle asked, and there were tears in her eyes.

'That's what I thought. That's what made me do it.'

'Do what?'

Henry looked uncomfortable and began folding a pile of shirts neatly. 'Auntie wouldn't send any flowers. She said it would only be expected if you were family. But I liked your Gran; she was good to me when we were kids, so I sent a bunch of flowers on my own with a little card. Nothing posh: just spring flowers, daffodils and tulips with a bit of mimosa. Well, your dad looked so sad that I wanted to do something to cheer him up; so when no one was looking I scribbled out my name, turned the card over, and wrote "To Gran, with love from Belle." '

Now Belle was crying in earnest. She didn't know what to say, so she just leaned across the counter and kissed Henry's cheek. 'Thank you. That was a lovely thing to do. I hope he saw them.'

'Yes. I stayed behind afterwards and watched as they put the wreaths around the grave. I saw his face when he read the card. It meant a lot to him.'

'I've been so selfish, but I mean to change. Have you seen him recently, Henry? Is he keeping well?'

'I think so. He looked fine last time I saw him.' Two spots of colour had appeared on Henry's cheeks; he looked agitated and wouldn't meet her eyes.

'I'll go and see him now, on the way home.' Belle was already turning towards the door as if eager to make amends for her neglect. 'He must be lonely living all by himself now that Gran's gone. I suppose Mam's still in that sanatorium. There must be something I can do for him.'

'I wouldn't, Belle.' Something in his voice made her stop her headlong dash to play the Angel of Mercy.

227

'Whyever not? He's my father; I know he'll be pleased to see me. He's all alone.'

'No, he's not.' Belle stared, her blue eyes huge in her heart-shaped face, as she waited for him to enlighten her.

'There's someone living with him.'

'Who?'

'Maud Carter.'

'That woman!' Belle saw a slow-moving film in her mind's eye. She was back in Duke's Road, standing in the doorway of her Mam and Dada's bedroom. Dada was there on the bed with a black-haired woman who looked like a gipsy. They were half undressed and she could see the comic sight of her father's skinny legs under the tail of his shirt, and the way Maud didn't even bother to cover her heavy breasts. Belle's face flooded with shame and disgust. 'How could he?'

Henry ran round the counter and put his arm around her to comfort her. She let her head rest on his shoulder. It seemed strange that after all the time they'd been apart they fitted together so perfectly, like the two halves of a puzzle.

'You've got to accept it, Belle. He's got his own life to lead and she makes him happy. I can hear them laughing sometimes through the wall, and they always sound as if they're having a good time.'

'But he can't marry her; at least not while Mam's still alive.'

'No. He moved her in after the fire at the Black Mill. Gutted it was, and now they're just waiting to pull it down. Worse than what happened in the war, some say. Arthur died in his bed although Maud tried to save him. It was a sight so I hear; Maud staggering through the door with Arthur in her arms. Her so big and him so small. But it was too late: he was dead already. She was very brave.'

'I wish she'd died in the fire,' Belle said bitterly.

228

'Don't say that. She's not a bad woman and she's good to your father. She had nowhere to go and he took her in. She's been there ever since and it seems to suit them both.'

'What do you think I should do, Henry?'

'Leave them alone. Later on you could write him a letter, and next time I see him I'll tell him I've seen you.'

'Thank you.' She moved away from him, straightening her coat and pulling on her gloves. Suddenly they'd run out of words and Belle felt it was time to leave. 'I'm glad I've seen you.'

He reached the door before her, and opened it as if she was a valued customer. She had no option but to step past him into the street. She couldn't leave like this, not knowing if he wanted to see her again. She must tell him about Joseph and Lucy. Before she could turn back to say the things she wanted she had to step aside to make way for a young woman pushing a pram who was bearing down on them.

The woman was pleasant enough looking, with a plump pretty face and pale hair covered by a headscarf. Her coat was loose and missing a button, and the baby in the pram was wailing lustily. Belle stepped aside, but the woman stopped and smiled at Henry.

'Sorry I'm late, love,' she said, slipping her arm through his, 'but I had to help your Auntie Mabel change the beds, and then baby wouldn't take his feed. I thought I'd never get out. Is Mr Hilton all right?'

'He's fine.' Henry was smiling at the young woman proudly and Belle's heart missed a beat. 'Belle,' he said. 'Don't go. I want you to meet my wife, Margery. Margery, this is Isabel Kelly. I've told you all about her.'

Belle's first feelings were of shock and then anger. How dare he! She might choose to forget his existence when things were going well, but she didn't like the idea that his feelings towards her had changed and he'd put someone else on her pedestal. She had to get away. She didn't remember saying goodbye or shaking hands; but now she was sailing fast towards the town where there would be crowds of people who would hide her.

Never in a thousand years had she imagined that Henry would be married. She'd been his first love, and now that awful girl called Margery had taken her place. She broke into a run but the height of her heels stopped her, so she slipped them off and ran in her stockinged feet, not caring if people stared. Let them stare! She'd lost Henry, and it was the last straw to her bruised ego. The pavement was rough and gritty and she'd soon laddered her stockings, so she slowed down to a walk and slipped her shoes on again. Now she could think more reasonably.

There was absolutely no reason for her to feel the way she did. After all, she'd married Joseph without giving Henry a second thought. He'd been a kind, caring boy and he'd grown up to be a kind, caring man, and he couldn't have known that Joseph was going to kill himself. So it was only natural for him to start looking around when he felt the need to settle down. Margery seemed to be a nice young woman and Belle tried to hope she'd be happy. At least her baby would have a proper father; not like poor Lucy.

She was passing the shops and although it was late some of them were still open. Belle liked shops and shopping, particularly when it involved clothes. She stopped outside a dress shop that was advertising a sale, and admired a silky dress with a full skirt, draped on a model in the window. It was a half-price reduction and worth every penny. Spending money always made Belle feel better and she had the wad of notes Henry had given her safely in her purse. She was just about to swing the door open when the lights went off inside. A woman with blonde hair, wearing a black dress, turned a card in the window from OPEN to CLOSED. Belle turned away dolefully.

Perhaps it was just as well she thought as she resumed her walk. What was the point of selling things because she was short of money, only to spend the proceeds on things she didn't need, just as an excuse to make herself feel better. If she used the money in her purse carefully, only buying essentials, it should last for several weeks. By then she might have come up with a plan to get them a regular income.

Deep in her private thoughts she found she'd walked almost down to the sea-front. In front of her was Prinny's Palace, better known as the Royal Pavilion: a fairy-tale place of onion-shaped domes and minarets, floating like a dream in front of her eyes. There the Prince Regent had entertained Mrs Fitzherbert under the twinkling light of the chandeliers. He hadn't been able to marry his love because she was a Catholic, but rumour had it that she'd borne him a child in secret. There seemed a similarity about the royal pair and herself and Henry. Belle stood for a moment lost in daydreams.

She turned her footsteps into a quieter road that ran behind the palace gardens. There was a bookshop, and a teashop, and a theatre that was disgorging its matinée audience. Everyone looked so happy clutching programmes and half-empty chocolate boxes, as they buttoned their coats and waited for their taxis or cars to take them home. Once, not so long ago, Belle might have been one of them, with a seat in a box or the front row of the stalls, and not a thought of the expense of her afternoon's entertainment. Now she could only watch from the sidelines.

Well, at least a cup of tea would cheer her up. She pushed the door of the tea-shop open and entered. It was a small cheap-looking place but the tea looked hot and strong, and she carried her cup to a table in the window. She'd treated herself to a plump bun with a sticky top and currants sticking out from the sides. Stirring three spoonfuls of sugar into her cup she sat back and relaxed, chewing on the bun.

The tea-shop was obviously a popular place as it was quite crowded. So when a crowd of young people burst through the door they had difficulty finding seats and at last congregated at an adjoining table. They were a jolly crowd about the same age as Belle, dressed in bright colours. The girls had heavy make-up on their pretty faces and even the men seemed to have the remains of black paint around their eyes. They were like butterflies from another world and Belle found herself listening to their conversation.

'Did you see my high kick in act three?' one young girl in a bright pink skirt asked her companions, flexing her leg muscles like a dancer. 'I nearly split my tights.'

They all laughed, and a young man ruffled the girl's hair teasingly. 'Darling,' he said. 'You were wonderful. What a pity the audience didn't seem to appreciate you.'

'Don't be horrid, Jerry,' the girl said, pretending to sulk. 'You know what matinée audiences are like. It'll be better tonight.'

'I hope so,' someone else said cheerfully. 'It certainly couldn't be worse.'

So they were actors and actresses from the theatre next door. Belle was interested because, although she didn't know anything about the stage, she was attracted to the colourful crowd at the next table. At that moment the door opened again and another girl burst in. She looked younger than the others, with short bleached hair and a tight red dress.

Someone called out 'Here's Mary; she's late as usual. Move up everybody.'

There was no room at the table, so the girl looked pointedly at the empty seat next to Belle, and asked, 'Is anyone sitting there?'

'No.' Belle smiled and the girl called Mary sat down with a plop.

'Are you an actress?' Belle asked, wanting to be friendly.

'No. I'm a dancer. Only in the chorus but a girl has to start somewhere. We're all in the musical next door.' She looked around at her friends and stretched her hands above her head as if she was exhausted. 'Phew!'

'What's the matter?'

'I stink!' Mary laughed. She was sniffing under her arms, not the slightest bit embarrassed. 'It gets ever so hot under the lights.'

'I suppose you'll be glad to get home and soak in a bath of hot water?'

'No such luck. We have to give another performance tonight and the digs I'm in hasn't even got a bath. We only get hot water if the landlady's feeling generous.'

'How awful. Where are you staying?'

'Just behind the station. They're all lodging houses there. It's a bit of a slum, but very convenient.'

'If you don't like it you should move somewhere else.'

'That's easier said than done,' Mary said gloomily. 'I suppose you don't know of anywhere? I'd give anything for a comfortable bed and a bath.'

Belle thought quickly. Before she could change her mind she said. 'I have some spare rooms, and a bathroom. The water's always hot.'

'Are you a landlady?'

'Yes,' Belle lied, wondering what a theatrical landlady was supposed to look like. 'But I have some vacancies.'

'Hey, folks,' Mary called to her friends. 'This lady's got some rooms to let.'

Before Belle knew what was happening they were all crowding round her asking questions.

'How many of us can you take?' the girl in pink asked.

'How much do you charge?' Jerry wanted to know.

'Can we move in at once?'

Belle tried to answer all their questions. She was in her element with these jolly people who seemed to accept her so easily as a friend. She wrote down her address and handed it to Mary, who seemed to be the leader.

'You can get in touch with me at that address,' she said.

'Let's drink a toast,' someone said. More tea was ordered and they shrieked with carefree laughter as they clinked their china cups in Belle's direction. She was quite disappointed when they left.

'You'll be hearing from us,' Mary promised.

'Come and see the show,' the girl in pink said, pressing two tickets into Belle's hand. 'It won't cost you anything. They're complimentary.'

Belle payed the bill and left, walking up the now deserted streets towards the clocktower. Things were changing, almost too fast, and she was growing up. One moment she'd been living the good life, and imagining that it would go on for ever, and now she was a widow, penniless but not beaten. There was a new spring in her step, and optimism in her heart. She saw a new career for herself as a theatrical landlady; and if it meant opening her door to people like the jolly crowd she'd just left, she couldn't wait.

It was going to mean a lot of reorganisation. She had no idea what Alice was going to say, as she'd probably have to give up her bedroom and move in with Lucy. But knowing the maid, and her devotion, Belle didn't think she'd raise any opposition. She'd have to buy some extra beds and things, but Mike Walker might be able to help her with that.

She found a sweetshop that was still open, and on a wave

of generosity decided to treat Alice and Lucy. She bought jelly-babies and dolly-mixtures for the baby and a box of milk chocolates for Alice, hoping it was the sort that had plenty of soft centres as she knew they were Alice's favourite.

She didn't buy anything for herself. Her days of treats and spoiling were over. She was now a working woman with responsibilities; and she had to learn the value of money and what it could and couldn't buy.

15

'Give us a whisky, darling. And have one yourself.'

'Thanks. I'll have a gin and tonic if it's all the same to you.'

Belle measured out the drinks. She mimed pouring the gin into her own glass so no one would know she was only drinking tonic. Then she slipped the extra money into her purse. It was one of the perks of the trade and all the barmaids did it. As she wasn't keen on the taste of alcohol she could earn quite a bit in the course of one evening.

Tonight had been quite a good example of a generous audience, and apart from the one man leaning on the bar everyone else had returned to their seats to watch the last act of the Agatha Christie play. The bar was full of the smell of cigarette smoke. Belle couldn't wait to clear up and get home so she drained her glass quickly.

'Come on now,' she said to the man. 'You're missing the end of the play and I'm waiting to close.'

He grumbled, but drank up obediently, and wandered back into the auditorium where the lights were dimmed. He'd probably have difficulty finding his seat in the dark, but that wasn't her problem. She pulled the red velvet curtains closed behind him and started emptying the ashtrays.

In four years Belle had changed. She'd filled out considerably and no one could now say that her figure resembled that of a boy. Her body was all feminine curves, and she dressed to show them off in tight-fitting black. The skirt just covered her knees, and the neckline plunged so deeply that a good deal of her bust was exposed. The customers liked that: a provocative figure across the bar was always popular. They knew they could look, but not touch. Her face was carefully made up. She used heavier make-up than in the old days and she'd copied the actresses she saw every day, and learnt how to enhance her best features. In the light of day it looked a bit unnatural, but it passed a treat in the artificial light of the theatre bar. Her hair, a mass of carefully arranged curls, was swept away from her face and piled high on top of her head, so that her neck and bare chest looked swan-like. From her ear-lobes dangled glittering ear-rings that swung like miniature chandeliers. She loved her outfit, which was almost a uniform, nearly as much as she liked her job in the theatre.

It had all started when she'd first become a theatrical landlady. The day she'd met Mary and the other members of the chorus who were dancing and singing in the musical comedy, was a turning point in her life.

True to her word the blonde dancer had turned up on Belle's doorstep with five friends in tow. Belle had been stunned: she hadn't expected so many.

Poor Alice had nearly had a nervous breakdown; turning out rooms and searching for extra towels and bed-linen. But however many sacrifices she made Belle still ended up two beds short, even when Alice offered to sleep on cushions on the floor. At last, in desperation, Belle had ventured down to the basement and knocked boldly on Mike Walker's door.

To her surprise she found an amused and sympathetic

237

ally. Mike had been waiting his chance to get to know the Merry Widow, as he called her, and this was a golden opportunity.

'Come in,' he'd said, ushering her into his dark, cluttered flat. 'I've got two folding camp-beds somewhere. Will that do?'

'Lovely,' Belle said doubtfully.

'Don't worry, I'll clean them up. And there's an iron frame somewhere. You can use pillows in place of a mattress.'

'How much?' Belle asked.

'They're free to you,' Mike said with a grin. 'And I'll even carry them upstairs for you – and put them together.'

As Belle got to know Mike better she found herself quite attracted to him.

And Mike: he was soon besotted. He admired Belle not only for her looks but for her enterprising spirit, and was prepared to help in any way he could. He didn't ask for anything in return – but he had high hopes.

To Lucy he soon became Uncle Mike. He liked the ugly little kid and felt sorry for her. She was now five and a half years old, tall for her age, with arms and legs like sticks. Her straight brown hair hung down her back in a thin plait no thicker than a piece of string, and her first pair of wire-framed glasses slid down her rather large nose. Sometimes Mike called her Lovely Lucy, to try to boost her morale, but they both knew he was only joking.

From those first lodgers a constant stream appeared. Not the stars, who could afford the expensive hotels on the seafront, but the chorus and the walk-ons, and the back-room boys and girls. Once she even had an author staying, who was following his play around England. He was so nervous on the last night because he'd been asked to make a speech, that Belle found him being sick in the bathroom at two o'clock in the morning. She ended up plying him with Ovaltine, and helping him to compose his speech, and before he went off to the theatre the next day made him say it to her over and over again until he was word perfect.

She felt at home with the theatre people. She admired their carefree extrovert way of life, and wished she could train as an actress. Now, at twenty-four, she was too old and had too many responsibilities, so she lived her life through her lodgers, enjoying the gossip and name-dropping, and trying to ape their mannerisms.

One day one of the girls came to her in a panic.

'Look at this,' she said, holding up her stage costume. 'I caught it on a nail in the green-room and there's an awful tear. Tomorrow's Saturday and I need it for the matinée. Whatever am I going to do?'

'I'll lend you a needle and cotton,' Belle said.

'But I can't sew for toffee.' The poor girl was almost in tears.

'Give it to me,' Belle said. She hadn't forgotten the skills that she'd learned at Lena Watkins's glove factory, or the way she'd made her own dresses before she'd married Joseph. So she soon set to and had the costume repaired so expertly that no one would guess it had ever been damaged.

Word got around back-stage. When some costumes were lost in transit from another theatre Belle was asked to make duplicates. Soon she was known to everybody at the theatre and was called in to do all manner of jobs. She helped the girls dress and make up, and stood by in the wings if there was a quick change. Sometimes she sold programmes or sat in a little glass-fronted booth in the foyer selling tickets, and sometimes she poured interval drinks in the bar. This was the job she liked best of all. Chatting and laughing with the public, all out in their best clothes, anxious to have a good time.

When she'd cleaned the last ashtray and put away the last glass, she unhooked her coat from the back of the door and slipped out through the velvet curtains. The play was nearing its close and the murderer was soon to be unmasked, so there wasn't a sound or a rustle from the attentive audience who were caught up in the plot. Belle had watched the ending the night before so knew exactly what was coming and how surprised they'd be at the dramatic conclusion.

Walking quietly so as not to cause a disturbance she passed out into the foyer. The doorkeeper was already pacing about with his bundle of keys in his hand, anxious to be off home. Mrs Smith, the pianist, who entertained with popular music in the intervals was sitting on a chair just inside the glass doors, her music case on her lap, waiting for her husband to collect her.

Belle called a cheery goodnight, and they smiled and waved to each other. Outside the theatre she stopped to pull on her gloves. It was just after ten, but the road was bright with overhead lights and traffic passing. She was trying to decide whether to catch a bus, of if she'd earned enough in tips to hail a taxi, when a dark figure stepped out of the shadows and in a false stage-whisper growled, 'Going my way, lady?'

She jumped, and then laughed in relief. It was only Mike Walker waiting to see her home. He often came down into the town to watch the ice-hockey or see a film. He wasn't much of a theatre-goer, but he'd watch for her to leave the theatre, only too well aware of the dangers that could befall an attractive young woman walking the streets of the town after dark. She slipped her arm through his and looked up into his friendly face. He was so solid and comforting. She felt safe with him, as she had with Dada when she was a child.

'Do you think we could stop for some chips?' she asked. 'I didn't have time for any tea and I'm starving.'

'Whatever my lady wants.' Mike made a mocking bow, doffing his hat so that his hair blew in the wind in a most attractive way.

They followed their noses when they smelt the familiar odour of fish frying, and joined a queue of hungry people outside a backstreet shop. There were so many fish and chip shops in the town centre that it was a wonder that they all managed to make a living. They bought pieces of cod covered in crisp batter and mouthwatering chips the size of a man's finger. They soaked the food in salt and vinegar and ate out of newspaper, resuming their walk in companionable silence. They knew each other too well to have to keep up a pretence of polite conversation.

Belle finished first and tossed her screwed-up paper into a bin. Then she greedily helped herself to the crunchy pieces Mike had been saving till last. He slapped her hand playfully.

'That's better,' Belle said with a contented sigh. 'When we get in I'll make some cocoa if you want to come up for a cup.'

'Great,' said Mike. 'I thought you weren't going to offer.'

'Only cocoa, Mike; and then straight downstairs. I know what's on your mind, but you can forget it.'

Mike grimaced, like a boy being refused a longed-for treat. They'd become sparring partners about the possible delights of Belle's bed, and although Mike would be quick to seize the opportunity if it was offered, Belle was adamant in her refusal. She accepted Mike Walker as a friend and nothing else, in the similar way she'd looked on Henry Murtell in the old days.

She knew that she was attractive to men, but she looked on sex, and other intimate relationships, as trouble. Hadn't her first innocent experience in the bluebell wood led to the

241

birth of Lucy? – a child she'd grown fond of in a rather distant way, but who was nevertheless a disappointment to her. Joseph had been attractive, but weak, and she didn't feel inclined to marry again and put someone else in his place. After all, why should she? She was doing very nicely on her own: working hard and keeping a comfortable roof over their heads, so why should she change things? Of course one day she might have to come to a decision, either about Mike or somebody else, but until that day arrived she was happy to let life run its course.

They were heading towards the borders of Hove and had to pass one of the notorious squares where tramps congregated. The houses on all three sides were so graceful and dignified, and in daylight the smooth grass and ornate railings made the area a sightseers' paradise, but at night it was like a scene from hell. Bodies sprawled, humped on the wooden benches amongst old newspapers and broken bottles, at their feet pools of their own vomit glistened green in the moonlight. A thousand sad eyes seemed to stare at Belle and Mike as they passed by. She was glad of his protecting arm, and averted her eyes from the unpleasant sight of human indignity.

They crossed over the main road into the narrower streets that wound away up hill. Belle's spirits returned. She started to hum a popular tune in her uncertain treble and Mike accompanied her with a whistle.

They were approaching a public house when they first heard sounds of an uproar. It was a better class tavern than the Black Mill had been, but even so the landlord seemed to be having difficulty calling time and getting his customers to go to their homes. In particular a woman seemed to be giving him trouble. He was struggling to get her through the doorway into the street while the other revellers swore and called out insults.

Mike tried to guide Belle well out of the way, but just as they were passing the landlord gave the woman a final push. She lost her footing and fell across the path, landing almost at Belle's feet.

'Keep walking.'

Mike spoke tersely, trying to hurry Belle along, but she drew back, suddenly curious about the poor woman. She didn't like drunkards but she wasn't frightened of them, particularly women, who usually resorted to abuse rather than violence. She'd evicted a few from the theatre bar herself, quite successfully. When Belle flashed her blue eyes at someone in anger they usually knew they'd met their match.

The woman at her feet was quite young. Belle felt almost sorry for her, wondering what sad story there might be behind her plight. There was blood on her knees where she'd laddered her stockings in the fall. She sat on the pavement rocking backwards and forwards, and rubbing her fists in her eyes like a child.

'Wait a minute,' Belle said to her companion. 'She's hurt herself.'

'Leave her alone and let's get home. She's probably only got herself to blame.' Mike suddenly sounded just like Joseph and Belle felt slightly irritated.

'I must see if she's all right.'

'Oh, Belle, do come on. Look at her: she's no better than those tramps in the square.'

Belle nearly took his advice and let him lead her away. Then she looked at the woman again and something about the shape of the head and turn of the cheek looked oddly familiar.

'You go on; I'm staying. I want to talk to her.'

Mike shrugged his shoulders as if he thought she was mad and walked away, his hands in his pockets. Belle dropped to her knees and put her arms around the woman's shoulders.

'Come on,' she said. 'Get up. You're not badly hurt.'

'I'm bleeding . . .'

'It's only a scratch. Here, bind it up with my handkerchief. It's quite clean.'

'Thanks. You're very kind. I think I had one too many, but someone was buying a round and I couldn't say no, could I?' She laughed harshly and then coughed. 'Sorry about this. I think I'm stone cold sober now.' She turned up a pale face to see who was helping her. Belle found herself looking into two hazel eyes that she remembered well.

'Flora! It is you, Flora, isn't it?'

'Yes.' The woman got to her feet slowly, and Belle saw without a doubt that it was indeed her old friend, Flora Smart. 'Do you know me?'

'Of course I do. Look, don't you recognise me?' Belle turned so that the light from the street lamp fell full on her face. Even then Flora still looked doubtful until Belle pulled the pins out of her hair, shook her head, and let the shining red curls tumble to her shoulders. Then Flora's face lit up with recognition and she grasped Belle's hands.

'Belle! It is Belle Kelly, isn't it?'

'Yes. Oh Flora, it is good to see you again.'

'Like this?' Flora looked down at herself. She was embarrassed by her shabby appearance, with her old friend looking so well turned out.

'Belle!' Mike was standing at the corner waiting impatiently. 'Are you coming?'

'In a minute.'

'You mustn't keep your fella waiting,' Flora said. 'I know what they're like. I'm fine now, Belle, honestly.'

'Are you sure?' Flora nodded. 'I can't just leave you like this.' Belle found an old envelope in her bag and scribbled on it with the butt of a pencil. 'Look, here's my address. Do get in contact if there's anything I can do for you.'

'Well, I don't know . . .' Flora took the envelope doubtfully.

'Promise?'

'All right.' Flora suddenly smiled and her face looked almost girlish again. 'I promise.'

Belle left her then. She rejoined Mike, but they walked the rest of the way home in silence. She seemed to have forgotten all about the cup of cocoa she'd promised him, and left him standing rather forlornly on the doorstep. It was the old story, Mike thought to himself: he put himself out for her, and just when he thought things were going his way something happened, and he was back to square one.

Upstairs, Belle let herself in with her latch-key. The light in the hall was left on all night because her theatrical lodgers came in at all hours. This week she had two vacancies because the cast in the Agatha Christie play was quite a small one, but next week they had a touring Gilbert and Sullivan company arriving and they'd have a full house. Belle made a mental note to get in plenty of throat sweets and honey and lemon drink, because she knew from experience the trouble singers had with their vocal cords.

There was a light on in the kitchen and she found Alice Battey still working although it was so late. The trays of china and cutlery were all laid up ready to be carried into the dining-room first thing, and Alice was busy measuring oatmeal into a porringer. It would be left to soak on a warm stove overnight so that it would cook quickly in the morning.

'Everything all right?' Belle asked, unbuttoning her coat.

'Yes, Mrs Belle. Lucy seems to have a bit of a cold and called me up a couple of times. I made her a milky drink and read her Squirrel Nutkin and she soon dropped off.'

'I'll look in on her on the way up.'

Belle walked up the stairs slowly. She was always tired after her stint at the theatre and usually dropped straight into bed and fell asleep almost at once. But tonight, tired as she was, she felt restless. It was probably seeing Flora again in such distressing circumstances; it was enough to upset anyone.

She pushed open the door to Lucy's room and stepped inside. There were two beds, as Alice still slept in the same room as the child, so that the other rooms were free for the lodgers. Lucy slept in the smaller bed, with a flickering nightlight standing on a saucer nearby. She was afraid of the dark and still needed the comfort of a light and a teddy bear to cuddle.

She was stretched out on her back with the eiderdown pulled up to her armpits. The bear's face poked out from under one arm and she was sucking her thumb. She appeared to be fast asleep. Belle looked down on her child with a sort of wonder, as if she was discovering her for the first time.

It was meeting Flora again and resurrecting memories long past of a boy child with golden curls. Flora's little boy, Peter, whom she loved, and when she'd become pregnant herself dreamed of recreating. Instead she'd given birth to this poor little ugly girl child, who sucked her thumb so vigorously that she would soon need a brace on her teeth. Peter must be nearly eight now Belle calculated. She wondered where he was, and if he'd grown from a pretty baby into an equally attractive child.

Lucy sniffed in her sleep and dribbled around her thumb. Belle put out her hand and gently pulled the child's hand away from her face. Lucy stretched and immediately put the thumb back; she might have know she'd wake her up. Two solemn eyes looked up at her from the bed.

'Don't suck your thumb, Lucy. Your teeth will grow crooked.'

The thumb was removed, but the child said indignantly, 'You woke me up.'

'I'm sorry, darling. Alice tells me you've got a cold.'

'Yes.' Lucy sniffed pathetically. 'And it's dark.'

'No it's not. You've got your nightlight. Before that burns out Alice will be up to keep you company.'

'If I had a brother or a sister I wouldn't need Alice.' This was Lucy's usual complaint and Belle ignored it.

'Do you want anything? A drink? A story?'

'Alice brought me a drink and read Squirrel Nutkin to me.' She had a way of making even a trivial conversation sound like an accusation. It was probably because Belle felt guilty about her feelings for her daughter and the way she always left her with the little servant. 'I need a hankie.'

Belle felt in her pocket, but she'd given her own handkerchief to Flora. She searched in the dressing-table drawers and found a neat pile, and handed the top one to Lucy.

'Now blow your nose and go to sleep again. Alice won't be long.'

'Leave the door open.'

'Of course.'

Belle left the room with her usual feeling of relief. She had a room of her own across the landing; she entered quickly, closing the door behind her with pleasure. It was the same room with big windows looking over the street that she'd shared with Joseph. Now she had it to herself. She'd refurbished it, and the heavy walnut bedroom suite had been replaced by smaller white painted furniture, and soft green carpets and curtains. The bed had a canopy of frilled lace, and the bedspread was white with a sprinkling of pink rose-buds.

Belle undressed quickly. She was too tired to hang her

clothes up, so she left them trailing across a chair to be put away in the morning. She put on the crisp linen nightdress with the frilly yoke that Alice had left spread out on the turned down bed and climbed in under the covers. Her tired muscles relaxed slowly as she stretched herself languidly on the soft pillows.

She started to think about poor Flora, and pondered on what could have happened to her. But her mind kept returning to the little boy, Peter, and she wondered where he was and if he still remembered her. She fell asleep, her head full of memories, and when she woke in the morning to another busy day she didn't have time to dwell on the events of the evening before.

Two weeks flew past and she'd almost forgotten her meeting with Flora. Mike Walker resumed his attentions, and Lucy's cold cleared up.

One morning Belle was busy checking a pile of linen just returned from the laundry when the front door-bell rang. She continued counting as she knew Alice would answer it.

'Mrs Belle!' Alice was calling up the stairs in a most unladylike way. 'There's someone at the door asking for you.' Belle lost her place, and muttered 'Botheration!' under her breath. She'd have to start counting the pillowcases all over again. She went out on to the landing and looked over the bannisters but couldn't see who was at the door. All she could see was Alice in the hall, waiting for instructions.

'Who is it, Alice?'

'I don't know. Some woman. Begging, by the look of her.'

'Give her a shilling out of my purse and send her away.' Belle turned to return to her work when a voice below halted her.

'It's me, Belle – Flora.'

It was indeed Flora Smart. She'd followed Alice into the hall and was looking up at Belle with such desperation in her hazel eyes that Belle was moved to pity. She forgot the laundry and ran down the stairs to greet her friend, and although aware of Alice's curiosity and disapproval told Flora to follow her into the dining-room. Then she turned to her friend and tried not to look shocked.

In the harsh light of day Flora looked even worse than she remembered. She hadn't been drinking and had obviously tidied herself up for the occasion, as if she wanted to make a good impression, but she was so shabby and thin, her brown coat threadbare and ill-fitting. Her hair that had always been so smooth and healthy-looking had lost its lustre, and her face was pale and lifeless, although she'd painted her mouth bright red. But her hazel eyes were the same, except that one was half-closed by an ugly bruise that extended into the hairline and part the way down her cheek. She saw Belle's look of horrified concern and put up her hand as if to cover it.

'Oh, Flora!' Belle said. 'What have you done to yourself? Have you had another accident?'

'Not exactly.' There were tears brimming her eyes and Belle pulled out a chair and made her sit down. 'Someone hit me.'

'Benjie?' Flora's husband had been a bit of a rough diamond in the old days, but Belle didn't think he was the sort to give his wife a black eye.

'No, not Benjie. I left Benjie a long time ago. Didn't I tell you? It was Brian.'

'Who's he?' Then Belle recalled a conversation they'd had a long time ago when Flora had mentioned a man she'd met in a pub. His name had been Brian.

'I moved in with him when I left Benjie over a year ago. He's not a bad sort; but he drinks a bit and gets into violent tempers. I've had worse than this.'

'Why do you stay with him?'

'Because I don't have anywhere else to go. I don't mind for myself because I've got used to it, although the neighbours cut us because we're not married. But . . .' Trying to explain was too much for her. The tears brimmed over and she began to sob helplessly. Belle put her arms around her and hugged her close in a vain effort to comfort her.

'Tell me, Flora. I won't criticise you whatever you've done. I'm your friend and I want to help.'

'Don't mind him hitting me: I suppose I deserve it. But he hit Peter.'

'Oh, Flora. How terrible!'

'I know.' Flora wiped her eyes and blew her nose. Belle waited patiently and soon Flora seemed to feel better and continued her story. 'I'd been out shopping and he was looking after the boy. Peter's nearly eight now, but he's young for his age and isn't good at standing up for himself. Brian says he's a sissy; he doesn't realise he can't help it. Anyway, when I got home Peter was crying, and when I looked I saw bruises on his legs. Brian said he'd been naughty.'

'What had he done?'

'He'd taken some biscuits without asking. I know he shouldn't have, but he hadn't had any breakfast because there was no food in the house. Brian bought the biscuits for himself when he went to fetch a newspaper. Peter was so hungry he helped himself to one while Brian wasn't looking, so he thrashed him.'

'What with?'

'His belt. It's made of leather. He beat me with it once so I know how it feels.'

'Listen Flora.' Belle had been thinking, and she knew there was only one piece of advice she could give her friend. 'You have to leave him. If not for your own sake, for Peter's.'

'I know. I've thought about it lots of times, but I'm not very brave. You see I've got no money and I've nowhere to go.'

'Well, you have now. You can come and stay with me.'

'What, here?'

Flora looked around the room: to her it seemed like a palace. She'd been living with Brian and Peter in two dreary rooms in one of the poorest quarters of the town. She could hardly take in what Belle was saying, let alone believe that she was being offered an avenue of escape.

'Yes,' Belle said, ideas for housing two new lodgers spinning through her head. 'I'm on my own now since my husband died; apart from my little girl, Lucy. I run this as a boarding house for theatrical people. My maid, Alice, can do with some extra help in the kitchen, so you can earn your keep. Peter will be good company for Lucy; she was only wishing the other day that she could have a brother or sister to keep her company. We'll put a camp-bed up in Lucy's room and you can come in with me. It'll be like old times.'

Belle's eyes were dancing with excitement and Flora couldn't help but catch her mood.

'Oh, you are kind, Belle,' she said, and pleasure had brought a bit of colour to her cheeks so that the bruise didn't stand out quite so vividly. 'I'll work hard, really I will. You'll never regret giving us a home. I promise that Peter will be good.'

'Of course he will. Where have you left him? Go and get him quickly, and your things, while I have a word with Alice about the beds.'

'I've only got what I'm wearing,' Flora admitted. 'Peter's outside in the street. I didn't like to bring him in. He does what he's told so he won't wander away.'

She's talking just as if her son was a pet dog, Belle

thought. 'Come on then,' she said. 'Let's go and get him.'

Belle ran through the hall with Flora at her heels and out of the front door into the street. A little boy was standing on the pavement with his back to them. A slender figure with a mop of fair curls, wearing grey shorts and a torn blazer.

'Peter,' Flora said excitedly, 'come and meet your Auntie Belle.'

The child turned to face them and Belle stopped in her tracks. Peter had changed from the pretty baby she remembered. His mouth hung open and his chin was wet with dribble, and his unfocused eyes wandered about in a vacant fashion, just as his father Sydney's had done when she'd known him. Belle's heart sank: Flora's child was obviously a little boy of limited intelligence. What had she let herself in for?

Flora, with her troubles, and her poor little son; two more people to be responsible for. She tried to hide her feelings, and forced a smile on to her face as she took Peter's hand and led him into the house.

16

'What are you hoping Father Christmas will bring you, Peter?' Lucy asked, as she tried to hang her stocking over the end bed-rail.

'Dunnow.'

'I want a doll. A little one with real hair that I can carry around in my pocket.'

'So do I.'

Lucy looked at the solemn little boy crouched on the edge of the adjoining bed. His blond hair was ruffled and his striped pyjamas were buttoned in the wrong holes. He stared from the sock dangling in his hand to the little girl busy beside him.

'Don't be silly,' Lucy said kindly. 'Father Christmas won't bring you a doll. You're a boy. You should ask for a car or a train set.'

'Want doll! Want doll!'

Peter's voice was rising anxiously and Lucy knew she had to try to calm him down. His face, pretty at first glance, soon gave away his low intelligence. He was seven years old but hadn't outgrown his toddler ways, behaving more like a child of three or four, although he was well-built and tall for his age. Recently he'd started to have fits. The doctor had been called after the last attack and had diagnosed epilepsy. They had to keep him as quiet as possible because if he got too excited it often triggered another fit.

'Here, let me do it for you.' Lucy took the sock from him and looped it neatly over the bed-knob. 'There! I like boys' things, so if you get an engine or a car we can share it. If I get a doll I'll lend her to you. All right?'

'Awl right.'

'Get into bed then. Auntie Flora will be up any minute.'

They climbed under the covers and pulled the quilts up to their chins. In the half-light and without her glasses Lucy almost looked pretty. Her face had filled out a little bit, and excitement had made her eyes sparkle, but her childish face seemed to be permanently frowning so that she already had a crease between her brows. Belle had cut her daughter's hair to try to encourage it to grow thicker. Tonight it was pulled tightly away from her pale face into rag curlers that coiled around her head like rows of snails. Tomorrow was Christmas Day and there would be a party. Belle was determined that Lucy should look her best, even if the child had to pay the price of sleeping in discomfort, or sitting propped up all night. Lucy put up with the torture to please her mother. She didn't want to look pretty or have curly hair: after all Peter had both without having to try, but it wasn't doing him any good.

The door opened and Flora flounced in carrying two cups of hot milk for the children's supper. She bustled between the beds in a surly fashion as if she was in a hurry.

'Come on now you two, drink up,' she said. 'I haven't got all night you know.'

There was a marked improvement in Flora's appearance since Belle had taken her under her wing. Her tartan skirt and red twin-set were smart, even if they were Belle's cast-offs. Good food had improved her skin and brought back the gloss to her brown hair, but the bright painted bow of her lips, and the sharp waves pressed into her hair by the hot tongs, made her look older than she was. Her gratitude at her friend's kindness had been short-lived, and there was a sulky impatience in her manner even when dealing with the children. Peter seemed, if anything, to bear the brunt of his mother's displeasure, and Lucy spent her time trying to protect him from her sharp tongue.

'Is Mummy coming up to say goodnight?' Lucy asked, sipping carefully. The hot milk left a frothy white line on her upper lip and she wiped it away on the back of her hand.

'Don't be so mucky,' Flora said. 'Haven't you got a hankie? And you . . .' she turned to her son who was slurping noisily, 'drink quietly or I'll take it away from you.'

Peter jumped nervously and a stream of hot liquid ran down his chin on to his pyjama jacket. Flora snatched the cup out of his hands and Lucy jumped to his defence. She'd thought by the threatening expression on Flora's face that she was going to strike Peter.

'Don't touch him Auntie Flora, or I'll tell Mummy.'

Flora turned away to fold Peter's clothes and Lucy knew that this time she'd won. Life was a perpetual worry for her. She was protective of her mother as well as Peter; but somehow along the way they'd missed out on the loving. In fact Lucy suspected that Belle loved Peter more than her. She had a way of smoothing his hair away from his face and embracing him fondly. Lucy tried not to be jealous because poor Peter needed all the affection and understanding he could get, but it was hard all the same. Between trying to win her mother's love and watching over Peter, Lucy found life very difficult. But she was born with the sort of spirit that saints are born with, and every disappointment whetted her steely determination to get her own way.

'There are carol singers in the street. If you're in bed I'll leave the door open so you can hear them.'

Belle had entered the room to say her goodnight to the children. Lucy was always taken aback at how beautiful her mother was; not common like Auntie Flora. Lucy recognised style when she saw it.

Belle was dressed all in green. A dress of soft green wool fell in drapes from her shoulders to her waist tightly belted with a shiny black band, then the skirt flared out like a sea-green bell with big square patch pockets. The neck was cut in a deep V with a turned-back collar, and on one lapel was pinned a silver brooch in the shape of a cat. Lucy knew this brooch was important to her mother because she often wore it, and she wondered who had given it to her, but didn't like to ask. Belle's curly hair caught the last of the light in the dim room and glowed like fire in the nape of her neck, caught into place by a ribbon that matched her dress.

Lucy sat up in bed, her arms hugging her knees under the multi-coloured quilt. From far away she could just hear voices singing 'Silent night, holy night' drifting up the stairs. The front door must be open as well because a frosty draught crept into the room and made her shiver. She would have liked to be out there with the carollers, muffled to the ears, and carrying a lighted lantern like the pictures on old-fashioned Christmas cards, stamping cold feet and blowing on numb fingers.

A door slammed and the voices faded. The magic moment had passed for another year; but there was still tomorrow, Christmas Day, to look forward to.

'Did you remember the pies?' she asked, as if daring her mother to admit she'd forgotten the traditional treat.

'Alice is coming with them now.'

As if on cue the homely figure of Alice Battey, cheerful

and white-aproned filled the doorway, carrying a plate of mince pies covered by a cloth.

'Not asleep yet,' she teased. 'Whatever can you be waiting for?'

'Mince pies,' shouted Lucy.

'Pie – pie,' chanted Peter, opening his mouth like a baby bird waiting to be fed.

Belle fed him first: sitting on the edge of his bed and holding the pie while he bit into the pastry.

'He should feed himself,' Flora said, bustling and banging around the room busily. 'He's not a baby.'

'The pastry's hot; he'll burn his fingers.' Belle went on feeding the child as if his mother hadn't spoken.

'He'll never learn.' Alice sided with Flora, but she knew Belle's feelings for the little boy, and seeing Lucy's face fed her in the same way until she was smiling again. 'And one for Father Christmas,' she said, holding up the remaining pie. Lucy remembered the routine from the previous year and it was placed in the hearth next to a small glass of ginger wine.

'Is everything ready downstairs?' Belle asked as Alice crossed to the door carrying the empty plate.

'I think so, Mrs Belle. I've been baking all afternoon. I cleaned and polished yesterday so there's only the table to lay up.'

'Flora can help you with that.'

'Oh, Belle!' Flora turned from the window where she'd been watching the people passing below. 'I'm going out. Can't we do it in the morning?'

'No, we can't,' Belle said firmly as she tucked Peter in first and then turned to do the same for Lucy. 'It will be much easier to lay the table tonight. Anyone who wants breakfast can eat in the kitchen as long as they're up early, and you can bring up a tray for the children. Later on you can help me with the tree. Mike's promised us a big one from the Open Market; he says it's cheaper if you leave it to the last minute. There's a box of last year's decorations packed away somewhere. Alice will tell you where it is.'

'I'm going out,' Flora said again stubbornly, two patches of colour staining her cheekbones and her chin jutting out.

'Not until everything's ready here,' Belle said quietly.

She was getting used to this battle of wills with her friend, and Flora usually gave in at the last moment. Flora liked a good time: to get down into the town where there were lights, jollity and crowds of people. Although she was grateful to Belle for giving her a home, she also resented the younger woman's authority over her.

Flora opened her mouth to argue, but changed her mind. After a brief goodnight to the children she followed Alice out of the room and down the stairs. Inside she was fuming at the unfairness of the situation. Belle often annoyed her with her airs and graces. Just because she'd been lucky enough to marry someone above her station she thought she could throw orders about. Flora overlooked how hard Belle worked, not only supervising the running of the house and its lodgers, but also her tiring job at the theatre. Added to that Flora was jealous of Mike Walker's attentions, seeing in his eyes his feelings for Belle, while she wasn't even allowed out on Christmas Eve to meet her date.

Alice returned to the kitchen to turn off the oven and take the last batch of pies out to cool. The scrubbed table was already groaning with good things: pies and puddings, sausage-rolls and scones, and the fruit cake already covered with marzipan and icing, but waiting to be decorated with crystallised fruits and red-breasted robins. The turkey was trussed ready in the larder, and Alice was a bit worried about cooking such a large bird. Usually they had a chicken, as turkeys were expensive and hard to come by, but the recipe book soon put her at her ease. She'd get up extra early, put the bird in the oven on a low heat, and then hope for the best.

'The cloth's in the dresser drawer,' she told Flora, wishing Belle had let the girl out. She was hopeless when she was in a bad mood, and Alice was used to running the house single-handed.

In the dining-room the leaves had already been pulled out on the table and Belle was counting places.

'How many will there be sitting down, Mrs Belle?'

'I'm not sure. Ten at least; probably more if Mike brings his brother. I've invited him. Will there be enough napkins?'

'I've bought some paper ones in case.'

'I hope the children will behave.'

'Lucy will; she's just like a little old woman sometimes. As for Peter, it'll depend what mood he's in.'

'Sit him next to me, Alice, and I'll keep an eye on him.'

'That's what his mother should be doing.'

'Shh!'

Flora had come into the room bearing the table-cloth and they quickly changed the subject. Between the three of them it didn't take long to lay the table with cutlery and the best glasses. Two tall candles stood in the middle amongst an arrangement of ivy and holly berries to give it a festive look. Belle was admiring the finished picture when she heard the front door open and a familiar whistle.

'It's Mr Walker,' Alice said, peering round the door. 'He's brought the tree.'

'In here, Mike,' Belle called, and the big man's shoulders appeared in the doorway bearing the biggest tree she'd ever seen. He had difficulty getting it through, and then found it was too tall for the room. In the end the roots had to be sawn off and even then the top branches pressed against the ceiling. He stepped back to view his handiwork, hoping Belle would be satisfied.

'You'll have to take some more off,' Belle instructed. 'Lucy's fairy has to go on top.'

Lucy had spent days under Alice's supervision making the fairy for the tree. The result was rather strange-looking, and not a bit fairylike, but it was important to her: a golliwog made by winding wool around a piece of card, with yellow hair and inked-in features, a band of pink cotton material bound around its middle for a skirt, and a wand made from a bent pipe-cleaner. Peter had made the star for the end of the wand, and for him it was a surprisingly neat piece of work – a five-pointed star cut from silver paper out of a cigarette packet and glued carefully into place. Even his mother had admired it.

Belle knew how important it was for the children to see the fairy in place when they came downstairs in the morning, so another foot had to be sawn from the tree, covering Alice's clean floor with pine-needles. She didn't complain; after all it was the season of goodwill and she could easily sweep the floor and put the room to rights.

Decorating the tree was a joint endeavour, with Mike balanced on a stepladder and Belle handing things up to him. Alice and Flora concentrated on the lower branches. They all admitted with pride that the finished tree was a work of art. The boughs were laden with coloured balls and strings of glittering tinsel. Lucy's fairy perched on the topmost branch smiling down on them.

Then there were the goodies to hang in easily accessible places. Bags of sweets for the children, cigars for the men, and embroidered hankies for the ladies. Lastly, the main presents in their gay wrappings had to be piled around the tree's foot. Lucy's longed-for doll, with a papier mâché head and stuffed body, had been dressed jointly by Belle

260

and Alice. It was larger than she'd asked for but would be loved nevertheless. The dolls' pram with hood and apron, just like the real thing, stood waiting for its owner on solid rubber wheels, with a label tied to its handle saying it was a present for Lovely Lucy, from Uncle Mike.

For Peter there was a clockwork train-set with rails and signals. He'd have difficulty working out how to put it together and wind it up, but Lucy would enjoy helping him.

The pile of presents grew surprisingly. The four grown-ups giggled and behaved like children themselves: catching the spirit of the occasion, and feeling the shapes inside the parcels and trying to guess the contents. Just as they thought they'd finished Belle ran out of the room, and returned carrying a long wrapped parcel she'd almost forgotten. She laid it carefully beside the others and saw Mike's curious glance. An explanation seemed necessary.

'It's for my father,' she said. 'I've invited him to dinner tomorrow.'

Mike laughed. 'Do you know,' he said. 'I didn't even know you had a father.'

'I haven't seen him for ages,' Belle confessed. 'We sort of lost touch when I married Joseph. It was my fault, I'm afraid. He's never seen Lucy, and I thought it would be nice for her to meet her grandfather.'

'Peter's got a grandfather and a grandmother,' Flora said a trifle petulantly, 'but they don't bother about us.'

'He probably won't come,' Belle said. Her thoughts were far away, remembering Dada and her childhood. 'I've bought him a present just in case.'

Alice prodded the heavy box. 'Whatever is it?'

'New garden tools,' Belle said proudly. 'To replace the rusty set Dada uses on his allotment. There's a fork, a spade and a hoe. He grows all his own vegetables – or at least he used to.'

'That must have set you back a bit,' Flora said. 'I'm not buying my mum or dad anything. They don't care about me.'

'If he doesn't come I can always take them back to the shop and get my money back. You're joining us for dinner aren't you, Mike?'

Belle felt the need to change the subject. She'd had to pluck up her courage to send that letter to Dada, not knowing how it would be received. As soon as she'd posted it she'd wondered if she'd done the right thing. But it was too late now to change her mind. He probably wouldn't come anyway.

'Of course I'm coming,' Mike said with a grin. 'You need me to carve the turkey; women never do it properly.'

'You can bring Johnnie if you like,' Belle said generously. Mike's younger brother was very quiet and always seemed to have his nose buried in a book. He didn't have Mike's sparkling personality.

'I'll ask him. I don't think he's doing anything. Sure there'll be room?'

'Of course there'll be room. It's Christmas: we'll make room.'

'How many have you got upstairs?' Mike looked up at the ceiling, in the direction of the bedrooms which were usually crammed with boarders.

'Only four. The rest of them have gone home for the holiday. The twins are still here; and Myrtle and Doris.'

All four of these remaining lodgers were appearing in the local pantomime. The only day they had to rest was Christmas Day itself, before starting the run with the Boxing Day matinée. The twins were Will and Stan Dent: a middle-aged couple who were always booked to play the broker's men. Myrtle and Doris were in the chorus, although Doris managed to get a speaking part as well this year. Three lines in scene three, introducing the fairy godmother. Myrtle was understudying the principal boy and was praying that some minor disaster would befall the actress playing the part. Not life-threatening, just twenty-four-hour flu or a sprained ankle would give her the chance to show what she could do, and get her noticed. They were all past their prime and looking forward to sharing a family Christmas. They'd spent too many years in cramped bed-sits, with only the crackle of a radio for company.

'Who's going to play Father Christmas this year?' Alice asked. She was crawling around the floor brandishing a dustpan and brush. They all turned and looked at Mike. He laughed.

'All right; but what do I wear so that they don't recognise me? You know what kids are like.'

'I've got an old dressing-gown somewhere,' Belle said. 'We can make a hood out of a red towel and trim it with a border of cotton wool.'

There was great hilarity while they were helping him get ready. There was enough cotton wool to make him a beard as well, and with the help of some spirit gum they finished the job to everyone's satisfaction. In the dim light of the nursery the children wouldn't recognise the Uncle Mike they saw every day. But Lucy and Peter were fast asleep and it was easy to stuff their stockings with nuts, fruit and sweets, and consume the snack that had been left in the hearth.

The job completed Mike joined the women in the kitchen where Alice had glasses of sherry ready, and more mince pies. It was time for the grown-ups to relax after a tiring day and look forward to watching the children's excitement on the morrow.

Peter and Lucy were awake early as was to be expected. Alice heard them chattering like birds as she prepared the breakfast. Soon the house was a hive of industry, with the lodgers giving a hand with the washing-up, and everyone wishing each other a Happy Christmas.

The only absentee was Flora. She'd managed to get out late the night before and hadn't returned until the early hours, tired and flushed with drink. So when she did manage to drag herself out of bed her head ached and her temper was decidedly frayed.

Peter and Lucy kept out of her way: they knew what she was like when she was in one of her moods. At her best she would ignore them, and at her worst they might feel the back of her hand around their legs.

The exchange of presents was a great success. Mike had bought Belle a long silk scarf, coloured smoky-grey and mauve. She immediately draped it around the shoulders of her green dress, and with her mane of hair loosened she looked like a beauty from a pre-Raphaelite painting. Mike couldn't take his eyes away from her, although Belle was far too busy to notice.

Johnnie, Mike's brother, arrived, smiling shyly at everyone. The children claimed him, and soon he was sitting on the floor with them clipping the rails of the train track together, and talking to Peter in a quiet reassuring voice.

Lucy watched, her new doll tucked safely under her arm. She'd already christened her Shirley, after Shirley Temple, her favourite film star. The doll was perfect; but her bear, who had been her night-time companion for as long as she could remember, wouldn't lose his place in her bed. Shirley would spend her nights in the dolls' pram, safely tucked under the hand-knitted blanket, just like a real baby.

The excitement was at its height, with Alice needing all her strength to wrestle the turkey out of the oven and carry it to the table. Mike was standing by with the carving knife, freshly sharpened and looking highly dangerous, and Flora was clattering plates in a desultory fashion. The door-bell rang. Everyone stopped what they were doing. 'Are you expecting anyone else?' Mike asked Belle.

'I don't think so.' Belle was busy counting heads. 'Answer the door, Alice.'

'I can't. My hands are full.'

'I'll go,' Myrtle said, and put down the pile of serviettes she was folding.

Belle was laughing at a slightly wicked joke Mike had just told her. She was whipping cream for the pudding with a fork. There was a blob of frothy white on her cheek and her hair was hanging over her face, so that her blue eyes peered from under a curly red veil of fringe.

'It's someone asking for Mrs Bishop,' Myrtle announced, standing in the doorway doubtfully.

Belle looked up. Nobody called her Mrs Bishop these days. Everyone had picked up Alice's way of addressing her employer, so those who weren't on Christian name terms called her Mrs Belle.

'Who is it?'

Before Myrtle could answer a man appeared behind her and Belle thought for a moment that she must be dreaming. It was George Kelly: her Dada. Although she'd sent him an invitation she hadn't thought for a moment that he would accept.

'Hello, Belle.' He pushed Myrtle aside and stepped into the room.

Belle dropped the bowl of cream and ran into his arms. He held her close in a bear-like hug, and it was just like old times before they'd grown apart. George saw an older, wiser Belle, who looked at him with the same candid blue eyes, that were brimming over with tears of joy and welcome. Gone was the willowy girl he remembered: she was all woman. He was proud of her beauty, and relieved that she'd lost none of her spontaneity and wild charm. She was his Belle, and he was delighted to see her again.

Belle saw a father who the years hadn't been so kind to. He was smaller, thinner, and his shoulders seemed to have developed a droop, as if he was used to carrying a burden. His face was lined and his hair greyer than she remembered, but the eyes were kind and full of curiosity.

'Oh, Dada,' she said. 'I'm so pleased to see you. I didn't think you'd come. It's been such a long time.'

'Well, I'm here now.'

'Dada, there's someone I want you to meet.' Mike looked up from his task of carving the meat but Belle was looking past him. 'Lucy,' she called.

A thin gangly child slipped into the room. A little girl with match-stick arms and legs, and hair that even rags couldn't entice to curl. Her pink frilly dress, bought new for the festivities, looked ridiculous. She was the sort of child who would look stylish in plain clothes with tailored lines. George thought the glasses made her look like a stuffed owl.

'Dada,' Belle said. 'This is your granddaughter.'

'Why you dear little thing,' George said, and he dropped on to one knee and opened his arms. Lucy wasn't afraid of the strange man; after all, she'd just seen her mother hugging him. She ran to him and let him embrace her as if she were coming home. He held her close, the sort of way she'd always wanted Belle to hold her, and she relaxed and felt safe for the first time in her young life.

'And what's your name?' he asked, and she knew he was really interested, not just being polite.

'Lucy.'

'Do you know, Lucy is my favourite name.'

'Is it?'

'Yes.'

266

'Are you sure?'

'Cross my heart and hope to die,' and George gestured a finger across his throat to demonstrate; but the smile on his face reassured Lucy so that she smiled in return.

'Have you got a little girl?'

'Yes.'

'What's her name?'

George paused for a moment and met Belle's eyes over the child's head. 'Isabel,' he said softly.

'If Lucy's your favourite name, why did you call your little girl Isabel?'

George sat back on his heels and laughed. The sort of laugh he hadn't enjoyed since Bess had been taken away from him. 'Why, Belle,' he said at last. 'You've got a sharp one here and no mistake. She's a chip off the Kelly block, if I say so myself.'

Everyone joined in the laughter then, even Lucy, who was pleased to be the centre of attention. She showed George her new doll, and he admired the pram, and the way Shirley just fitted into it as if it had been made for her.

Then Peter joined them to see what was going on, his new engine clutched in his hands. George admired the toy, and seemed to think Peter was very clever to be able to turn the key all by himself without breaking the spring. He won the boy's heart by confiding that he could never do it successfully until he was much older than seven years, and Peter was, without a doubt, his favourite boy's name.

There was so much noise, chattering, and laughter going on that no one was aware of Alice standing in the doorway trying to make herself heard. At last she banged a tin tray with a wooden spoon to get everybody's attention.

'Dinner will be cold if you don't come to the table at once,' she announced.

She didn't have to say it twice as there was an immediate

stampede of hungry people towards the dining-room. Belle found herself alone with her father and felt suddenly nervous. 'You are coming to dinner, aren't you?' she asked.

'No, Belle. I can't stay. I'm sorry.'

'Why not? I invited you, and Lucy will be disappointed.'

'Well, the thing is . . .' George seemed embarrassed and Belle waited for him to go on. 'I didn't come on my own. Maud Carter's outside in the street waiting for me. I said I wouldn't be more than ten minutes.'

Then Belle did something she never thought she'd do. 'Alice,' she called. The little maid ran into the room, wiping her hands on her apron. 'There's a lady waiting outside. Her name's Maud Carter and I'm going to invite her in to join the party. I want you to lay another place at the table.'

And when Maud came in, she hadn't changed a bit. Big and jolly, with not a single strand of grey in her jet hair. A black cape over her tight shiny red dress, and her large feet in flat lace-up shoes for comfort.

It was the season of goodwill, and Belle stepped forward to meet the woman who had taken her mother's place in her father's affections. Their hands met warmly, and Maud's face was so friendly that Belle couldn't help saying, 'Happy Christmas, Maud, and welcome.' And she meant it.

17

'I know she's your friend, but I'll swing for that girl one of these days.'

'Whatever is the matter, Alice?'

Belle had come into the kitchen to find Alice clattering saucepans together. It was unusual to find her in a state.

'It's Flora again, Mrs Belle. Who did you think I meant?'

Belle sat down at the table with a sigh. There was tea in the pot, still hot, and she filled a cup and stirred in two spoonfuls of sugar. 'What has she done now?' She sipped her tea and waited for Alice to tell her about the latest calamity.

'It's not what she has done, it's more what she hasn't. She promised faithfully to come down early and lay up, but the lazybones is still in bed.'

'I expect she came in late again last night.'

'I don't know why you put up with her, Mrs Belle; really I don't. She never says please or thank you, and she's not a bit grateful to you for having her here.'

'I don't want gratitude. I told you, she's an old friend. She'd do the same for me.'

'That's what you may think,' Alice said darkly. 'The moment she walked into this house, all pale and woebegone,

269

I said to myself, "Here comes trouble," and that's exactly what she is.'

'She's had a bad time. Try to be patient with her.'

'Patient!' Alice laughed. 'What she needs is a good old shake-up to pull her to her senses, if only for the little boy's sake.'

'I'll have a word with her when she comes down.'

'It's about time you did, Mrs Belle, if I may say so. Have you finished with the pot?'

'Leave it,' Belle instructed. 'I'll clear everything away when I've finished; and I'll ask Flora to take the children out to give you a rest. I'd do it myself but there's a matinée this afternoon.'

'I'll sweep the front steps then.'

Alice left in a whirl of activity, leaving Belle finishing her tea and deep in thought. Alice was right of course: something would have to be done about Flora. Sorry as she was for her she was turning out to be more of a hindrance than a help. And as for Peter: she neglected him shamefully. Belle had felt so sorry for her and had tried to give her time to settle in. But right from the start Flora had made use of them and expected Alice to behave more like her servant and Peter's nursemaid than a person with equal responsibilities.

When Flora at last came down she would have a talk with her and point out how she wasn't pulling her weight in the household. She'd warn her, in a friendly fashion, that if things didn't improve she would have to leave. Belle wasn't looking forward to the task as her friend took offence easily, but it had to be done. Belle had ceased long ago to feel sorry for Flora and wondered how many of her troubles she'd brought on herself. But she did feel sorry for Peter.

The little boy had settled in with them quickly, and she'd seen a change in Lucy since she'd found a friend and companion. Although he was two years her senior she looked after him as if he was still only a baby, and it had helped him grow in confidence; he was like her little shadow, following her everywhere.

The terrible vacant look Belle had noticed in his eyes when she'd first seen him wasn't nearly so pronounced now, as if the stimulation of loving people around him had helped to boost his intelligence. But the epileptic fits had become more pronounced, and seemed difficult to control as he grew older. Belle dreaded to think what would happen to the little boy if he only had his mother to care for him. This was the main reason why she'd let the present situation continue for so long.

Belle had finished her tea, washed up, and cleared the kitchen before Flora made her appearance. She was dressed in a crumpled dressing-gown and had obviously just got out of bed. She fumbled in her pocket for a squashed cigarette packet and lit up as she wandered around the kitchen.

'God, I feel terrible,' she said, rubbing the sleep out of her eyes with her fists. 'Isn't there any tea left?'

'I've tipped it away: it was stewed anyway.' Belle hung up the damp tea-towel and began to wipe the draining-board a little bit too energetically.

'That's all I need! Why didn't Alice call me?'

Belle turned around to face her friend. Now was the moment; if she didn't take the opportunity now it might be even more difficult to do it later on.

'I don't think that's Alice's job do you?'

'I never said it was her job; but it wouldn't have hurt her. I'm meeting someone important this morning and I want to look my best.'

'What about Peter?'

Flora stared at her. She seemed surprised by the sudden change of tone in Belle's voice.

'Aren't you taking him with you?'

'Of course not.' Flora grimaced. 'He can stay here with Lucy. Alice will look after both of them.'

'Alice is busy today. She seemed to think you were going to give her a hand this morning.'

'I overslept.' Flora was wide awake now and on the defensive. Belle guessed she was in for a difficult time. 'Is that a crime?'

'Not unless it happens as often as it does to you.'

'I've had enough of this.' Flora was on her feet and about to head for the door. 'I'm going back to bed.'

'Oh no you're not!' Belle stopped in front of the door to prevent Flora escaping. 'Sit down, Flora, I have to talk to you.'

Flora sank back into her chair and blew out a trail of smoke. Belle sat down in the chair opposite.

'Well, what is it?'

'It's you,' Belle said. 'You're not pulling your weight around here.'

'So who's complaining – Alice?'

'No,' Belle lied, not wanting to cause enmity between the two women. 'I am. We had an arrangement, if you remember. You were going to help with the cooking and housework, and in return I'd give you and Peter a home.'

'Well?'

'I've kept my side of the bargain, but I can't remember the last time I saw you working in the kitchen, unless you count boiling a kettle to make yourself a pot of tea.'

'It's Alice,' Flora said, trying to look hard done by. 'She says I don't do things properly, and it's quicker to do them herself. She doesn't give me a chance.'

'All right,' Belle said, thinking quickly. 'Perhaps it was a mistake to expect two women to share a kitchen. But there are other things you can do.'

'Such as?'

'I'm going to make you responsible for keeping the bed-rooms cleaned and looking after the children. You can start by changing the sheets, and after dinner you can take Lucy and Peter out.'

'But I told you, I've got a date.'

'Then you'll have to cancel it, won't you.' Flora's face stirred Belle to pity. Perhaps she was being too hard on her friend. 'Don't look like that,' she said. 'Alice is busy and I have to work at the theatre, but you can have the evening free. I think that's fair, don't you?'

Flora had no option but to agree. She disappeared, and Alice and Belle smiled at each other. They could hear her making an awful lot of noise over their heads, but at least she seemed to have got the message and decided to do some work. At dinner time she joined them at the table and gave a hand serving and handing round the plates. But she hardly said a word and seemed sunk in her own private thoughts, but that was better for everyone than her usual arguments and surly tantrums.

Peter ate his steamed fish and rice pudding. Then he climbed down from his chair, announcing to everyone, 'Train.' They all knew that this meant that he was going back to the nursery to play with his train-set.

'No,' Flora said, grabbing him by the shirt-tail before he could reach the door. 'We're going out.'

'Train!' Peter said crossly, struggling to get away.

'Where are we going?' Lucy asked. She was surprised at the unexpected turn of events, but guessed that if Auntie Flora was taking Peter out she would be included.

'Wait and see,' Flora snapped, not wanting Alice or Belle to guess what she had in mind.

Lucy was trying to help Alice by carrying the dirty plates to the sink, but Flora pulled her away, telling her to wash

273

her hands and change her shoes while she did the same for Peter. When she came downstairs Lucy was already waiting in the hall; clean and neat in a summery frock and white sandals, her straight hair tied back with a wide ribbon bow. Peter still looked distressed but Lucy smiled at him and held out her hand. He soon forgot his train-set.

It was a lovely day for a walk: sunny, with just a hint of a sea breeze to keep it pleasant. Lucy wondered why Flora was wearing her best peacock-blue dress, and also high-heeled shoes. They seemed most unsuitable for a walk with two active children. She guessed that if Peter got out of hand it would be her job to do the chasing, as Flora certainly wouldn't be able to run very fast. Not that she minded; the most important thing was that Auntie Flora must be kept in a good temper.

At the bottom of the steps Flora guided the children to the right. Peter smiled happily.

'School?' he asked hopefully.

This was one of his favourite walks, to the nearby infants' school where Lucy was already a pupil. Every day, in term time, he watched his friend going through the school gates into the excitement and mystery of the playground. Then Alice, who usually accompanied them, would take his hand and pull him gently away. He hated being apart from Lucy for even part of the day.

The trouble was Flora couldn't find a school that was prepared to take him. He was eight years old and education was compulsory, but his history of fits and mental disturbance had made him a difficult pupil. He was disruptive with children, apart from Lucy, and the authorities had assured Flora that a place would eventually be found for him at a special school that would be able to cope with his needs. But he had to wait his turn as places were limited, and in the meantime he could only watch through the school gates as Lucy and the other children enjoyed themselves.

His favourite walk was to the school gates, to stare at the big red building that was beyond his grasp, and dream of the day when he would be allowed to join the children inside.

'No!' Flora said, damping his hopes. 'We're not going to the school today: it's the holidays. We're going on a bus.'

Peter's disappointed face brightened. He liked riding on the big red buses, particularly when he could sit on the top deck, right at the front above the driver, and pretend to steer. Today he was in luck: although they were only going three stops the downstairs was full and the only vacant seats were upstairs, so the children's spirits rose. They disembarked at the Open Market, half falling down the steep winding stairs while the driver waited impatiently for them.

Across the road was a play area called The Level, where the boys played football, and on Bank Holidays the travelling fairs pitched their tents and parked their caravans; it had a paved playground with rusty metal slides and creaky swings. It was a rough area, frequented by drunks, and Lucy knew her mother wouldn't approve of Auntie Flora bringing them here even in broad daylight. A child had recently suffered a bad head injury falling from the top of a slide on to the paving stones. Peter, with his unsteady legs would have to take care.

Flora, either unaware of or disregarding the danger, led the way. Pushing Lucy in front and trailing Peter by the hand she guided them across the road. Peter was immediately attracted by a shallow paddling-pool, half-full of dirty water, in which floated empty cigarette packets and stubs.

'No,' Flora said quickly and sat down on the nearest bench. The wooden slats were broken in places, and there were dirty newspapers and other rubbish blowing around their feet from a nearby overflowing bin.

'Can we go on the swings?' Lucy asked hopefully.

'If you're careful,' Flora said. 'Will you take care of Peter?'

'Of course.'

Lucy felt important. She was used to this task and the little boy usually obeyed her. With his mother he would argue and get upset.

The two children wandered away hand in hand. Flora opened her shiny handbag and got out her powder compact and a comb. She was late for her date and the pubs were already closed, but she could still be lucky. Bill had seemed keen enough and might have waited around somewhere hoping that she'd turn up. She started titivating herself up just in case: repainting her lips and powdering her nose, and making sure that every wave and curl in her hair was in place. In her compact mirror she could see the public house where they'd arranged to meet. She was too busy watching to keep her eyes on the children. After all, she told herself, they couldn't come to any harm. Lucy was very self-sufficient for her age, and if Peter got into trouble she would soon come and tell her.

Peter was fascinated by the paddling-pool. He liked water of any kind, and no tap in the house was safe from his exploring fingers. Regardless of his clothes he stretched out on his stomach on the hard ground and dabbled his fingers in the dirty water.

'Fish?' he said hopefully, looking up at Lucy who was crouched on her haunches beside him.

'No fish,' Lucy said.

She picked up a stick and threw it into the pool. Peter reacted by wanting to do the same, although bits of paper and stones were the same as sticks as far as he was concerned. Lucy remembered her Winnie the Pooh book at home, and the game the bear and piglet had invented called Pooh-sticks. She found a broken plank on a nearby heap of rubbish and placed it across the corner of the pool as a bridge; and then showed Peter how to drop pieces of twig into the water and, by stirring up a current with her hands, race them under the improvised arch.

Peter soon caught on to the game, although he got rather wet in the process. Lucy glanced across the playground to where Auntie Flora was sitting, half-expecting her to come across and reprove them. But Flora was still occupied with her comb and mirror.

When Peter got bored with the game she took him to the swings and held the seat while he climbed up. He liked the movement as long as it didn't swing him too high. When Lucy sat on the seat next to him and began working it with her legs so that she was soon swinging over his head, he began to cry with fear. It's not fair, Lucy thought as she slowed down. Much as she loved him he wasn't her responsibility, and she shouldn't have to keep him amused all the time. The slide looked exciting, but she didn't dare climb the metal ladder to the top as Peter would be bound to follow her. It was much too high and dangerous for him.

'Come on,' she said, pulling him off the swing. 'Let's play hide-and-seek.'

Peter obediently followed her. She led the way to a corner of the playing-ground which was bordered by rather battered privet bushes. Dogs had adopted this corner for their own private lavatory. Drunks and children used it as a short cut to the main road; there were plenty of gaps and broken branches so that it resembled a badly made set of giant false teeth.

Lucy told Peter to hide first while she counted up to fifty; then she would come and find him. The little boy trotted off. His idea of hiding was to sit behind the nearest bush with his eyes tightly closed. As he couldn't see Lucy he presumed that she couldn't see him, even though his legs and feet and part of his head were in full view.

'Got you!' Lucy shouted, leaping on him and tickling him under his armpits so that he yelled in delight. 'Now I'll hide. You go and sit on that bench and count to ten, then you must come and find me.'

'All right.'

He trotted away on rather unsteady legs; counting as he went. He could just about count to ten, but then she knew his attention would wander. He might even forget why he was counting.

She pushed her way through a gap in the hedge, holding her breath because of the smell of dog's urine. She was on an island. In front of her was the tall church of St Peter's, standing on the junction of the London and Lewes Roads. Cars and buses sped past at a terrifying pace. If she put out her hand she could almost touch them. A taxi cab came almost too close and a spray of loose gravel shot up into her face, stinging her skin and eyes so that she felt tears on her cheek – or was it blood?

She wiped the wetness away with her hand and watched a pigeon trying to find a place to land. Brave bird, she thought as it fluttered helplessly; or was it a stupid bird? At last it made a safe landing a few inches in front of her and hopped about searching for crumbs. Someone had thrown away half a sandwich. It had lain there for days, unnoticed, and was now green with mould. The pigeon didn't seem to mind, so why should Lucy? She broke the bread into pieces and was pleased when the bird came right up to her to be fed. She forgot Peter and Auntie Flora, and the dangerous road, and was happy in her own private world where she was alone with the pigeon.

Peter counted carefully to eight and then forgot what came next; so he counted to eight again. Then he opened his eyes and looked around. His mother was still sitting on the bench a long way away so that was all right. But he couldn't see Lucy. Of course, now he remembered, they were playing hide-and-seek and it was her turn to hide and he had to find her.

He wandered to the nearest bush and pulled a green branch aside, but there was no one there, only dirty earth and human rubbish. He started for the next row of bushes, but something twinkled away to his left and distracted him. The sun was shining on the water in the pool, disguising the floating dirt with sparkling ripples. He forgot Lucy and went to investigate. When he got closer he saw that it was only dirty water again, with bits of twig floating on the surface. He liked this place even without Lucy beside him; and as long as he could see his mother in the distance he felt safe.

A child yelled excitedly close by. He saw the big slide towering up into the sky, and a little boy with a dark head and a blue jersey hurtling down towards the ground. The child was laughing when he got to his feet, and immediately ran back to the ladder and climbed skywards to repeat the experience. It looked frightening, but it couldn't be, because the boy in the blue jersey was laughing and shouting 'Watch me!'

Peter was caught up in the other child's excitement and wanted to share it. He shouted as loudly as he could 'Watch me!' and glanced over his shoulder hopefully, but Flora wasn't looking. How surprised she'd be when she saw him at the top of the slide: just like the King of the Castle. He followed blue jersey up the ladder impatiently. At the top the other child sat down and shuffled on his bottom trying to get comfortable; then he changed his mind, and for variety turned around and positioned himself on his front with his head facing the ground and his grubby shoes almost in Peter's face. With a whoop of delight he let go and slid downwards to the ground, and then jumped to his feet and ran off towards the swings.

Peter didn't think: what that boy could do, so could he. He looked around to see if Lucy were watching him, but there was no sign of her. Holding on to the safety-rail he turned around as he'd seen the other boy do and lay down on the platform with his head hanging over the drop. Then he closed his eyes tightly and let go. The wind whipped his fair curls away from his face as he gathered speed, and he didn't feel the blood on his knees caused by the friction of his delicate skin against the metal runners. He didn't know how to slow down when he reached the bottom so slid at top speed off the end, rolling over and over and bumping his head on the concrete.

Flora finished admiring her image in the mirror and closed her handbag. She'd missed Bill, and he wasn't coming back to find her as she'd hoped. She stretched her legs out in front and studied her ankles, and the stockings with the clock heels Bill had given her. He was a commercial traveller peddling ladies' lingerie and all she knew about him was his name: William Smith, and that he was heading east when he left Brighton. He'd probably gone already and she'd never see him again.

She was feeling cross and sorry for herself, blaming Belle for her disappointment. A hand landed on her shoulder, making her jump, and she looked up into Bill's smiling face.

'Hello, Flo. I thought I'd missed you.'

'I was late. I couldn't get away any earlier.'

'Well, you're here now, darling.'

Flora moved along the bench to make room for him and he sat down, closer to her than he need, and took her hand.

He was a short, dapper little man, in his mid-forties. His dark hair was flattened greasily across his head as if it had been painted on, and he had round watery eyes in a pale face and a pencil-thin moustache adorning his upper lip. Tidily dressed in a navy-blue pin-striped suit with tiny feet in pointed shoes poking out from under the wide trouser legs, he placed his trilby hat carefully down beside him. He opened his mouth to say something but Flora was never to know what it was, because at that moment Lucy screamed.

She'd pushed her way from her hiding-place in the bushes just as Peter started his descent, and watched with horror as his small body shot off the end of the slide and hit the ground. She reached him first, and when Flora joined them she was already nursing his bruised face in her lap. Although there was blood on his legs and a big lump already coming up on his temple he was trying to sit up.

At the sight of his mother he started to cry, thinking she was going to tell him off, but all she said was, 'That was a silly thing to do. You might have really hurt yourself.'

'He has hurt himself,' Lucy said. 'Look at his knee.'

'Why didn't you keep an eye on him?' Flora said crossly.

She was relieved that Peter seemed to be all right and was prepared to pass the blame on to Lucy. She could see Bill watching them and wondered what he was thinking. She hadn't told him she'd got a kid because she hadn't wanted to put him off. Lucy promised to stay with Peter so Flora returned to the bench.

'What was that all about?' Bill asked curiously.

'Nothing. He didn't hurt himself.'

'You didn't tell me you'd got kids.'

'I haven't,' Flora said quickly. 'They're not mine. I'm just looking after them for a friend.'

'Good.' Bill took her hand again. 'Because I was hoping we could come to some arrangement.'

'What sort of arrangement?'

'I told you I'm going east. I want to be in Dover by the morning so I'm leaving this evening before it gets dark. I was hoping you'd come with me. My car's parked down by the Steine. What do you say?'

Flora didn't know what to say. He could have been offering the moon for all the use it was to her. Of course Peter was the problem. Without him she could have disappeared into the sunset in Bill's car just like the leading lady in a film, or the heroine of one of the romantic novels she liked to read. When Peter had been a baby she'd loved him: he'd been so small, helpless and pretty. But the older he grew the more of a liability he seemed to be. If she hadn't lumbered herself with a kid life would have been altogether different.

When Bill left her Flora hadn't agreed to anything – but she hadn't refused anything either. He kissed her a brisk goodbye. 'I'll be waiting outside the Palace Pier if you can make it,' he said. She watched his dapper little figure trot away and turned back to gather up the children. Life seemed hopeless and she couldn't help feeling depressed.

The journey home was a nightmare. Flora was cross and dragged Peter roughly by the hand. He seemed tired and listless but she was glad to see that his hair covered most of the bruise on his forehead, so with luck Alice and Belle wouldn't notice and ask questions. The graze on his knee didn't look nearly so bad after she'd wiped it clean with her handkerchief.

Lucy was quiet as well. She wasn't tired, she was frightened. Peter's fall had scared her; she felt responsible and was still waiting for Auntie Flora's wrath to descend upon her. She needed to tell someone, Alice or her mother, but guessed this would only make the situation worse. Even to her childish eyes Peter's apathy and pale face was the result of more than a tiring afternoon. Before they reached the house he was sick in the gutter.

'Good boy,' Flora said grudgingly. 'Alice would be cross with you if you were sick indoors. Are you all right now?'

Peter nodded his head weakly.

'My, he looks peaky,' Alice said as they crossed the hall. 'Whatever is the matter with him?'

Flora steered her son towards the stairs. 'He's just tired: Lucy got him over-excited. I'm taking him upstairs to lie down.'

'But it's only half past four.' Lucy thought she was being put to bed as well.

'You can come with me, Miss, and have some tea,' Alice said. 'I've made sandwiches and jelly, and someone's got to eat it up.'

Lucy followed her into the kitchen and tried to force some food down, but she really wasn't very hungry.

In the nursery Flora put Peter to bed in his clothes. His eyes closed almost before he was lying down and she quickly closed the door and went into her own room to think. She felt weary and was glad to slip off her shoes and sink down on the bed.

She fell asleep and dreamed that she was spinning through the countryside in a luxurious open-topped sports car, with Bill at her side telling her how much he loved her. When she woke, only half an hour later, she felt confused and her head ached. She supposed she'd better show her face downstairs and see what jobs Alice expected her to do. First she'd better check on Peter.

He was lying on his back and his face was in shadow. She presumed he was still asleep. He'd been sick again and his head had slipped sideways off the pillow. He didn't move.

Flora picked up the pillow and hugged it to her as she looked down at her son. There was a foam of dribble on the

283

side of his mouth and his face, in repose, looked even more vacant than when he was awake. She suddenly hated him for being alive and standing between her and the life she could have, travelling around with Bill.

An idea came to her: an idea so daring that a cold sweat broke out on her neck. He was so helpless; it would take no more than a minute to press the pillow down over his face and hold it there. With luck everyone would assume that he'd had a fit and choked to death. It wouldn't matter what they thought because she wouldn't be here; she'd be miles away driving through the countryside in Bill's car, heading for a new life.

She was still standing there clutching the pillow when she heard a sound behind her and swung round. Lucy was standing in the doorway, her eyes huge in her thin face.

'Go away!' Flora hissed, but Lucy seemed frozen to the spot, so she put out her foot and pushed the door to in the child's frightened face.

18

Flora wasn't missed until later that evening. Alice was too busy to notice her absence as the house was full of boarders; there was a big cast playing at the theatre that week. Every bed was occupied so there was plenty to do. It was only when Belle came home from work after the matinée that anyone noticed that something was amiss with Lucy.

'That child's sickening for something,' Alice said when Belle pointed it out. 'I hear there's measles about.'

'That's all we need,' Belle said. She stretched her arms lazily; it had been a busy afternoon with not an empty seat in the auditorium and queues in every interval. 'What's the matter, Lucy, are you feeling ill?'

The child was sitting at the kitchen table with her crayons and colouring-book spread out before her; but she wasn't occupied with the pictures, just idly scribbling any old how. Her teddy bear was clutched tightly under one arm for comfort, which was always a bad sign. The doll, Shirley, had replaced the bear in her affections during the daytime, and she only fell back on the bear for comfort when something was wrong.

Lucy shook her head and bent over the page to hide her face, but she couldn't hide from her mother her drawn expression, or the unshed tears in her eyes.

'Where's Peter?' Belle asked, thinking that the children might have had an argument. It would be unusual, but it could explain Lucy's strangeness.

'He was tired,' Alice said, 'So Flora put him to bed. She was out with the children all afternoon, so whatever you said to her worked a treat, Mrs Belle.'

'Good.' Belle was pleased. 'That's a good omen; perhaps she's got the message at last. But Lucy certainly looks as if she's sickening for something. Would you like me to read to you?' she asked the child. 'Or we could play a game.'

'Can we play Happy Families?'

They collected the pack of cards and retreated to a corner of the room where they wouldn't be in Alice's way. Belle won the first two games easily, although she cheated to try to give Lucy the pleasure of winning. The child was so pre-occupied it didn't work and Belle began to lose patience.

'Come on Lucy, look what you're doing. You've got Mr Bun the Baker in your hand. I can see it.'

Lucy wasn't in the mood for a reprimand and the tears spilled over. She dropped her playing cards and they fluttered to the ground around her chair. Belle scooped her up into her lap and the child seemed grateful for the unusual show of affection. Belle and Alice exchanged questioning glances across her dark head, and then, thinking they'd be better left alone for a while, Alice picked up a pile of the children's newly pressed clothes and left the room.

The house seemed very quiet as she climbed the stairs, but that was to be expected as the lodgers would all be at work. She suddenly remembered Flora and wondered where she was. The door to the nursery was closed so Peter must still be asleep. She frowned: if Flora let him sleep much longer he wouldn't be tired when bedtime came. She would go into the nursery quietly and put the clothes away;

that should rouse him as he wasn't a heavy sleeper. She turned the knob and pushed the door open.

Peter was lying on his back, stretched out on his narrow bed. She was just about to speak to him, to tell him to put on his shoes and come downstairs, when she saw that his eyes were staring in a strange unblinking fashion at the ceiling. She stepped nearer and saw the bruise where the curly hair was pushed back from Peter's temple, the pinched nose and blue texture of the skin around his mouth as well as traces of dried froth. The pillow which should have been under his head was part-way across his body. She suddenly realised that the little boy was dead.

He couldn't be! She was imagining things. He was playing a dreadful game with her and would suddenly smile and shout 'Boo' or some other silly exclamation. She put out her hand and touched his bare leg to attract his attention, but the skin was cold and felt like rubber under her trembling fingers. Then the realisation hit her and she dropped the pile of laundry and ran from the room.

Downstairs Belle was still comforting Lucy. Over her head she heard the slam of a door and running feet, and looked up expectantly. She didn't quite know what to expect, but when Alice appeared in the doorway she was alerted by the expression of horror on the maid's face that something dreadful had happened. She put Lucy gently away from her and got to her feet.

'What is it?'

'Peter!'

'What's the matter with him? Is he ill?'

'I think you'd better come and see, Mrs Belle.'

'You stay here and look after Lucy.'

Alice immediately crossed to the child who had begun to whimper quietly. She dropped to her knees and put her arms around her as if she wanted to shield her.

Belle ran up the stairs and burst into the nursery. What she saw there was even worse than she'd anticipated. Although something told her it was too late she flung herself down on the bed beside the motionless form and tried to bring back warmth into the cold limbs with her own body, and breathe life into the flaccid mouth. There was nothing she could do and the effort made her sob with helplessness, and then with anger. Where was Flora? Where was the child's mother when death was claiming its tiny victim?

She ran from the nursery, her breath coming in painful sobs, and screamed for Flora. Wherever Flora was she didn't respond, and Belle soon guessed rightly that she wasn't even in the house.

The room she shared with Alice told its own tale. The maid's half of the room was neat and tidy; but Flora's bed was a tangle of discarded clothes, and the drawers in the chest were pulled open and empty. Flora had packed in a hurry taking only an overnight bag and a change of clothes. There was no letter or message of any kind: nothing to indicate where she'd gone.

Alice looked up as Belle returned to the kitchen.

'Flora's gone,' she said tonelessly. 'I've searched upstairs. She's taken some of her things.'

'Shall I telephone for a doctor?'

Belle sat down in the nearest chair and sank her face in her hands in a gesture of despair. 'I don't think a doctor will be any good. I think it had better be the police.'

'Sh!' Alice indicated Lucy who was listlessly hugging her teddy bear. Then she crossed to Belle so that they could speak in low voices. 'Is he . . .?'

'Dead? Yes. Poor little soul.' Belle was dry-eyed. She wanted to cry but the pain was too great. Later, she told herself, when she was alone perhaps she would allow herself to cry.

Alice went out into the hall to make the telephone call, and then returned to take Lucy away. Belle waited nervously for the arrival of the law. When they arrived she was pale but composed and showed the two uniformed men into her small private sitting-room. The doctor who'd accompanied them disappeared upstairs where Alice was waiting outside the nursery door.

Mike Walker appeared while she was still telling her story. He'd reached home to find a police-car parked outside and scenting trouble came upstairs to investigate. Belle found she was pleased to see him. He was so large and reassuring, and it was easier to talk to the older of the two policemen with Mike's strong hand on her shoulder. When she'd finished they found themselves alone, and neither of them seemed to know what to say.

'You look exhausted,' Mike said at last. 'Can I get you a drink?'

'A sherry would be nice.'

There was a drinks table in the corner and he filled two glasses. He handed Belle one, and then pulled up a chair and sat beside her. The alcohol was welcome; he was pleased to see her relax slightly and the colour return to her cheeks.

'Feeling better?' he asked, and refilled her glass without asking.

'A bit. That poor little boy. I loved him . . .' her voice tailed away.

'I know. Is he really – dead?'

'Yes. I couldn't believe it at first. I tried to revive him, but it was no use.'

'And you think his mother, Flora, had something to do with it?'

'She must have. If she didn't, why has she run away?'

'Perhaps he had one of his fits . . .'

289

'He's had fits before, but they haven't killed him. Stop making excuses for her, Mike. There was a wound on his forehead and the pillow had been pulled out from under his head. He was dead, and had been for some time by the look of him, and his mother has disappeared without a word to anyone. I can't believe Flora would do such a thing, but if I can't help being suspicious what must the police think?'

'I don't know. I can hear someone coming downstairs.'

There was the tramping of heavy feet and then the thud of the front door closing. The sound of car engines jumping to life drew Mike to the window. He pulled the lace curtains aside and peered into the street.

'They've gone.'

'Peter?'

'They've taken him with them.' He was glad she hadn't seen the tiny covered stretcher being carried from the house, or the curious by-standers watching avidly for any scandal.

'It's all right. It's over.'

He'd said the wrong thing and he knew it. Belle was on her feet, blue eyes flashing, a veritable virago of pain and anger. 'It's not all over Mike; how can you say that? For me it's just beginning.'

He wanted to ask her what she meant, but at that moment Alice tapped on the door and entered without waiting for an invitation. Extraordinary events seemed to ask for extraordinary behaviour. Lucy, still white-faced and red-eyed, was clinging to her apron.

'They've gone,' she said bluntly. 'But they're coming back tomorrow.'

'Thank you, Alice,' Belle said. 'Is that all?'

'There's a reporter on the step. I didn't know what to say.'

'I'll come,' Mike said, crossing to her side. He was reassured to see that Belle had come out of the first shock. Anger would help her cope and delay the feelings of acute grief. Lucy looked up at him: all eyes. 'You stay with your mother,' he said, drawing her into the room. Then he left with Alice, closing the door behind them.

Belle and Lucy looked at each other across the vast expanse of carpet. Their grief was the same, but their worlds seemed to be far apart. Lucy was full of sorrow because her little companion was dead and she was all alone again. Belle's main feeling was guilt, looking at her daughter as if she was really seeing her for the first time.

She knew she'd failed Lucy, pushing her aside to shower affection on Flora's little son. It wasn't her fault that she wasn't born the child Belle had dreamed of. Her eyes filled with tears at the pathetic little figure in front of her: plain, small and unhappy. A belated instinct stirred in her. She saw herself as a child again; pushed aside while Bess doted on her brother Charlie. Bess, who'd never come to terms with her son's death and ended up mad, and locked away in an asylum. Was that the sort of future she was building up for herself? Perhaps she was being given a second chance to right the wrongs – perhaps it wasn't too late.

She opened her arms and Lucy hesitated for only a second, and then ran into them. They clung together, both feeling the relief of tears.

Lucy stopped crying first because she still didn't realise the terrible thing that had happened. All she knew was what Alice had told her: that Peter was dead. Dead meant gone for ever; like the pet rabbit she'd had last year who'd been killed by a stray cat. Her mother's tear-stained face moved her, and in her childish thoughts Belle was now in the place Peter had occupied. She must protect her mother, as she'd tried to protect him.

Belle sat rocking her child for what seemed to her an

eternity. She didn't want the spell broken, because that meant acknowledging what had happened. She looked down and met again Lucy's eyes; they seemed to be begging her for some sort of an explanation. Young as she was, Peter had been her friend and companion over the last few months. She had to tell her something.

'Lucy, listen to me,' she started gently. 'There's been an accident. Poor little Peter has died.'

'I know.' Lucy's voice was no more than a whisper. 'I saw him.'

'What do you mean you saw him?' Belle couldn't keep the sharpness out of her voice. But it wasn't directed at Lucy; it was directed at Alice who she thought must have allowed the child to go into the room before the body had been removed.

'I saw him on the bed. I was frightened because of the way Auntie Flora was looking at me. She was bending over Peter with the pillow in her hands.'

'And what happened then, Lucy?' Lucy had fallen silent as if the memory of what she'd seen was too much for her. 'What did Auntie Flora do? You must tell me; I have to know.'

'I don't know.' Lucy started to cry again. 'She pushed me out and closed the door; but I was frightened in case she put the pillow over his face. If she did that, he wouldn't be able to breathe, would he?'

'No, darling,' Belle said. 'You're quite right – he wouldn't be able to breathe. You've done the right thing by telling me, but now you must try to forget it.'

Lucy relaxed and put her thumb into her mouth, a thing she hadn't needed to do since she was a baby. The bear was still clutched under her arm. Slowly her eyes closed and her breathing deepened. When Mike came back into the room he paused for a moment in the doorway to admire the picture they made: the pretty mother with her halo of flaming hair nursing the sleeping child with unusual tenderness.

'It's late,' Belle said. 'And long past her bedtime. She's exhausted.'

'Let me help you.' Mike took the small figure in his arms and followed Belle out of the room. She led the way up the stairs.

'We can't put her in the nursery after what's happened,' she said as they reached the top landing. 'There's Flora's bed in Alice's room . . .' That didn't seem suitable either. 'She can come in my bed until we can make other arrangements.'

Belle's bed was plenty big enough for two, and she pulled back the covers so that Mike could lay the sleeping child down. She didn't stir, even when Belle tenderly removed her clothes and slipped the embroidered lawn nightdress over her dark head. The eiderdown pulled up to cover her, and a small light left on to drive away night terrors should she wake, Belle bent over and pressed a gentle kiss on the pale cheek. Then she followed Mike out of the room.

'I'll leave the door open in case she wakes up. Alice will hear her.'

There was a new determination in Belle's step as she walked down the stairs with Mike close behind. He was surprised to see her unhook a light summer jacket from the hall-stand and slip it over her dress.

'You're not going out, are you?' he asked. 'It's late.'

'I know.' She turned to face him with her hand on the door-knob. 'There's something I have to do.'

'Surely whatever it is can wait until the morning. You must be exhausted as well.'

But Belle didn't look exhausted. She always found action

293

stimulating and now she looked full of fire and energy, as if the terrible events of the evening had fuelled her to some battle she had to fight, and win.

'Oh, Mike! If I went to bed now I wouldn't be able to sleep. How could I?' and she told him in a few words what Lucy had confided in her. 'I'm going to find Flora.'

'The police will do that. It's their job, not yours. Anyway, how do you know where to look for her?'

'I don't,' Belle admitted. 'I can only guess. She likes bright lights and people. If she's done what I suspect she'll be needing a drink – more than one probably, to drown her sorrows. She could have headed for any public house that would be prepared to serve her. There are hundreds in Brighton, not to mention Hove.'

'That's what I mean. How do you know where to start looking?'

'I've no idea. I'm going to start at the one where we found her. You were with me Mike, when the landlord threw her out into the street. At least she's known there, and they might have seen her.'

'That's a rough area even in daylight. I don't think you should.'

'Don't tell me what I should or shouldn't do, Mike Walker. You're not my husband, and I do as I please.'

She stood in front of him, with her blue eyes flashing with determination and her hands on her hips. He loved her more at that moment, when she was prepared to fight him and anyone else who stood in her way, than he'd ever loved her.

'All right,' he said. 'If that's what you want to do. I can't stop you or make you see sense. But I'm coming with you.'

She was pleased; it was what she'd been hoping for but hadn't liked to ask. She had to avenge Peter's death and couldn't wait for the law to take action. While they were going through all their legal procedures and red tape Flora could slip through their fingers. After listening to Lucy's story Belle believed, without a shadow of a doubt, that her suspicions were justified. Flora had indeed murdered her own son.

In the dark street Belle slipped her arm through Mike's. It was a small enough gesture but her way of saying thank you. He pressed her hand gently with his to show her that he understood. It was very quiet, but there was a full moon and the pavements seemed flooded with silver. The trees that lined the streets in military precision shimmered in the ghostly light, and Belle hugged her jacket close around her body and shivered.

'Are you cold?' Mike asked, immediately concerned.

'No. I think someone just walked over my grave.'

They had no problem finding the public house where they'd discovered Flora. It stood out like a beacon of light amongst the rows of houses climbing the hill. The doors were wide open, and the customers seemed subdued by the warm summer evening. It appeared to be a peaceful place after the trauma of their earlier visit.

Belle hesitated in the doorway. She was used to bars and drinkers but she still found the smell of alcohol and stale smoke distasteful.

'We'll go in and have a drink,' Mike said, taking the initiative. 'Do you recognise the barman?'

'I'm not sure.' Belle studied the bluff red-faced figure pulling pints. She couldn't be sure if it was the man who'd ejected Flora into the street.

Mike ordered drinks and passed the time of day. The barman seemed friendly. They discussed the news and the weather and then Belle interrupted, thinking Mike had forgotten the reason why they were there.

'We're supposed to be meeting a friend,' she said, trying

295

to sound casual. 'Her name's Flora. I wondered if you know her?'

The barman scratched his balding head as if he was trying to activate his brain. 'We get a lot of people in here. There's at least two Florences and a Flo. What's your friend's other name?'

Belle nearly said Smart and then thought quickly. Flora would be using her married name more likely. 'Mann,' she said. 'Her name's Mrs Flora Mann.'

'Don't know anyone of that name, lady.'

Belle tried to describe Flora. 'She's about my age, with brown hair and hazel eyes,' she began, but the barman shook his head.

'I don't recall anyone of that description, tonight or any other time. Now, if you'll excuse me.' He turned away to serve another customer, having lost interest in Belle and her enquiries. They had no option but to finish their drinks and leave.

'What now?' Mike asked, waiting for Belle to take the lead.

'I've no idea. Let's try the sea-front; there are lots of late-night bars along the promenade.'

They walked down Preston Street. The shops were closed, but a few restaurants were still lit up and busy. Candles stood in dark bottles in the windows of pseudo-foreign dives, where flies hovered over spilling dustbins in back alleys and greasy slops were emptied down outside drains.

But the promenade, when they reached it, was like walking into a fairy paradise. A mile or more of twinkling lights were strung from lamp-post to lamp-post, so that the pavements were almost as light as day. The fronts of the hotels were illuminated, as were the two piers stretched out into the sea, with domes and minarets like giant mushrooms.

The clank of the turnstile mingled with distant music, and Belle grabbed Mike's hand and dragged him across the road between the busy evening traffic.

'Where are we going?'

'The West Pier. I've suddenly remembered Flora saying there's a dance-hall there. She's been there a couple of times at least.'

'Come on then.'

Mike paid their entrance fee and they pushed their way through the turnstile. Their shoes made a hollow sound on the wooden slats, and they could hear the gentle murmur of the waves breaking on the shingle below. It seemed an awfully long way to the end of the pier. Most of the tiny shops that traded in the daytime were closed and shuttered: there was no call for ice-cream or sticks of brightly coloured rock after dark. But a fish and chip bar was still doing a roaring trade, and there were still people roaming around an illuminated arcade selling funny hats and souvenirs.

The strain of the music increased and a waltz rhythm reached their ears. Mike smiled: he recognised *The Merry Widow* waltz that he always associated with Belle. Her foot-steps were slowing down as if she were tiring and he guessed her earlier burst of energy was really a cover to hide her feelings of pain.

'Let's sit down for a minute.'

He drew her to a bench set in an alcove outside the dance-hall. Through the open door the dancers whirled round and round; the women's colourful skirts swirling wide as they were propelled by their partners in time to the music. They were lucky not to have a care in the world.

'Belle,' he said softly. He took her hand, surprised at how small it was. 'This may not be the right moment, and I know how you must feel, but I want to talk to you.'

'Talking won't bring Peter back.'

'I know. But it's not about Peter; I want to talk to you about us.' She didn't interrupt as he half-expected, so he carried on. 'I've been waiting to ask you for a long time – if you'll marry me?'

'Oh, Mike!' she let out a long sigh and he pressed her hand hopefully. 'Not now.'

'Why not? You've had a bad time today with Peter, and the police and their questions. It's not going to get better for a while. You need someone to support you before you break under the strain. I love you, Belle: let me be the one.'

'No, Mike. I'm sorry.'

'Why not? Don't you love me a bit?'

'I don't know, Mike. I don't think I know what love is.'

'I don't understand you.'

'I'll try to explain.' For a long moment Belle was silent, staring out at the dark sea as if seeking inspiration. She didn't want to hurt Mike; he'd been too kind to her for that. 'I don't think I know what love is, or what I want from life. Oh, when I was younger I thought I knew it all. I wanted to be a success and get out of Duke's Road where I'd been brought up. Joseph was a stepping-stone to that new life and I thought I loved him. But it was all an illusion and it didn't last. I'm not a very nice person, Mike. You're too good for me.'

'Don't say that . . .'

'But it's true. But I really did love Peter. He was a darling baby, and even when I knew the worst about his condition I still loved him. After what she's done I have to find Flora, to bring her to justice.'

Her voice was rising ominously and Mike was frightened. If she broke down it mustn't be here, in this lonely place, where it would be difficult to summon help.

'You don't know for sure that Flora had anything to do with it. You're only surmising by what Lucy said she saw.'

'Then why did she run away?'

'I don't know. I'm just frightened that what happened today is going to become more important to you than Lucy – or me.'

'I told you that I'm not a very nice person.'

'But you are, Belle.' On impulse Mike turned and put his arms around her. She didn't push him away which was a good sign. 'You're brave and honest, and everyone who knows you admires you for the way you've coped since Joseph died. The fact that you loved that little boy so much proves that you are capable of love. You're just frightened to trust your feelings to anyone. I can wait; I want you to know that, because one day I hope you'll learn how to love me. But Lucy can't wait, she needs you now. Perhaps what's happened to Peter, although tragic, could be the best thing that could happen to Lucy, if it brings you two closer together.'

They sat there in companionable silence, the star-spangled night surrounding them like a soft blanket. The music from the dance-hall had faded away and couples, their arms around each others waists, wandered out to get their breath back. Belle envied them their easy trust and sharing. She hoped Mike was right: that one day she would be able to accept his love and give hers in return. She hoped it would be soon.

A couple passed them, and walked to the rail to look down into the water. The woman was wearing a blue dress and she was laughing gaily. Belle felt pleased for her. They leant against the rail, talking quietly, but the man must have said something annoying because the woman's voice rose angrily and she tried to push her companion away. They stood there for a moment locked in a struggle, silhouetted against the moon, and then the man made a sharp comment and walked away.

The woman turned, her hands pushing a lock of hair into place. The moonlight fell directly on to her peacock-blue dress turning it to silver, and Belle saw that it was Flora. She let out an exclamation, and jumped to her feet before Mike could stop her.

'Flora!'

'Hello, Belle. What are you doing here?' She seemed surprised and looked more uncomfortable than upset. Certainly not the behaviour of a potential murderess.

'I've been looking for you.'

'Why? You said I could have the evening off.'

Belle didn't know what to say. She glanced at Mike for guidance but he too seemed lost for words.

'What about Peter?'

'Peter! What about him?'

The casual way Flora mentioned her little son enraged Belle. The terrible words burst from her: 'You must know – he's dead!' The look on Flora's face almost made Belle think she'd made a mistake; and then she saw in her mind's eye the helpless little figure on the bed and her heart hardened. This woman wasn't the girl she'd giggled and joked with at Lena Watkins's glove factory; this woman hated her son enough to smother him with a pillow. 'And I think you killed him,' she said.

'What are you talking about?'

'Peter's dead, Flora,' Mike said, stepping out of the shadows and joining them. 'The police want to talk to you.'

Flora's face was a picture of conflicting emotions. Suddenly a wail broke from her, and before either Belle or Mike could stop her she ran past them into the shadows towards the shore. Belle reacted spontaneously and raced after her, stumbling over the legs of discarded deck-chairs. In front of her flitted the blue and silver figure and she knew she mustn't let it out of her sight. She was panting

300

with exhaustion as she neared the turnstile, hoping the barrier would slow Flora down, but she seemed to slip through effortlessly.

A sob of despair broke from Belle's throat. Then she saw the tall square shape of a uniformed policeman pacing solidly along the promenade. All she could do was shout as loudly as she could.

'Stop that woman! For God's sake stop that woman!'

The policeman heard her and stepped forward barring Flora's way. When Belle and Mike reached them he was holding the struggling Flora in a vice-like grip.

19

The newspapers had a field-day. Reporters knocked on the door at all hours of the day and night, and cameras clicked as soon as anyone appeared. At first Belle thought it was necessary, after all they were only doing their job; but as the days went by and there was no let-up she became rather tired of the unasked for publicity.

'MURDER HOUSE' screamed a popular tabloid, from its front pages in letters two inches high. Underneath was a picture of her home with the backs of Alice and Lucy disappearing through the front door. There was a crowd of sightseers around the bottom of the steps, and the little child was peeping over her shoulder in a puzzled fashion.

'Well, it's news,' Alice said grimly, slamming down her iron on the board in a vicious fashion. 'Some people have got nothing better to do.'

'I know. Mike says there'll be no let-up until the trial ends.'

'And they decide whether she's innocent or guilty?'

'Yes.'

'And then what?'

'I don't know.' Belle didn't know, but she had a vivid imagination. 'If she's found guilty of murder she could be sent to the gallows. After all, Ruth Ellis has only just been hung for the murder of her lover. They won't let her off just because she's a woman. I can't bear it, Alice. I want Peter's death avenged, but hanging a woman in cold blood seems nothing short of barbarous.'

'A lot seems to depend on that man, William Smith's story.'

'He could be lying. I never heard Flora mention anyone of that name.'

'Why should she?' Alice sighed and ironed neat creases in a cotton sheet before adding it to the pile. 'She kept quiet about a lot of things she was up to because she knew we didn't approve.'

Belle had had to make a statement about how she'd found the body and what she'd noticed about it. Of course she had mentioned the bruise, and the position of the pillow as if someone had pulled it from under his head and left it across his body.

Lucy had confided to her mother the details of the fall from the slide, and Belle had told a policewoman, not wanting the child to have to undergo questioning. She was upset enough already.

When Flora's photograph was first published, Bill Smith, already travelling through Kent, came forward, and his story was soon splashed all over the papers. How he'd met the accused a couple of times in Brighton and become friendly. She'd seemed restless and said she had no ties, so he'd asked her to accompany him. But she hadn't turned up at the appointed time or place, so he'd left without her. The most damning part of Bill's testimony was when he related the accident to the child and the way Flora had disowned him. Anyone who could do that lost sympathy with the magistrates and the public.

Flora's account of what happened on that day also lost

her support. She appeared callous and unemotional as she admitted that she'd intended running away with William Smith and leaving her child behind. She'd gone to the wrong venue: mistaking the West Pier for the Palace Pier. By the time she'd realised her mistake she was too late and he'd left without her. Her employer, Mrs Isabel Bishop, had however given her the evening off, so she'd gone dancing on the West Pier instead, fully intending to return home later. When questioned about her son, she swore an oath, that he was alive when she left him. He'd slipped off of the pillow in his sleep, and she'd picked it up and placed it beside his sleeping body. She denied fiercely the insinuation that she'd smothered the boy, and insisted that she'd cared for him, and would never have harmed him.

'I've finished the ironing,' Alice said. 'At least work keeps my mind off things and stops me brooding. But I'm worried about you, Mrs Belle. You've lost all your energy and I don't like the way you mope about the house.'

'I'm all right.'

'Aren't you going to the theatre today?'

'No. I thought I'd clear out the nursery. We can't leave it standing empty for ever and it'll make quite a nice guest-room. Lucy can stay in with me for the time being.'

'It's not for me to say, Mrs Belle, but I think it would be better for you to go back to work. I can do the nursery.'

'I know, but they told me to take as much leave as I want. I think they find me a bit of an embarrassment.' Alice stared, so Belle tried to explain. 'It's those reporters, Alice, the ones Mike sent away. Somehow they found out where I work and started making a nuisance of themselves, trying to get a story from the manager. He wasn't very pleased. I thought I'd better take the hint and stay away until the fuss died down.'

'Why can't they leave us alone and let us get on with our lives?' Alice asked indignantly, not expecting an answer.

She marched out of the room to be confronted by a figure flying at top speed down the stairs. It was Maisie Minor, their newest boarder, the prompt and understudy at the theatre that week. She was running so fast that she didn't see Alice, and ran straight into her, making her drop the pile of ironing.

'Oh dear; I am sorry,' Maisie said.

'Can't you watch where you're going?' Alice was on her hands and knees picking up her dropped linen. 'Look at these pillowcases; I'll have to press them all over again.'

'I've said I'm sorry,' and suddenly Maisie burst into loud sobs. Alice was astounded: whatever was the matter with the girl? Was she soft in the head or something?

'Here, pick these towels up for me and stop crying.' Maisie did as she was bid, and then hovered around Alice as if she were trying to pluck up courage to say something. 'Did you want something, Miss Minor?' she asked at last.

'Yes. Well, I suppose I ought to see Mrs Bishop, but perhaps you could give her a message.'

'Is something wrong?'

'Oh, no!' Maisie said a little too emphatically. 'It's just that I think she ought to know that I'm leaving.'

'When?'

'Today.'

'Today!' Alice was so taken aback that she nearly dropped the laundry for the second time. 'But it's the middle of the week. I thought your play was booked until Saturday.'

'It is.' Maisie looked embarrassed and fiddled with the belt of her dress. 'I'm moving in with another actress: the junior lead. She's got a double room right in the centre of town.'

'But why, Maisie?' asked Alice, dropping the Miss Minor. 'Aren't you happy here?'

305

'I was.' Maisie fiddled again, and looked back up the stairs as if she were frightened of being pursued. 'But it's the ghost . . .'

'Ghost!' Alice burst out laughing. 'What are you on about, you silly girl? There aren't any ghosts in this house.'

'Yes there are.' Maisie clung to Alice's arm, and the maid could see that the young woman wasn't joking: she was really frightened. 'It's that little boy who was murdered in his bed. He came into my room wearing a cap and a little grey suit. I woke up and saw him.'

'Maisie, listen to me,' Alice said in her most consoling voice. 'You've let your imagination run away with you. We're all upset about what happened, but just because Peter died doesn't mean to say he was murdered.'

'But they've arrested his mother . . .'

'I know; but only on suspicion. We've got to wait until the police have finished making enquiries. And then there'll be a trial. She may be found innocent you know.'

'Never! I think she's an evil woman.'

'We have to give her the benefit of the doubt,' Alice said nobly. 'Anyway, she's innocent until proved guilty, as they say on the pictures.'

Maisie dropped her voice in case anyone else was listening. 'Well, I think that little boy's come back from the dead to try and tell us something.'

'Nonsense; you were dreaming. It was that cheese I served up for supper last night. It was a bit strong, and it always gives me nightmares.'

Maisie clutched her arm. 'But I saw him again this morning. He was coming out of the nursery as I was leaving my room.'

Before Alice could reply Maisie screamed and pointed up the stairs to the first-floor landing. 'There he is again, just going into the bathroom. Oh, I can't stand it! This house is haunted, do you believe me now?'

'Stay here and hold this.'

Alice thrust the pile of linen into the trembling woman's hands and ran up the stairs two at a time, reaching the bathroom door just as it closed in her face. Silly woman, she said to herself: a real ghost would have floated through the panel, not turned the key with that determined click.

'Lucy!' she called. 'Unlock this door.' There was no answer so she rapped on the wood with her knuckles. 'I know you're in there. Unlock this door at once and come out.'

After a moment's silence she heard the flushing sound from the overhead cistern and grinned. There was nothing supernatural about a ghost who has to use the toilet. The key grated in the lock and the door slowly opened. Lucy stood in the doorway, an innocent little figure in a blue gingham dress and white socks.

'What are you doing?'

'Nothing, Alice. Just going to the lavatory.'

Alice pushed her aside, her eyes searching the small room. There was only a bath, wash-basin and linen basket, but she soon found what she was looking for tucked down behind the radiator: a screwed-up jacket and shorts and an old cap.

'You naughty girl.' Alice waved the cap under the child's nose. 'Don't you know it's wicked trying to frighten people? Poor Miss Minor was really scared. Did you go into her room last night?'

'Yes, Alice.'

'Wearing Peter's clothes?'

'Yes, Alice.'

'But why on earth . . .? It was a dreadful thing to do.'

'I'm sorry.' Lucy stared at the maid as if she wasn't a bit

sorry, and she hardened her heart. Much as she loved the little girl she couldn't imagine what motive there could have been behind her cruel impersonation. 'I'd been dreaming that Mummy loved Peter more than me, and when I woke up I saw his clothes folded on a chair. I thought if I looked like a boy she'd love me too, so I put them on and went looking for her. But I was sleepy and must have gone into the wrong room.'

'It was very naughty, Lucy. I don't know what could have come over you.'

'I said I'm sorry.' Lucy stopped giggling and a sullen look settled on her childish face. 'You won't tell Mummy will you?'

'I certainly will, you naughty girl. And if I don't Miss Minor will. She's so frightened she wants to leave, and you know how important it is for us to have every room full. You're to go downstairs right this minute and apologise.'

'I won't! You can't make me.'

'Yes I can you wicked girl. Come here this instant.'

Alice grabbed for Lucy's hand but the child evaded her. Quick as lightning she slipped past the bulkier figure of Alice and ran down the stairs.

'Stop her!' Alice yelled, leaning over the banisters and waving her arms at Maisie Minor.

The startled woman dropped the pile of sheets she was still clutching and put out a detaining hand, but Lucy was too quick for her. The front door was standing half-open, and without slowing down she ran through the opening and down the steps.

Alice reproached herself afterwards, when she had time to think clearly. She'd felt so cross she'd only half listened to Lucy's explanation as to why she'd dressed up in Peter's clothes. She should have felt sorry for the child who found it necessary to dress herself in a dead boy's clothes to try to win her mother's love; not told her off and frightened her into running away. Hot in pursuit, she might have caught up with Lucy quickly if she hadn't become entangled in the fallen laundry, which after all the excitement and being passed from hand to hand was now littered all over the hall.

Lucy had no idea where she was running to. She might have turned to the right, towards the school; or left, to become entangled in the many little streets branching from the area called the Seven Dials. Or she could have tried to run across the road and been knocked over by a bus or a lorry.

As luck would have it she didn't get the choice, because on reaching the bottom of the steps she ran head-first into a man who was standing on the pavement. He was carrying a basket on his arm full of vegetables, and the impact of the child made him spill carrots, onions, and potatoes all over the ground. A big cabbage bounced into the road and was shredded by passing wheels. It was George Kelly, on an uninvited visit to his daughter.

'Hey there,' he said, looking down at the child with a smile. 'What's the hurry?'

'I'm running away.'

Lucy recognised George. It was the nice man who'd come to see them on Christmas Day, and had played with her and Peter. Her mother had told her he was her granddad: although she still wasn't sure what a granddad was.

'Does your mother know?' George asked, calmly picking up the vegetables and returning them to his basket.

'No,' Lucy said, handing him a carrot.

'And where were you thinking of running away to, Lucy? It is Lucy, isn't it?' said the kindly man who had once told her that Lucy was his favourite name.

'London,' said Lucy quickly, being the first place she could think of.

'That's a long way. You'd have to go in a train, and you'll need money for the fare.'

'I've got sixpence in my money-box.'

'Not enough I'm afraid. I'll tell you what . . .' George seemed to have an unexpected idea and his smile won Lucy over with its brightness. 'I live in Duke's Road. That's only a bus ride away, so you could afford to run away and stay with me.'

'Could I? Would sixpence be enough?'

'More than enough. But I think we ought to go and ask your Mam first; so that she won't be worried.'

Lucy was happy to take her grandfather's rough hand and let him lead her back up the steps. She liked everything about him: from his baggy working trousers hitched up with braces, to the cloth-cap set straight on his greying hair. He liked everything about Lucy too, although she wasn't a bit like her mother to look at. Some sort of throwback, he wondered, to old Bridget Kelly. She certainly reminded him of someone, but he couldn't think who it was.

They met a flustered Alice in the doorway, with Maisie still hovering helplessly in the background. She recognised George as Mrs Belle's father, and didn't like to tell the naughty child off in front of him. Instead she tried to smile, and stood aside for him to enter.

'It's Mr Kelly, isn't it, sir? Mrs Belle will be pleased to see you, I'm sure. She's in the kitchen; I'll go and tell her you're here.'

'There's no need.' George loosened Lucy's hand so that he could remove his cap and tuck it in his pocket. 'Lucy can show me the way. I think kitchens are the best rooms in the house.'

'Why?'

'Because they're the heart of the house, where the best

310

things happen. It's always warm there because of the cooking and eating; and everybody's busy because there's so much to do.'

'We don't eat in the kitchen. We've got a dining-room,' Lucy said, stating a fact. 'But sometimes I eat at the table with Alice because I make a mess. I like that.'

'If you come and stay with me you can eat in the kitchen every day, because I haven't got a dining-room.'

'Haven't you?'

Lucy looked at George, surprised that anyone could be so lucky as to live in a house without a dining-room. She found theirs too big and formal, with its long table, dresser full of china, and the big roll-topped desk in the window.

'Mummy, it's Granddad,' Lucy said excitedly, pulling George through the doorway. Belle was sitting listlessly at the scrubbed table, deep in thought. Her face brightened when she saw who the visitor was.

'Oh, Dada, I am pleased to see you again; and so is Lucy by the look of her.'

'It's a sad time for you all,' George said, putting down his basket. 'I read all about it in the papers, so I thought I'd bring you a present from the allotment. You can see I've made good use of those tools you gave me.'

Belle picked up a carrot and sank her teeth into the raw juicy flesh. 'They taste as good as ever. I always said you had green fingers.'

'Have you Granddad?' Lucy uncurled his hands and peered at the palms. They didn't look green to her. Just pink like everybody else's, with hard skin from handling a spade. She copied Belle, biting into a carrot, surprised at how good it tasted: as scrunchy as an apple, only sweeter. Alice made her eat boiled carrots sometimes, saying that they would help her to see in the dark. She thought they were horrible, and as she was never allowed out after dark she didn't see why she had to eat them. 'I'm running away,' she announced. 'I've got sixpence in my money-box and Granddad says that's enough for the fare.'

'I ran away once,' Belle said, smiling at the remembrance. 'I'd had a telling off for being late home from school. Mam said I couldn't have any tea so I said I was going to run away.'

'What happened?' Lucy was interested. She couldn't imagine her mother as a little girl, although she supposed she must have been once, a long time ago.

'I got as far as the church and then it started to rain. I met Father Joe and he lent me his umbrella on condition I went straight back home.'

Lucy wanted to ask who Father Joe was, but the two grown-ups were happily laughing at their recollections. She was so pleased to see her mother smiling again that she didn't want to butt in and spoil everything.

'So I thought,' George was saying, 'that she could come and stay with Maud and me. Just until after the inquest. It's no place for a child, being photographed and hounded by reporters. And it'll give you a break.'

'It's very kind of you,' Belle said thoughtfully. 'It would make things a bit easier I admit. Once the court case is over they'll soon lose interest in us and we shall be able to get back to normal. It's bad enough for me, but Peter was her only friend and I still don't think she really understands that she'll never see him again.'

'We worried about you in the same way when Charlie died.'

'You did; but Mam only thought about herself.' Old wounds were being opened, wounds that she'd thought had healed years before. She was surprised to find that the pain was still there.

'Don't say that, Belle,' George said gently. 'You were only a child. You didn't understand.'

'I understood that it was always Charlie this, and Charlie that. She never had time for me.'

'That wasn't her fault. She did try when you were a baby, but you were always an independent little thing. You didn't seem to need her, or anybody – but Charlie did.'

Belle fell silent. She'd never thought that the rift between her and Bess could have been partly of her own making. She looked at Lucy, still munching her carrot greedily. Mothers and daughters, she thought: was it always so hard for them to get on and understand each other?

'Have you seen Mam lately?'

'Yes. There's no change. They say she could go on for years, or she could just slip away quietly. I suppose that would be best. I mean, she's not going to get any better.'

Poor Dada, Belle thought. His voice was still gentle when he spoke about his wife, although she was in the way of his making an honest woman of Maud. But Maud Carter would wait for him. There he was, grey-haired and bent, but he'd been a bridge for her when she was a child, and now he was offering the same for Lucy. A bridge out of stormy waters into a quiet harbour. They fell silent, and then Belle became aware of Lucy standing watching them, a question in her eyes.

'I can go with Granddad, can't I?' she asked.

Belle looked over the child's head at George. He nodded and winked.

'Of course you can,' she said, pleased but sad at the way Lucy's face lit up. It would be good for the child to get away from the memories the house held for her, but sad because she seemed so keen to go. Maud Carter would be at Duke's Road, but her opinion of that woman had changed since the visit on Christmas Day. At first Belle had only invited the

313

woman into her house out of politeness and it being the season of goodwill, but afterwards she'd had to admit that the blowzy creature was good company. Everyone had taken to her, and she'd organised games and helped Alice in the kitchen as if she'd been doing it all her life.

'You'll need some things,' Belle told the excited child. 'We'll go and get them now, shall we?'

'Don't pack much,' George shouted after them as they headed upstairs. 'Just a change of clothes.'

'I must take Teddy,' Lucy whispered as she helped her mother pack the folded clothes into a little cardboard suitcase. 'He'd miss me.'

She insisted on carrying the case downstairs herself, and under her other arm was tucked the beloved bear who was rapidly becoming quite bald in places from too much loving. She walked trustingly up to her grandfather, who was waiting on the front step, and slipped her hand into his.

Belle bent down to kiss her daughter goodbye, and there was an unexpected lump in her throat as she watched the two figures walk away. They stopped at the corner to turn around and wave for the last time, and then she hurried back into the house and closed the front door. Alice was waiting for her in the hall.

'It's that Mr Newman,' she said. 'He insists on speaking to you. I told him you were busy but he says it's important, and can't wait. He's in the dining-room.'

'Thank you, Alice,' Belle said, crossing the hall towards the half-open door. 'I'll go and see what he wants.'

Basil Newman and his wife Margaret were the latest in the succession of boarders. They were appearing in the Noel Coward play, *Hay Fever*, at the little theatre perched on the end of the Palace Pier. They were different types of artists to the ones Belle was used to. Older, and rather set in their ways, they'd insisted on single beds and meals served in the privacy of their room. It was making extra work for everybody, but if they were satisfied with their accommodation Belle was hoping they'd recommend her to their friends. She saw her little boarding-house attaining the status of a small hotel, given time, with celebrities staying there.

Mr Newman was standing in the window in front of Joseph's desk staring out into the garden. He was a tall thin man in a dark suit relieved by a flowery cravat, and an eyeglass that Belle suspected was only for show. He turned around as she entered the room and inserted the glass into one eye, screwing up his face to hold it in place. He looked slightly ridiculous. Belle had to compose her face to stop herself smiling.

'Alice said you wanted to talk to me, Mr Newman,' she said politely.

'Yes indeed, Mrs Bishop,' he said in rather theatrical tones, dropping the glass so that it swung to and fro across his waistcoat on a black silk ribbon. 'My wife, Margaret, is very upset.'

'I'm sorry to hear that. Is your room unsatisfactory?'

'No, no. We're very comfortable. But when we booked in on Monday you didn't tell us about the murder.'

'No,' Belle replied calmly, trying to keep the irritation out of her voice. 'I didn't see any reason to – in any case we still don't know for sure that it was a murder.'

'But a little boy died.'

'Yes. We were very fond of him. It was sad, but life has to go on.'

'That's what I told Margaret.'

'So what's the problem?'

'We've decided to leave today and find other accommodation. You see, we had a child once, a son, and he died. Margaret is still very sensitive about these things.'

'I'm sorry, Mr Newman. I didn't know.'

315

'So I'm sure you understand; and of course we'll expect a refund.'

'Whatever you want.' Belle opened the door, anxious to bring the interview to an end. 'We haven't tried to keep the matter a secret you know; we just didn't think it was anybody else's business. Most of our regular boarders are too busy with their own lives to be interested. Some aren't even aware of what happened.'

'I think you're wrong there, Mrs Bishop.' Basil Newman had crossed to the door, but paused dramatically to deliver his last line. 'I've talked to most of them, and they, like my wife and myself, were quite surprised that you hadn't been frank with us. I think several feel as we do and are thinking of moving elsewhere. We thought it was our duty to enlighten them.'

'I'm sure you did!'

He minced past Belle into the hall and she watched him climb the stairs. Alice was standing in the kitchen doorway and they exchanged glances.

'The Newmans are leaving – that makes three with Miss Minor. I wonder who'll be next?'

'Because of Peter?'

'Yes. I thought actors were worldly characters who took the highs and lows of life in their stride. I even thought if they found out they might take a morbid interest in the details. I was prepared to cope with that.'

'They're just human beings, Mrs Belle, like you and me. They don't want tragedy to touch their safe little worlds. Don't worry, it'll blow over and everyone will forget.'

'I hope so.'

'But I think you did the right thing sending Lucy away. She's usually so good, but she's been getting up to all sorts of mischief. And your father seems a kind man; she'll be safe with him.'

316

Belle smiled. 'I know. But the house will seem empty without any children.'

'You mustn't brood, Mrs Belle,' Alice said firmly. 'Why don't you go out somewhere? You need a break to take your mind off things. I'll see to Mr and Mrs Newman – and try to talk some sense into the others before they start to get ideas.'

'That would be nice. Mike's always complaining that I'm too busy to go out with him.' Belle looked at her watch. 'He's usually in by now; if I go and change I can surprise him.'

Alice was pleased to see how Belle's face had lit up at her suggestion. 'Put on your green dress, and the little hat that goes with it, then he won't be able to resist you.'

The green dress was her favourite and a perfect complement to her red hair. She dressed carefully; twirling in front of the long mirror to admire her reflection. She was twenty-five and still young enough to be interested in her appearance. But gone were the days when she bought indiscriminately and needed new clothes for every occasion, just to keep up with the current fashion. Now she bought to last. Simple, classic designs that showed off her full womanly figure to perfection.

She painted her lips a delicate pink and powdered her nose, frowning as usual over the sprinkling of freckles. They were always worse in the summer and she still hadn't found a remedy for them. Her coppery hair curled round the little green hat that she wore tilted slightly to one side. She smiled with pleasure. Mike would be pleased with the trouble she'd taken. As a final touch she dabbed perfume behind her ears and tucked a clean lace handkerchief into her belt, before running down the stairs like a child going to a party.

The basement door was closed and there was no sign of

life. She guessed Mike and his brother, Johnnie, were relaxing over a meal. She knocked twice, her heart sinking slightly: had she gone to all this trouble only to be disappointed? But no, at the third knock she heard footsteps approaching and was so relieved that when the door opened she spun on her heel to show off her dress and said gaily, 'I'm glad you're in, Mike. I'm banking on you taking me out to dinner.'

'I'm sorry, Belle,' Johnnie said, for it was Mike's young brother who opened the door. 'Mike's been called away. He won't be home for the rest of the week – he told me to tell you but I haven't had the time.'

20

'Get up on the bed and keep still. We're not going to hurt you. '

The bed was narrow, the thin mattress covered with a cold waterproof cover. Wearing only the stiff cotton night-dress the prison had issued, Flora climbed up obediently. The lights were so bright and the room so bare that she felt like a guinea-pig about to be vivisected. She screwed up her eyes against the unshaded bulb hanging directly overhead and tried to pretend she was somewhere else.

'Open your mouth.'

Flora's eyes flew open. The nurse had retreated to a corner of the room and was unwinding a huge rubbery tube. It reminded Flora of pictures she'd seen of poisonous snakes. The nurse's place had been taken by an elderly doctor wearing gold-rimmed glasses who was bending over her, his fingers searching for her pulse. He looked kindly but she hoped he wouldn't be able to find it. Then he'd have to pronounce her dead and they'd all leave her alone.

'Pardon?' she said, dragging herself back to the events in hand.

He took the opportunity while her jaws were unclenched, to ram the end of the tube into her mouth, holding her nose with his other hand so that her eyes streamed with tears of pain.

'Relax,' he instructed. 'Just swallow and it'll soon be over.'

The end of the horrible tube made her gag. She arched her back on the hard bed and tried to turn her head away from her tormentor. But the nurse had joined the doctor, and while one held her still with a muscular elbow in her stomach, the other forced the tube down her throat until she longed to scream with the pain and humiliation. They carried on a conversation over her prostrate body as though she was of no account and couldn't hear them.

'What did she take, nurse?'

'Aspirin I think. One of the warders found her slumped in her cell.'

'How many?'

'No idea. Not enough to kill herself if that's what she intended. They're all the same: attention seekers.'

'Do you know where she got them?'

'Saved them up, doctor. At least that's what they usually do. Keep complaining about headaches, and then hiding them away until they think they've got enough. We try to watch when we issue any medication, but they're up to all the tricks of the trade. Hiding them under their tongues, and then spitting them out instead of swallowing them is the usual way.'

'Then we'd better make the experience so unpleasant for this one that she'll think twice before trying again.' The doctor spoke in such a gentle voice that Flora, looking up into his eyes, couldn't believe the expression she saw there. He was enjoying himself, she would swear. His eyes were glistening with suppressed excitement and he was licking his lips in anticipation. 'Relax,' he said again as Flora tried to fight back. 'If you make it difficult for us, my dear, we'll have to force the tube up your nose instead, and that really is painful. So it's up to you; one way or the other we'll pump the poison out of you.'

When it came the vile-smelling concoction of fluid and bile missed the waiting bucket and spattered their spotless uniforms. They exchanged furious glances and continued with added force. It took two hours to complete the job, and they both looked exhausted when the prisoner had been punished enough.

The pain was terrible. As they carried her back to her cell, which she shared with two other women, she was still vomiting blood through cracked lips. The others were at work in the prison laundry and she would have the luxury of being left alone for a while; even though the spy-hole in the door meant she was constantly under surveillance.

The last few weeks had been a nightmare: she woke sometimes imagining that the things that had happened to her were still a dream. She tried hard not to think about Peter, who was dead, and who she was accused of killing. She hadn't done it, she remembered that, even though in her heart of hearts she'd wished many times to be released from her responsibilities. But she hadn't killed him. Even she couldn't do an awful thing like that. On the fateful day she'd stood beside his bed looking down on his little body with the pillow in her hands, and for one fleeting second she'd realised how easy it would be; but then Lucy had interrupted her and she'd thrown down the pillow. Belle loved the boy; she would give him a home and Flora would have her freedom.

She'd packed some things in a bag and slipped out to meet Bill. A new life was what she'd craved: travelling about the countryside where no one would find her. But she'd gone to the wrong pier, and Bill had waited and when she didn't turn up he'd left without her. It was the same old story: she'd messed things up again. Well, Belle had said she could have the evening off after looking after the children all day so she'd gone dancing instead. The first news she'd heard about her son's death was Belle's announcement on the end of the pier.

But no one believed Flora's story. They'd asked why she'd run away. She'd tried to explain about being upset and wanting to run home to see for herself, not away, like a guilty person would.

So what had she to live for? Her son was dead and her life in ruins. She didn't think she could face the magistrates' court and all the questioning. So she'd taken matters into her own hands and tried to end it all; but she'd even failed in that. The handful of pills she'd secreted wasn't enough to do the job properly. Perhaps if she was convicted the hangman would make a better job of it.

They said you were innocent until a court of law found you guilty, so she couldn't understand why she'd been sent to this prison for female offenders. Everyone was awaiting trial for some offence or another, but the degradation they lived in while they waited was a punishment in itself.

She would never forget that day, only a few weeks before, when she'd stood in the dock and been remanded in custody, pending enquiries and a post-mortem. Then there'd been the drive in the van with the blacked-out windows, through the Sussex countryside towards the women's prison which was to be her home until they decided what to do with her. Two policemen in dark uniforms and a young policewoman built like an Amazon accompanied her. They were very kind, offering her barley-sugar sweets and trying to chat about the villages and towns they were passing through; but Flora refused to be aroused from her misery. It was all right for them. When they'd handed her over at the prison gates they'd be free to go about their business, while she, who loved freedom more than anything, would be locked up in a cell in some monstrous building.

The exterior of the prison was not as forbidding as she'd expected. It was a long, low structure behind high walls, with many gates where passwords had to be exchanged. In the courtyard women in grey shapeless garments were pounding around with stony expressions on their faces. It was exercise time, and they were supervised by a large woman in a blue uniform with H.M.P. stamped on the sleeve.

In the reception area she'd been strip-searched by a female warder, who handled her roughly and grinned all the time as if she enjoyed Flora's discomfiture. Then she'd been handed a garment similar to the ones she'd seen the women wearing in the yard, grey in colour and made of coarse material, cheap toiletries, a towel and a nightdress. She'd watched as her own belongings were labelled and packed away in brown paper.

Next she'd been ushered into a room where an officer, who was obviously of senior rank, sat behind a desk rustling a sheaf of papers. There was nowhere for her to sit, although by now she was so tired that she felt almost fit to drop. She stood on a square piece of carpet in front of the officer's desk, and waited for what seemed an interminable time while he ignored her. At last he stacked his papers neatly, consulted his watch, and then looked up as if surprised to see her.

'Name?'

'Flora Mann.'

'From now on you'll answer to A77964 . You will work in the kitchens, under supervision of course. And try to keep out of trouble.'

A warder who was standing right behind her prodded

her in the small of the back. She thought that this was a signal to say she'd been dismissed, but as she turned away she saw the officer still regarding her and his expression looked more human.

'Just a word of advice,' he said. 'Don't tell anyone what you're in here for. Anyone who's committed an offence against children gets a bad time.'

'But I'm innocent!' The words burst from Flora's lips before she could stop them.

'That's not for you to decide. I'm only warning you. By the way, they've given you leave to attend the funeral when the body's released. Do you want to go?'

Flora nodded; but the sudden reminder made her eyes flood again with tears. Much as she dreaded it she had a duty to her son. She only hoped the authorities would make it easy for her. It was the publicity she dreaded.

The formalities over, she was taken to her cell. It was a bare room with a barred window, containing the basic comforts and necessities for three women. There were bunk beds along one wall, and a single in line with the door. Flora guessed this was hers, because the others were made up with coarse sheets and army blankets. A pile of bedlinen was folded on the thin flock mattress of the third bed, and she made it carefully, glad of something to do.

She was just tucking in the last corner when her companions entered and Flora was glad to see that they appeared friendly, if curious. She remembered the officer's warning and was careful not to give away the reason for her being there.

The two women introduced themselves as Joan and Dorothy. They were happy to tell Flora all about themselves, expecting her to be interested. Flora listened politely: after all, if she had to share a cell with them she might as well try and be friendly in return.

324

Joan, a woman in her forties with gaps in her teeth and prematurely grey hair, told her story in excited little bursts. 'It's the drink that's to blame – they wanted to send me to a psychiatric hospital to dry me out – during one of my binges I attacked a policeman – I cut one of them up so badly he had to be stitched up – thirty stitches to his face, and they think he'll lose the sight in one eye.' She sounded almost proud of her achievement, and not a bit sorry for the injured policeman.

The other woman, Dorothy, was about Flora's age. A merry extrovert, who was doing time for burglary. She had a partner, a man ten years her senior, who she admitted was her lover. He'd left her to take the rap for their last break-in, where they'd stolen silver and jewellery worth hundreds of pounds from a country house. Dorothy didn't seem a bit repentant for her crime; just sorry she'd been caught.

'Paul will be waiting for me outside. I'll join him as soon as they let me out. He's planning something really big and if it's successful he's promised to marry me. We're going to live somewhere abroad – in luxury.'

The loud clanging of a bell had brought their reminiscences to an abrupt end, and Flora was given her first introduction to the dining-room, and prison fare. Cold meat, hacked into grey wedges, and limp green salad, with chunks of stale bread spread thickly with margarine. Biscuits, hard enough to break your teeth, washed down with stewed tea black and steaming, in chipped enamel mugs that could have done with a good scouring.

But she was hungry and felt better when she'd eaten. Around her women shrieked and scrambled for the last hunks of bread as if they were starving, although there was plenty to go round. Food seemed to be the only thing they got pleasure from. Flora was glad when the meal ended.

When she saw her cell-mates, Dorothy and Joan, get up from the table and head for the door she started to follow them.

A hand, with a grip like a vice, clamped itself around her upper-arm, and a voice hissed in her ear, 'And where do you think you're going?'

Flora didn't know what to answer. She could say, 'To my cell,' but that sounded stupid: as if anybody would go there voluntarily. To say, 'To my room,' sounded even sillier. So she just stood there trying not to look stupid. The female warder, for that was who it was, although her muscles were those of a wrestler, then asked, 'Laundry or kitchen?'

'Kitchen,' Flora answered, remembering the officer's words.

'Then clear the tables and load the trolleys. I know it's your first day but hard work never did anybody any harm.'

Flora joined a team of women prisoners who were silently wheeling the empty trolleys between the rows of tables. They didn't talk, and the only sound was the clatter of spoons and enamel plates and mugs. She was handed a bucket of luke-warm soda water and a greasy rag, and followed behind, wiping down the surfaces as instructed. When the dining-room was cleared to the warder's satisfaction she followed behind the trail of grey-garbed women as they pushed their loads along a cold bare corridor to the kitchen.

The corridor had been cold and draughty, but the kitchen was stifling, as the rows of ovens were already baking the following day's fare. The cook, who had a round red face and black beady eyes that darted to and fro like a curious bird's, immediately spotted the newcomer and summoned her over.

'You,' she said in quite a friendly voice. 'Can you make bread?'

'Yes,' said Flora. She'd sometimes helped Alice when

she'd tried her hand at home bakery.

'Knead that then.'

Flora found herself standing over a huge basin with her hands wrist deep in a glutinous mound of grey dough. She hadn't even had a chance to wash her hands. She began to work the mixture until her back ached and her arms felt as though they would drop off. She didn't dare stop because the cook worked beside her busily: hacking away with a chopper at a bloody piece of meat, and tossing fatty portions into a stewpot on the stove behind her.

So began Flora's initiation into the life of the kitchens. The prisoners did the donkey-work, the scrubbing and the cleaning, until their hands were cracked and bleeding. They cleared the tables and pushed the endless trail of trolleys carrying evil-smelling food to the dining-room, so that when they finally sat down they had no appetite. After all, who would fancy drinking vegetable soup when they'd seen the cook tasting it and shuddering. The only chore they weren't allowed to do was anything that involved knives, in case they got fancy ideas. So chopping vegetables was out, as was slicing and buttering bread.

'Anyone would think I was convicted already,' Flora muttered to herself one day soon after her futile suicide attempt, as she made her third trek of the day with the heavy trolley. As she entered the room the warder with the muscles like iron called her over.

'The doctor wants to see you,' she said. 'Follow me.'

'Not again,' Flora sighed.

She was fed up with being questioned and prodded by these faceless officials. If they were so convinced of her guilt that they treated her like a criminal already, why didn't they just say so and then leave her alone? She was too tired to fight back anyway, and it would be a relief to admit to anything they wanted, even if it was a lie.

She was shown into a bright consulting room that even had patterned curtains at the windows. There was a long examination couch against one wall, padded with green leather cushions, and the desk-top had a potted plant in full bloom upon it. The doctor who sat behind the desk and motioned Flora to a chair was quite young, and handsome as well. He had sleek blond hair and a pale blue linen suit that looked expensive and matched the colour of his eyes. The heavy gold ring on his left hand, and the photograph of the beautiful woman by his telephone, showed that he was happily married.

'I'm Hugo Price,' he said, smiling at Flora. 'I'm a medical psychiatrist and I've been asked to see you.'

'What for?' She didn't like the word psychiatrist. They treated mad people; and she wasn't mad – or was she?

'I have to write a report for the magistrates' court before your case is heard. So I thought we could have a little chat and you could tell me, in your own words, what happened. Take your time; anything you say will be just between you and me, and needn't go any further unless I feel it necessary.'

Flora relaxed. This was more like it: at last someone was going to listen to her and treat her like a human being. This man was on her side, that was the main thing.

She told her story in fits and starts, with some prompting from Doctor Price, who didn't even seem to be taking notes. He was doodling casually on his blotting-pad. She told about Peter falling from the slide and being sick on the way home; and the way she'd put him to bed as a caring mother should.

'And you didn't call a doctor?'

'No, why should I? It was only a fall. He was always falling about.'

'But surely the symptoms you describe, vomiting and

sleepiness, were signs that he could have been suffering from concussion?'

'I never thought of that.'

'Or were you hoping that the fall might be fatal if you didn't get treatment on time?'

'Whose side are you on?'

'Yours of course, Flora. I can call you Flora, can't I? I'm on your side, whether you're innocent or guilty.'

'But I am innocent!' Even to her own ears the emphasis put on the word innocent sounded false.

'You think you are . . .'

'I am!'

She was getting angry, and wondered if this was what Dr Price intended. To goad her on until she snapped and said what he wanted to hear. Well, she wasn't born yesterday, she'd keep her temper under control and try to win his sympathy. She needed an ally if she didn't want to spend years in this prison, like some of the women she'd spoken to who had learnt to be content with their lot and seemed to have forgotten what life was like outside the gates. Flora valued her freedom and would go to any lengths to regain it, even if it meant telling lies.

Hugo Price leaned back in his chair and smiled. He was so good-looking that her heart missed a beat; she could fall in love with a man like this even if he was a doctor. The expression on his face was kind and he looked as if he liked her as well. She sat upright in her chair and pulled her shoulders back, tilting her chin provocatively, only too aware of the horrible prison dress and lack of make-up.

Doctor Price looked at the young woman in front of him sadly. This was the part of an interview he always hated: when he had to encourage them to relax so that they would unburden themselves, and then use their confidences against them. But it was part of his job and he'd taught himself not to be too sensitive to the tragedies he met every day, working in the closed community of a prison. He guessed that this woman was imagining herself in love with him, and he only had to pander to her fantasies to get at the truth.

'Now, Flora,' he said kindly. 'I want you to tell me about Peter.'

'Why? Peter's dead.' Saying the words brought the fact home to her. She allowed a stray tear to run down her cheek and didn't wipe it away.

'Did you kill him?'

'No!'

Doctor Price noticed the pain in her voice and saw the tears. He looked into the moist hazel eyes that were staring at him from under heavy lids, and the full mouth that couldn't help pouting sensually even at a moment like this. This woman would react to any male who showed an interest in her. He knew that this was the moment to get under her skin and get her to admit the truth while her defences were down.

'I think you've been very brave, Flora,' he said gently. 'You've had a sad life. A failed marriage through no fault of your own, and then a lover who was violent towards you. But through it all you still cared for your son. It must have been difficult for you.'

'It was.' Now the tears were genuine and Flora wasn't using them to get attention. 'Peter was such a good baby.'

'And even when he was diagnosed as epileptic, you still stood by him.'

'Yes.'

'Then your friend, Mrs Bishop, gave you a home. You went to work for her, taking Peter with you.'

'Belle has a child too: a daughter. So they were company for each other.'

330

'It sounds like an ideal arrangement.'

'It was – at first.'

'So, what happened to change things?'

'I met a man. I fell in love. I'm still young enough for a man to find me attractive, doctor.'

'Of course you are, Flora. I think you're very attractive.' Flora took the bait and preened herself; tossing her unwashed hair out of her eyes as if she were a girl on her first date. 'I'm sure the judge will take a sympathetic view of your case. After all, a healthy child is a burden, and a sick one, like Peter, must have drained you. A magistrate would understand if you broke under the strain.'

'That's it,' Flora said, almost triumphantly. 'It was too much for me. I thought I was going to break down, and there was Peter fast asleep on the bed and Bill waiting for me, so I . . .'

'Put the pillow on his face?'

Flora had to think fast. She had been going to say 'So I ran away.' But Hugo Price was sympathetic and seemed to understand. If she said 'no' he might think she was being difficult, but if she said 'yes' he might fight for the court to show compassion. Sometimes she did indeed wonder if she'd given in to the feeling that had overwhelmed her when she'd stood at Peter's bedside. If she had placed the pillow over his face and held it there – was it a fact, and not just something she'd imagined? Doctor Price was waiting for an answer. She must say something before he lost patience with her. He repeated the question.

'Flora, did you or did you not put the pillow over Peter's face.'

His sympathy was more important to her than his enmity.

'Yes,' she said in a low voice.

'And held it there with the intention of killing him?'

331

'Yes.'

Doctor Price stopped looking at her. He'd started writing rapidly, covering a sheet of paper in front of him with his small neat handwriting. Why didn't he look at her, tell her not to worry, that everything was going to be all right, because he understood and was going to stand by her?

'Doctor Price.'

'Yes, Mrs Mann?' He was looking at her again, but the smile had gone now that it had served its purpose. His eyes were cold and grey, and he was tapping his fingers on the polished wood of the desk-top impatiently. Why had she thought him handsome? He was just a man with unnaturally blond hair and an effeminate manner. 'Did you want to add anything?' He looked at his watch. 'I have another patient waiting for me.'

'No,' Flora said forlornly. 'I don't want to add anything.'

On the strength of her confession to Doctor Price Flora was persuaded to plead guilty, but a request was made for compassion on the grounds of diminished responsibility.

She was driven to the court in a dark prison van, and sat in an underground cell waiting to be called. There was no clock, and her watch had been stolen by a fellow prisoner, so she had no way of judging the passing of time. She could have asked the two policewomen who sat with her, but they were too interested in discussing their prospective boyfriends. One did remember her existence when she was unwrapping a bar of chocolate, and offered her a piece. It was Flora's favourite kind, but she shook her head dumbly: the imagined taste of the chocolate made her stomach turn over. After an eternity of waiting the door clanged open and a cheerful policeman beckoned her.

'Come on, love. They're waiting for you.'

Flora followed his dark figure up the stairs. Someone had

lent her a navy-blue suit and a pair of black court shoes, but the person who owned them was at least two sizes larger than her. She had to keep hitching the skirt up and wished she dared ask for the loan of a safety-pin, and the shoes slapped their heels up and down as she walked. At least they'd let her wash her hair, and she'd even managed to find a lipstick somewhere, and that gave her much needed confidence.

The cell had been gloomy, and the bright lights in the courtroom dazzled her eyes so that she put up her hand to shield them. So many people: rows and rows of them, some in gowns and some in civilian clothes, all staring in her direction.

'Good luck,' the policeman whispered. 'Soon be over.'

Then she was in the dock; her eyes lowered so that she wouldn't have to look at the judge who kept clearing his throat as if he had a cold. She didn't want to look at the man who held her future in his hands. She was allowed to sit down, and was glad of that because her brain kept losing track of the things that were going on around her. It would have been awful if she'd fainted.

She watched Doctor Price stand up and tell his story. She wondered why she'd thought him so handsome, because now, in a dark suit, he looked very ordinary. He read her admission of guilt to a shocked courtroom and Flora wondered why she'd been so stupid as to allow him to trick her. He was followed by a succession of witnesses including Bill Smith who she hardly recognised, and Alice Battey who told her story about finding the body. But then Belle was called to the stand and a stir of interest ran round the court.

After the homely figure of Alice and the way she answered the questions put to her in a monotonous voice, Belle was a refreshing change. She'd dressed carefully for the occasion in a brown dress with yellow trimmings, and had attempted to tame her hair with a tortoiseshell comb, but nothing could hide her physical attraction. In a soft voice she answered the questions as honestly as she was able, but when asked if she had suspected her friend of being the cause of the little boy's death she had to admit that she had.

Flora clenched her fists in her lap so that the nails almost made the skin on her palms bleed. Belle had been her oldest friend, and now even she had turned against her. In her tortured brain she had to blame someone for her misfortunes, and the pretty woman on the witness-stand, who was being listened to with evident admiration, filled her with jealousy and hatred. It was Belle who had alerted the police and was the cause of all her troubles. When this was all over and she was free again she'd get her own back. Belle Kelly had better look out because she, Flora Smart, would pay her out, however long it might take.

After Belle the pathologist came forward. He cleared his throat and glanced at his notes before telling the court his conclusions. 'I carried out a post-mortem, and in my opinion the child Peter's death was caused by an attack of epilepsy, probably aggravated by the fall. He had inhaled vomit, and if the accused had indeed tried to smother him, she would have been too late, because he was most certainly dead already.'

After that the case was wound up quickly. Flora couldn't be convicted of murder if her son had died of natural causes. The case was concluded.

21

'Tell me about the allotment again, Grandda.'

George and Lucy were sitting on the back doorstep sharing a sandwich. It was an early day in November and still warm for the time of year, although the child was wearing a tartan kilt and a green sweater that was too big for her. It reached almost to her bony knees, and the sleeves were rolled up so that her hands were free. Belle would have been horrified at her ungainly appearance, but Lucy didn't care. She knew she wouldn't ever be pretty so she'd decided to try to be interesting instead. Anyhow, in Duke's Road clothes were worn for warmth and comfort, not to be admired.

'What do you want to hear, lass?'

'About the robin.'

'It was years ago,' George started reminiscently, rubbing his stubbly chin with a workworn hand. 'Your mother wasn't so much older than you are now. She loved to come and help me dig but it was winter and the ground was frozen. Cold and bare it was and as still as still, and we couldn't get the spade into the earth however hard we tried.'

'What was Mummy wearing, Grandda?' Lucy knew the story almost by heart, she'd heard it so many times, but she never got tired of the telling.

'A little red coat and hood.'

'Just like Red Riding-Hood's?'

'Exactly – and boots.' He didn't tell her that the boots had been her brother's cast-offs, and she'd hobbled along beside him trying not to cry because of the blisters. To Lucy the boots sounded romantic. Soft leather with a lining of white fur was how she imagined them. She could almost see her mother with her pretty face and red curls trotting beside Grandda like a fairy child. 'We made tea in the shed on a primus-stove, and your mummy had to keep her mittens on so as not to scald her hands.'

'And then the robin came.'

'That's right. Just like a picture postcard it was, lass. The earth all brown and frosted with lace like the icing on a cake, and the rusty old spade sticking out of the ground with the little fellow with his red breast perched there on the handle, singing fit to burst.'

'Tell me what Mummy did.'

'Why, she held out some crumbs, and he was so hungry he came right up and pecked them out of her hand. And the next time we went he was there waiting for us; and he'd brought his little wife along with him, although she wasn't nearly so pretty. And your mummy gave them names. Can you remember what she called them?'

'Robbie and Rowena,' Lucy finished with a deep sigh of satisfaction. 'I wish a robin would come and visit us.'

'I'll make you a little bird-table when I find the time,' George promised. 'And you can put out bits of bread and bacon-rind in the winter. Then all the birds will come: not only the robins.'

'Will I still be here?' Lucy asked hopefully.

'I don't know, lass. But even if you're not, you can still come and visit me.'

'And Maud?'

'Of course. Maud will be here too.'

'Good.' Lucy smiled contentedly: she trusted him implicitly. 'She's kind and funny, and she makes me laugh.'

She got to her feet and walked a few steps away from her grandfather, her feet flat and splayed as she tried to copy Maud Carter. It was a wickedly accurate imitation, and a hoot of laughter from behind them showed that her game had been taken in good part. Maud was standing there, arms akimbo, black hair streaming, and her heavy figure bulging out of a bright red hand-knitted dress. Lucy had the grace to blush and made patterns in the dust at her feet with the toe of her shoe.

'You'd better say sorry to Maud, Lucy,' George said. Lucy obediently murmured an apology.

But the big woman clapped her hands. 'Do it again, kid,' she begged. 'You're a right little mimic and no mistake.'

So Lucy did it again, and Maud held her fat sides and laughed until her eyes streamed, and George applauded enthusiastically. 'I don't know who she gets it from,' he admitted.

'We'll have to put her on the stage. She'll make us a fortune.'

Lucy ran to them in alarm. 'I don't want to go on the stage, Grandda,' she said. 'I want to stay here with you and Maud.'

George put his arms around her and assured her that she'd never have to do anything she didn't want. The sun came back and the smiles returned: Lucy was happy again. The air was suddenly filled by an ear-splitting screech, and Maud blundered back into the kitchen to turn down the flame under the whistling kettle.

'I'm brewing some tea. Who wants one?'

George was always ready for a cup as long as it was dark and sweet, so he followed Maud indoors leaving Lucy to her own devices. There was so much to explore in the garden, she was always finding fresh corners and unexpected delights. George still kept his allotment as regimented as a market garden, so he didn't have time to do much to the plot in Duke's Road. It was left to run wild, with untamed trees and bushes, and long grass dotted with late daisies and the bushy golden heads of dandelions. The only path was the one Maud trod daily from the back door to the washing-line, on which flapped a set of George's long underwear, and a pink stretchy object rather like a concertina that danced in the breeze.

Lucy pottered her way towards the bottom of the garden. Here it was even more overgrown, with the wall dividing it from its neighbour crumbling in places. There was a laburnum bush that George had told her was her mother's favourite spot; in the spring she would see it covered with yellow flowers. The oak tree, that was nearly six foot tall, had had its beginnings as an acorn growing in a milk-bottle. Lucy loved these stories about her mother's childhood, and looked again with awe at the bushy oak, whose leaves were now golden and brown. It was hard to believe that it had such humble beginnings.

She bent down to pick a long strand of grass, and held it between her thumbs as Grandda had shown her to make a whistle. She hitched the bulky sleeves of her jumper up and blew gently, but the resulting squeak wasn't very satisfactory. She was standing still, smoothing out the grass blade to try again, when a movement caught her eye. She was sure she was imagining things when a small grey rabbit nosed its way out from under a nearby bush and loped its way across the turf directly in front of her. Lucy held her

breath in delight and watched the twitching nose and swiv-
elling eyes of the friendly animal. It didn't seem at all
scared, and she bent down slowly and held out her hand
hoping it would let her stroke it. But the movement
alarmed the creature and it leapt away on its strong back
legs, and with a flip of its white scut sped past her, ears laid
back, and disappeared under some nearby bushes. Lucy
was hot on its tail. Thinking it might have a secret burrow
she leapt head-first after it in pursuit.

It was dark with foliage, and when she felt something
move under her hand she expected it to be warm and furry.
But it wasn't: it was cool and smooth and wriggled like an
eel under her clutching fingers. Then she saw a brown san-
dal and a grey knitted sock and jumped back with a start. It
was a human leg she'd grabbed, and it belonged to a little
boy who was cowering amongst the fallen leaves, cuddling
the rabbit in his arms.

The two children stared at each other wide-eyed. They
both had thin white faces and straight brown hair; but the
boy was younger, probably a year or so younger than the
girl. Lucy recovered from the shock first. She was surprised,
but rather pleased to see the child. Much as she loved Maud
and Grandda they were grown-ups, and a child to play
with would be a nice change.

'Hello,' she said. 'Why are you hiding?'

'I'm not,' the boy said bravely. 'I was looking for my rabbit.'

'I thought he was a wild one. I didn't realise he belonged
to anybody.'

'Do you want to hold him?'

Lucy couldn't resist taking the soft little body into her arms.
She sat down on the ground beside the boy and made a lap in
her kilt. The rabbit seemed content to lie across her knees
while she stroked him, but his nose never stopped twitching.

'I had a rabbit once,' she said.

'Did you? What happened to it?'

'It died. What's his name?'

'Peter.'

Lucy froze and her face went white as chalk. 'It can't be. Peter's not a name for a rabbit.'

'Well it is; so there!'

There was only one Peter for Lucy, and the painful memories of her little friend came flooding back. She pushed them away, and handed the pet roughly back to its owner.

'Well I think it's a silly name – and it's a silly rabbit,' she said, and crawled through the tunnel of leaves back into the daylight.

'Come back!'

The shrill voice was so full of longing. Lucy hadn't really wanted to go, so she stopped and crawled back into the den.

'My name's Lucy,' she said as she crossed her legs and looked curiously at her new friend, who smiled shyly. 'What's yours?'

'Alan. Alan Murtell.'

'And what are you doing in my garden – Alan Murtell?'

'It's not your garden. It belongs to Mr Kelly.'

'So? Mr Kelly is my grandfather.' Lucy said it with pride. She was still getting used to the idea of having a real live grandfather. It was a new and exciting experience. 'He'll box your ears.'

'No he won't. He gives me sweets.'

'Does he?' This information took a few minutes to sink in and she wasn't sure she liked it. Grandda bought her sweets, but she was a relation. What business did he have buying things for this strange little boy? She felt threatened. 'I expect he feels sorry for you,' she said, trying to sound grown-up. 'Where do you live?'

'Over there,' Alan pointed vaguely at the crumbling wall. 'With my Mum and Dad, and my Auntie Mabel. Peter – I mean my rabbit – escaped from his hutch and got through that hole, so I followed to get him back. I won't get into trouble, will I?'

'Not if I don't tell.'

'If you promise not to, I'll let you choose his name. He's quite new and doesn't answer to Peter anyway.'

'If he was mine,' Lucy said thoughtfully, 'I'd call him Smokey.'

'All right,' Alan agreed.

They played with Smokey for a while, feeding him on grass and dandelion leaves. Lucy loved the way his wet nose tickled her fingers as he daintily helped himself. She liked this rabbit, particularly now he'd been renamed, and she liked his owner. Peter had been older than her, but mentally younger; but Alan, although her junior, was bright as a button, and she thought it would be fun to have him living next door.

'I'm having a firework party,' she suddenly announced.

'Why?'

'Because it's nearly Guy Fawkes night. Grandda said I could. He's going to help me build a bonfire and buy me some fireworks. And Maud promised to turn out some old clothes so I can make a guy.'

'Can I come?'

'I don't know. You may not be old enough.'

'I expect they'll let me come if you ask them.'

'You'll have to bring something.'

'I haven't any money.' Alan's face fell. He'd been to a birthday party the week before and had had to take a present. He thought the same applied to bonfire parties.

'You don't need money. You could bring some potatoes that we can cook in the fire. Maud says they're better that

341

way: like chestnuts at Christmas. Or perhaps your mummy would have some apples or biscuits to spare.'

'I'll ask her.' Alan's face had brightened.

He'd never heard of Guy Fawkes, but he knew all about fireworks. Last year his dad had taken him on the bus to Lewes to see the procession. He'd been little then and had sat high on his father's shoulders so that he could have a good view. He remembered being frightened by the revellers in their strange costumes, but the fireworks had been wonderful. The night sky had been full of showers of coloured stars and the bangs of the rockets had been exciting, not scary at all. He was just about to ask Lucy whether she was going to have any bangers when he heard a voice calling his name. It held a ring of authority and he knew it was time to go.

'That's my mum calling. I'd better go in.'

'I'll let you know about the party.'

'All right.'

Still clutching his rabbit he crawled towards the wall and found the gap he'd used to enter. It wasn't a large hole but the little boy was quite ingenious. He pushed Smokey through, and then followed feet first. The last thing Lucy saw of him was his dark head although she stood on tiptoe to try to see him reappear on the other side. All she saw was his dirty hand waving to her as he hurried towards the house.

Lucy burst into the kitchen excitedly; her hair was standing on end, and bits of dry grass were sticking out of the holes in her jersey.

Maud looked up from her mug of tea and wiped her mouth on the back of her hand. 'You look like a hedgehog,' she said.

'Whatever have you been up to, lass?' George asked. He pulled her on to his lap and poured milk from a bottle into a cup.

342

'Only playing.' Lucy buried her nose in the rim and made big gulping noises Belle wouldn't have approved of. When she came up for air her upper lip was edged with foam, just like an old man's moustache. 'I met a boy called Alan. I've invited him to my party.'

'What party?' Maud topped up the fat brown teapot with water from the steaming kettle. 'That's the first I've heard of any party.'

'Granddad promised, didn't you?' She nuzzled closer in his arms and her grip on the cup tightened. 'You said I could have a Guy Fawkes party, with a bonfire and fireworks.'

'So I did, lass,' George said. 'So you've met little Alan Murtell, have you?' The smile had gone from his face and Lucy wondered if she'd said something wrong.

'Yes. You didn't tell me there was a little boy living right next door. I can have a party, can't I, Grandda?'

'If Maud says so. She makes all the decisions around here.'

Lucy looked at Maud beseechingly. The big woman grinned and sank back in her chair, her feet splayed and legs apart, and her fat white thighs overflowing the narrow seat.

'Of course you can, love,' she said. 'I'll see to the food. You'll get the fireworks, won't you, George? And don't get anything too dangerous: we don't want any accidents.'

'What about me?' Lucy asked, wanting to have a share in the preparations. 'What can I do?'

'You have the most important job,' George said, planting a kiss on top of her head so that she wriggled with pleasure. 'You can collect the sticks for the bonfire and stuff the guy with newspapers.'

'And I can ask Alan, can't I?'

'Of course you can. That'll be four of us. And how about your Mam?'

'Oh, Grandda, can I?' Lucy hadn't seen Belle since that day, almost a month ago, when her grandfather had invited her to stay. She'd had the most exciting time of her young life discovering the charms of the little house in Duke's Road and making friends with Maud. But the best thing had been listening to stories about her mother when she'd been a little girl. Sometimes, but not often, she'd been homesick and missed her. 'Can I write her a letter?'

'No time.'

George frowned. The fifth of November was only two days away and he had no telephone. But there was a box on the corner of the road so he could telephone her. He couldn't bear to disappoint the child, although he wasn't sure if Belle would want to visit her old haunts.

His call came at the right time. Belle had been feeling rather dejected and was even beginning to miss Lucy. She still hadn't returned to her job at the theatre, and although there were plenty of things to do at home, helping Alice and trying to sort out her business affairs, she often felt lonely and depressed.

Mike still hadn't returned and she hadn't heard a word from him. It was so unlike him just to go away without saying goodbye or telling her when he'd be back. Johnnie didn't seem to know anything either; but he was a man of few words, and even if he did know something he wasn't letting on. Her greatest fear was that Mike had gone off with some other woman, and if he had, it was surely none of her business. He'd asked her to marry him and she'd as good as turned him down. He was an attractive man with normal appetites and yet she'd kept him dangling on a string, expecting him to be there when he was wanted. Perhaps she'd been too sure of herself and her attractions and he'd got fed up with waiting. If only he'd write or telephone she'd know where she stood; but the days went by, one after another, and there was still no news.

So when the phone rang at last she ran to it on flying feet, prepared to say she was sorry; her heart sank when she heard her father's voice. At first she nearly turned down his invitation. The last thing she wanted to do was go back to Duke's Road and be reminded of the squalor she'd been brought up in. She might see Henry Murtell and his wife again and that would be embarrassing.

'I am rather busy, Dada,' she said when George pressed her to come to the party. 'I can't make any promises.'

'You must try, lass. Lucy's so looking forward to you coming.'

'I'll see what I can do. Tell Lucy that I'll try and make it, but she mustn't be disappointed if I can't.'

This wasn't very satisfactory when he reported back to Lucy and saw her face drop. She was sitting cross-legged on the kitchen floor, stuffing the legs of an old pair of trousers Maud had turned out for the guy.

'I expect she'll come,' George said.

'It doesn't matter,' Lucy said in a quiet voice; but he knew that it did.

Preparations went ahead, and when the day of the party arrived they'd all caught Lucy's excitement. The bonfire was ready on a safe patch of ground where flying sparks wouldn't do any damage. Lucy's guy, dressed in George's old clothes, was perched on top grinning down at them. Its face under a greasy old cap had been Maud's final touch, and strongly resembled George. Maud swore the resemblance was purely accidental, but there was a wicked gleam in her eye all the same.

Lucy's favourite job was scrubbing the potatoes, and pricking their skins with a fork ready for baking. She had to stand on a chair at the deep white sink and drop the potatoes into a bowl under the running tap. They made a satisfactory splash and water sprayed everywhere, but Maud didn't reprimand her as Alice might have done.

Maud was too busy mixing the punch in a china bowl edged with flowers from the washstand. It was her own recipe: starting with lemonade and fresh orange juice, and ending with a dash of stout and the remains of a bottle of port. She'd managed to curb her drinking habits for George's sake, and now they only occasionally went on a spree. With a child in the house she didn't want to set a bad example, but it was supposed to be a party and a nip would keep out the cold. When she'd finished Lucy peered into the bowl and wrinkled up her nose. 'It smells nasty,' she said.

'Taste it,' Maud said, slicing lemons and scattering them on the surface, together with mint leaves coated with sugar. But Lucy wouldn't be persuaded, and announced that she would stick to lemonade, and so would Alan.

The best thing was, although this was a party, she didn't have to dress up. After all it was dark and cold in the garden, so the main thing was to be warm and comfortable. So she wore the old green jersey again, which seemed to grow bigger every time she put it on.

Alan arrived through the hole in the wall and carefully laid out his contributions: a bundle of sparklers and a bag of sausage rolls.

George told the children to stand well back and then lit a match and held it to the dry tinder. The little spark became a flame that danced in the night air, before dividing into two and burning higher and brighter. Soon the heart of the fire was red and glowing, and woodsmoke curled up into the sky above the rooftops and silhouetted chimneys. When the first flame reached the guy George lit a firework, warning the children to keep out of the way, and they all let out a cheer as a stream of coloured stars shot up into the sky.

Alan got so excited that he did a sort of war dance and

Lucy joined in, stamping her feet and letting out blood-curdling shrieks of delight. It was everything they'd expected. At the height of the excitement Belle arrived.

The first person to see her was Henry Murtell. He'd been standing in the darkened window for the last hour watching the street, because Alan had told them that Lucy's mother would be coming to the party. He fooled himself by thinking there was no other room in the house he could go into; because his wife Margery, and Auntie Mabel, were making tomato chutney in the kitchen and he was in the way. He could hear their friendly chatter from afar, and the jangling of glass bottles. The spicy smell tickled his nose: he sneezed and took off his glasses to polish his lenses. Without his spectacles the street outside the window looked misty and mysterious, the street lights glowing yellow, their edges blurred. He quickly replaced them on his nose and the scene sprang to life, clear-cut and three-dimensional.

Henry had been deep in thought while Belle was walking up the road, and to him it was as if she'd appeared by magic. She was standing on the pavement looking up at the house next door: her old home. She was wearing a silvery-grey two-piece and a jade green blouse with a floppy bow at the neck. The light from the lamps shone on her coppery curls, highlighting them in gold, and picking out the little silver cat brooch she wore pinned to her lapel. Henry thought she was as beautiful as ever even if she had put on a bit of weight. It suited her. He compared her with his wife, who was pretty but homely, and his heart turned over in remembrance.

After inspecting the house Belle ran lightly up the steps, her bag on its long strap swinging over her shoulder. She disappeared from Henry's view.

He wandered back into the kitchen where Auntie Mabel, in her usual grey dress that matched her hair, was washing up at the sink. Margery was sealing the jars with waxed paper and elastic bands. She stood bent over the table in an ungainly posture to ease her back, her cheap print overall tied loosely over her swollen belly. She smelt of onions, vinegar and sweat. Belle had always smelt of wild flowers and newly cut grass, and he suddenly wondered why he'd married Margery. Then he remembered: it was because Belle had married that rich fellow named Joseph Bishop. He'd heard, only recently, that Joseph had died, so if he'd waited and not married the next girl that came along he could have had the girl he'd always loved. Now it was too late, although Belle was free. He was tied to Margery and he had little Alan to think of, not to mention the new baby that was due at Christmas. He picked up the nearest jar and put it down again quickly: it was hot and burnt his fingers.

'What are you doing?' Margery asked crossly. 'Can't you leave things alone?'

'I thought I'd give one of these to Mr Kelly. It was kind of him to invite Alan to their bonfire.'

'You'll have to wait until they've cooled down. I'll take a couple of jars round in the morning.'

Henry wandered aimlessly to the back door and leant against the frame, his hands in his pockets. He could hear the shrieks of the children as another firework shot skywards, but he couldn't think of another excuse to go into the garden. Auntie Mabel gave him a reason. She turned from the draining-board, a teapot in her hands.

'I should have emptied this while it was still light,' she moaned. 'It stains the porcelain when I tip it down the sink.'

'I'll do it,' Henry said quickly.

Mabel Murtell was particular about her roses, and also about waste. She always emptied the used tea-leaves round the base of the plants, having read somewhere that it made a good mulch. He chose the rose-bed growing nearest to the wall and picked his way carefully so as not to trample anything underfoot. He bent double to complete his task, and then stood up casually to see what was going on in the neighbouring garden.

The fire was burning low, the heart red and glowing. Maud was bent over raking the potatoes out of the ashes with a poker. Her face was flushed with heat and her red skirt hitched up showing the tops of her stockings and her bulging white thighs.

Lucy and Alan were standing as close as they dared. their faces bathed in orange light as they waited patiently for their supper. George was counting the remaining fireworks into an old biscuit tin. He held a pocket torch between his teeth to see better, and his cap was pushed to the back of his head.

Henry took in the dimly lit scene quickly, and then his glance fell on the pale figure standing on the grass on the other side of the wall. It was Belle, so near he could almost put out his hand and touch her. One rounded arm was leaning on the trunk of a tree, and in her hand she held a glass. She seemed deep in thought as she watched the group around the fire. She was one of them – but alone at the same time.

'Hello, Belle.'

She jumped back into the present, but it took her a few moments to recognise the tall, thin man peering shortsightedly at her over the crumbling wall. Then he made the familiar gesture of brushing a falling lock of straight brown hair out of his eyes, and she realised who it was.

'Why, Henry Murtell,' she said in a teasing voice. 'You made me jump. Why don't you come over and join us?'

'I haven't been invited.'

'I'm sure that doesn't matter. Is that your son?'

'Yes. That's Alan.'

'And he's made friends with Lucy.' It was on the tip of her tongue to say "our daughter" but she stopped herself in time. The glass of punch Maud had insisted on her accepting was going to her head. She looked around for somewhere to put the glass down, and said, 'Lucy's my daughter.'

'I'm glad they're friends,' Henry said. 'There's not many kids around here for him to play with. Not like there was when we were young.'

'No. I suppose most of the families moved away. Have a drink.' She pushed her glass into his hand before he could refuse. He took a sip to please her, and then coughed and put his hand over his mouth.

Belle grinned, just as she had when she was young and out to tease him. 'Horrible isn't it?' she said in a low voice.

'It's not very nice. What's it supposed to be?'

'Maud calls it punch. She says it's her own invention.'

'As long as she doesn't try to patent it.'

'Unless it's for rat-poison.'

They giggled together, their heads close. George looked around and saw them. He frowned slightly and his glance wavered from Henry to the little girl nibbling her hot potato spiked on the end of a fork. He shook himself: it wasn't any of his business, and he'd always liked Henry. Carrying a plate in each hand he left the rosy circle made by the fire, and with a smile handed a potato to Belle and one to Henry.

'I suppose Margery's not up to these sort of games?' he said pointedly. 'She must be getting near her time.'

'Not for another six weeks.' Henry blushed slightly. 'It's due before Christmas.'

'I suppose you both want a girl this time?'

Henry didn't have a chance to answer because a child screamed behind them. George had left the tin of fireworks unattended and Alan had gone to investigate. He'd picked up a jumping-jack and thrown it into the fire where it had ignited almost at once. It was harmless, but noisy, and was jumping and crackling across the grass. Lucy was terrified and ran towards the grown-ups for protection.

Belle gathered the frightened child into her arms and explained to Henry. 'She's terribly frightened of fire. I don't know why, but she always has been.'

'That's nothing to be ashamed of,' Henry said staunchly, looking at the little girl for the first time. 'So was I at her age.'

22

Mike drummed his fingers on the steering-wheel as his old van rattled along the country roads towards Guildford. He hoped it wouldn't break down before he met Stan at the crossroads where they'd planned a rendezvous. He'd never driven so far out of town before and wasn't sure if the van was up to the journey.

It had all been a spontaneous arrangement; with Stan persuading him at the last minute that it would be worth his while. Stan had seen an advertisement for a country house sale in a newspaper and had driven up to reconnoitre. There'd been an auction, and he'd brought back some really good saleable items of furniture, which he'd flogged for a profit to an antique dealer in the Lanes. Now he'd got the bug and suggested that Mike accompany him.

They were going to go round the villages of Kent and Surrey, visiting private houses, and making offers for bits and pieces people didn't need any more.

'OK,' Mike said. 'As long as there isn't going to be any funny business.'

'Funny business! What do you mean?'

'We must pay a fair price.'

'Don't you want to get a bargain?' Stan asked with a grin.

'Of course; but I don't want to see anyone taken advantage of.'

Mike hadn't known Stan for long and didn't completely trust him. He'd hoped that Johnnie would have come as well: he was useful at lifting things and could take his turn at the wheel, but his brother wasn't interested.

When he was ready to leave he went up the front stairs to tell Belle where he was off to, but there didn't seem to be anybody in although he waited around for nearly half an hour. He nearly wrote a note and pushed it through the letter-box, but then he saw the time and was anxious to be off. So he left a message with Johnnie instead, and drove off. After all he should be back at the end of the week, and it might do their relationship good to be apart for a few days. Perhaps she'd miss him.

Sometimes he wondered if Belle cared for him at all, or if she was just making use of him. He wanted to marry her, he'd made that plain, and he was even prepared to take on her funny little kid, Lucy, and be a father to her. He wasn't getting any younger and it was about time he settled down. Johnnie wouldn't mind, he was happy on his own. But Mike wanted a proper home and a family, and he loved Belle, with her red hair and impulsive ways. The way she'd pulled herself up when she'd been widowed and turned her home into a boarding-house – even taking in that girl, Flora, and her little boy, with such tragic consequences. He said he'd wait for her, and he meant it, but he wasn't going to sit around like a lap-dog answering her beck and call. Perhaps he'd broach the subject of marriage again when he got back. If she missed him she might be in a better frame of mind.

Stan was waiting at the crossroads. You couldn't miss his tumbledown truck, which was in a worse condition than Mike's. His bald head was bobbing in and out of the window.

'You're late,' he yelled as Mike drew up alongside. 'I thought you'd changed your mind.'

'I missed a turning further back. Which way now?'

'Follow me.'

The engine started with a cough and a roar, and Mike followed close behind. Occasionally he was overtaken by another vehicle and fell behind, trying not to lose sight of the rattling truck.

They drove through a country town where there was a market in progress, and narrowly missed being delayed by a flock of sheep. Back on a straight strip of road heading north, Mike saw Stan slow down and take a left turning, just in time to indicate to the traffic behind and follow. It wasn't a road: it was the forecourt of a public house and Stan was climbing down from his cab. His bald head was wet with perspiration which he was mopping with a dingy handkerchief.

'Opening time,' he said, smacking his lips. 'Time for a dram.'

Mike had no option but to follow him into the public bar. They'd chosen the busiest time of the day when the thirsty farm workers were bent on refreshment. Brown arms in homespun shirts were raised to pour the foaming ale down parched throats. The softened vowels of the countrymen were singing or praising the skill of the darts players. Occasionally a shout of adulation at some score would be heard, and the men would slap each other's shoulders and call for a fresh round.

'Sit down,' Stan said. 'I'm buying.'

Mike found a bench in an alcove, highly polished from the seats of a thousand pairs of corduroy trousers, and sat down. He'd expected a pint in a tumbler or tankard, not the bowl-shaped glasses Stan carried carefully so as not to lose a precious drop. It was brandy, and Mike was so thirsty that he drank it down hardly appreciating the mellow flavour. He hadn't eaten since an early breakfast and it hit his stomach with a warm kick, and spread a glow throughout his body. A second one was easier, and suddenly Mike didn't mind the delay in their journey; after all there was nothing to hurry for. The company was congenial, and he grinned at Stan's red beefy face with affection.

'My round,' he said, and staggered to his feet to place his order at the bar. 'Same again.'

He couldn't remember afterwards how many more rounds were ordered and drunk, or how soon the evening closed in around them and the time flew by.

Their host, an agreeable fellow, was used to letting his guests sleep off their drinking bouts. It was better for them than sending them out into the night to stagger home and end up in a ditch; or drive away and kill someone on the road. When he called 'time' the last drinkers had the choice of braving the darkness, or helping each other into the back room where there was always a pile of blankets and a sweet-smelling sack of straw to collapse on.

Mike knew no more until he awoke with a thumping head as the first light streaked the window. Stan slept beside him sharing a mattress, his snores vibrating the very foundations of the old house. He shook him awake roughly, ignoring the curses it brought forth, and the two men staggered out into the yard where there was a cattle trough and a pump. The water was cold as ice as he sponged his face and head, slapping his skin until it tingled. Then he shook himself as he had no towel, and ran his fingers through his thick hair in place of a comb.

When they returned to collect their belongings their host was serving up breakfast: great piles of sizzling sausages and bacon, with double-yolked eggs the colour of butter, and triangular slices of fried bread as thick as your finger, washed down by tea from a pot so large that it needed two hands to lift it.

Mike felt better quickly. He looked for a telephone so that he could call Belle, but Stan distracted him. He was busy planning their campaign.

'I've been given these four leads,' he said, consulting a tattered notebook. 'Two in Millstream – that's a village a couple of miles away. The next turning on the right leads straight there. A chap called Hamilton's got some old pine furniture that might be worth a bob or two, and who knows what you may find under the cobwebs.'

'I'm not an expert,' Mike said doubtfully.

'I didn't say you were.' Stan grinned cheerfully and tapped his nose with his pencil. 'But you've got an eye for a bargain, I can see that. All you need is charm and the gift of the gab, like me.' He tore a sheet out of his notebook and handed it over. 'You do those. I've written down the names and addresses. I'll do Greenacres. That's a private house in the village of Sweetham. An old girl lives there all alone. A sort of recluse, so she should be an easy touch.'

Mike felt uncomfortable. It didn't sound honest somehow: Stan talking about easy touches and bargains and an old woman living on her own. But it wasn't his business. He'd go to the address in Millstream, and if there was anything he fancied he'd make a fair offer. He just hoped Stan would behave himself.

They separated and Mike waved until the rickety truck disappeared in a cloud of dust. Then he climbed into the driving seat of his van, rolled down the window, and drove off, taking the turning Stan had indicated.

Millstream was a small village. It consisted of one row of workmen's cottages leading to the dilapidated ruins of a water-mill from which it got its name, a dairy farm, and a few outlying houses.

The first address he found straight away. It was an attractive grey stone house by a stream, and although there was an old fashioned bell-pull that clanged at a distance, when he pulled it nobody answered the door. He tried again, and then stepped carefully across the flower-bed to peer through one of the front windows.

No wonder no one was answering the door, the room inside was empty, only bare boards and walls with square patches where pictures had once hung. The inner doors were all open and he could see an uncarpeted passage, and a hall with uncollected mail scattered below the letter-box. He was too late; whoever had lived there had sold up and moved on a long time ago.

Mike climbed back into the van and drove on to the next address. It was called The Old Rectory. The owner, Mr Hamilton, was in the garden, and when Mike introduced himself he was given a warm welcome. Dusting off the knees of his corduroy trousers and pulling off his gardening gloves, Mr Hamilton ushered his guest inside.

'I've only been here a couple of months,' he explained. 'Bought the place furnished, lock, stock and barrel, because the owner died suddenly. Moved all my own furniture down from my London flat, and now I can't move. Just piled it all in the little room at the back until I can get a buyer.'

He flung open a door and Mike saw what he meant. There were beds and mattresses leaning against the wall, a long refectory table jammed under the window, and boxes of books and upturned chairs everywhere.

'I heard you had some pine stuff you wanted to sell,' Mike said hopefully.

Mr Hamilton pushed his way between a pile of boxes and moved a small chest of drawers aside. 'There's a pine dresser here somewhere; and some stools if you're interested. I'll be glad to get rid of them. This room is going to be my study, but I have to clear it first.'

The dresser was fairly old but not in very good condition. Mike felt sorry for the man. 'I'll give you twenty-five pounds if you'll throw the stools in as well,' he said.

'That sounds fine.' Mr Hamilton looked pleased. 'I hope you make a profit.'

'I will. I know just where to place them.'

Mr Hamilton was so delighted he even gave Mike a hand loading them into the van, and waved cheerfully as he drove away.

Where next? Mike was still looking out for a telephone box to ring Belle. The only one he passed wasn't working so he decided to go and find Stan.

A house called Greenacres, in the village of Sweetham, was where he'd been heading, and Mike soon found a crossroads with a sign telling him which turning to take. Sweetham turned out to be even smaller than Millstream and Greenacres was the only private house.

Stan's truck was parked on a sweep of gravelled drive, so Mike pulled in behind and peered through a forest of over-hanging greenery towards the house. It looked very old. It was built of solid grey brick, with small windows with diamond-shaped panes sunk deeply into the thick walls. Ivy climbed almost to the roof of mossy tiles, and a rose rambled over a trellised porch. A crazy-paved path curved through an untidy garden to the front door. The plants had grown and seeded themselves and the result was a patch-work of late summer colour.

Mike felt as if he was walking into another world as he approached the door which was standing open. No hope of finding a modern invention like a telephone in a place like this, he thought. The first town they drove through on the way back, he'd insist on stopping and making that call to

Belle. The first thing he heard was Stan's voice, loud and persuasive, and he stopped to listen.

'Not worth much, Miss Grey,' Stan was saying. 'But out of the kindness of my heart I'll give you five.'

'Five? Five hundred I suppose you mean.'

The speaker stepped into his line of vision, a little old lady, not much taller than Lucy. She was dressed in old-fashioned black, from her neck to the pointed toes of her button boots. Her face was wrinkled by a million lines, and her fine silver hair was coiled into a tight knob on the top of her head, and draped with a fragile piece of lace. Although she was so small she stood proudly upright and held an ivory cane with a silver top in one veined hand.

'Five hundred pounds!' Stan's incredulous voice reached him. 'You must be joking. I said five – five pounds I meant.'

'But my father had it insured. He said it was worth a lot of money.'

'How long ago?'

'Oh, not that long. About twenty years I suppose.'

'That's what I mean, Miss Grey. Prices drop in twenty years.'

'I thought they rose.'

'You don't want to believe everything you read in the newspapers.'

Mike had to admit Stan sounded very convincing. He moved closer to see what the offer of five pounds was for. It was a picture leaning against a table leg, and there was a gap over the fireplace where it usually hung. It was an oil painting of a group of scantily clad maidens bathing in a lake. The heavy gilt frame alone was worth the five pounds Stan was offering.

'Well, I don't think I want to sell it anyway,' Miss Grey said firmly, thumping the ground with the tip of her cane. 'You'd better hang it back on the wall.'

'Please yourself.' Stan picked up the picture and carried it back to the fireplace. 'Hey, what's this?' He put the painting down again and peered at a pair of vases set amongst other china on the mantelpiece. He picked one up in his rough hand to inspect it.

'Please be careful,' the old woman said nervously. 'That's a *Cloisonné* vase.'

'Is it?' Stan was holding it up to the light. 'I thought it was Japanese.'

'It is. It was made at the Kyoto factory by an artist called Hayashi Kodenji so I was told. They must be seventy or eighty years old and I'm very fond of them. Look at the flowers and butterflies.' She pointed out the delicate tracery of a wing and the petal of a chrysanthemum.

'How much?'

'Put it down – it's not for sale.'

Stan put the vase back and moved to the table, searching in his pocket for his wallet. He extracted a bundle of notes and peeled off two tenners.

'Here.' He held out the twenty pounds as if he was offering her a fortune. 'I'll take the vases instead of the picture.'

'I told you – they're not for sale.'

'Come on now, what use are they to you?' Stan was busy hanging the picture back in its place. He'd left the notes on the table as if he'd struck a deal. Mike could see that Miss Grey was looking upset; he wondered if it was time to intervene. 'I'll send you a receipt.'

'I don't want a receipt. I'm not selling you my vases or anything else, so you can leave them alone and get out of my house – or I'll call the police.'

'How?' Stan looked around. 'I don't see a telephone, lady, and I'm bigger than you.'

'How dare you.' Miss Grey might be small and frail, but she'd been brought up to be treated like a lady. Her word had always been obeyed, so she stood up to Stan although she barely reached his shoulder. 'I'm not afraid of you,' and she poked him in the stomach with the end of her cane.

The effect on Stan was like a fly irritating an elephant's thick hide. He turned on her, an ugly expression on his face.

'I'm having these vases, lady, whether you like it or not. If my money's not good enough for you, I'll take it back,' and he grabbed the notes and thrust them into his pocket, at the same time reaching out a greedy hand for the nearest vase.

Mike stepped forward out of the shadowy doorway. He'd listened to enough. He'd guessed Stan wasn't completely honest and was prepared to overlook small extortions, but intimidation and theft from a helpless old lady enraged him.

'Do what Miss Grey says and take your hands off her belongings, Stan.' His voice was firm and his handsome face flushed with anger.

'Whose side are you on?' Stan seemed surprised to see him. 'I thought we were partners.'

'Not any more.'

'Come on now, Mike. This lady and I had made a bargain. All fair and square. But now she's trying to change her mind.'

'It didn't sound like that to me.' Mike turned to Miss Grey and led her to the nearest chair. 'Do you want to sell those vases?'

'No.' Her voice was tiny and slightly cracked, like the tinkling sound that comes when you tap a valuable piece of old china. 'I don't want to sell him anything.' She emphasised the HIM firmly, and glanced in Stan's direction.

'That's not what she said earlier.'

'You heard the lady: she doesn't want to sell anything. I suggest you pick up your money and go.'

'Oh, now I see what you're after: you want to get rid of me so you can sweeten the old girl up and get the things yourself. You can't get rid of me that easily; I wasn't born yesterday.'

Mike ignored him; he was too busy making sure that Miss Grey was all right. She was sitting bolt upright in her chair, but the hands resting on the top of her cane trembled slightly.

'I told you to go.'

Suddenly Stan lost his temper; he strode across the room and put his ham-like fist on Mike's shoulder, swinging him round. He had a reputation for liking a fight so Mike decided to hit him first. His fist caught Stan unawares and he staggered backwards, his hands to his jaw. Mike walked calmly past him and pushed the front door open wider, hoping he'd get the hint.

Stan shook himself like a bull getting ready to charge, and then thought better of it. He walked to the door with his head down and his shoulders hunched. Mike relaxed too soon. Stan was almost past Mike when he suddenly changed his mind and charged, one fist landing in his stomach and winding him, and the other catching him on his temple. Mike grabbed the side of the door for support, missed his aim, and slipped downwards, catching his head on the iron doorstop in the shape of a prancing greyhound. Everything went black.

The first thing Mike heard as his senses returned was birdsong. He kept his eyes closed while he tried to locate the bits of him that hurt most. Every muscle in his body ached as if it had been hit by a sledgehammer; but his head hurt most of all.

'Are you feeling any better?'

The speaker was close beside him. He made an effort and

opened his eyes carefully. At least he opened one eye, because the left one didn't seem to be obeying orders. He put up one hand and felt it gently, exploring the puffy mound of flesh that had once been his eye-lid, and then discovering a neat pad of lint just above the hairline, held in place by sticking plaster. He was lying on a long couch, which in the trade was known as a day bed, with his head on a cushion and a tartan rug tucked neatly around him. Miss Grey sat beside him at a small table. She was turning the key on a musical box, and the rippling notes filled the quiet room like birdsong.

'How did I get here?'

'I helped you. Luckily I kept my father's old wheelchair,' and she pointed to a wicker contraption on giant wheels. 'You were too heavy for me to lift. But your legs aren't hurt, and I couldn't leave you lying on the floor just inside the door. Someone might have tripped over you.'

Mike wanted to laugh, but it was too painful. He'd tried to protect this little woman from Stan and ended up so much the worse for wear.

'Has he gone?'

'Oh, yes. I wanted him to stay and help me. I mean he could have lifted you easily, but he couldn't wait to get away. If he's a friend of yours you didn't make a very good choice. And then he left his money on the table. I had to leave you and run outside to give it back to him before he drove away. I suppose the van is yours?'

'Yes.'

'There's a nasty dent in the side now. He was in such a hurry he backed into it trying to turn round. Would you like a cup of tea? I haven't anything stronger. There's vintage wine in the cellar but I haven't been down there for years. There's no light, and it needs a man to open the trap door.'

'Tea will be fine.'

'And then perhaps you'll feel strong enough to get upstairs to bed.'

'You're very kind, Miss Grey, but I mustn't impose upon you. I'll just have the tea and then I'll be on my way.'

'Oh, no, you mustn't do that. Your head wound is really nasty. I would have called a doctor and he could have stitched you up, but I've never bothered to have the telephone installed and now, at my age, it's hardly worth it. Complete rest is what you need. That's how we treated my father when he fell off his horse and cut his head open. He didn't believe in doctors and was right as rain in a few weeks.'

All the while she was talking she was busy preparing the tea. The pot was silver, with a monogram he couldn't read on the side, and the cups were so fragile he could see the light through the porcelain. She handed him a cup as if she were offering him nectar. It looked and smelled like no other tea, with a slice of lemon floating on the top, but no milk. The sugar was in cubes, and she dropped two lumps into his cup with silver tongs.

Mike felt as if he were in another world and wondered if he were dreaming. Perhaps the blow on the head had affected his reason. But he was content just to lie there and be waited on by Miss Grey. When she enquired whether he felt strong enough to follow her upstairs he went obediently.

The head injury must have been worse than he thought because he lost track of time. He seemed to do nothing but sleep, and in one of his brief periods of consciousness he wondered if she'd slipped something into his tea. Not for any evil purpose, she wasn't that sort of old lady, but something herbal made to her own recipe.

The first time he woke properly he looked around with

interest. From his massive bed, hung with faded silk drapes, he could see all round the room he was in. It was a long, low chamber, with a beamed ceiling and polished wooden floor riddled with knots and worm-holes, and scattered with tatty fur rugs. The furniture was huge and old and there was a lot of it. The walls were hung with pictures and faded sepia photographs, and every available surface was crammed with china and silver. He was thankful Stan hadn't seen this room, or he might not have gone so easily.

The feather mattress was so comfortable that he slept again. The next time he woke it was the middle of the night. The room was dim and the curtains were pulled over the diamond-paned windows, but Miss Grey was sitting in a chair beside the bed playing a game of patience at a folding card-table. A silver candelabrum stood behind her, the flames from its candles leaping in the draught so that flickering shadows danced around the walls.

'How are you feeling?' Miss Grey asked, laying down her last card with a satisfied smile.

'Better, I think.'

'Good. Do you play cards?'

'I used to play whist – but I haven't for years.'

'What about *vingt-et-un*?' She was shuffling the pack expertly as she put the question.

'No.'

'It doesn't matter: you'll soon pick it up. It's a variation of pontoon, and everyone knows that.'

They'd played three hands before Mike felt his eyes drooping again. He was feeling better, but the fact that an old woman had beaten him at a simple game of cards showed him that he wasn't completely recovered.

After that they played cards every day, or she read to him. He hadn't asked her to, but as she sat beside his bed with the book held close to her eyes, she fell into the habit of reading aloud. She started with Tennyson, but when he mentioned he'd been fond of Dickens when he was a boy, she read him her favourite chapters from *Oliver Twist* and *A Tale of Two Cities*.

One day when she was about to leave the room he stopped her.

'Miss Grey, do you think I could have a pen and some note-paper?'

'What for?'

'I want to write a letter.'

'If you're sure you're feeling well enough.' She propped a writing-tray across his knees, and provided him with everything he needed. The pen felt strange with its old-fashioned nib, much used and scratchy, but he managed to fill four sheets of paper telling Belle about his misfortunes, and promising to return as soon as he was well enough to drive. On the last page he repeated his proposal and assured her that he would wait for her, but on reflection he tore that sheet up and just signed his name.

Just then Miss Grey arrived with a loaded tray. 'I've scrambled you some eggs for your lunch,' she said. 'I hope you like them.'

'I like eggs cooked any way,' Mike assured her.

'And then we'll read some Thomas Hardy.'

A leather-bound book was tucked under her arm. He held out the sealed envelope.

'Could you post this for me?'

She took it with a nod and a smile and tucked it behind a grinning Staffordshire dog on the mantelpiece. A few days later he noticed that it was still there.

Even so, under her gentle ministrations he did begin to feel better. He began to notice that the leaves were falling from the trees outside the window and the nights were drawing in.

The first time she allowed him to get out of bed he slowly made his way down the stairs draped in the dead Mr Grey's dressing-gown. His legs felt heavy and weak and he barely recognised his pale face in a passing mirror, but the bruises were gone and the head wound healed. He must have suffered some sort of concussion when he fell on the iron doorstop to have laid him low for such a long time.

There was a newspaper on the table, with Miss Grey's reading glasses neatly folded on top. He had a shock when he glanced at the date and saw that it was October. It was late summer when he'd begun the trip with Stan, and now it was autumn. He must have been away at least six weeks. He dreaded to think what reasons Belle might have imagined for his absence. At least Johnnie wouldn't worry or send out a search party. He wasn't like that. When he returned his brother would greet him casually as if he'd only been away for a few days.

He called out for Miss Grey. He wanted to ask for his clothes, and tell her he had to be on his way if he could get the van started. What could he do to repay her kindness? She wouldn't want thanks, but he could send her a gift when he got back to Brighton. He didn't know what sort of things old ladies like – apart from flowers. Perhaps Belle would be able to suggest something suitable.

Where was she? She was usually within earshot, but he couldn't hear the tapping of her cane or her high silvery voice. The kitchen was deserted although there was a kettle steaming on the range, and the back door was wide open. She must be outside – gathering herbs, or putting out crumbs for the birds.

He saw her from the doorway. She was sitting on a bench under a trellis of rambling rose, but she didn't turn when he called her name. Her eyes were closed and her lips blue and clenched, and her thin little hands were pressed to her

367

bodice as if to ease the pain. Her laboured breathing rasped in and out in time with the rise and fall of her chest as he looked down at her.

Gently he lifted her into his arms and carried her into the house.

23

It was a dreary wet November afternoon and Belle stood in the window staring out into the street. It was still raining; silver spears of water lashed against the glass and made her shiver. November was such a dreary month: nothing to look forward to but the cold chill of winter, and months before the warmth returned and the sun shone again.

A bit like her life, Belle thought. All the colour and warmth in the past and nothing in the future. A sudden gust of wind rattled a loose pane and she crossed her arms over her chest for warmth.

'Mrs Belle.'

'Yes.'

Alice was standing in the open doorway: a plump parcel in a dark blue dress, her fat feet laced into walking shoes. Belle wondered vaguely why she wasn't wearing her apron. Even when she went out to the shops she left it on under her coat. It was a standing joke between them.

'I hope you don't mind, Mrs Belle, but I'm going out.'

'In this weather, Alice? It's pouring down. If you forgot to get something on that list I gave you I'm sure we can manage without. There's only the sisters to cook for, and they'll be happy with eggs. We can have the rest of the pie left over from yesterday.'

'I wasn't going shopping.'

Belle gave Alice her full attention. The maid's life had always revolved around the house and the boarders for as long as Belle could remember. She'd never mentioned a family or any ties, and had never bothered about time off. Belle was so used to her constant support and presence that she'd never even considered what life would be like without her.

'I'm sorry, Alice,' she said. 'Of course you're free to go out whenever you want. You don't have to ask me first. It was different when the children were here . . .' She paused briefly as her thoughts wandered back to a fair curly-haired little boy. 'But until Lucy comes back from my father's house, and the rooms are full again, we can both do what we like.'

Alice was busy buttoning herself into a gabardine coat, and pulling a felt hat shaped like a basin on to her head. 'The sisters don't want supper tonight anyway. They're playing at the Excelsior.'

The sisters were Emily and June Hunt, who were at present the only boarders. They were professional musicians, Emily on the cello and June on the violin; they were half of a string quartet playing the local hotels.

'You'd better take an umbrella or you'll get soaked.' Alice nodded, smiled, and turned to the door. Belle was puzzled and her curiosity got the better of her. 'I know it's none of my business, Alice, but where are you going?'

'To tea with Arthur's parents.'

'Arthur! Arthur who?'

'Arthur Pratt – whose parents own the bakery.'

Belle's head spun at this news. 'But you hardly know him.'

'He's been delivering our bread for two years now, Mrs

Belle, and I always invites him into the kitchen for a hot drink when the weather's bad. He's been bothering me for a long time: you know, saying daft things and asking me out. But I never had the time or the inclination.'

'Oh, Alice, I'm sorry. I didn't know.'

The news of Alice's private life came as a revelation to Belle, but there was no reason why she couldn't have an admirer. She wasn't old, and she'd proved herself to be a good cook and housekeeper. She'd be a good wife to the right man, and obviously Arthur Pratt had recognised her good qualities.

'There's no reason why you should have known. After all, it was my business and you had other things to concern yourself with. Anyway, he asked me again last week, and I thought it was the right time to say yes.'

'He's asked you to marry him?'

'Yes. Whatever else would he ask me? There's nothing much to do here with the place pretty well empty, and Lucy gone. You could see to it yourself blindfolded. Well, the old 'uns, Arthur's mum and dad, are retiring. Arthur's taking over the shop himself and employing a boy to do the rounds. I'm pretty good in the kitchen, and there'll be plenty to do looking after them all. You won't miss me.'

'Oh, Alice I will!' It had suddenly dawned on Belle just how much she was going to miss this homely little woman who'd been part of her life for so long. She ran across the room and flung her arms about her with one of her spontaneous gestures.

'I'm so pleased for you – really I am. It was unexpected, that's all. Such a surprise – but a lovely one. I hope you and Arthur will be very happy.'

'We shall, Mrs Belle. Don't you worry about that. We're both hard workers and don't expect much from life. Not like you with your dreams.'

'What are you talking about?'

'I've seen you: head in the clouds when your feet should be set firmly on the ground. You should have accepted that nice Mr Walker when he asked you. You've been on your own quite long enough.'

'Alice!' Belle couldn't help smiling. The change in her circumstances seemed to have gone to Alice's head. She didn't usually talk so openly. 'What do you know about me and Mike Walker anyway?'

'Enough. And what I don't know I can guess. He's dotty about you and always has been. Even before Mr Bishop died so tragically he couldn't take his eyes off you. But he's always behaved like a gentleman; even to me. And now you've sent him away.'

'I haven't, Alice – truly.' Belle turned her face away, but not before Alice had seen tears in her eyes. 'He went away weeks ago, of his own accord and without leaving a proper message. Nobody's heard from him: not even Johnnie.'

'Perhaps he's had an accident.'

'I thought of that; but surely then we'd have heard. The police would have had to let his brother know if anything had happened to him.'

'That's true.'

'I think he got tired of me. After all he's a very attractive man and I probably wasn't the only woman in his life.'

Belle tried to speak lightly but the quaver in her voice gave her away. She was pleased for Alice: she deserved happiness, but she had to hide the feeling of loneliness that the news had brought her.

As she stood at the window watching the dark figure under the big umbrella trotting away towards the baker's shop, and the floury arms of Arthur Pratt, it was as much as she could do not to cry. She'd never felt so alone in her life before, and the empty echoing rooms that had once been so

372

full of life seemed to close in around her.

She thought back over her life. It seemed to be full of a succession of people she cared about leaving her. First Charlie, urging her to run home, and promising to follow – but he never did. Then Mam and Joseph, Peter and Flora, and more recently Lucy and Mike. Losing Alice seemed to be the last straw.

On top of these things was the ever-worrying lack of money. With a full house and her jobs at the theatre, life had been pleasant enough, but not luxurious. Belle liked nice things for herself and Lucy, so there hadn't been a chance to save much. She was still young and hadn't anticipated her income drying up. But Peter's death had changed things. People were more sensitive than she'd imagined they would be, and although Flora had been cleared of murder, the intent was still there.

She was lucky if she had more than two rooms occupied these days, and with overheads this meant she was often working at a loss. No one had contacted her from the theatre about returning to work, and once when she was passing she'd peeped inside. There was a new woman, dressed in polished silk and with freshly coiffured hair, sitting behind the grille in the box-office. She was too proud to make enquiries. If they didn't want her back she wasn't going to press things.

She walked through the deserted rooms to the dining-room. Joseph's desk still stood in its usual place in the window, and she rolled back the lid. Raindrops were trickling down the glass but the sky looked brighter, as if the downpour would soon be over. There'd been a letter from the bank only that morning but she hadn't had time to open it. Now she slit the envelope open with the ivory paper knife and pulled out the statement it contained. It wasn't as bad as it might have been; her account was still in the black.

But unless she did something soon to boost her income she was going to be in trouble. She closed the desk with a thump. She'd think of something: she wasn't like Joseph who when confronted by disaster took the easiest way out. Her back might be to the wall, but she was still fighting.

She couldn't stay long in the quiet stillness of the house, with all its memories, a moment longer. Fresh air was what she needed. Exercise to stimulate her brain into fresh ideas, even if it was raining.

There was a mackintosh hanging on the hall-stand, left behind by some lodger ages ago. It was faded and old but she didn't care; she wasn't likely to meet anyone she knew. It wasn't a bad fit either, and there was a deep hood to cover her curly hair. She didn't bother about boots or an umbrella although there were both in the rack.

Outside everything was dripping: the trees lining the street and the bushes in the front gardens. The gutters gurgled as dirty water swirled past a blocked drain. It had made a miniature lake on the pavement in which a small child in wellington boots was paddling. Belle smiled at him, and he grinned back cheekily.

'You going out, Belle?'

She looked over the area wall and saw Johnnie standing outside his front door in his shirt-sleeves, inspecting the weather.

'Just for a walk. I need some fresh air.'

'Don't get wet then.'

'No. It's almost stopped.' She was about to turn away when she stopped. 'Have you heard anything from Mike?'

'No.'

'Aren't you worried? I mean, it's been weeks. Something must have happened to him.'

'Not to Mike. He'll turn up when he's ready, don't you fret.'

'I'm not.'

She turned away and walked briskly along the road. She didn't know where she was going but the exercise made her feel better. The rain had almost stopped; there was just a thin mist of drizzle, like a curtain, enveloping the houses and blurring their outlines. She pushed back the hood of her coat and ran her fingers through her loose hair, enjoying the dampness that made the red curls cluster tightly to her white forehead. Cars and buses passed her, and once a red fire-engine clanging its bell, although she couldn't imagine an emergency on such a wet day.

The earlier heavy rain had kept everyone indoors, but now the housewives were out catching up with their shopping. She avoided the large stores and their temptations, and found herself in the Open Market where everything was cheap.

She hadn't been there for years. It was part of her childhood where she'd clung to Mam's hand while she haggled over the price of fruit and fish. In front of her was a pile of yellow bananas, freckled with brown, and she recalled the first banana she'd ever tasted. When the war was over and fruit from foreign parts began to appear in the shops Dada had brought home one banana. To Belle it had seemed strange and exotic; she'd enjoyed peeling back its damp skin more than she'd enjoyed it's strange taste. Now fruit was cheap and plentiful and she bought a pound of the largest bananas forgetting that there was only her to eat them.

The traders were yelling their wares, trying to cut each other's prices, and soon Belle had been persuaded to buy apples as well.

Her shopping tucked under one arm, she wandered back into the main road, a half-eaten apple in her hand. She felt quite wicked: after all she tried to discourage Lucy from eating in the street, telling her that it was unladylike. But today she didn't feel like the Mrs Bishop who tried to behave like a lady. She was Belle Kelly again: a rough urchin who tagged around the streets with a bespectacled boy called Henry Murtell.

Belle stopped in her tracks, her teeth sunk deeply into the sweet juicy flesh. Someone bumped into her and pushed her impatiently out of the way.

Of course, she should have thought of Henry before. He was still around, and the shop he'd taken over from Jim Hilton was only a stone's throw away. She'd be able to talk to Henry; be honest about the position she was in and ask him to advise her. She threw the apple core into the gutter, just missing a scavenging dog, and almost ran towards the narrow turning where the second-hand clothes shop was situated, half-afraid that if she didn't hurry she'd find it gone, just like the important people in her life.

But it was still there, and it looked prosperous. The window was dressed with models wearing sensible day-clothes, all in good condition but a third of the price asked in the nearby shops. There were boxes of cheaper items, shoes and woollens, but everything was clean and there was no rubbish.

Belle pushed open the door and heard the jangle of the bell. Her way was barred by racks of winter overcoats, and she had to fight her way through the stock to reach the counter.

Henry was busy with a customer. He'd just sold a middle-aged woman a tweed two-piece, and was wrapping it up into a parcel and tying it neatly with string. He saw Belle and coloured slightly, but then smiled his old delighted smile. He looked as if he was going to drop everything to give her priority. She shook her head at him and pretended to examine a row of dresses. Henry pushed his glasses up his nose and turned his attention back to his customer.

'That'll be one pound and ten shillings, Mrs Moss.'

'It's to wear to my daughter's wedding. I wanted something smart, but warm for the time of year. Do you think it will be all right, Mr Murtell?'

'I'm sure it will.' Henry took the two pound notes she offered him and handed her four half-crowns in change. 'Take it home and show it to your husband; if he doesn't like it we'll find you something else.'

'You're very kind.' Mrs Moss dropped the coins into her capacious bag and picked up her parcel. 'I was delighted with that crêpe dress you sold me last week. My friends all admired it and wouldn't believe me when I told them it only cost seven and six. I'm recommending you to everyone.' She hurried to the door and poked her head outside. 'Good. It's stopped raining at last; and don't forget Mr Murtell, if you do get any real silk blouses I hope you'll keep them for me.'

She was gone and Henry and Belle were alone. They hadn't seen each other since the firework party, and then Belle had been wearing her best and looked like a lady. Today, in the old blue mackintosh, with her red curls tumbling damply over her shoulders and her freckles showing up clearly on her white skin devoid of make-up, she was the old Belle. The Belle he still half-loved and yearned for. She smiled at him as he came round the counter to greet her, a tape measure hanging round his neck, and a silly grin on his face. She took the two remaining apples out of the paper bag, sunk her white teeth into one, and handed Henry the other.

'Come inside so we can talk.'

He drew aside the curtain separating the back room from the rest of the shop. It was the room where Jim used to live

377

among the piles of unsorted rubbish; where Queenie the
cat had presided over a continuous succession of kittens.
Henry had converted it into an office. There was a desk
and chair, a bookshelf filled with ledgers, and a small settee
with the inevitable tabby cat curled up in the corner. Belle
wondered if it was a descendant of the original Queenie.

'You're doing very well,' Belle said, wandering around
looking at everything with interest.

'I can't grumble. Of course I owe it all to Jim. He taught
me everything, and then let me take over when he went
into that home.'

'How is he?'

'Fine. I go and see him every week, and take Alan with
me sometimes. He likes to see him. He doesn't go out at all,
but he plays chess and cards. Sometimes all the old people
are taken out for trips in a special bus. It's not a hospital –
it's a private place.'

'Who pays for it?'

'He does. Everyone thought he was poor, but we found
out he had quite a bit of savings. I suppose you could call
him a miser. He didn't trust banks, and kept bundles of
notes all over the place. Biscuit tins, teapots, mattresses.
He'd even stuffed an old cushion with notes, sewn it up,
and let the cats sleep on it. Anyway, there's plenty for him
to live in comfort for the rest of his days.'

Talking of money reminded Belle of the reason she was
there. She tried to put on a casual expression, and perched
on the edge of the desk swinging her legs.

'I need your advice, Henry. We're old friends and I
thought you might be able to help me.'

'I will if I can.'

'I need a job, badly. I thought you might need an assistant.'

Henry's eyes nearly started out of his head. His heart

raced. To have Belle working here with him in the shop: to see her every day would be his idea of heaven. But he didn't need an assistant. He'd managed things on his own all these years, with just a bit of casual help from his wife Margery. But he could afford it.

'I've never thought of it,' he said honestly.

'I'd be ever so grateful – and you wouldn't regret it.'

She was unconsciously flirting with him and he knew it. She always used her feminine wiles to get her own way, and she hadn't changed. Margery would be bound to find out and he couldn't see her approving; or Auntie Mabel for that matter. No, he'd got to be firm; he didn't want to upset his wife just when the new baby was due in a matter of weeks. There must be some other way he could help Belle.

'I don't think I could afford to employ anyone on a regular basis,' he said, removing his glasses and nervously inspecting the lenses so that he had an excuse not to look at her. 'But if you're hard up I could give you a loan.'

'No thanks.' Her voice was sharp with disappointment. She really had thought she'd only have to smile at Henry and he'd be only too pleased to fall in with her wishes. 'I don't want any favours. If you lent me money you wouldn't get it back for ages. I need a permanent job with a regular wage.'

'Have you looked in the paper? There are usually plenty of jobs advertised there.'

'No I haven't. I expect most of them want someone with experience. I'm not an expert at anything except sewing.'

'Don't put yourself down, Belle. You could learn to do anything you set your mind to. I've got yesterday's evening paper here. Let's have a look and see what they have to offer.'

They spread the paper on the desk and studied the columns listing job vacancies. There seemed to be quite a lot of them. There were no openings for barmaids, which was a job she could do; or box-office staff. There were plenty of openings for domestic servants but the pay was low: only about half a crown an hour. She would have to work around the clock, scrubbing and polishing other people's homes, to earn enough to get by. But Alice had been doing it for years and never complained. Belle pushed that reminder away.

'Here's something that you could do.' Henry held a page of newsprint up and read aloud. ' "Mature lady wanted. Good at machine and hand sewing; to make gloves and other accessories." There's a telephone number.'

'I haven't made any gloves for years.' Belle had lost interest and was fiddling with the ink-well on Henry's desk. It had a silver top and looked expensive. It showed how well he was doing.

'But you can't have forgotten. You used to make them for yourself, as well as your own dresses; and very pretty they were too.'

Belle thought back. She had liked sewing once upon a time. Particularly the sequined evening-gloves she'd made at the factory, and the stage costumes for the theatre. It might be better than nothing.

'Does it give a name as well as a number?'

'Yes. Mrs Watkins.'

Belle grabbed the paper out of Henry's hand and studied the advert. 'It's Lena Watkins without a doubt,' she said. 'Where I used to work. She's advertising for experienced staff. I don't fancy going back to a job on a factory bench but I suppose it would be better than nothing. She'll probably snap me up if I apply. What do you think, Henry?'

'I think it's a good idea.'

'I'll give it a try. If I can't stand it I can always keep my eye open for something better.'

She was busy tearing the printed square out of the paper when the shop bell clattered. Someone had opened the street door.

'I'll have to go. I've got a customer.'

Henry pulled the dividing curtains aside and then stopped in his tracks. Belle heard hesitant footsteps and then a voice she recognised.

'I want a black suit.'

'Mr Kelly!' Henry advanced into the shop and led George to a chair. The older man looked drawn and pale, as if something terrible had happened to him and he was still in shock. 'Belle,' he called over his shoulder. 'It's your father.'

'Dada!' Belle ran into the shop and knelt on the floor beside the huddled figure. 'What's happened?'

George stared at his daughter. He didn't seem to be at all surprised to find her in Henry's shop. He took her hand and pressed it tightly. His hand felt cold and rough to the touch.

'I need a black suit. Bessie's gone.'

'Mam – gone. Do you mean she's dead?'

'Yes. I had this telegram from the hospital.' He searched in his pocket and pulled out a crumpled piece of yellow paper. He handed it to Belle. All it said was, 'Elizabeth Kelly passed away. Please contact.' It was signed by some doctor with a signature she couldn't read.

'Maud was out with Lucy, so I went down to the box on the corner and telephoned. They said it was very sudden, and she didn't suffer. Just slipped away in her sleep they said: quite peaceful. So you see, I must have a black suit to put on before I go and see Father Joe to arrange the funeral.'

'I'll find you something.' Henry began to search through the racks.

'Your Gran always kept something black in the wardrobe just in case. She said everybody did that in Ireland because there was so much death about. I haven't needed a mourning suit since she passed away; and then I borrowed one.'

'Here – try this.' Henry had come forward with a jacket. George stood up helplessly. He seemed to have lost the power of motion. It took both Belle and Henry to remove his old working jacket and slip his arms into the new one. 'There's a mirror in the corner.'

His reflection was slightly comic. His lined face with its halo of wispy grey hair, and then the smart black coat over his striped flannel shirt, and his baggy trousers held up by braces and a thin leather belt. Confronting his image in the mirror seemed to bring it home to him that his Bess was dead. A tear slipped down his cheek and he didn't bother to wipe it away. Belle was standing behind him; he could see her in the glass.

'She was a good woman,' he said simply. 'I loved her once.'

'Of course you did, Dada.'

'You thought she was hard and unfeeling, but she wasn't like that when I first met her. She was pretty and gay, just like you. She wanted to be a lady and have nice things. I promised them to her. But life got at us; and then the war came.'

'And Charlie died.'

'It was my fault.'

'No it wasn't, Dada; it wasn't anybody's fault. It was a bomb.'

'I didn't mean that, Belle. Charlie was our son, but you were my daughter. My little Brighton Belle: that's what I called you. She said I spoiled you, and I did. You came to me with your childhood troubles and I'd side with you. She was jealous of you because she thought I cared for you more than her. So she turned to Charlie.'

Belle thought of Lucy. Was it always like this between

mothers and daughters, fathers and sons? Jealousy rearing its ugly head and spoiling relationships. She only knew that she loved her father more at that moment than she'd ever loved him. His pain was her pain; his mourning her mourning.

'You look very smart,' she said softly. 'I'll come with you to see Father Joe.'

'No. I'm all right now.' He took the black trousers Henry was holding out and disappeared into the back room to change behind the curtains. When he reappeared he'd recovered his composure and dried his face. 'Thanks, Henry,' he said, touching the young man briefly on the shoulder. Then he turned to Belle. 'I'll be off then. Don't worry, Maud will look after me; and Lucy. I'll let you know about the funeral.' He stepped out into the street and walked briskly away.

Belle turned a tragic face to Henry. 'He didn't pay you for the suit,' she said. 'I expect he forgot.'

'I wouldn't have taken it anyway.'

'You'll never make a profit, Henry Murtell, if you give your stock away,' Belle said angrily.

Suddenly she was crying; great tearing sobs that shook her body. Her sorrow was too much for Henry: he put his arms around her shaking shoulders and gathered her to him. She smelt sweet and damp, and her skin was as soft and smooth as he remembered from the day, so long ago, amongst the bluebells. Her red head dropped on to his shoulder and seemed to fit exactly. He touched her hair with his lips: it tasted salty with its exposure to the mist and rain.

'I'm sorry about your mother,' he said. 'But it must have been a happy release.'

'I suppose so.'

'And your father's taken it well . . .'

'Don't talk, Henry.'

She tipped her head childishly to look up at him. He saw her big blue eyes brimming with tears, her freckled face, and her full red lips, and his heart turned over. She saw Henry Murtell: safe and familiar, always there to comfort her when she needed him. When he kissed her she didn't push him away; after all he was Lucy's father although he didn't know it. The fact that he had a wife didn't seem important when she needed comforting. She returned his kiss and he thought he detected passion. He didn't recognise the desperation in the way she clung to him and tried to lose herself in his embrace.

'I'll take you home,' Henry said gently.

'There's no need. I'm perfectly all right.'

'I want to.'

'What about your wife? Won't she be worried about you?'

'She'll be fine. The baby isn't due for two more weeks and Auntie Mabel's there. I'll close the shop early and take you right to your front door. You've had a shock and I think you need company.'

'Thanks, Henry, but I'll be all right.'

But Henry insisted. He locked the door and pulled down the shutters, while Belle waited patiently on the pavement. The rain had cleared and the sun was shining weakly, making everything sparkle. The world smelt fresh and clean.

Belle was determined to walk although Henry suggested the bus would be quicker. She wanted to keep on the move; every time she stopped she saw pictures of her mother flash before her eyes. Those last pictures of a mad stranger with a scarred face staring at her with hatred. Not the pretty, gay young woman her father had fallen in love with.

All too soon they turned the corner into the road where Belle lived. His arm was around her waist, guiding her, protecting her. Suddenly she stopped and froze in her tracks. Henry followed the direction of her eyes to see what had caught her attention. It was a battered old van parked at the side of the road. The cab door opened, and a big man with a handsome face and thick unruly hair swung himself down to the ground.

'Mike!' Belle shouted, and her voice was alive with welcome. She shook off Henry's hand and ran, and the man grinned and swung her off her feet in a bear-like hug.

Henry was forgotten. He turned away sadly and slowly retraced his steps.

24

The happy reunion between Mike and Belle was short-lived. Mike had seen the tall, thin man with the round shoulders and glasses, and wondered who he was. He'd also noticed the lovesick expression on his face, and the way his arm was around Belle in a familiar way as if he owned her. Mike couldn't help wondering what she'd been up to in his absence.

As for Belle, she listened silently to the story about Mike's accident, and the way he'd stayed on to care for Miss Grey after her heart attack, and although it sounded above board she did wonder if he was making it up to pacify her.

'It was the least I could do,' Mike said as he accepted the cup of tea Belle handed him. They were sitting in the basement kitchen as Johnnie was out somewhere. Belle had helped him unload the van and carry the things down the stairs. 'She was so kind to me after Stan left. I couldn't just leave her.'

'You say she had no telephone. Why didn't you write a letter? I was worried; all this time and not a word.'

'I did write.'

'Well it never arrived.'

Belle was busy clearing things away. She hated mess and

386

disorder, and Johnnie had got the flat in an awful state without his brother to keep an eye on him.

'I don't think Miss Grey could have posted it. Don't do that,' he instructed as Belle plunged a pile of dirty plates into a bowl of soapy water. 'I'll wash them up later.'

'I've never seen such a mess,' Belle grumbled. 'You need a woman to keep you in order.'

'Who would you suggest?'

They were sparring. Pleased and relieved to see each other but angry at the same time. Mike couldn't forget Henry's face, and Belle was full of suspicions. He wanted to grab her by her tousled head and kiss her; tell her he loved her, and beg her to marry him.

'What's the matter, Belle?' he asked, sensing that there was more to her unhappy face than the fact that he'd been absent so long. So she told him about her mother dying and that she needed time to adjust.

'I'm sorry,' Mike said. But he didn't know how to comfort and reassure her. Words seemed inadequate somehow. When she finally left him to go upstairs they were locked in a private duel, like two strangers.

Alice was still out, having tea with her fiancé's parents, and the house felt cold and empty. Belle peeled off the old mackintosh after retrieving the newspaper clipping from the pocket. She sat at Joseph's desk and read Lena Watkins's advert again. To go back to the factory would be a step backwards. However badly she needed a job, was she prepared to start all over again? Belle thought deeply. The trouble was her pride, always something she had to fight, before common sense came to the fore. She couldn't afford to be fussy, so she put her pride in her pocket. After all, it was a job, and she was desperate to find some sort of employment. She picked up the telephone and dialled the number before she could change her mind.

A voice she didn't recognise answered. She gave her name as Mrs Bishop and said that she was experienced in the trade. She was careful not to mention that she'd worked for Mrs Watkins before, as it might cause unnecessary probing into her past. An appointment was made for her the following day and the address given was a road in Kemp Town. Mrs Watkins had obviously changed her premises since Belle had left her employ.

Belle arrived early; not like ten years before when she'd arrived late with laddered stockings. She'd dressed carefully, wanting to make a good impression. Her tan coat with the swing back was fashionable, although it was last year's model. She'd smoothed her hair back and secured it with a brown velvet ribbon, so only a few tiny kiss-curls escaped and framed her face. Only the way she clutched her handbag tightly between gloved hands gave away the nervousness she was feeling.

Mrs Watkins had extended her premises into a double-fronted shop. It was a smart establishment glistening with new paint. In one window there was a simple arrangement of gloves and scarves, and a faceless bust wearing a straw boater decorated with trailing ribbons. In the other was a casual arrangement of dried flowers in autumn tints. A young woman with tight blonde curls and a fixed smile was turning the pages of a book of samples on the glass-topped counter.

'Can I help you?' she enquired in a refined voice as Belle approached.

'My name is Mrs Bishop. I have an appointment to see Mrs Watkins. I telephoned yesterday.'

'Please wait here.'

The young woman disappeared through a glass door with PRIVATE painted on it in black and gold lettering. Belle wandered about and stopped to inspect an assortment of gloves laid out in a glass case. They were expensive and showy, but she considered they were inferior in workmanship to gloves she'd made in the past. Output and demand had increased, but a lot of the work seemed to have been done by machines; not the fine hand-sewing Belle had been taught.

'Come this way. Mrs Watkins will see you now.'

Belle followed the girl through a door into the workroom. It was twice the size of the old place, and the women sitting behind the rows of sewing-machines were older and seemed to take their work more seriously. There was no happy chatter or suppressed laughter; only the monotonous whir of the machines.

The photographs of film stars that had graced the old walls hadn't found homes in this new building. In their place were pale tinted prints of painfully thin women, leading equally thin dogs, their thin scarves blowing backwards in invisible winds.

The row of small windows, although hung with bright curtains, overlooked a gloomy warehouse. Belle thought with nostalgia of the panoramic view of Brighton they'd had from the old workroom. She was ushered through a door at the far end, and felt as if she'd stepped back ten years in time, and was fourteen again.

Lena Watkins seemed to have picked up her whole sitting-room and transferred it lock, stock and barrel to the new premises. There was the same shiny leather armchair, and the chintz-covered settee, slightly shabbier but still remembered. Even the walls had been covered by the same brown and green embossed paper.

On a small table set in the window stood the brass cage containing the moth-eaten grey parrot. Mrs Watkins, smaller than she remembered, but still sharp and birdlike in mauve silk with her gold-rimmed spectacles balanced on the end of her nose, was feeding Warlock with sunflower seeds.

'Mrs Watkins, I need a job.'

She'd decided not to beat about the bush. She couldn't afford to. Although it was nearly seven years since Belle had left Lena Watkins's employ she wouldn't have been forgotten. She'd grown up and changed inside, but that was all. It was better to be honest, and hope she'd be remembered for her good workmanship. But Mrs Watkins wasn't looking at her; she was too busy feeding the parrot who hadn't changed at all.

'Mrs Bishop?' she said doubtfully, pushing a grape between the bars.

'Actually, it's Isabel Kelly.'

That name caught Mrs Watkins's attention and she turned from the cage, pushed her glasses back up her nose into a better position, and stared at Belle. Warlock seemed to recognise her first. He screamed, and ruffled his feathers so madly that a shower of pips and shucks flew through the air. A frayed grey feather stuck in his owner's hair, giving her the appearance of an Indian brave.

'So it is!' Mrs Watkins sounded neither pleased nor surprised. 'You see, Warlock remembers you. Why didn't you say who you were? I was told to expect a Mrs Bishop.'

'I am Mrs Bishop now . . . But my husband is dead. I'm a widow.'

'So am I.'

Belle thought of poor inoffensive Mr Watkins and wondered briefly what he'd died of. Certainly nothing exciting, or dramatic, like Joseph. He'd been a grey character, who would have passed away from some minor ailment. Nobody would have noticed, or cared particularly. Certainly not his wife.

'I'm sorry,' was all she could think of to say.

'So you want to come back and work for me?'

'If you'll have me.'

She waited with baited breath, but Mrs Watkins didn't answer immediately. She just picked up a brass hand-bell from the table and rang it loudly. The expression on Warlock's face was a picture. He seemed to screw up his beady eyes, and ruffled his feathers again as if he were trying to put his wings over his ears. The ringing sound was still echoing around the room when hurrying footsteps were heard outside. The door burst open after only the briefest tap, to admit a woman dressed in a navy-blue suit with her hair curled around her ears in tight earphones.

'Joyce!' Belle said in delight, seeing another familiar face. 'Joyce Binns.'

'Goodness gracious!' Joyce strode into the room and inspected Belle from head to foot, as if she couldn't believe her eyes. 'If it isn't little Isabel Kelly. And quite grown up.'

'I'm twenty-five,' Belle said, laughing. 'And I've got a six-year-old daughter.'

'I don't believe it.' Joyce rolled her eyes skywards, showing her surprise at the passing of time. 'Are you coming back to join us? I hope so. You were a good worker and we've missed you.'

'If Mrs Watkins will have me.' Belle looked hopefully at the woman who was trying to sooth the startled parrot's feelings.

'Of course we'll have you,' Mrs Watkins almost snapped, as if annoyed that Belle hadn't read her mind. 'You're worth two of any of those women out there. Some of them don't seem to know one end of a needle from the other. They do the straight machine stitching, but I still need good embroiderers and hand sewers. We make bags, and belts and scarves now, as well as gloves, so there's plenty of work.'

'Thank you, Mrs Watkins.' Belle's shining eyes showed her delight. She'd got herself a job, and she wasn't afraid of hard work.

'Come with me, Belle,' Joyce said, taking her arm. 'I'll show you round, and introduce you to everybody.'

'Just one thing.' Mrs Watkins stopped them before they could leave the room. 'Don't forget: the newest employee has to clean out Warlock's cage. That's one rule that hasn't changed.'

Belle's face dropped. Not that horrible parrot again! And then she heard a chuckle, and it was Mrs Watkins actually laughing. She'd been teasing her, and showed a side of her character Belle had never seen before. Even Warlock seemed to see the funny side: he threw back his head, showing a scraggy neck almost devoid of feathers, and made a fair imitation of his owner's laugh.

Joyce showed her round and gave her the VIP treatment. She introduced her to the other women as one of the best workers they'd ever had. Belle was given a demonstration on one of the machines, but she remained unimpressed. She could see nothing creative or rewarding about turning a wheel and letting a sewing-machine do the work.

The other women, although friendly enough, were much older.

'We can't get young girls to do the work these days,' Joyce explained. 'They don't find it glamorous enough. They all seem to want to be typists or hairdressers. Or work in shops and offices where they can be seen by the public.'

'When I left school I didn't have much choice,' Belle said.

'Nowadays there's plenty of jobs for school-leavers. It's only married women whose children have just started school who need to supplement their incomes. They don't mind the monotony.'

Belle was given her own corner of the workroom where

she could work undisturbed. The difficult and delicate work was brought to her, and she found she'd forgotten none of the skills she'd been taught. Her curly red head was soon a familiar sight, bending over a piece of fabric, pulling the silky thread backwards and forwards and weaving delicate patterns.

Mrs Watkins was so delighted to have her back that she willingly gave her the two days off she needed for family commitments, and without docking her salary. The first was for her mother's funeral, and the second, Alice's wedding.

Bess was buried on a grey winter's day, and Father Joe was called upon to officiate. He was showing his age now and was suffering from various crippling ailments, including rheumatism. He was also overweight and his blood pressure was dangerously high. But he'd watched over the Kelly clan for so many years that when George approached him he'd agreed willingly. He had a new young priest, appointed to help him with his parish work, but he knew George would have been disappointed to see a stranger walking beside the coffin.

Two men in black suits carried Bess into St Anne's Church, and placed the simple pine box with its brass handles reverently down on the trestles before the altar. Belle and George walked behind. George was wearing the suit Henry had given him, and Belle wore a black coat and a little pill-box hat. She looked taller and thinner in her high-heeled court shoes, her head bowed sadly. She towered protectively over her father even so.

The church was cold: nobody had bothered to stoke the boiler. Father Joe was usually fussy about his church being a place of welcome, even for sad occasions. In the summer he liked to keep it cool and airy, a place to rest your feet and refresh your soul; and in the winter it needed to be warm and cosy in order to entice people out of their homes. These days he couldn't be bothered; it was enough that he'd forfeited his morning nap to struggle into his egg-stained cassock and waddle into the church.

The new priest, his deputy, was still young enough not to notice the cold, and believed in spartan living. He preached that suffering sharpens the soul, and too much comfort is bad for you. They had long arguments late at night in the presbytery and the young man usually won, but only because Father Joe let him. Joe believed in warmth and comfort and love, in that order, bringing people nearer to God. He was a man of the people, and knew that people were important. If you gave them too much pain, too much suffering, they closed the door and began to doubt the very existence of God.

Once he was in the familiar pulpit he felt better and was glad he'd made the effort. He looked out on the sparse congregation: George Kelly and his daughter Isabel – her with the red hair. There were two nuns in the front row rattling their rosaries, and a tramp rustling paper. Two figures at the back he didn't immediately recognise, but Belle had spotted them out of the corner of her eye and was surprised. A middle-aged woman with iron-grey hair and a coat and hat to match, and a youngish man in a dark suit with rounded shoulders and glasses. It was Henry and his Auntie Mabel, come to pay their last respects. Belle was pleased and hoped her father had noticed them. They all knew Mrs Murtell's opinion of the Catholic Church and its followers; she must have made a special effort to put in an appearance.

The words flowed from Father Joe's lips automatically. He didn't need to read them, he'd said them so many times over so many dead bodies. The sweet smell of incense wafted through the cold air as he prayed for the soul of Elizabeth Mary Kelly.

The bearers lifted the coffin back on to their shoulders as if it were a feather-weight. Surely nobody, even in death, could be that light or small.

There were only the black hearse and one funeral car, but they drove so slowly through the town centre that they brought the busy traffic almost to a standstill. Why, we're almost like royalty, Belle thought, looking out of the window at the women bowing their heads and the men doffing their caps as they passed. As they neared the cemetery the procession picked up speed, and the springs under the seats bounced as they turned sharply through the gates and climbed the widening hill between the rows of graves. Granite tombs with undecipherable names, angels with open books, green chippings raked smooth as ice within a stone framework. Every one a memorial; every one different.

The grave-digger had done his job and tactfully disappeared to eat his lunch, to reappear later on when the hole was ready to be filled.

'I hope the relatives don't grieve too long,' he muttered. 'I don't get paid overtime.'

As they approached, the cars slowed to a dignified pace. Everything looked black and white on this cold winter's day. White marble against a colourless sky and the black shapes of leafless trees, so the splash of purple by the grave stood out in contrast. It was Maud Carter, wearing her best dress waiting for her George.

Belle glanced at Father Joe. Would he think Maud's appearance on this solemn occasion to be a sign of bad taste? Surely she should have kept a low profile until her predecessor had been decently laid to rest?

But Father Joe had other ideas. He beckoned her forward to the graveside during the committal. They made a grand pair: both elephantine in height and breadth; he in black and white, she in voluminous deep purple. Her hat was like a cartwheel which the wind, blowing in from the Downs, threatened to snatch. They all made the token gesture of scattering a handful of earth on to the coffin-lid. The two solitary wreaths, from George and Belle, were placed each side.

They turned away, more relieved than overcome by grief. Who could be anything but relieved that the misery Bess had suffered over the years was at an end and she was now at rest. Belle felt almost guilty as she walked away; but she was glad that the funeral was over and she could now get on with her life.

'Who's coming back for the wake then?' The words were spoken by Maud who was still hanging on to her hat. 'That's what they have in Ireland, don't they, Father?'

'They do that.' Father Joe was struggling across the uneven turf towards the car. 'When my father died we held a wake that went on for three days. It's supposed to be held while the body is still in the house, but these days it's just an excuse for a party.'

His face was red and he was sweating profusely. It took three of them to heave him into the back of the car, where he collapsed against the padded cushions and mopped his brow with a handkerchief the size of a tea-towel.

By the time they arrived back at Duke's Road they all felt more cheerful. George had loosened his collar, and Belle and Maud had removed their hats. Maud kicked her shoes off and lumbered into the kitchen to put the kettle on, while George led the others into the front room which had been opened up specially for the occasion. The leaves on the table had been pulled out to accommodate the food, and the plates disappeared under the sandwiches and sausage rolls Maud had prepared. Belle was grateful for the cup of tea she was handed, but everyone else helped themselves from a sherry bottle left conveniently open on a tray with an assortment of glasses.

'This is a sad occasion . . .' Father Joe started to say as if it was expected of him.

'No, it's not,' George said, and stared at the old priest as if daring him to start an argument. 'Bess was a fine woman when I married her, but she's only been living half a life since Charlie died. She wanted to die a long time ago so that she could be with him. That's why she threw herself through that window.'

'So be it,' Father Joe said, sipping his drink as if it were nectar. 'She's at peace now and we must be thankful.'

'God works in a mysterious way,' Maud said, padding around on her bare feet, a plate in each hand.

She started humming to herself and Belle was glad it was a hymn. Some of Maud's bawdy ditties would hardly be suitable for the occasion. They were all surprised when Father Joe joined in. Mellow and comfortable after two glasses of sherry he broke into, 'There is a green hill far away,' beating time with his chubby fingers on the arm of the chair. He had a surprisingly tuneful voice for a man of his age, and soon George and Maud had joined in to accompany him in 'All Things Bright and Beautiful' and 'Onward Christian soldiers'.

They seemed to be set for a musical evening if they hadn't been interrupted mid-verse by the arrival of Lucy.

She stood shyly in the doorway in a comfortable old cut-me-down dress, with a straggly piece of green ribbon dangling from her hair. George noticed her first and he held out his arms in welcome and she ran to him. Belle looked disappointed. George whispered instructions into the child's ear and she turned to her mother, greeting her politely and holding up her face for a kiss. Belle hugged her daughter, but Lucy couldn't help noticing the frown of disapproval at her untidy appearance. The hug seemed to be given as a duty; not like the bear-like hug she'd exchanged with her grandfather.

They'd discussed together whether it would be suitable for Lucy to attend her grandmother's funeral, but decided against it. After all they'd never known each other, and Lucy was really too young to understand. She stared wonderingly at the food, and Father Joe, and her mother dressed all in black. She seemed to be silently accusing the grown-ups of having a party behind her back.

'What have you been doing today, Lucy?' Belle asked.

'We sent her next door,' Maud explained. 'The Murtells have got a new baby so Margery couldn't come to the funeral. You like Margery and Henry, don't you love?' She handed the fattest sausage roll left on the plate to the child.

'And Alan. I like Alan best: he's my friend.'

So Henry was a father again for the third time. Belle's heart turned over at the plain little creature, in her shabby clothes, biting into the pastry as if she were ravenous. Would she ever dare tell her about her parentage; and if she did would she understand? She thought of her mother who'd just been laid to rest, and the mysterious bond that seemed to bind mothers and daughters, and at the same time form a wedge that drove them apart. For the first time she caught a fleeting glimpse of how Bess must have felt sometimes, and she warmed slightly to the feeling. Perhaps it meant that now she could stand back and see the mother/daughter situation with the eyes of an adult.

'Is the new baby a boy or a girl?' she couldn't help asking.

'A boy. His name's Ben, and Margery lets me hold him sometimes.'

Another boy. Everyone seemed to be having boys, and all she'd been able to produce was this one puny daughter. Suddenly she was overcome with love for Lucy and hugged her close. Just for a moment she wondered if Bess had ever felt like this, and she as a child, had rejected her mother's advances.

'I think it's time you came home,' she said on impulse.

'I don't want to.' Lucy wriggled in her grasp. 'I want to stay here. I can, can't I?' she asked, turning beseeching eyes on Maud and her grandfather.

'Let her stay a while longer,' George said. 'We're only just getting to know each other.'

Belle wanted to argue. She felt they were all in league against her; but when she thought it over carefully she saw that it was for the best. She would be at work all day, and Alice would be married soon and moving out to live at the bakery. There would be no one at home to care for the child and she was still too young to be left on her own. At least at Duke's Road she was loved and wanted. Belle decided to leave things as they were for the present.

Alice's wedding was a bit of an anti-climax after the funeral. No one, however hard they tried, could have turned that plump pudding into a radiant bride. Belle tried. She made her a blue dress, cut in simple lines to slim down her figure, and trimmed a big brimmed hat with artificial flowers to hide her dull hair. But if Belle was disappointed in her artistic achievement, Arthur Pratt the baker thought Alice was beautiful; and after all, he was the one marrying her.

The old 'uns were lured from their retirement to see their son married. They smiled and nodded and clicked their false teeth as they sat on the hard chairs provided by the Registry Office. When the solemn pronouncement was made that Arthur and Alice were now man and wife, they actually applauded.

Belle was asked back to the rooms over the shop for a celebratory tea, and looked with trepidation at the cream cakes and sugary pastries that were laid out for the occasion. She feared for her waistline as she accepted a cream-horn, one of Arthur's specialities, but couldn't help licking her lips in appreciation.

When she let herself into her own home later that evening, leaving Alice in the bosom of the Pratt family, the loneliness of the empty house surrounded her like a tangible force. The only sound was a radio playing dance music somewhere close by. Perhaps Mike Walker was feeling as lonely as she was and had switched on the music to cheer himself up. Alice had sent him an invitation to the wedding but he'd apologised for his absence, pleading a previous engagement. But he'd sent a fluted glass vase wrapped in silver paper for a present.

'Isn't it lovely,' Alice had said proudly as she showed it to Belle. 'I don't know where I'm going to put it though. It's so fragile, and Arthur and the old 'uns are always breaking things.'

Belle took off the clothes she'd worn to the wedding and stretched lazily, shaking loose her hair. She had to be up first thing in the morning so as to be at work early to make up for the time she'd taken off. She thought sleep would come rapidly but the music kept her awake. She tossed and turned in her lonely bed wondering where Mike was and what he was doing.

In the basement Mike turned up the radio even louder to keep himself company. He thought of Belle upstairs alone and longed to know what she was thinking. She had become so independent and self-contained that he was frightened to push himself forward in case his attentions were unwanted. Some day soon, he hoped, she'd need him, and he'd be waiting.

The winter mornings were dark and frosty. Belle was muffled to the ears as she waited for the early bus to take her to

Kemp Town. She alighted after her twenty-minute ride along the sea-front almost opposite the front door of the shop. It had a large sign hanging outside proclaiming that Lena Watkins sold only the best gloves and accessories.

Usually the windows with their displays of finery were illuminated, even at this time of day. It was Carol Jenkins's job to switch on the lights and remove the shutters when she arrived. Carol was the blonde receptionist with the curls who had greeted Belle on her first day. Mrs Watkins employed her to grace the desk and look ornamental. She was the only young member of staff, apart from Belle, and was no good in the workroom, as she could neither sew nor understand the workings of the machines.

Belle was surprised to see the windows still in darkness, but as she crossed the road she saw Mrs Watkins's tiny form struggling with the shutters. They were heavy and Belle quickly went to the help of the older woman.

'What's happened to Carol?' she asked. 'Is she ill?'

Mrs Watkins shook her head so that her long ear-rings jangled. She gave her familiar little snort which showed something had displeased her.

'I told her not to come in today; not after what happened yesterday.'

Belle carried the shutters into the shop and leant them against the wall. She didn't know Carol very well, but what she had seen of her hadn't impressed her. Several times she'd caught the girl flirting with some of the male customers. Usually they were sent by their wives to collect goods or place orders, and Belle hoped the wives weren't aware of the giggling innuendos that went on over the counter. She was surprised that Mrs Watkins hadn't put a stop to it long ago. As for Belle, she hadn't considered that it was any of her business. Her job was in the workroom, and the staff's morals were up to them. Mrs Watkins looked upset and Belle waited for her to unburden herself.

'I'm giving Miss Jenkins her notice, and I've told her I won't give her a reference.'

'Why? What's she done?'

'I knew about the way she makes eyes at anything in trousers, and I overlook it as long as the wives don't complain. I'm not a prude, and a pretty face behind the counter is always good for business. But yesterday, when I cashed up, I found the till was short by three pounds.'

'Perhaps she made a mistake. Gave too much change or something.'

'It's not the first time. Only last week I checked the till-roll and found a discrepancy; so yesterday I marked a note. She asked one of the women to do some shopping for her, and lo and behold she handed her the marked note from her purse.'

'I can't believe it, Mrs Watkins. Did you call the police?'

'I threatened to, but it would have been very unpleasant. She didn't deny it anyhow, so I gave her instant dismissal. I said I'd send her wages on to her.'

'So what will you do now, Mrs Watkins? Advertise for a new receptionist?'

Belle had already unwound the warm woollen scarf and taken off her coat, ready to take her place in the workroom. She had a busy day ahead of her: trying to catch up with the work that would be waiting after her day's absence.

'I don't need to advertise.' Mrs Watkins was smiling. 'I need someone honest, hard-working, and attractive to the eye. Someone I know I can trust. You'll get a good rise in your salary if you accept the post, Mrs Bishop.'

25

Early morning sunlight filtered through the dusty window high-lighting the untidiness of the basement kitchen. The sink was piled with unwashed dishes and the table littered with the remains of the last meal.

Mike sat, in his shirt-sleeves, contemplating the brown dregs in the bottom of his cup. He was unshaven and looked as melancholy as his dreary surroundings. A cheerful whistle outside made him look up. Through the window he could just see two trousered legs descending the area steps. The letterbox rattled, and the postman climbed back to the street level.

'Post!' Mike yelled at Johnnie, who had just wandered out of his bedroom wearing only the bottom half of his pyjamas. He was stretching and yawning sleepily. 'Get it will you.'

'Bills, bills, and more bills.' Johnnie appeared in the doorway, an assortment of envelopes in his hand.

'Throw them away.'

'You'd better open them. There might be something important.' He tossed one after the other on to the table-top until there was only one remaining in his hand. 'This looks interesting.'

'Open it then.'

'It's addressed to you: M. Walker Esq. What have you been up to Mike?'

'Nothing that I know of.' Mike took the long brown envelope and studied the postmark. 'Guildford. Who do we know in Guildford?'

'One of your fancy women?' Johnnie was grinning.

'I should be so lucky.'

'You'd better open it and see.' Johnnie was busy pouring himself a cup of tea from the pot, leaving a trail of drips across the surface of the table. Mike slowly slit the envelope open with a sticky knife and pulled out the sheet of paper it contained. Johnnie watched him, his nose buried in his cup. 'What is it?'

Mike didn't answer, but his expression had changed. He read the letter through with close attention, and then turned to the top of the sheet and read it through again. Then he silently handed it across the table to his brother.

'Read it.'

Johnnie did as he was told, and then turned to Mike a face transformed with amazement. 'Amelia Grey. Who's she?'

'You remember – I told you about that old woman I helped last year. I only knew her as Miss Grey, but it must be her. It says Greenacres, and that was the name of her house.'

'It says here that she's died.'

'I'm not surprised. She must have been in her eighties. She was a real character. Sometimes we played cards half the night and she usually beat me. I didn't know her name was Amelia . . .'

'Mike!' Johnnie was leaning across the table excitedly. 'Haven't you taken in what it says here? This is from her solicitor; they've been trying to trace you because, in her will which she made just before she died, she's made you her sole beneficiary.'

'I'd better read it again.' He did so, quickly and with his full attention. 'Good lord! Johnnie you're right. I get the house and contents, minus death duties, of course.'

'You're rich! congratulations.' Johnnie reached across to take his brother's hand and pump it up and down.

'It looks like it.' Mike still looked half dazed, the good news was almost too much for him.

'You'll be able to marry Belle now.'

'What did you say?'

'You heard me – you'll be able to marry Belle now. That's what you want, isn't it? You've been too proud to ask her before. I suppose you thought she wouldn't accept you when you had nothing to offer her.'

'I have asked her before.'

'You're a dark horse, Mike. Don't tell me she was daft enough to turn you down?'

'She said she'd think about it.'

'When was this?'

'Last October; when all that business with Flora was going on. She seemed so alone; I thought she needed some sort of support.'

'Not the best time to propose marriage: in the middle of a crisis.'

'And then that business with Stan blew up, and I was away for weeks recovering from the blow on the head and nursing Miss Grey. I did try and write, but she said she didn't get the letter.'

'I suppose she thought it was all an excuse and you'd found someone else?'

'I don't know what she thought. I could feel she didn't believe my explanation; that she thought I was lying. I suppose you can't blame her.'

'She'll believe you now: you can show her this letter.'

'I don't know that I want to.' Mike was carefully folding the precious piece of paper up and replacing it in the envelope.

'Mike!' Johnnie was beginning to look exasperated. 'What's come over you? You hardly ever talk about her, and she never comes down to see us like she used to. What's happened?'

'I'm not sure. I still love her if that's what you're wondering.' Mike stopped, he was trying to find the right words to explain to his brother what was on his mind. 'I fell for her a long time ago; when her husband was still alive, if you want me to be honest. I thought she was the prettiest thing, the way she used to prance along the street pushing Lucy in her pram. Of course I didn't do anything about it because she was a married woman. But when she was free she seemed to turn to me, and I thought there was hope.'

'So what happened?'

'She became too independent I suppose. She didn't seem to need anybody. When she thought I was lying to her I began to doubt whether she'd ever really cared for me at all.'

'What are you going to do?'

'Wait a while. I've learnt patience. If we're meant for each other something will happen. I'm a great believer in fate.'

Johnnie looked doubtful. He cared about his brother and wanted to see him happy. 'Don't wait too long,' he said. 'Or you might lose her.'

But Mike thought he'd lost Belle already. He still couldn't get out of his mind the picture of a round-shouldered man with glasses, and the way his eyes had followed Belle before he'd turned away in the street. Belle had welcomed him home that day in her usual impulsive way, but since then she'd kept her distance, and when their paths met she was polite rather than friendly.

'There she goes. She's early today.'

Johnnie had crossed to the window and was looking up. From that position he could see the front path and steps leading to the street. Mike joined him.

They could see Belle's shapely legs in high-heeled shoes, and the line of her slim-fitting turquoise skirt hugging her hips. As she reached the pavement the rest of her body was in his line of vision. His heart skipped a beat. She was wearing a matching bluey-green jacket, cut short to the waist, and trimmed with a row of tiny pearl buttons, over a white blouse that foamed with lace. Her hair was carelessly piled high at the back of her head, with loose curls escaping and tumbling to her shoulders. She stopped on the pavement to wait for someone who'd followed her from the house. A little girl appeared at her side. Belle took the child's hand in hers and they walked together.

'I didn't know Lucy was back,' Mike said, turning away now that there was nothing to watch.

'I don't think it's permanent,' Johnnie said. He might be quiet and serious in his outlook, but he was also interested in human nature, and nothing much went on in the neighbourhood that escaped his notice. 'Belle has her to stay when she's not working, and the rest of the time she still lives with her grandfather and his woman-friend.'

'That sounds like an odd arrangement. The poor little kid deserves a safe secure home.'

'The sort you could give her.'

'Shut up, Johnnie!' Mike strode angrily across the room to rinse his cup. 'I'll do things in my own good time.'

Johnnie smiled and shut himself in his bedroom to dress, leaving Mike to his private thoughts. They had a busy day ahead, moving a load of heavy furniture from one side of the town to the other. Mike was glad; keeping busy would stop him thinking about Belle.

*

407

'I don't want to go shopping. I want to go to the park.'

Belle sighed, and looked down at her little daughter. Lucy, now seven years old, had a mind of her own and had become increasingly difficult of late.

Her own father had now been a widower for over six months; but even so it had come as a surprise when he'd confided to her that he and Maud Carter were getting married in August. She also found that she was pleased at the idea. Maud for all her common ways had become a good friend, and she looked after George's welfare in a casual, affectionate manner.

Lucy adored staying at the house in Duke's Road and would have been quite happy to live there permanently, but Belle had at last decided that she wanted Lucy back with her for some of the time at least.

She missed the child and she was lonely in the big house on her own. Now that Lucy had become friendly with Alan Murtell she didn't talk about Peter half so much, and her childish innocence seemed to have blotted out the terrible happenings of the previous year.

Sometimes Belle worried about the two children becoming too close. They were after all half-brother and -sister, although she was the only one who knew that. When she saw them together, their dark heads close, a thrill of fear stabbed her. They were so alike: thin and pale, just like their father; and Lucy still wore glasses to correct her eyesight. She even had Henry's gesture of brushing a stray lock of straight brown hair out of her eyes.

'Please be good, Lucy,' she begged, as the child pulled her hand away and began to hop up and down from the kerb into the gutter. 'We're meeting Maud to buy you a pretty dress for the wedding. Then I have to go to work, so she's taking you home with her. I'll give you some money to buy an ice-cream at De Marcos.'

'Will Granddad be there?'

'I expect so.'

'All right.'

Lucy slipped her hand back into her mother's. An ice-cream and an afternoon with her grandfather was a good enough enticement for her to behave. Buying a new dress would be boring, particularly if they tried to fit her out in something pink and frilly. She'd have to face that problem when the time arrived.

Maud was waiting for them under the life-size statue of Queen Victoria. They walked through the Pavilion Gardens towards the shops. They had to walk slowly so that Maud could keep up with them. These days she was finding her weight a burden, and she plodded slowly beside them on her flat feet, panting breathlessly at the unusual exertion. The red silky dress that she was wearing didn't help. It seemed to reflect the heat, and above the tight bodice her plump face was streaked with perspiration, and her black hair hung in damp strands.

She perked up however when they reached the cooler interior of a big store. The fashion department was spacious, with an overhead fan keeping the air moving. There were chairs to rest on as well and she sank down gratefully, slipping off her tight shoes and wriggling her toes.

'We'd like to see some summer dresses, suitable for a wedding,' Belle told the assistant, a strait-laced figure in black crêpe.

'Can I go and look at the toys?' Lucy asked, heading for an archway leading to the next department where she could see rows of dolls.

'Don't go far away.'

Belle spent a difficult half-hour squeezed into a changing cubicle with Maud, trying to button that woman's surplus flesh into a variety of unsuitable dresses. Yellow velvet trimmed with a black silk fringe wasn't Belle's idea of a bride's outfit. Neither was a floating confection of blue and orange stripes that caught Maud's eye. In the end they compromised over a dress in peach-coloured silk, with a big white collar and a sash. It was a bit girlish for a woman of Maud's age and size, but it was smart and she seemed to like it.

Belle didn't need a new outfit, she planned to wear her favourite dress made of cream cotton. She called Lucy in from the toy department where she'd been playing with a dolls' tea-set made of real china.

'For your birthday,' Belle promised, pulling her away.

'But that's ages. Not until next year.'

'Christmas then.'

Lucy glowered, but followed her mother obediently. Maud had been busy searching along the racks of children's dresses and was holding one up as they joined her.

'Don't you think this one's lovely?' she asked Belle.

'It's rather bright. What do you think, Lucy?'

'I'm not wearing that!' the child said emphatically.

Belle didn't blame her. The dress was made of bright yellow satin, with rows of glittering frills stitched to a square yoke. It hung from Maud's hand like a buttercup yellow bell. But Maud insisted on Lucy trying it on, and the wriggling little creature was stripped of her cotton dress and the fancy creation slipped over her head. It did nothing for her at all, and she scowled at the grown-ups furiously.

'I don't think the colour suits her,' Belle said doubtfully. 'Yellow always makes her skin look more sallow than it already is.'

'Well I think it's ever so pretty, and I'm paying,' Maud said. 'You like it, don't you, love?' Lucy shook her head. She felt stupid in the silly dress and was near to tears. 'You look ever so sweet; just like a fairy.'

'I don't want to look like a fairy. I want to look like a girl.'

'Perhaps we can find her something else,' Belle said, appealing to the assistant with a quick glance behind Maud's broad back. 'Have you anything in blue? I always think she looks better in blue.'

Maud was still set on the yellow, but Belle stood her ground. She sided with Lucy. When the child fell in love with a simple blue linen dress with not a frill in sight, just a row of tiny covered buttons in the shape of acorns down the back and a single box pleat, Belle insisted that it was exactly right. To please Maud she bought a straw hat with a little brim that shaded her childish face, but she made the assistant remove the bunch of artificial flowers pinned to the side and replace it with a blue ribbon band.

They finally left the store loaded with parcels and pleased with their purchases. Maud seemed to have forgiven them for not liking her first choice of the yellow satin, and had treated Lucy to the china tea-set she coveted. She never held a grudge, and liked to see everyone around her happy.

'Let's go and have a cup of tea,' she insisted. 'And I'm paying.'

There was just time before Belle had to catch the bus to work. They found an open-air café in front of the Royal Pavilion, and sat at a little white table under the shady trees where every evening flocks of starlings roosted for the night. Lucy had a glass of lemonade and sipped it carefully as she admired her new tea-set.

It was a pleasant spot, with the sea to the south and the Downs behind them skirting the town. Unfortunately the drunks and tramps also found it congenial, and groups of ragged figures were always to be found huddled on the benches around the fairy-tale palace. Police and park-attendants did their rounds and periodically moved them on. They would pick up their belongings and wander off in the direction of the seafront leaving a trail of litter and empty bottles behind, only to reappear when the coast was clear to claim their favourite seats. Belle felt sorry for the homeless drifters. Many of them came down on the train from London thinking that the pavements of Brighton were paved with gold. They were soon disillusioned and ended up in hostels, on park benches, or even under the pier, where at least they were fed with hot soup by a local charity.

A ragged couple passed them and sank to the ground against some ornate railings. The man had his arms about the woman in a bold intimate way, and they were sharing the contents of a bottle.

Maud decided that it was time to take Lucy home. Belle watched the fat woman and the skinny child slowly walk away towards the bus stop. Just before they disappeared from sight Lucy turned and waved to her mother. She was smiling again. content that the shopping expedition she had been dreading had been concluded to everyone's satisfaction.

It was time for her to get to work. Mrs Watkins had given her the morning off to do her shopping, but she'd promised to be back at her post by twelve o'clock. She had time for a leisurely stroll through the gardens before catching the bus to Kemp Town. She had to pass the couple on the grass to reach the road. The woman's face was hidden in her companion's shoulder, but Belle couldn't help noticing with distaste the way the man's hand was groping inside the woman's bodice, kneading her breasts with his dirty hand. Belle had to step over their legs which were stretched across the path. The woman moved as she picked her way over them and she tripped and almost fell to the ground.

'Mind where you're going,' the man growled. He waved his empty bottle threateningly at Belle.

'I'm sorry.' She'd dropped her bag and some of the contents had spilled out. She knelt down to retrieve her purse.

'Can you spare us the price of a cup of tea, lady?'

Belle placed a shilling in the palm of the tramp's hand. She felt genuinely sorry for him, but she was also afraid of his anger if she refused.

'That ain't no lady. Give her the money back.'

It was the woman who had spoken. Belle felt a chill run up her spine at the words and the tone of the woman's voice. From under the brim of the battered hat she wore the ragged woman was staring up at Belle, and she saw the familiar hazel eyes under their heavy lids. Those eyes were the most remarkable things about Flora, and they were the only things still recognisable under the filthy exterior.

Belle had often thought about her old friend, and wondered what had happened to her. Now here she was, half-drunk, and living with the poorest dregs of society. Belle's heart went out to her in pity. Whatever she had or hadn't done, she didn't deserve to end up like this.

'Listen, Flora,' Belle said, ignoring the man who'd quickly slipped the shilling into his pocket. 'There must be something I can do to help you.'

'Hark at Lady Muck.' The sound that issued from Flora's lips was meant to be a laugh, but there was no humour in it. 'The last time you helped me I ended up on remand.'

'I'm sorry if that's what you think. Perhaps I can make amends in some way. What do you need the most: money, food, a place to sleep?'

'I need to forget the day I met you, Isabel Kelly. With your false promises of friendship and your fine ideas.'

Belle didn't know whether to take the hint and leave, or try further persuasion. She turned to Flora's companion for help, but he'd drained his bottle and was once more waving it aggressively in her direction.

413

'You heard what Flo said. She wants to be left alone, and that goes for me as well.'

'All right; but you know where to find me if you change your mind.' Belle opened her purse and took out a pound note. She held it out to the ragged couple. 'Take this and get yourselves something to eat.'

The man stretched out his hand eagerly, but Flora suddenly came to life and screamed at him, 'Don't touch her filthy money! I'd rather starve than take anything from her.' And she spat in Belle's direction. Although she drew back quickly a gob of spittle landed on Belle's shoe. She couldn't help wrinkling up her nose in disgust.

Flora and her companion seemed to find this funny, and as she turned away she heard them laughing and shouting insults after her.

She hurried through the crowd of pedestrians thronging Castle Square and boarded her bus. She sank into her seat with relief; but she was shaking and had difficulty extracting the coins from her purse to pay the conductor. Well at least she'd tried. If her path crossed Flora's again it would be better to give her a wide berth. You couldn't help people like that. Even so, as she let herself into the shop under the sign that read 'Lena Watkins – gloves and accessories made to order', she could still see Flora's face. It would be a long time before she would be able to forget the bitter hatred in those hazel eyes. Where once she'd had a friend, she now had an enemy.

As she took off her jacket she looked around the shop. There was a long list of jobs she had to do to catch up with her morning's absence, including rearranging the window display, and filling out an order-form for the company who supplied buttons and embroidery silks. In between she had to answer the telephone and deal with any customer's enquiries.

The early part of the afternoon was busy and Belle managed to push away the unpleasant morning meeting. She took a large order from Lady Duvet, who usually sent her maid with specified instructions. Today she came in person to choose the materials to match her autumn wardrobe. She was a tall, thin woman of striking appearance who most people considered intimidating. Belle however got on with her well, and always undertook the hand-sewing on any gloves she ordered – often taking the work home to finish at her leisure.

After Lady Duvet she had to help two giggling young women choose chiffon scarves to match their summer dresses. When they left, delighted with their purchases, she started on the window display. She was busy with an arrangement of dried seed heads, poppies and honesty behind a tall stone jar containing sunflowers. Their bright heads were the size of dinner plates. Mrs Watkins came from the back room to join her.

'I thought I'd use these new silk scarves with the designs of peacock feathers as a background to the new evening gloves.' Belle stepped back to view her handiwork.

'You certainly have some original ideas, Mrs Bishop.' Lena Watkins looked pleased. 'I've had a letter from a women's magazine; they want to do a spread about us.'

'How exciting,' Belle said. 'That will give you some publicity for the winter collection.'

'I'd like to put the new lines on show somewhere.' Mrs Watkins was busy inspecting the other window which was still full of cotton goods.

'We need more space,' Belle sighed.

'That's what I want to talk to you about. Come here.' Belle followed her employer to the door. Mrs Watkins was looking along the street at an adjoining shop which had recently closed down. There was an estate agent's board outside saying the remains of the lease was for sale. 'Would that be enough space, Mrs Bishop?'

'But would there be enough work for another factory, Mrs Watkins?' Belle wasn't sure what Mrs Watkins had in mind.

'Not another factory – a showroom, with changing cubicles. Subdued lighting and soft music. I think it's time we expanded again – this time into lingerie.'

'We'd need extra staff.'

'Of course. Home-workers like we used to employ. Only the best. I'd need someone to train them and be my personal assistant. Would you be interested, Mrs Bishop?'

Would she indeed! Belle's face lit up at the idea Mrs Watkins was proposing. 'I'd be more than interested,' she said frankly.

'Good. I always knew you had potential; and so did Warlock,' said Mrs Watkins. 'How much money can you put down?'

'Money?'

'Of course. If we're going into partnership you'll need to invest something as well. When I retire you can take over, lock, stock and barrel. I can make you a wealthy woman, Mrs Bishop.'

The talk of investing money had spoilt Belle's excitement. She was living more than comfortably on the money she earned, but she hadn't the sort of capital she'd need to buy her way into a business.

'How much?' she asked bluntly.

'Two thousand: that should be enough. Now I know you haven't got that sort of money just lying around waiting, so I can give you time to raise it if you're interested. How about six months? You must have contacts, or a bank manager who would give you a loan. Are you still interested?'

Belle was interested but she also knew that it was

impossible. She couldn't see any way of raising that amount of money in such a short space of time. If she owned her own home she could have put it up as collateral, but she was still only a tenant. She spent sleepless nights and restless days trying to find a way to realise her dream – without success. She would never be a partner and equal to Lena Watkins. She was destined to be just an employee.

Maud and George's wedding day arrived to change the passage of her thoughts. It was the brightest, jolliest wedding Brighton had seen for a long time. The town centre was decked out with flags for a conference, but to the bride they were there to welcome her noisy arrival at the civil offices. The dress of peach silk was a great success, and after hours of cajoling Belle had managed to coil her long black hair into a knot at the back of her head. A big-brimmed white hat, set at a rakish angle, gave Maud the appearance of a plump imp when she smiled at George as he stood beside her. Belle suddenly realised what a striking woman Maud was, and her heart reached out with affection to the kindly woman who had now taken her mother's place.

Their arms about each other's waists, the happy couple led the way across the road to have their photographs taken in front of the Royal Pavilion. They looked so pleased with life, and each other, that they might have been royalty themselves.

A ground-floor room had been rented at the King and Queen public house for a buffet meal. Maud seemed to have invited everyone she knew and the room was soon packed with jolly well-wishers, many of whom Belle had never seen before. Maud was popular and everyone had turned out to congratulate her on her big day. George had nothing to do but move around among the guests shaking hands, with a silly grin on his face. Soon the party grew so large that it overflowed into the courtyard outside which was hung with cages of singing birds and baskets of flowers.

Belle saw Lucy with the hem of her new frock already hanging down, sharing a piece of wedding-cake with Alan Murtell. Then she spotted Henry arriving with his wife, Margery, at his side, a plump eight-month-old baby in her arms. They hadn't seen her because she was positioned behind a pillar trailing with rambler roses, but Belle couldn't help noticing the way Henry fussed over his wife, pulling forward a chair for her and relieving her from the weight of the heavy child.

She'd sensed that he was aware of her although he wasn't looking in her direction. After all, she knew very well that he'd only married Margery because she, his first love, was unattainable. But Henry's love brought her no comfort. Everyone else seemed to have someone to keep them company. She was the only one alone. She was toying with the idea of joining Henry and his wife, to see if she could exert the same power over him as she had in the old days. She'd taken half a step in their direction when a hand fell on her arm, staying her.

'A splendid sight, isn't it, Isabel Kelly?'

It was Father Joe. He'd not been asked to officiate at the nuptials as Maud had insisted on a civil wedding, but he'd been delighted at his invitation to the reception.

'Yes, Father,' Belle agreed. 'Doesn't Maud look happy?'

'I wasn't referring to our Maud. That lady has got what she deserves, and she's waited long enough for it.' Belle's eyes followed his. It was Henry and Margery he was looking at. She suddenly felt the old priest could read her mind and hid her nose in her glass to hide her discomfort. 'I was referring to the Murtells: such a lovely family, and so devoted. Your Lucy and their Alan get on so well together. They might be brother and sister, they're so close.'

He knew her secret; she could tell by the way his booming voice had dropped low for her ears alone. He was warning her not to break up the happy family.

'A toast! A toast to the bride and groom,' someone was calling, and a fresh glass was thrust into her hands. She moved away from Father Joe and stood on her own in the crowd. She had a good view of the wedding party. George was toasting Maud as they gazed into each other's eyes. They had the rest of their lives before them. Henry had slipped his arm around Margery's shoulders, and was gazing down at his baby son devotedly.

Everyone seemed to have someone of their own, someone to turn to, except her. Even Lucy was standing by the bride and groom holding little Alan's hand, and everyone was saying what a pretty picture they made.

Belle couldn't bear to watch. She turned away with tears in her eyes.

26

The reception carried on its merry way well into the evening. The room at the King and Queen had been booked until closing time, so although the bride and groom would be leaving for their honeymoon, there was nothing to stop the party continuing. At seven o'clock a taxi drew up with packed suitcases already stowed away in the boot. They were to travel to Worthing to spend two nights at a sea-front hotel.

Belle had tried to persuade them to go somewhere a bit more adventurous; after all, Worthing after Brighton was like going home from home. They were both sea-side holiday resorts with piers and promenades, and only a few miles apart. But George was adamant. 'If I have to go anywhere it's got to be a place where I'll feel at home – and I must be able to see the sea. What do you say, Maud?'

'It's fine by me,' Maud said. 'I've never been to Worthing.'

She didn't mind where they went now that she had George for keeps and a gold band on her plump finger.

There was such excitement as the guests helped the pair into the car for the short ride to the railway station. Someone had tied one of George's old gardening boots on to the back, and there was so much confetti they had to grope their way, half-blinded by the coloured snowstorms. Everyone cheered and waved as they drove away, and then returned to fill their glasses and tuck into the remains of the food.

Everyone got merry, but nobody spoilt things by getting drunk As the sky darkened, and the evening air cooled the revellers pleasantly, hundreds of tiny flying insects hovered around the outside lamps, assuring them that the good weather was set to continue.

Father Joe, nostalgic and mellow with wine, changed the tempo of the evening. He heaved himself to his feet and struck an attitude, before giving them a rendering of the old song 'The Lost Chord' by Sir Arthur Sullivan. Then a couple sang a passable duet. Nobody knew who they were, but by this time nobody cared. They could have wandered in from the street for all it mattered.

'Why don't you get up and recite one of your poems?' Alan Murtell whispered to Lucy. 'I dare you.'

Lucy couldn't resist a dare. 'I know a poem,' she announced in a loud voice.

Someone hauled her on to a chair. Alan was now safely hidden behind a nearby pillar waiting to see if his friend would fluff her lines. It had seemed exciting as the grown-ups stepped back to give her room and patted her encouragingly as they helped her up. But when she looked out and saw the sea of faces, all turned towards her, all waiting for her to entertain them, her heart sank.

'Come on, kid,' someone shouted. 'You can do it.'

Lucy stood there, her thumb in her mouth, looking out at her audience and trying to remember the first line of her poem. Her mind had gone blank and she couldn't remember a word. She wished Maud was there beside her egging her on to perform. But Maud and her grandfather were a

421

long way away on a train, and she was alone.

And then she saw her mother. Belle was standing alone, under a flowery arch of honeysuckle. The long strands of creamy scented blossoms haloed her red head and matched the milky colour of her dress. She looked so beautiful that for a moment Lucy couldn't breathe. Belle was watching her daughter with an encouraging smile on her face.

Lucy took a deep breath and started, 'There are fairies at the bottom of my garden.' She faltered once in the first verse but looked at her mother again: Belle smiled and nodded as if she were doing fine. After that Lucy relaxed and began to enjoy herself. She gave quite a performance, waving her arms about to indicate the King and Queen of the Fairies 'floating down upon their car'. When she reached the final line, and paused dramatically so they could try and guess the identity of the Queen of the Fairies, and ended with 'Well – it's me!' she brought the house down.

She was a huge success. Someone lifted her from the chair, and she was passed over people's heads until she was set down beside her mother. Belle was smiling so proudly that Lucy flung herself into her arms – a thing she'd never done spontaneously before. They hugged each other.

'Was I all right?' she asked.

'You were wonderful. I'm so proud of you.' And Belle meant it.

It wasn't because her little daughter had shown her cleverness or because everyone around was praising the child. It was because Belle had suddenly seen her daughter through the crowd: the little figure in her blue dress, so frightened as she faced her first audience, but so brave. Some belated feeling had stirred in Belle's heart, and she'd reached out in love to Lucy to spur her on. Their eyes had met just for a moment, and it was as if there was an invisible cord between them, like the umbilical cord that had joined them before birth; but this one would never be broken.

After that someone produced a violin and a merry jig was played to set feet tapping and the younger ones dancing. At the height of the revelry Belle and Lucy stole away. The child's energy had started to flag and she was ready for bed. But there was a new companionship between them as hand in hand, like a couple of conspirators, they crept away into the dark.

Lucy had never been out in the dark streets before but she felt safe walking beside her mother. She tried to match her footsteps, and gazed around her in wonder at the fairy lights and flood-lit gardens. Brighton at night was mysterious and exciting, and she fell in love with it there and then.

The house was dark when they reached home, although there was a dim light shining through the basement curtains. The van was parked in the road so Mike must be at home, as well as his brother. Belle was groping in her bag for the doorkey, while Lucy was hovering behind her having a last look at the dark street.

'Mummy, there's someone over there watching us.' Lucy, suddenly afraid, clutched at Belle's skirt.

'Where? I can't see anybody.'

'Over there – in the garden of that house. I saw someone staring; and then they dodged behind the wall.'

'You're imagining things. That's because you're tired. Let's go inside and I'll make you a hot drink and put you to bed.'

'I'm not imagining things. I did see someone.' Lucy insisted as Belle ushered her inside the front door.

The house was dark and silent, but when they'd switched on the lights, and a saucepan of milk was heating on the stove, everything looked more cheerful. Lucy drank her cocoa at the kitchen table while Belle was running her bath. Alice always used to supervise bath times, and it felt strange to the little girl to have her mother soaping her back and warming the towels. Belle didn't even seem to mind getting splashed – although Lucy didn't do it deliberately – and she was wearing one of her best dresses.

Lucy chose to sleep in the single room at the top of the stairs. She still avoided the old nursery and the memories it held of Peter. Belle tucked her in and asked if she wanted a story.

'Squirrel Nutkin,' Lucy said, curling up into a ball and watching Belle folding her clothes into a neat pile. 'But you don't have to read it to me: I know it by heart.'

'You'd better tell it to me then.'

So Lucy told her mother the story of the rude squirrel and the way he tormented the wise old owl. Belle was struck again by the way she acted the story out. Lucy was a clever mimic and Belle realised for the first time how gifted she was. Her plain face lit up as she became involved in the story. Her eyes sparkled and she looked almost pretty. When she'd finished she turned to Belle for approval.

'Very good,' Belle said, clapping her hands. 'I think you should have acting lessons. Would you like that?'

'No.' Lucy's face dropped, and she looked worried. 'Don't send me away again.'

'I didn't mean you'd have to be sent away. We can probably find some classes you can join here in Brighton. Maud could take you.'

'Do I have to go back and live with Maud and Granddad?'

'I thought you wanted to.' Belle sat down on the edge of the bed, pleased that Lucy was old enough to confide in her. 'You always say you love Duke's Road, and you'd like to live there all the time.'

424

'I know – but I miss you, Mummy. I think I'd like to come back here and live with you. Just you and me, Mummy. That's all I want.'

'I'll have to think about it,' Belle promised. 'There'd be no one here to care for you while I'm at work. Or take you to school.'

'I'm nearly eight; I can go on my own. And we could still go and visit Maud and Granddad, couldn't we?'

'I'll see what I can arrange. Now go to sleep or you'll never wake up in the morning. I'll leave the door ajar; if you want me I'm in my usual room at the end of the passage.'

Belle leant over to kiss her, and Lucy reached up and twined her arms around her mother's neck. They smiled into each other's eyes as if they liked what they saw there.

Lucy was so tired that her eyelids began to droop before Belle had left the room. She switched out the light, leaving just the tiny glow of the night-light beside the bed. In her own room she undressed quickly, and wrapped in a warm gown sat at the dressing-table to brush her hair.

She felt excited, pleased that Lucy wanted to come back and live with her permanently; she hadn't realised before how much she'd missed her. It wouldn't be easy, she knew. She'd have to employ someone, at least part-time, to take Alice's place. But it would be worth it. They were both alone in the world, but now that Lucy needed her it seemed to have opened up the floodgates of love between mother and daughter.

Belle's thoughts recently had been full of schemes to raise the money to go into partnership with Lena Watkins. It had been the height of her ambitions to be part-owner of the showroom and factory. She wanted it badly, but it faded into insignificance beside Lucy's need of her.

Still sweeping the brush through her hair she wandered to the window and looked down into the street. She saw something move in a gap between two houses. There was someone over there; she could see the pale smudge of a face turned in her direction. Lucy hadn't been imagining things.

Belle pulled the curtains to shut out the night. It was probably some homeless tramp trying to find a place to bed down for the night. It was sad, but the town was full of such cases and there was nothing she could do about it. In the morning she'd investigate and if there was someone there, sleeping rough, she'd offer breakfast or the loose change in her purse. So happy was Belle with the reunion between her and Lucy that she felt at peace with the whole world. Sleep came easily.

Across the road there was a movement in the shadows. The dark form crouching behind the wall detached itself and searched for a more comfortable position. The ground was hard, but at least it was dry, warm and dark. When you come this low you like the dark, because then you don't have to face up to what you have become.

Flora, huddled in her filthy rags, raised a bottle to her lips and loudly cursed the moon and stars for shining so brightly. She wasn't completely drunk, but she hoped there was enough left in the bottle to complete the job.

The other bottle wrapped in newspaper was tucked safely in her pocket. She'd stolen it from one of the night creatures as they'd dozed drunkenly under the pier. She recognised the sharp odour and clear violet colour of meths. Years ago she'd used methylated spirits to heat water on a portable stove, and had liked the smell and the pretty blue flame. She pulled the bottle out of her pocket and unwrapped it carefully before unscrewing the cap. Then she tipped it slightly so that her finger just touched the liquid and brought it to her lips, curious about the taste. No, she wasn't that far gone yet!

She placed the bottle on the ground in front of her as if it were treasure, and turned her eyes on the house opposite. She'd seen Belle in her cream dress, and Lucy all in blue, come home so happily, so gaily, as if they hadn't got a care in the world. What right had they to be so happy? She hated Belle because she had everything: a home, a child, and pretty clothes. She, Flora, had nothing. She didn't stop to analyse or point the blame – Belle had succeeded and she had failed, so somehow Belle must be to blame. When Peter died and Belle, who called herself a friend, had notified the police, Flora had sworn she'd have her revenge. She'd paid her price: the time she'd spent on remand had been more than enough. Now it was Belle's turn. Belle and that little brat Lucy had to pay the price as well.

Hidden deep in her leafy den, like a wild animal, Flora kept her solitary watch on the house opposite. She saw the lights go out downstairs and the light in the front bedroom go on. She recognised Belle by her flaming hair as she stood in the square of light, the brush moving rhythmically in her hand. Flora's hands trembled as she lifted the bottle to her lips to drown the throb of anger pulsing through her body. Damn Belle Kelly! She deserved to burn in hell!

But still she bided her time. A cat, thin and homeless as herself, stalked silently out of the bushes. Its yellow eyes glowed with evil as it stepped across her sprawled legs, as if she was of no account. She kicked out with her foot, delivering a blow on the animal's flank. It drew back its head and hissed viciously before vanishing as silently as it had come.

Flora still waited. A door opened nearby. There came the clinking of glass as milk-bottles were put outside, and then the thud of the door closing, and the scrape of metal as the bolt was shot home. Footsteps passed along the street and paused a few feet from Flora's hiding place. A match was struck to light a cigarette and she could just see the features of a man bending over the tiny flame. The dead match was flung away into the bushes to land at Flora's feet. The footsteps hurried away.

At last all was silent, dark and still. Even the moon had hidden its face behind a cloud so as not to be a witness to Flora's revenge. She pulled up her skirts, searching through the layers of clothing until she found the remains of a cotton petticoat. The elastic snapped as she pulled it down and stepped out of it. It didn't matter; it would serve her purpose and she wouldn't be needing it any more.

Picking up the bottle of methylated spirits in one hand she crossed the deserted road and approached the house. The windows were now dark, except for a glow behind the basement curtains. Belle would be in bed by now, thinking herself safe and secure. But nobody, not even Isabel Kelly, was safe from Flora's revenge.

It took no more than a minute to dowse the petticoat in the contents of the violet bottle and stuff it through the letter-box The next part of her plan wasn't so easy. She had three matches in a box, but the first one snapped just below the head as she tried to strike it. The second one flared successfully, but a sudden gust of air caught the flame and extinguished it before she could push it home. The third one behaved itself. She held the box with the fingers of her right hand inside the letter-box, and struck the match with her left. It flared brightly and she kept quite still, knowing that this was her last opportunity. The flame ate into the match until it nearly reached Flora's fingers, and then it leapt into the box with a greedy splutter and burnt brighter. At the right moment Flora dropped the flaming match-box and pulled her fingers quickly away.

She waited for a minute, counting slowly, and then pushed the flap forward a fraction so that she could peer into the hall. It had worked according to plan. The flaring box had landed on the spirit-soaked rag, and it was burning with a merry blue flame directly under a row of coats hanging in the hall. A chuckle of delight issued from Flora's cracked lips, but she stifled the sound quickly in case it alerted a late passer-by. Then pulling the collar of her coat up around her face she stumbled down the steps and along the path. When she reached the pavement she broke into a hobbling run, and like some evil demon disappeared into the darkness.

In the silent hall the blue and orange flames danced about in the draught. The doormat made of dry plaited cord was well alight, and the flames leapt higher trying to reach the corner of a coat to feed their hunger. They made it by climbing the length of a cotton scarf, and then running along the shoulders of the coats, leaving a trail of sparks in their wake. One bold spark found Belle's old straw hat which she wore in the garden in the summer. With a fizz and a crackle a flame shot around the brim. The flaming mass fell to the floor igniting everything inflammable on its way.

Upstairs in the dark bedroom Belle slept dreamlessly; her red hair curling across the pillow, and one white arm flung out from the covers. She'd got used to sleeping in a silent empty house and wasn't tuned in to her daughter's restless stirrings.

Lucy had been dreaming. She was in the garden of her grandfather's house in Duke's Road, and they were having a firework party. George was lighting the bonfire, and Alan was standing beside her holding a lit sparkler in his hand.

'Put it out!' she said, frightened that her friend would burn himself. She put out her hand to take it from him. But the sparkler flared higher and she saw that it wasn't Alan Murtell, but Peter, looking at her with sad eyes, his golden curls falling over his forehead. The flames of the bonfire burned brighter; she could smell woodsmoke and an unpleasant acrid aroma. It wasn't her grandfather any more but Auntie Flora stoking the flames with a metal poker with prongs on the end. She was laughing as she plunged the red-hot prongs into the heart of the fire. The flames leapt up towards the guy perched on top, and it was her mother balanced there wearing her cream dress – her hands were stretched out towards Lucy as if begging for help. But Lucy was too small, and every time she tried to step nearer the fire Flora drove her away. The flames were climbing higher and higher so that they would soon reach Belle, and the smell of smoke was choking her . . .

Lucy woke with a little cry of terror. She wasn't in the house in Duke's Road, but in her mother's home. She felt so damp and uncomfortable that for a moment she thought she must have wet the bed, a thing she hadn't done for years. But it was just the heat and the perspiration bathing her body. Her throat was dry, and although she opened her mouth to call her mother, it hurt so much no sound would come.

The night-light was still flickering on its saucer. She'd forgotten to ask her mother to leave a glass of water beside her bed in case she was thirsty in the night. Maud always remembered without being asked. There was a tooth-glass in the bathroom so she could get herself a drink.

She climbed out of bed and pulled on her dressing-gown: a thing her mother was fussy about. It went back to the days of the boarders when you might meet a stranger on the way to the bathroom. The door was still ajar and Lucy pulled it open. She expected to see the strip of patterned carpet leading to the other rooms, and the well of the stairs, bright with the shaded light that was left on all night. But she couldn't see a thing because the landing was full of smoke.

A cloudy mass of pungent smoke billowed up the stairs and drifted lazily along the passage. She could feel it already irritating her lungs and tickling her throat, making her want to cough. Still half-asleep and half-awake she wasn't sure what was happening, until she looked over the banisters and saw the red hell in the hall below. The wooden rails were already well alight and flames were climbing steadily towards her, cracking the varnish on the wood with a popping sound and leaping in the draught.

Lucy froze, her hand over her mouth, the dressing-gown cord trailing behind her. This wasn't a bonfire, or a jumping jack out of control. The staircase was on fire, and she and her mother were trapped upstairs in the burning house. She wanted to scream a warning, but although she opened her mouth she couldn't force a sound between her lips. The flames were crackling nearer and the smoke was becoming more dense.

A shower of sparks exploded close by and the sudden noise brought her to her senses. She gathered up the hem of her gown into a bundle and fled down the passage on bare feet towards her mother's room.

Belle was fast asleep, her head resting on her arm, her face composed and peaceful. Even in the midst of her headlong flight Lucy couldn't help thinking how pretty her mother was. Just like the Sleeping Beauty in her fairy-tale book. She stood in the doorway with the smoke billowing relentlessly behind her, and then with a spring leapt on to the bed, pummelling Belle with her tiny fists, tears of terror blinding her.

'Mummy! Mummy! Wake up!' she sobbed.

Belle stirred in her sleep and tried to push her away; but the smoke was already beginning to creep across the room and she coughed and turned over. She heard Lucy calling her from a long way off and opened her eyes, surprised at the furious little creature who seemed to be attacking her.

'What is it, Lucy? Have you had a nightmare?'

'Fire!' Lucy sobbed. 'The house is on fire.'

Belle was wide awake: she saw in an instant the danger they were in. The flickering light from the flames was already nearing the landing, and in a matter of minutes would engulf the upper part of the house. When that happened there would be no escape for either of them.

'The window!' she cried, leaping from the bed and running across the room. Even the floor beneath her feet felt unusually warm to her bare soles. 'Stand back.'

The window had always opened easily; in fact Belle usually left the bottom open a couple of inches when the weather was warm. But she'd felt extra tired and forgotten. Now in her haste she couldn't move the sash.

Sobbing with the exertion she tore at the frame uselessly, while Lucy huddled on the bed watching her. At last, in desperation, she grabbed the chair that stood in front of her dressing-table, and holding it like a battering ram hurled herself at the window. The glass shattered with an almighty crash. Regardless of the sharp knife-like edges Belle leant out into the street, her head and shoulders framed in the jagged opening.

'Help!' she screamed. 'Save us! There's a little girl up here – we're trapped.'

The street was empty. It was one o'clock in the morning and everyone was at home, safely tucked up in bed. There was no one abroad to hear Belle's frantic cries. Only a cat with yellow eyes lurking in the undergrowth in the garden, but he didn't care.

The smoke was billowing closer, curling in grey coils along the passage. The only way to escape was to climb higher, hoping someone would be aware of their plight and come to their rescue. Lucy seemed dazed, unable to take

432

instructions, so Belle grabbed her hands and dragged her out of the room. Above them was the attic: a low, curiously shaped chamber where they hoarded unused nursery equipment, Christmas decorations, and other unwanted items they had no immediate use for. Belle couldn't remember when she'd last been up there, but she knew there was a skylight in the roof. If they could reach it in time it might be a means of escape.

Pushing Lucy in front of her she mounted the narrow uncarpeted stairs and opened the trapdoor. With encouraging sounds she urged the child forward into the gloom. They were surrounded by the ghostly shapes of packing-cases and cardboard boxes. There was a dank musty smell which was perfume after the acrid smell of smoke and burning wood.

Somewhere below she heard a dull thud as if something had collapsed under the onslaught of the flames. She held her breath and then groped her way towards the window. It was set at an angle into the roof and was grimy with dirt, but she could just see the moon in the night sky: pure and silver like a precious coin.

She could reach the frame easily. There was a metal catch that looked simple to release. All she had to do was push the skylight open and scream for help before the flames reached them. Her hands were cold and trembling and she had to take a deep breath to control them. The latch was rusted into place; nobody had opened the window for years; she couldn't make it budge an inch.

'Mummy,' Lucy said in a tiny voice. 'I can't breathe.'

'I'm trying to open the window, and then we can get out and be safe. Don't be frightened. Someone will know we're up here and come.'

Her words seemed to reassure Lucy, but Belle wasn't as confident as she sounded. There was no one to know they were up there. She couldn't open the skylight, and eventually the flames would reach them, if the floorboards didn't collapse first and throw them helplessly into the inferno below.

Belle sank down on the floor where she could see the moon, and putting her arms round the whimpering child, held her close. Lucy twined her arms around her mother's neck and rested her head on her shoulder. They were as close as mother and daughter could be, and their defences were down.

Mike had sat up late thinking. He'd had another letter from Miss Grey's solicitor asking what he intended to do about his inheritance. Johnnie had told him to marry Belle, carry her away to Greenacres, and live happily ever after. Mike knew it wasn't as simple as that.

He sat at the kitchen table, his feet propped on the edge of the sink. All around him were empty coffee cups and overflowing ash-trays. He wasn't going to turn in until he'd decided on the future.

There were three options. He could sell up, invest the money and carry on as if nothing had happened, hoping that one day Belle would need him; or he could risk her refusal, put his cards on the table, ask her again to marry him, and if she accepted carry her away to Greenacres; or lastly he could admit defeat, sell up and go a long way away, and try to start a new life and forget her. He rather thought the last one was the one he would have to choose. He lit the last cigarette in the packet, determined that by the time he'd stubbed it out he would have made a decision. As he drew the smoke into his lungs he heard a scream.

Someone fooling about in the street? A domestic argument? An accident? It didn't concern him at this time of night; let the police deal with it. He crossed to the window to close the curtains and saw the moon like a silver ball floating over the rooftops opposite. But why was the house front so bright? Not with silver moonlight, but a rosy flickering glow against the night sky.

Curiously he opened the front door and strolled into the area. He was immediately alerted by the crackling of flames and the smell of burning. He glanced upwards and saw to his horror that the inside of the house was an inferno. If Belle was in there, and still alive, he had to reach her – but how?

He saw the broken glass in the bedroom window. He had a ladder in the back of the van that might just be tall enough to reach the sill. If he could get inside he might be in time. He rushed back into the flat calling for Johnnie, instructing him to run to the nearest telephone and call the fire brigade.

Mike pulled out the ladder and extended it to its full height so that the top rung just reached the window-sill. There wasn't time to be afraid. He climbed upwards two steps at a time, and ignoring the jagged glass leapt into the room. The floorboards were beginning to smoulder and he had to grope his way across the smoke-filled room, but he was reassured by the fact that it was deserted. So were the other bedrooms. If Belle was still inside she must have climbed higher, away from the flames.

He ran up the attic stairs and immediately took in the situation. Two figures huddled in the gloom under the window. They seemed half-conscious, either with fear or the inhalation of smoke. But Belle looked up at him and moved aside so that he could reach the window. Her face was white as paper in the moonlight, but at least she was alive.

His strong fingers grappled with the clasp, and then he pushed the glass with his hands and the frame creaked upwards. A blast of fresh air, smelling of honeysuckle and

435

salt, rushed into the dark attic reviving the occupants.

'We'll go up on the roof,' Mike said, pulling a wooden box under the opening for Belle to stand on.

When she was safely through he followed with Lucy in his arms. They crouched there on the slanting tiles, with the child between them and the pavement far below. Belle was shivering.

'Someone will see us,' Mike said, putting his arms around her.

'Perhaps they won't. Perhaps we're going to die.'

'Sh! Don't talk like that in front of Lucy. Someone will come. Johnnie phoned the fire brigade.'

Belle clung to him; her eyes clear blue and her hair blowing backwards. 'Just in case they don't come. Just in case we die – will you kiss me, Mike?'

Suddenly the danger seemed unimportant. Mike's arms around her, strong and safe, made the fire and everything else fade into the background. She clung to him as if he was her lifeline, and all the love that had been dammed up for so long overflowed. He could see it in her eyes, in the way she trembled under his touch as she waited for his lips to meet hers.

But the kiss had to wait, because just as his lips were touching hers with the gentleness of a lover, they heard the clanging of a bell. The fire-engine had made good time through the empty streets and drew up outside the burning house.

Soon they would be rescued. Soon the flames would be dowsed. But as the flames died, the flames of love were stirring in their hearts, to grow stronger before the night was past.

27

'It's incredible!'

Belle was standing on the grass verge outside Greenacres looking up at the house. It certainly looked its best on this late September day, covered in unpruned roses and wisteria.

Mike came up behind her holding Lucy by the hand. 'Do you like it?'

'It's like a dream come true. And it really belongs to you?'

'Us.'

They'd been married two weeks, and it had been the happiest two weeks of Belle's life. After the traumatic events of the fire, when she'd thought she'd lost everything and life would never be the same again, she'd found instead that the best times were only just beginning.

She hadn't accepted Mike's proposal out of gratitude, or the need of a companion because the days were dark. She'd accepted because when he kissed her on the roof-top, before the firemen reached them to lead them down the ladder to safety, she'd known that this was the man she really loved.

More than Henry, the father of her child; more than Joseph, who she'd been attracted to because of what he could give her. More than any man she'd met or imagined.

She was left with nothing. Everything she owned had been lost in the fire; and she hadn't been insured. All she had was Lucy and her job. Her dream of buying herself into Lena Watkins's business was now further away than ever.

Mike couldn't have much more. But at least he still had his shabby old flat which seemed to have escaped unharmed, his van, and Johnnie. So feeling as she did it was easy to imagine that marriage between them might work. Her pride, which had always been a barrier between them, was now gone. They could start to build a new life.

Mrs Watkins had given her an extended period of leave to get married and sort her affairs out. Her job was waiting for her, but only when she felt able to pick up the reins. She didn't need a honeymoon. The joy of waking up beside Mike in his poky bedroom, with Johnnie whistling outside and the gutted rooms upstairs, was a daily reminder of what she'd gained, not lost.

Mike had deliberately not told her about Greenacres because he wanted to see her face when he showed it to her. So he'd waited. That morning over breakfast he'd decided the time was right.

'What are you doing today?' he'd asked.

'Nothing much. Why?'

'I thought we'd collect Lucy and go for a drive.'

'Where to?'

'Into the country.'

'That sounds like a lovely idea.'

Lucy was excited, she thought they were going on a picnic. Belle wondered why the back of the van was piled with boxes and bags, as if they were going for a month, not just a day. The only ones he'd confided in were Johnnie and George. He didn't want them to worry if they didn't return that night.

Before they got out of the van, while Lucy was staring at the pretty house and Belle was worrying about parking on private property, Mike had enlightened them. Greenacres belonged to them: it had been left to him in the will of Amelia Grey, the old lady he'd befriended. They were going to make their home in it for a few weeks until they decided whether they wanted to live there permanently.

It was the sort of house Belle had once dreamed of living in. Bigger and better than the one Joseph's mother still owned. She would feel like the lady of the manor living in a house like this.

'Would you like to live here?' she asked, turning to Lucy. But the child had already scampered away to explore the garden. 'It's perfect for a child,' she said to Mike, thinking of the gardens in Duke's Road: with only a wall between the narrow gardens.

'Come and see the inside.'

Belle followed him up the path to the front door, where he'd stood listening to Stan threatening Miss Grey. The skirt of her green dress billowed around her bare legs, and her hair hung in curls from a matching ribbon. She was twenty-six, but she still looked like the young girl he'd first seen pushing a pram along a Brighton street. He'd thought she was pretty then; now he thought she was beautiful.

The key was large and ornate and he had difficulty turning it in the lock. When the heavy door was open he hesitated on the step; then stepped aside to let her precede him. A grandfather clock with a painted face was ticking a welcome. It was the heart-beat of the house itself. As if, although Amelia Grey was dead, her house was still very much alive.

Belle wandered through the large, airy rooms in a dream, running her finger along the grain of a beautiful piece of old wood, or stroking the curved side of a specimen of antique porcelain. She couldn't believe that all this belonged to Mike, and he'd kept dark about it so he could spring it as a delightful surprise when the moment was ripe.

'Do you think you'll be happy here?'

'Oh, Mike! Can you doubt it?'

'Come and see the upstairs.'

The bedrooms with their four-poster beds and chintz curtains delighted her. She flung herself full-length on a patchwork quilt, faded with age, but beautiful in its mellow antiquity.

'Do you think Amelia Grey made this?'

'We'll never know.'

'The stitching is so fine. Better than mine.' He lay down beside her and took her in his arms. He hoped wherever Miss Grey was she could see them, and know how happy they were. Belle put up her face like a child to be kissed. She smelt of grass and wild flowers and a heady sensuality.

'Have I told you that I love you?' he whispered in her ear as he caressed her tenderly.

'Not since breakfast.' Her eyes were dreamy and her nose freckled by the sun. His hands were arousing her, and she stirred with pleasure under his touch. He wanted her fiercely, as he'd never wanted a woman before. He knew this was one woman he'd never get tired of. Suddenly Belle stopped and pulled away, smoothing her wild hair and pulling down her green skirt in a modest gesture that provoked him even more.

'We mustn't. Lucy might come looking for us.'

'Damn Lucy. I suppose I'll have to wait until she's in bed.'

'Aren't I worth waiting for?' she said demurely.

'I'd wait for you for ever.'

He put out his hands to pull her to him, but right on cue Lucy ran into the room. She was beaming all over her thin face, and her cheeks were flushed with colour. She looked almost pretty, even with grubby hands and a tear in her dress.

'There's a funny little garden where everything smells of Christmas,' she announced. Belle guessed that she must have discovered a herb garden that would give out a mixture of sweet and spicy smells. 'And there's a bush in the shape of a giant bird, and a slope you can roll down, and nobody to tell you off if you squash the daisies. And right at the bottom of the garden there's a little stream – and I found some blackberries.' She held out her stained fingers for their inspection.

Belle laughed. 'So you like it here?'

'It's lovely: as long as we can all live here together.'

'That's the idea,' Mike reassured her. 'From now on, whereever we live, it'll always be together. Now we'd better go and decide where you're going to sleep.'

'I've chosen already.' Lucy took his hand and dragged him to the door. 'I saw a little window right at the top: just like Rapunzel's. So I climbed the stairs until I found it. It's a lovely room. There are two beds so Alan can come and stay. But . . .' the smile slipped a little. 'I can't see the sea, although it's ever so high up.'

'We're too far inland to see the sea, Lucy.'

'I can't smell it either. I shall miss that.'

'You'll get used to it.'

'I suppose so.' She brightened up quickly, anxious to tell him what else she had discovered. 'There's a box that plays a tune when you wind a handle, and the banisters are wide enough to slide down and . . .'

'What else?'

'I wish Alan was here.'

'He can come and stay, we promise. And Maud and Granddad, and anybody else you miss.'

Lucy was content and rushed out of the room to see what other wonders she could discover. So began a succession of long, quiet, sun-filled days, full of country walks and pottering in the garden. Early nights when the air was so still that the windows were left wide open, and the song of the birds woke them from their dreams. Belle would wake lazily, stretching out a bare arm to make sure that Mike was beside her and it wasn't all an illusion.

Lucy was happy, but she still begged and begged for her friend Alan to come and stay. A visit was arranged, just for a day, and Mike drove to Brighton to collect him. While he was there he thought he might as well collect Maud and George as well. When the van door opened and they all tumbled out, Belle and Lucy didn't know which one to embrace first.

Such a day they had exchanging news and showing the visitors the charms of Greenacres and its surroundings. Maud fell in love with the kitchen and the old iron range. 'I'll swap it any time for my old kitchen,' she declared. 'There isn't room to swing a cat in the one in Duke's Road. I'm covered in bruises from trying to dodge the corners.'

George inspected the garden and advised Mike on the quickest way to improve the vegetable plot. 'If you set to work quickly, you can have it under control before the winter sets in,' he said.

Lucy and Alan greeted each other with whoops of delight. They disappeared into the garden, not to resurface until they were hungry.

Belle had got used to cooking on the range and had made meat and potato pies for the grown-ups, and sausages and baked potatoes for the children. Mike had investigated the cellar and brought up a bottle of table wine. They decided not to include the cellar in the guided tour, as the dusty bottles might have proved too much for Maud and George.

It was the sort of family party Belle had always longed for. Three generations of the Kelly family side by side at the same table. All close, happy and loving. Mike proved a good host: teasing Maud, talking about plants to George, and turning a blind eye to the table-manners of the children. Their excited reunion had got a bit out of hand.

While Belle cleared away, Maud waddled into the drawing-room and collapsed contentedly on to the big sofa and slipped off her shoes. Belle handed round cups of coffee and they all relaxed. The visit was proving a great success.

The good food had pleasantly tired the grown-ups but it seemed to have stoked up more energy in the children. They couldn't keep still, so Lucy took Alan upstairs to show him her bedroom. He bounced on the beds in turn, declaring that his mattress at home was much softer.

'My mummy says it's unhealthy to sleep on a soft mattress,' Lucy said loftily. She didn't like criticism, even from Alan. 'Look out of the window. You can see the little wood at the bottom of the garden.'

'But you can't see any houses.' Alan was peering over her shoulder.

'Of course you can't, silly. This is the country. There aren't any houses for miles and miles.'

'I don't think I should like that. I like lots of houses around me: it makes me feel safe.'

'I pretend I'm an explorer,' Lucy said dreamily. 'I'm high up in the rigging of a ship, like in *Treasure Island*, and wild beasts are waiting for me in the garden.'

Alan looked down at the tangle of greenery below. 'I can't see any wild beasts – not even a cat.'

'It's only a game. Have you forgotten already how we used to pretend?'

'It's easier to pretend at home.' Alan looked worried. He didn't want to upset Lucy but be couldn't pretend just to please her. 'I mean, we used to pretend the rainwater butt was a pond, and that the garden went on for miles and miles. But here there's a real pond and the garden does go on for ever. So there's nothing to imagine.'

Lucy knew exactly what he meant. It was a bit like dreaming about the presents you wanted for your birthday. If you got exactly what you asked for it was always a bit of an anti-climax.

'Look at the birds,' she said, pointing down at the lawn. 'They're ever so tame. We put bread out for them, and sometimes they come right up to the kitchen door.'

'What are they?'

'The small ones are tits, and the others are wrens I think. At least that's what Mike said.'

'Where are the sea-gulls?'

'There aren't any, silly. We're miles from the sea.'

'I don't think I should like that: not being able to see the sea-gulls.'

After that things slowly got worse. Mike organised a game of cricket but Lucy got bored. She missed a catch because she was picking daisies, and Alan waded into a patch of nettles and got stung.

Indoors things weren't going so well either. Maud had got her second wind and was wandering about the drawing-room looking at Miss Grey's collection of china and glass. She was a bit like a bull in a china shop. Belle held her breath every time her fat white hand delved into a cupboard to pick up some delicate piece that caught her eye. The inevitable happened. She dropped a Staffordshire figure that Belle knew was quite valuable. It wasn't so much the damage that upset Belle; it was the way Maud dismissed the accident.

'It's only an old piece of china,' she said. 'I'll get you something much nicer to replace it. I saw some funny china cats in a gift shop in Brighton when I was shopping the other day. Much prettier than that old thing.'

Belle tried not to look upset. She swept the pieces up and took them out to the dustbin. George was sitting on a bench under a shady tree, looking out over the countryside. His old cap was tilted on the back of his head and he gripped his pipe between his teeth. It was unlit because he'd given up tobacco, but he liked the feel of it. He moved along the seat so Belle could sit down beside him. She didn't know what to say so waited for him to speak first.

He took the pipe out of his mouth slowly and looked into the empty bowl. 'Mike's a good man,' he said at last.

'Yes.'

'And I can see you're happy.' Belle nodded. 'And Lucy. I've never seen her looking so healthy. Of course, we miss her. I know Maud does. But it's right that she should be with you: like a real family.'

'Do you like the house, Dada?'

'It's a bit posh for me. And large; I'd be lost in all those rooms. But it's all right for you youngsters with lots of energy. I was just wondering what it'll be like out here in the winter?'

'Oh, Dada!' Belle couldn't keep the smile off her face. 'You talk as if we're living out in the wilds, away from civilisation. There's a village only just down the road with a church, a pub, and a shop. The coast is only ten miles away. We can be in Brighton in half an hour.'

'I was thinking of snow and power-cuts – that sort of thing.'

'What about them? You have snow in a town; and

445

power-cuts aren't confined to the countryside.'

'I know. But in a town there's always someone on call. That's why it's important to have good neighbours.'

'I don't need neighbours. I've got Mike and Lucy.'

'But Mike will have to go back to work sometime, and Lucy to school.'

'So? I'll be alone here. I don't mind, Dada. I can learn to be a proper housewife.'

'As long as you're happy.'

'I'm happy.'

'What about Mike?'

Belle turned to face her father. She didn't like this probing into her affairs. His questions were stirring undercurrents in her mind. They'd always been there, but in the day-to-day contentment of her life she'd denied their existence.

'Mike's happy. He has no reason not to be: after all it was his idea to come here in the first place. He wanted us to have a new life.'

'You don't have to run away to have a new life.'

'We're not running away! I don't want to listen to you.'

'Why not? Because you don't want to hear the truth?'

'Stop it, Dada.' Belle's voice was almost begging her father not to put into words what she feared might be true.

At that moment Lucy and Alan began to fight. It was only over the ownership of a tennis ball, but Lucy had flung herself at the little boy and he'd tripped and sprawled on the ground. Lucy was sitting on his chest pummelling him with her fists. Mike had been lounging on the grass nearby, and he threw himself into the fray. Cross and red-faced at his step-daughter's behaviour, he slapped her bare legs before dragging the two children apart.

'They don't look very happy to me,' George said in a low voice.

'The children are over-excited and Mike's not used to it. What makes you think he's not happy here, Dada? Have you been talking to him?'

Suddenly Belle felt that she had to know the worst. She'd been living in a dream-world where it was always summer. But like everything in life it would come to an end someday, and then she'd have to face reality.

'I didn't mean that he's not happy with you, Belle. I can see there's nothing to worry about that. It's this place: it's too beautiful, too rural. You'd have to be a countryman born and bred to appreciate it.'

'And Mike's not.'

'No. Neither are you, Belle. You're a town bird like me. We pump up our energy by pounding along the streets, and smelling the smoke and petrol. Once the sun goes down and you're shut indoors, you'll be pining for the bright lights, the shops and the seaside.' He waited for Belle to retaliate, but she didn't. She was looking past him at Mike crossing the lawn towards the house, a struggling child held firmly in each hand. 'He's a town bird too, Belle,' he said gently. 'He's bored already. When he was showing me the vegetable garden I tried to tell him what jobs he should do before the weather sets in. He didn't want to know. He just said "Tell me again if we're still here." '

'Thank you for telling me, Dada,' Belle said.

She slipped her hand through his arm and they walked across the grass to follow Mike and the children into the house.

Mike drove off with their visitors leaving Belle to do the clearing up. Maud had offered to wash the dishes but she had refused. Maud was a guest, and was to be treated as such. Lucy had cheered up sufficiently to kiss everybody goodbye, including Alan; but after she'd waved the van out of sight she disappeared on one of her own private concerns.

The evening sped past and Belle had to search for Lucy in the half-dark. She found her happily paddling in the stream at the end of the garden, and led her back to the house to get ready for bed. She'd expected tears and defiance, but neither was forthcoming. Lucy was good and loving, full of the joys of seeing Alan and Maud and her grandfather again.

Belle sat beside her daughter for a while after she'd drifted off to sleep. She had a lot to think about, and was glad that Mike was taking his time returning home. He'd probably stopped for a drink, or been delayed by a build-up of traffic on the road.

She was sitting up in bed reading when she heard the van rattle across the loose gravel, the slam of the door, and Mike's whistle.

He came to her at once, as if he couldn't bear even an hour's separation. She held up her face for his kiss. He undressed slowly, folding his clothes neatly on a chair at the foot of the bed. Then he crossed to the window, pulling back the curtains and opening the casement wide.

'It's a beautiful evening,' he said. 'I wished you'd come with me.'

'Lucy was tired, and I wanted to clear up.' She closed the book and put it down on the bedside table. He was silhouetted against the window. The naked man's body that she loved, his rounded muscles outlined in silver. She loved him so much it hurt. 'They were our first guests. It was lovely to see them again, and show them everything. I hadn't realised how much I missed them.'

'Don't sound so sad, Belle.'

Mike turned from the window and approached the bed. Belle held out her arms in welcome and he embraced her.

She felt so soft and fragile in his arms he was afraid of crushing her. He stroked her body through the thin stuff of her nightdress and she moaned softly like an animal, stirring languidly under his caresses. She was so beautiful in the moonlight with the red curls hanging loosely on her shoulders, framing her white face, and the little pulse that flickered in the hollow of her throat. He pressed his lips to that spot and she arched her back beneath him. The narrow strap of silk on her shoulder slipped, revealing her pale bosom heaving with emotion.

He wanted to take her gently, as if she were a precious thing, but desire got the better of him. His hands were rough, tearing her gown in his sudden eagerness to possess her. When he found her he entered without mercy, hating himself for what he was doing. At last, exhausted, he tried to roll away, disgusted with himself, expecting her to be disgusted with him. But her arms held him tight, surprisingly strong.

'I'm sorry Belle! I'm sorry!'

He began to weep, and Belle didn't push him away. She held him close. She'd never seen a man cry before. It was awesome and beautiful that one so strong could be so weak. But the fact that he could weep without shame made her love him all the more. She'd never been stirred so deeply by any of the other men in her life: Dada and Charlie, Henry and Joseph, and Peter. The other deep stirrings of love were for Lucy. Different, but just as deep and strong. The protective feeling that only a mother can have for her daughter. It didn't include expectations, or fear, or envy: it was love without chains.

Mike fell asleep in her arms. She felt fulfilled, happy, stronger than she'd ever been. She knew what she wanted, and she thought she knew what was best for all of them.

When Mike woke it was morning and he was alone in the

PEGGY EATON

big bed. Usually it was his habit to get up first, while Belle was still sleeping, and make her a cup of tea. He liked to spoil her, and she enjoyed being cosseted. He got out of bed and crossed to the window, pulling on his trousers at the same time. It was a grey day; summer was drawing to a close, but the mist would clear soon and then the sun would come out.

He could see Belle in the garden. She was wearing her green dress and was gliding across the grass like a dancer on her bare feet, her full skirt floating around her, and her hair flaming with a life of its own around her shoulders. He adored her beauty, and her wildness, and the way she'd comforted him last night with such tenderness.

He dressed quickly and ran down the stairs to join her. She was standing on a little rise of ground, peering through the trees. Her eyes were shaded by her hand, and all she could possibly see was the green curves of the South Downs. He walked up behind her, not making a sound on the soft turf, and slipped his arms around her waist, pulling her to him. She leant back, the curve of her body fitting in to his. They were like two halves of the same puzzle.

'What are you looking for?' he asked.

'I thought I might be able to see the sea.'

'We're too far away.'

'I woke up, Mike, and I thought I could smell it. You know: the salty smell of brine, and the greasy smell of oil and fish. Some people hate it, but I'm used to it. It was so strong that I was sure I would be able to see the sea from the window. But I couldn't. Do you know, I couldn't even remember which direction it was in.'

'Does it mean that much to you?'

Belle rested her head on his shoulder knowing that he would understand.

'Yes, it does. I didn't know how much. I was born within

450

sight and sound of the sea and I've always loved it. I think I'd die if I thought I'd never see it again.'

Mike laughed; but it was a kind laugh. 'It's only the other side of those hills. I can take you there in half an hour.'

'To stay?' She turned in his arms to face him, and now the tears were in her eyes. Those beautiful blue eyes he loved. 'I can't live here, Mike. Not for ever. I'm a Brightonian, and I have to live within sight and sound of the sea. Dada understands – when I was little he used to call me Brighton Belle.'

'What about Lucy?'

'Didn't you see her face yesterday, when she said goodbye to Alan and the others? She was longing to go with them, I could see it in her eyes. That's why she was naughty when they arrived. It wasn't because she didn't want them to come, it was because she wanted to go home with them and she knew they'd have to leave her behind.'

'I'll put Greenacres on the market tomorrow.'

'Do you mind?'

He shook his head. She could see by the expression on his face that he didn't mind a bit.

'To tell you the truth Belle, I'm getting bored. I've lived in the town all my life and I don't think I can stand the silence of the countryside much longer. Yesterday, after I took your family home I dropped in to see Johnnie. He's packing up and going to live up North because the whole house has to be demolished, even our flat. The heat of the fire cracked the walls and it's no longer safe to live in. Then I drove up to Kemp Town to have a look at that shop you've been offered a partnership in. There's plenty of scope there, and I could help with the alterations. There's a flat over the top as well. If we sold up here we could buy our way into the business just as I know you've always wanted. What do you say?'

Belle didn't have to say anything. Mike could tell by her

eyes that it was the best present he could have given her.

While they'd been talking the mist had cleared and they were bathed in sunlight. There was a rush of wings, and a bird, off course, landed with a squawk at their feet. It was a sea-gull, who'd come to guide them home.

28

'Well, what do you think?'

Belle stood in the empty shop and looked around. On her face was an expression of delight and her blue eyes were wide with wonder.

'It's wonderful' she said. 'Look, Mike – at the size of the windows – and the floor space. We could have a fashion show, with mannequins.'

'Now you're getting carried away.' Mike crossed to her side, but he was also looking pleased.

'No I'm not, am I Mrs Watkins?'

Lena Watkins was hovering in the background jangling the bunch of keys she'd used to let them in. She looked older, her hair was almost completely white now and her body seemed to have shrunk, but her beady eyes were still as sharp as ever and the gold-rimmed glasses still had the habit of sliding down her long hooked nose. She peered over the top of them at Belle and Mike, and snorted.

'If she is, Mr Walker, it's only because she can see the potential. Added to the main shop we shall commandeer most of the main road.'

'That's what I'm afraid of.' Belle frowned slightly. 'You don't think we're aiming too high?'

'Belle Kelly afraid!' Mrs Watkins snorted again. 'I've never known you afraid of anything. You were never afraid of me, or Warlock. Don't start being afraid now.'

It was the first time she'd ever called Belle by her Christian name. Firstly it had been Miss Kelly, and then Mrs Bishop, followed by Mrs Walker. It sounded strange to be called Belle, but it was a step in the right direction. If they were going to be partners it was just as well that they started off on a friendly footing; although Belle couldn't imagine calling Mrs Watkins Lena. The idea made her smile.

'What are you grinning about?' Mike asked.

'I'll tell you later.'

'Of course you can see how the previous owners let the place go. That yellow paint is awful.' Mrs Watkins started bustling about exploring corners and flinging open doors. She stopped at an adjoining wall covered in peeling plaster and rapped on it with her knuckles. 'This will have to come down.'

'Why?'

'We'll replace it with an arch; that will make the two shops into one. That will give us even more floor space.'

'Won't we have to have planning permission?'

There was something in the tone of Belle's voice that made Mike look up. He'd met that sharpness before and guessed that it meant something was wrong. He hoped that she wasn't going to be awkward or start an argument.

'That's no problem if we do have to,' Mrs Watkins said. 'I know someone on the town council.' Mike walked through an open doorway. It led into a back room which had obviously been used as a store. There was a pile of old sacks in one corner, and when he investigated he found they contained a mixture of dusty rice and mouse droppings.

'Did this used to be a restaurant?' he asked.

'Yes. But not an English one. Run by Indians I think. At least their name was Patel.'

'That explains the smell of curry.' Mike pushed up a window to air the room. 'What will you use this for?'

'Another workroom. The light's good, and there's room for a long table to take the sewing-machines.'

'I think this would be the best room to partition off into cubicles,' Belle said. She stood there with her hands on her hips and her head on one side, as if deep in thought. 'It would make an ideal changing-room because it's not overlooked. White paint, with a touch of gold-leaf, I think, and red velvet curtains.'

'Not white, dear.' Mrs Watkins said firmly, pattering across the room to close the window Mike had opened. 'White is so cold. Egg-shell blue I think. I've already seen a colour chart and put in an order.'

'But . . .'

Belle was going to start an argument; Mike could see the warning signs. Her blue eyes were flashing dangerously, and the light catching her hair made it look as if it were on fire. He put his hand gently on her arm.

'Perhaps we should talk about that later,' he said, turning to the older woman. 'What's the living accommodation like?'

'Very nice. There's one big bedroom, and a smaller one that will do for the child. Then there are two other large reception rooms, and a spacious kitchen.'

'And a bathroom?' Belle asked. 'I must have a proper bathroom.'

'Well no. There's only an old-fashioned lavatory. But there's plenty of room to build one. Come and see.'

She opened a door and led the way up a flight of steep uncarpeted stairs. By the time she reached the top she was panting and stood still to get her breath. Belle and Mike walked past her.

The flat was large, filling the whole of the upper floor. The rooms were big and airy with large windows.

'I like the view,' Belle said, sitting down on the bedroom window-sill. It was as wide as a seat and the promenade and foam-capped waves could just be seen between a gap in the houses.

'On a clear day you might even be able to see the French coastline,' Mike said. 'Do you like it, Belle?'

'There's hardly any cupboard space. Where would we put everything?'

'I'll build you some fitted cupboards. What's this?' He tried to open a door in the far corner but it was stiff. Then tugging with all his might it suddenly gave way and he staggered backwards into the room under a deluge of old clothes that had been bundled inside. Belle burst out laughing.

'That'll teach you to mind your own business, my lad.'

She picked up an old pair of dungarees, and putting her arm around its empty waist in a ballroom hold, waltzed across the floor.

'I thought for a moment they'd left behind the family skeleton,' Mike said ruefully. 'Is this an "excuse me"?' He whipped Belle's baggy partner away and pulled her into his arms. 'Do you remember when I used to call you the Merry Widow?' he asked, humming the famous Franz Lehár tune softly into her ear.

'And I called you the cheeky bounder in the basement.'

'Well, have you made up your minds?'

Lena Watkins was standing in the doorway expectantly. They broke apart quickly, and Mike began piling the coats and trousers back into the cupboard. 'What do you say, Belle?' he asked over his shoulder.

'I like the flat,' she admitted, looking around again. 'And there's plenty of scope for improvement downstairs, but I still think you're wrong about the back room, Mrs Watkins.'

'Wrong!' Lena Watkins eyes gleamed. She wasn't used to being told she was wrong.

'I wasn't planning on another workroom,' Belle continued. 'I think we have enough machinists already. I was hoping you'd agree on employing people to work from their own homes, like we used to. There's a whole workforce out there. Untapped labour. Skilled hand-sewers with young children who would be glad of a few hours' work without having to disrupt their lives, or the lives of their families.'

'But that's why women are asking for playgroups and nursery centres. So that they can return to work and have somewhere to leave their children.'

'That's all very well,' Belle said quickly. 'I've given the matter a great deal of thought and I know what I'm talking about. You seem to forget I had the same problem when Lucy was little.'

'But you went out to work,' Lena Watkins snapped. She was seeing a new side to Belle: a side of the red-haired woman who was out to improve the world. 'You told me you worked in a theatre bar.'

'So I did. But I was lucky, I had a woman at home who helped me with the housework. She was always there to care for Lucy when I needed her.'

'Well then!' Mrs Watkins said as if Belle had proved her point. 'You were fortunate.'

'But I still took work home with me. Sewing and alterations to stage costumes; and I had the worry of running a boarding-house. That wasn't easy.'

'I didn't say it was.'

'Anyway,' Belle tossed her head. 'I wasn't thinking about me; I was thinking about people like Flora.'

'Flora? You mean Flora Smart?'

'Yes.'

'That trollop.'

'She was my friend.' Belle looked sad at the remembrance of a girl with sleek brown hair and cheeky hazel eyes.

'I understand she came to a bad end. I read all about it in the newspapers. Didn't she murder her baby?'

'No, she didn't,' Belle said quickly. 'But she still got punished. She didn't stand a chance. I realise how lucky I am.' She put out her hand to Mike to show him that she knew who was responsible for her luck.

'I did the best I could for her,' Mrs Watkins insisted. 'She came to me and asked for work after the child was born, but she had no one to leave it with. But I did give her outwork for a time.'

'But it was so poorly paid – it was hardly worth it.' Belle's eyes flashed now that she was in her stride. 'I'm talking about paying women a fair price to work from home. People like Flora need to earn more than pin money. They also need to feel valued, and useful to society.'

'I'm a businesswoman. I can't afford to hand out charity.'

'Charity . . .'

'Belle,' Mike said warningly. 'Let's change the subject. I think Mrs Watkins is waiting for our decision.'

Lena Watkins turned on her sparrow legs and headed for the stairs as if she was glad to be back on a safe subject. 'Let's go next door to my office and continue the discussion there.'

After a last quick look around Belle and Mike followed her. The door safely secured they trooped back to the shop, through the showroom with its colourful displays and into the workroom, towards Lena Watkins's private sitting-room.

Belle loved the familiar hum of the machines, and the dedicated way the women leaned over their work. Once she'd been one of them and her heart went out to them. They hadn't had her opportunities. If she came here, as a partner with an equal say in things, she'd see that they got a better deal. Perhaps she could even talk Mrs Watkins into helping the unfortunate with child-care arrangements.

As they entered the room they were greeted by the noisy parrot, Warlock. Belle still hated the vicious bird and had once sustained a sharp peck from his beak. He let out a shriek of welcome when he saw her.

'He always misses you,' Lena Watkins said complacently. 'Give him one of his grapes; that'll keep him quiet.'

Belle crossed to the brass cage and held out some fruit. Warlock ruffled his moth-eaten feathers and put his head on one side, staring at Belle expectantly through the bars. Then, perched on one scaly leg he put out his other claw in her direction to take the grape delicately, but before she could withdraw her hand he gave her a warning peck. She drew back quickly. Mrs Watkins snorted with delight at her pet's antics.

'Sit down,' she said, indicating the settee. 'I think I have some sherry left somewhere.' She poured the golden liquid into glasses and handed them around. 'I think a toast is in order, and then we can get down to business.'

Belle looked uncomfortable. She glanced at Mike but he seemed to be waiting for her to take the initiative. 'Don't you think that's a bit premature?' she asked.

'I hope not.' Mrs Watkins sipped from her glass, smacking her lips in appreciation, but Belle put hers down on a side-table. She wasn't going to drink the other woman's sherry until she'd cleared up a few points.

'Mrs Watkins,' she said. 'I think my husband will agree with me. We're very impressed by the new shop, but we still have a lot of things to discuss.'

'I don't see why. I thought it was decided that you

wanted to come in with me. It'll be to your advantage.' She put her glass down with a thud on the table by the parrot's cage. Warlock squawked indignantly, as if he agreed with his mistress. 'I hope you're not going to change your mind?'

'I think you'll agree that it's only fair to ask for a bit longer to think about it.'

'How much longer?'

Belle glanced at Mike. 'Another twenty-four hours,' Mike said, 'if that's all right with you.'

'But my solicitors have already drawn up the documents. They only need signing. He's bringing them along this afternoon. I said you'd be here.'

'Then I think you've been a bit premature, Mrs Watkins,' Belle said. 'Mike's right; we'll let you know our answer this time tomorrow.'

'Well I just hope you haven't been wasting my time,' she turned her back on them and busied herself at the parrot's cage.

Mike beckoned Belle away. They left the room and almost bumped into Joyce Binns who was marching past with a pile of letters for her employer to sign. She greeted Belle eagerly.

'Is everything all right? I mean, will you be coming in to run the place? Oh, dear!' she put her hand to her mouth. 'I hope I haven't spoken out of turn, but you know how news gets round in a place like this.'

'Don't worry,' Belle assured her. 'It's not a secret. It's just that nothing's settled yet.'

'I do hope you will. We need someone young with modern ideas. Poor old Watkins is getting a bit past it, although I shouldn't complain. She's been good to me, and I'm no spring chicken myself.'

'None of us are getting any younger,' Mike said with a smile.

'Well, thumbs up,' Joyce said, and strode off towards Mrs Watkins's sanctum.

'Come on,' Mike said. He put his hand under Belle's elbow and guided her out into the street.

They turned towards Brighton and followed the winding road through Kemp Town. They walked for some time without speaking, but it was a companionable silence, as if they were both going over the events of the last hour carefully.

The massive church of John the Baptist towered in front of them. Belle noticed that the main doors were open and suddenly had a longing to step inside. She hadn't been in a Catholic church since her last visit to St Anne's and that was for her mother's funeral mass. But her brain was in a turmoil and she knew the soothing influence the quiet interior of a holy place could bring. Mrs Maria Fitzherbert was buried under the floor of this ancient church and there was a memorial stone recording the event. She must have knelt in the polished pews during her troubled life with the Prince Regent, asking for guidance just as Belle was preparing to do.

Mike stepped back a pace. He wasn't a regular churchgoer although he respected other people's beliefs. 'I'll wait outside,' he said. 'Take as long as you like.'

It was like stepping back into her childhood, dipping her fingers in the holy water and making the sign of the cross. The interior of the church was dark and echoing. Although the summer was past the heating hadn't yet been switched on. Belle shivered slightly, aware of the tapping of her heels on the worn stone slabs of the nave. She curtsied towards the altar, and a late ray of sunlight pierced the coloured glass in the massive stained-glass window and fell on her uplifted face. She half-expected Father Joe to come waddling out of the vestry, but he was still holed up in his own dilapidated presbytery.

461

Someone, not very proficient, was practising on the organ high up behind her in the choir stalls. It made a pleasant accompaniment to her thoughts. Everything had seemed so simple: selling Greenacres, and returning to Brighton to throw in her lot with Lena Watkins. The reality of the enterprise hadn't struck her until today. As partners they should have an equal share in everything, including the responsibilities and decisions for alterations. But Mrs Watkins had had things her own way for so long that Belle feared that she wouldn't be prepared to compromise and give up her sole rights. If she didn't, was Belle prepared to back down into a subordinate position?

'No!' she said loudly.

Her voice travelled around the church and echoed up to the high rafters. The organist must have heard her because the music stopped suddenly. In the silence Belle wondered if the musician was waiting to hear what she would say next.

She drew the collar of her brown coat up around her face and closed her eyes over her folded hands. She knew there were no magical answers to her problem. God wasn't going to give her any divine guidance. But the act of quieting her thoughts made her feel calm. She suddenly knew the answer wasn't here: it was outside with Mike, the husband she'd promised to love and honour.

The church was so quiet that a feeling of fear began to overwhelm her. Was Mike still outside waiting? She needed the confirmation that she wasn't alone. Struggling to her feet in a panic she dropped her bag and had to halt her headlong flight to gather her things together. The music had started again, and to the strains of the 'Trumpet Voluntary' she half-ran from the church.

The porch and front steps were deserted. Where was he? And then with relief she saw his broad figure sitting on a low wall contemplating the distant sea. He looked so safe silhouetted against the sky that she let out a long sigh. Hearing her quick footsteps he rose to his feet.

'What is it?' Quick to recognise her change of mood he was all concern. Her pale face and distressed frown told its own story.

'I thought you'd gone.'

He held out his arms and with a little cry she went into them. She wanted to weep, but she was twenty-six years old and much too mature to give way to the privilege.

'Gone? Don't be silly. Where would I go without you?'

'I don't know.' Belle shook back her hair helplessly. 'I suddenly felt as if I was all alone.'

'Look, Belle,' Mike said. 'I don't know what the matter is, but I think we ought to talk. Where do you want to go?'

'Let's go down to the sea. That always helps to make me feel better. It's something to do with the fresh air and the smell.'

'I didn't know the smell of fish turned you on.'

'Silly.'

They were talking friendly nonsense, but at least Belle was smiling again. The colour had returned to her cheeks. With his finger Mike touched the freckles sprinkled across the bridge of her nose, the result of the weeks they'd spent in the country.

The route to the promenade was down a narrow street. It was lined with cheap hotels and boarding houses, sprouting ROOMS TO LET invitations. The season was over, but the hoteliers were still vying for the last of the holiday trade. A man wearing a hessian apron was busy sweeping the steps of a house with a stiff broom. The hard bristles made a satisfying rhythmic sound as they scraped across the stone slabs. He looked happy and contented with his work and Belle envied him.

Mike's arm was around her waist. As she relaxed he prompted gently. 'Now, are you going to tell me what's the matter?'

'I don't know. It's so difficult to explain.'

'Try.'

'I thought it was what I wanted – but now I'm not so sure.'

'The partnership, you mean?'

'Yes.' Belle turned her heart-shaped face up to him and her blue eyes were misted with unshed tears. 'It's not the shop. That's ideal. And the work would be a challenge. I've never been afraid of hard work; and I love the flat with those huge windows.'

'It's Mrs Watkins, isn't it?'

'Yes,' Mike had put into words her own fears. 'I don't think she's ever likely to forget that I was once Isabel Kelly, a scruffy little girl straight from school, who arrived late for work on her first day with a torn stocking.'

'And now look at you: a lovely young woman with the world at your feet. With an adoring husband and a doting daughter.'

'Sometimes, even now, I feel fifteen again.'

'With the wind in your hair, you look it.'

Belle frowned. 'I don't think Mrs Watkins will ever loosen the reins and treat me as an equal. You saw how she was about the room – and she had no business ordering the paint without consulting us first.'

'Perhaps if we explained to her how you feel,' Mike suggested.

'She'd never understand. Why should she? She's had years and years of experience and she wants to pass it on to us.'

'Is that so bad?'

'Yes.' Belle stopped walking and turned to Mike. 'I don't

want it easy. I want us to make our own mistakes and learn by them. I'm grateful to Mrs Watkins, but I know I can do better – you must think me terribly vain and pig-headed.'

'Of course you are. That's why I fell in love with you in the first place. I knew you'd never be boring.'

'I feel so guilty.'

'What about?'

'I made you sell Greenacres and come back to Brighton on a wild goose chase. I said it was what I wanted, and I really believed that it was. I'm letting you down.'

'Listen Belle,' Mike's voice was serious. 'Nobody made me sell Greenacres. I was as keen as you were to get rid of the place. It wasn't the right life for us and we would have made a worse mistake trying to stick it out. And I think you're right about Mrs Watkins – she's used to doing things her way. It's not her fault, it's just the way she is. She's not going to take our money and expect us to be her employees.'

'So what's the answer?'

'To set up on our own.'

Belle was silent for a moment, digesting the proposition. When she spoke again her voice was soft with disbelief. 'You mean, open our own showroom?'

'Why not?'

'But could we? Would we have enough money? What if we failed? It's a frightening thought.'

'We'll take those questions in order.' Mike said, holding up four fingers. 'Of course we could. Mrs Watkins did, and she probably started with less than us. As to money: I've no idea how much we'll need; but there are such things as bank managers and loans. We might succeed and we might fail; but if we do fail we'll still have each other and that's the most important thing. It's your last question that puzzles me most.'

465

Belle thought back. 'I said something about being frightened.'

'That's the one. And Mrs Watkins said she'd never known you afraid of anything.'

'Oh, Mike!' Belle was looking more cheerful. 'Why did I have to be plagued by those dreadful doubts? Of course we can do it.'

'That's settled then. I'll phone Mrs Watkins in the morning and tell her we've changed our mind.'

'She'll be furious.'

'Only for a while; then she'll forget about us and find someone else.'

'I hope so. Where are we going?' They'd reached the seafront. Mike grabbed her hand and was leading Belle across the main road, in and out of the heavy traffic.

'You're my wife,' he said with a possessive smile. 'And it's about time I had you to myself.'

Belle knew what he meant. Since their return from the country they'd been staying with her father at Duke's Road. Maud and George welcomed them with delight, assuring them that they could stay as long as they liked. Lucy was also pleased to be back in the familiar environment. Alan was only next door so she wouldn't be lonely.

But it was a small house. Belle had forgotten how small, and nobody had any privacy because the walls were paperthin. Lucy had her usual room: the slip-room at the top of the stairs where Belle and Charlie had slept when they were children. Belle and Mike had Gran's old room, which was next door to the main bedroom. There was only space for a double bed, but not much else. At first it had been fun, but the novelty of roughing it had soon worn off.

Mike led the way down the steps to the beach. Belle followed, leaving the smoky fumes and noise of the traffic far behind. It was deserted down here at this time of year now that the ice-cream vendors and gift shops had put up their shutters. There were just stretches of shingle, and blue sea as far as the eye could see. On the right was the Palace Pier, now deserted. They might have been ship-wrecked on a desert island as far as the world was concerned.

At first they ran, revelling in the freedom, their shoes scrunching over the pebbles. Laughing like children at the screams and antics of the gulls soaring on the wind, on the lookout for scraps of food. Belle lost a shoe and then, find-ing it kinder on her feet, removed the other one. She ran to the water's edge and let the ripples run across her toes, soaking her stocking. Mike watched, delighted by her bold-ness, as the wind whipped her coat about her legs and her red hair streamed backwards in the wind.

A long strand of wavy seaweed passed and she paddled further out to retrieve it.

'Don't catch cold,' Mike called.

'I won't. The water's still warm from the sun. Why don't you come in?'

Mike shook his head although he was laughing at her wildness. At last she waded ashore with the strands of wet weed dangling from her hand and her pocket full of shells. Her legs were wet to the knees as was the bottom of her brown coat, but her cheeks were flushed and her eyes bright as twin stars.

'Look at you – you're soaking,' Mike said, as if he were talking to a naughty but much-loved child.

Belle slipped on the sharp pebbles and almost fell and he put out his arms to steady her. It seemed only natural then to pull her in to a close embrace. He held her tightly and looked down into her upturned face. Her smile was so inviting that he had to kiss her. It was long and satisfying, and when at last he let her go she looked sad.

'I've missed you,' he whispered, his face buried in her hair.

'I thought you'd grown bored with me.'

'Never.' His finger traced the line of her jaw and then slipped under her chin to tilt her head backwards so that he could kiss her again. 'I can't make love to you with your father the other side of the wall. He might hear us, and it doesn't seem right somehow.'

'I know. I feel the same.'

He kissed her once more, and then moaned as if he were in pain. 'I want you so much.'

'I know. We'll find a shop and a flat and make love every night.'

Mike grinned. 'In the shop or the flat?'

'Both if we feel like it. Don't worry, Mike, something will turn up. I must take these stockings off.' Belle lifted the side of her shirt to release a suspender and Mike was made aware of the smooth whiteness of her thigh.

'Here, let me.'

He led her to an opening in the cliff face, where lovers before them had carved their initials in the chalk. She knew what he was going to do and sank down willingly on the hard ground, allowing him to roll down the damp stocking. Her toes curled with delicate abandon as his hand trembled on her cold skin. As his fingers undid the buttons of her coat she shrugged its constricting weight from her shoulders and stretched voluptuously. She was wearing a narrow skirt and white blouse and the fastenings were difficult for Mike's untrained hands. Belle had to help him.

As he discovered her body it seemed, to both of them, to be the first time. Every curve and hollow was a mystery to him, to be explored with determination. He wound the trailing strands of seaweed around her full breasts. The clammy texture was exciting and her nipples stood erect in

468

glorious anticipation. Before her feelings got the better of her she remembered briefly another occasion when she'd experienced gratification in the open air. It happened in the depths of a bluebell wood, and Henry Murtell had been her inexperienced teacher. Now she was older, had a child, and knew what to expect. But she still felt the wonder and excitement, as if she were a young girl on the brink of her first sexual awakening.

To Mike she had all the appearance of a beached mermaid, with the feminine allure of a siren. He stroked her pale skin until it was rosy with love under his hands. Then he gently covered her nakedness with his own body.

His weight crushed her and for a moment she was overwhelmed. Then she welcomed him, stretching up her arms and winding them around his neck, drawing him down even closer. Only the sea-birds heard their words of love and moans of desire – but they'd seen many strange sights and weren't particularly interested.

29

Later in the afternoon Belle and Mike started for home. The sky had clouded over, and they walked through the town hand in hand like young lovers. Belle's stockings were rolled in a damp bundle in the pocket of her coat and her bare legs were prickled with goose-pimples.

'My shoes have rubbed a blister on my heel,' she complained.

'Let's take a short-cut through the Lanes; then we can take shelter if it rains.'

Mike pulled her into a narrow cobbled entrance where there was only room to walk two abreast. The Lanes were a landmark in the town, and the most ancient part. Many of the buildings still had the original features, and walls several inches thick. When the town had been a fisherman's village it was called Brighthelmston, and was renowned for its secret passages leading to the shore and nearby Rottingdean. In the old days smugglers and brigands would have known every twisting corner of the narrow streets, plying their dubious trade regardless of the law of the land.

Today, most of the houses had been converted into shops, and visitors searched the area for antiques. Where once it had been the home of the poorest members of the community, it was fast becoming a valued shopping-centre, with high-class gift shops equalling the number selling antiques.

Belle would have liked to window-shop but Mike hurried her forward. He turned a corner, and when he looked back found he'd lost her so he retraced his steps. Belle was standing on the cobbles staring at a shop-front, which in his hurry he'd overlooked. There was something in her expression that caught his interest.

'What is it?' he asked.

'That shop. It's for sale.'

The premises in front of them had been converted from one of the old fisherman's cottages into a shop selling china and glass. In one corner of the window stood a huge Chinese vase and part of a dinner-service. Apart from that the interior was empty, the bare floor scattered with straw and packing-cases. On the glass frontage was displayed an estate agent's notice saying the shop was indeed for sale.

'I wonder what they're asking,' Belle said dreamily.

'More than we can afford.'

'But look at the position. This is where all the wealthy people come when they visit Brighton. They spend money here. It could be a little goldmine.'

'Even if we could afford it, there wouldn't be space for a workroom.' Mike was peering through the glass trying to see into the interior. 'It's just a shop with a sort of office at the back.'

'And another floor above.' Belle stepped back and was looking up. 'Look at those little windows; there must be living accommodation up there. There are no curtains so it could be empty as well. Look, there's a side-door, so it's self-contained. I wish we could get in and look around.'

'We'd be wasting our time.' Mike was smiling at her

enthusiasm. 'It'll be too expensive, and too small, I tell you.'

'But we wouldn't need a workroom, Mike. We'd be employing women to work from home. Machinists and hand-sewers – only the best. We'd only need a showroom and an office.'

'And what are you going to make and sell – gloves?'

'And other things. All the frivolities women yearn for. Scarves and handkerchiefs, romantic underwear and nightwear. Do you know the latest in nightwear are pyjamas? But not the old-fashioned kind. These are made of pure silk and cut from a Chinese design: you know, a high-necked jacket with masses of oriental embroidery. I saw a picture in a fashion magazine. They're all the rage in Paris.'

'And what would you call this dream emporium?'

'I don't know,' Belle said with a smile. 'I haven't thought that far yet.'

'I'll find you a shop, Belle.' Mike sounded as if he meant it. 'Somewhere we can afford to rent. It might not be in such a good position, but it'll be a start. If it hadn't been for the death duties we would have had enough with Miss Grey's legacy.'

They turned away. Mike spotted a pin glittering between the paving-stones and bent down to pick it up. 'Here,' he said pushing the spike into the lapel of Belle's coat. 'Do you remember the saying, "See a pin and pick it up, and all the day you'll have good luck"?'

'That's it!' Belle said, looking down at the sliver of silvery metal. 'That's what we'll call the shop – NEEDLES AND PINS. What do you think?'

'Very appropriate. What would you have hanging outside – a giant sewing-machine? And seats for the customers shaped like giant pin-cushions?'

'Why not?'

They walked away without daring to look back. It was

good to have dreams; sometimes dreams were better than realities. The rest of the walk back to Duke's Road was uneventful but they'd lost their earlier exuberance. Belle opened the front door and Mike followed her inside. The house seemed unusually quiet. There was no Lucy waiting for them in the hall, or music playing from the kitchen wireless.

'Where is everybody?' Mike said.

'I don't know. Lucy must be home from school by now. Maud usually starts to get tea about this time.'

Belle had taken off her coat and was hanging it on one of the hooks inside the front door among the overcoats and mackintoshes. They looked up at the sound of heavy footsteps on the landing above. It was Maud. There was a solemn expression on her usually merry face and her black hair was falling down. She was trying to secure it on top of her head with a dangerous looking hair-pin as she walked down the stairs.

'Is everything all right?' Belle asked, suspecting the worst. 'Where's Lucy?'

'In her room. I put her to bed as soon as she came in. She was that fretful I couldn't do anything with her. Crying and carrying on. Not a bit like her usual self.'

'I'll go up to her,' Belle said quickly, thinking it was an unusual way for Lucy to behave. She'd always been a healthy child although she was stick-thin and pale. She might have the appearance of a weakling, but she was wiry and energetic. It took a good deal to upset her these days.

Belle opened the bedroom door quietly. Maud had pulled the curtains over the window but there was still plenty of daylight. Lucy was lying on the narrow bed under the window, on top of the multi-coloured quilt that was frayed and faded with age. At first Belle thought she was asleep, but the stiff posture of her body, stretched out so uncomfortably, and her wide open eyes proved her wrong.

'Lucy.' Belle walked across the rag rug to the bed and looked down at the child. 'What's the matter?'

'I was sick – all over Nellie Brown.' The childish voice was tearful, full of misery.

'I'm sure you couldn't help it.'

'But Nellie's my best friend at school. It's awful being sick all over your best friend.'

'Perhaps you'd eaten something that upset you. What did you have for lunch?'

'I had school dinner. It was horrible.' Lucy shuddered at the memory.

'No wonder you were sick. What was it?'

'I don't know. It looked like one of Maud's old white knitted vests. Teacher said I had to sit there until I'd eaten it all up.'

Belle tried not to smile; she couldn't imagine anything worse than being made to eat an old woollen vest. 'I expect she was thinking of the poor people,' she said. 'She didn't want you to waste good food.'

'It wasn't good food; I told you, it was horrible. Maud said it was tripe.'

'No wonder you were sick. Do you feel better now?'

'No. I don't feel sick any more, but I'm too hot.'

Belle leant over her daughter, noting the unusual flush of colour in her cheeks, and the anxious restless eyes. She put her cool hand on the child's forehead and felt an unnatural glow of heat.

'Why don't you undress and get under the covers,' she suggested. 'I think you're running a temperature.'

'Is that because I was sick?'

'Probably.'

Lucy was always so independent, but this time Belle had to help her. She lay quietly while her mother undressed her; pulling a freshly laundered nightdress over her head, and drawing the bedclothes gently up over her thin, unre-sisting body.

'I'm just going downstairs to talk to Maud. Is there any-thing you want?'

'A glass of water. My head hurts.'

'Close your eyes and then it'll feel better.'

Lucy did as she was told. 'You'll come back?'

'Of course.'

Belle left the room pulling the door closed behind her. She was worried. Lucy hadn't had a day's real illness in her short life; only the odd cold or childish complaint. Maud was in the scullery, peeling potatoes at the sink. She looked up as Belle entered the room, a question in her eyes.

'I think she's sickening for something,' Belle said, filling a large tumbler with water. 'She's hot and listless and says she's been sick.'

'Has she had any of the childish illnesses?' Maud asked.

'No. Have you heard of anything going around?'

Maud wiped her hand on the coarse cloth of her working apron and stretched to ease her back. 'Little Ben Murtell had the measles, but he's better now. I haven't heard of anything else. She's always in there playing with Alan; you know how close they are. I can't keep her away.'

'I'll take her into my bed tonight so that I can keep an eye on her. Mike won't mind.'

Mike didn't mind; he was the complete family man. He even carried Lucy along the passage, and helped Belle tuck her up in his side of the big bed.

'If she's no better in the morning I think we should call the doctor,' he said.

'Maud says they've had measles next door,' Belle said, handing him his folded pyjamas. 'It could be that.'

'What about you?'

'I had it as a child. Charlie brought it home from school and we were sick at the same time.'

Temporarily reassured Mike left her to nurse the child. Neither of them got much sleep that night. Mike found Lucy's bed hard and narrow and he'd got out of the habit of sleeping on his own. Belle slept in snatches next to the fractious child.

By midnight Lucy's face was flushed an unhealthy shade of red. She tossed and turned, complaining of the heat and the way her head ached. The night seemed endless. Belle was relieved when the morning arrived, bathing the room in its cold light. A concerned Maud knocked on the door, bearing a cup of tea and enquiring about the patient's condition.

'She's not so hot,' Belle said, looking at Lucy who had at last drifted into a quiet sleep. 'I think the worst must be over.'

'You'd better still call the doctor,' Maud said, gently pulling the sheet aside to make her own inspection. 'It looks to me as if she's got a rash.'

Maud was right. The child's chest was mottled a rough uneven pink. Belle left her sleeping peacefully and went downstairs, pulling on a dressing-gown over her night clothes, to find Mike. He was helping George demolish an old wooden lean-to at the back of the house. They were going to finish the job by chopping it up for firewood to reduce the winter's fuel bills. He 'downed tools' and promised to go along to the surgery straight away. Doctor West's receptionist said he would make a home visit later in the day.

By the time the doctor arrived Lucy had woken up and looked considerably improved. She was propped up against the pillows drinking orange-squash and insisting she was hungry when the overworked doctor entered the room.

476

'You don't look very sick to me,' he said with a smile, sitting down on the edge of the bed and waving his stethoscope about. 'I think you just wanted a day off school.'

'I've got spots,' Lucy said proudly. 'Look.' She pulled down her nightie to show them off. 'And I was sick all over Nellie Brown.'

'I hope it was a good aim.'

'It was: all over her skirt and new shoes.'

'Is it measles?' Belle asked, coming in to the rooms to hear the doctor's verdict. 'They've had measles next door and she spends a lot of time in there.'

'Yes – it's measles.' Doctor West removed his glasses and tucked them into his breast pocket. 'But not your common or garden variety. Oh, no! This young lady's got German measles.'

Lucy preened herself: it sounded important.

'What's the difference?' Belle asked.

'The difference is that it's quite a minor complaint, with none of the repercussions you get from the ordinary kind. Lucy tells me that she's feeling better already; but you must keep her away from school, and other children, until the rash has completely gone. We don't want an epidemic, do we?'

'Is there any treatment, doctor?' Maud was hovering in the doorway, waiting to get her question in.

'No. Just lots of patience and loving kindness; and a dollop of spoiling is always a good thing.' He got to his feet briskly. 'I'll see myself out.'

Lucy recovered quickly. The angry rash began to fade after a few days and she began to behave like her usual self. The incident was almost forgotten until one day Belle discovered she'd developed a similar rash.

'Do you feel all right?' Mike asked, full of concern when

she showed it to him. 'I feel fine. Never better. I remembered having measles, but I suppose they weren't the German kind.'

'Shall I call in Doctor West again?'

'No. I'm not ill like Lucy was. I'll just keep away from people until it's gone.'

Belle didn't intend measles to interfere with their lives – German or otherwise. She had other things occupying her mind. The most important was that she suspected she was pregnant. It hadn't been confirmed, but she remembered the symptoms she'd had with Lucy in the early weeks. If her suspicions were correct, she'd conceived during the delightful afternoon when Mike had made love to her on the empty beach.

At first she'd been dismayed. They'd talked about having children in the early days of their marriage but neither of them had been terribly serious, although they hadn't done anything to deliberately prevent it. Belle never had been particularly maternal. She loved Lucy now, but the thought of another daughter was daunting. But what if it were a son?

A little boy to love as she'd loved Flora's son Peter. The thought still stirred her heartstrings although she'd never admitted it. And there was no doubt in her mind that Mike would be a perfect father. He was so good with Lucy even when she was at her most difficult, so he would be even better with a child of his own.

She hugged the secret to herself, afraid to tell anyone, even Mike. He'd be so disappointed if it was a mistake, and she still wasn't sure how she felt about things. And at the back of her mind there was always the fear that it might be a girl.

The weeks passed, the days grew shorter and Christmas approached. The new year dawned mild and wet making everyone sneeze and shiver around the fire. Then the temperature dropped suddenly and it began to snow. Icicles hung from the window-frames and the trees in the garden were silhouetted against the brooding sky with their white burden. Lucy and Alan built a snowman, and cried and fought each other when it melted prematurely. George built them a toboggan out of some of the wood from the lean-to, and taught them how to steer it down Duke's Road, using their feet as brakes, so that they didn't go careering across the main road.

George and Maud revelled in having a full house, and stopped asking when Belle and Mike were going to find a home of their own. They liked having the family all together under one roof. Belle stopped looking at the empty shops she passed, and even began to wonder if she'd been wise in turning down Lena Watkins's offer.

Then one day in March when the first signs of spring were in the air, and Lucy had found the spear of her first snowdrop under the oak tree, everything changed.

Belle's spirits had been low. The cold weather had made her feel heavy and sluggish; but that day the sun shone with a new warmth, making the blood pulse more strongly through her veins. She looked in the mirror while she was brushing the tangles out of her red hair and was surprised to see that she was still pretty.

'I must tell Mike about the baby,' she told her reflection in the glass. 'I'll tell him as soon as he gets home.'

He'd been out a lot lately, busy over some private enterprise, and sometimes she'd wondered if he was planning to go back into the furniture business. When she'd asked, he'd just kissed her, instructing her to 'wait and see'.

She was drinking tea with George and Maud when they heard the scrape of his key in the lock. Lucy had been occupied with a jig-saw, but she'd found it difficult and left it to run and meet him. His large frame filled the doorway and he was bent almost double under a heavy package he was carrying. But there was a cheeky grin on his face as they all turned to him expectantly.

'I've brought you both a present,' he said, looking straight at Maud and George, his eyes twinkling over the top of the parcel. 'Clear some space on that table will you, Lucy.'

Lucy threw the half-made puzzle back into its box, ignoring the pieces that dropped on to the floor. The present looked much more exciting than the silly old jig-saw. Everyone watched as Mike removed the protective wrappings, disclosing a polished wooden cabinet with a small window in the front.

'What is it?' Maud asked.

George shook his head; he didn't know either.

'I know! I know!' Lucy shouted, jumping up and down with excitement. 'It's a television set!'

'Clever girl,' Mike said, unrolling wires and connecting the box up to the electrical supply. Electricity was still a new innovation to the house in Duke's Road.

'Is it safe?' Maud asked. She was frightened of all the new contraptions people were beginning to install in their homes – like refrigerators and washing machines. She was convinced that things worked by electricity would be likely to explode or catch fire.

'Of course it's safe,' Mike assured her.

He turned a knob on the front of the box and the window glowed. Then, after he'd twiddled about at the back, a blurred image suddenly flickered across the screen. It was the moving picture of a man playing a violin.

'It's magic!' Lucy said, her eyes wide with wonder.

'It's clever,' George announced. He patted Mike on the back as if his son-in-law had invented the thing himself.

'I'll turn the sound up,' Mike said, and marvel after marvel, they could hear the music as well as watch the musician.

'I'm going to fetch Alan,' Lucy declared, defying any of the grown-ups to stop her. 'He hasn't got one.'

She bolted out of the door while Mike was still busy trying to explain the mysteries of the television to George, and repeat his assurances of its safety to Maud.

'You are good to them,' Belle said, as the older couple positioned themselves in front of the screen. 'What a lovely surprise.'

'I've got a present for you as well. Come outside.'

She followed him into the hall. They had to wait while Lucy charged past, followed by an equally excited Alan Murtell. He'd heard about the magic boxes and couldn't believe that the Kellys had really got one. If it was as good as he hoped he'd try to persuade his dad to buy them one.

At last they were alone. Mike took Belle's hand in his and pressed something hard into her palm. She uncurled her fingers and found she was holding a long brass key.

'What is it for?' she asked slowly, not wanting to jump to conclusions. 'It looks like the key to a front door.'

'It is a door key. A shop door key.'

'You mean . . .?' Belle's eyes were as big as Lucy's had been at the sight of the television set.

'NEEDLES AND PINS. Proprietor – Isabel Walker. From her adoring husband.' She couldn't believe it, and there were still questions in her blue eyes, so he tried to explain. 'The shop you set your heart on – in the Lanes. Suitable for smugglers, highwaymen, and makers of fashion accessories.'

'Oh, Mike!' She wanted to cry. 'You said we couldn't afford to buy it.'

'We can't. I put my solicitor in touch with the owners,

and they negotiated terms. I've bought the lease. What do you think I've been doing the last few weeks?'

'I had no idea, but I didn't dream of this. When can I see it?'

'How about today? I've had workmen in helping me do the alterations to the flat upstairs. They've just about finished so it's time to show it to you. But the shop is your responsibility: I want you to make the decisions there. You've no idea how large the living-quarters have turned out to be, now that we've pulled down a few walls and rearranged things. There are three bedrooms, if you include the attic, although two would have been enough. Lucy will be pleased, it means she can invite Alan to stay.'

'We're going to need three bedrooms, Mike.'

Now was the time. She blushed slightly with the news she was now anxious to share with him. He read in her eyes what she was trying to say.

'You mean . . .?'

'Yes, we're going to have a baby. Sometime in August I think, although I haven't seen a doctor yet.'

He didn't spoil it for her by telling her that he knew. They were so close in everything that he'd suspected from the beginning, and had been waiting for her to confirm his suspicions.

He pulled her into his arms and held her tightly. Then, remembering her condition, held her away from him at arm's length. Her figure was so shapely that even the slight swelling that was their child was lovely to his eyes. His hands travelled down her body, from the slope of her shoulders, over the twin mounds of her breasts, until they reached her belly. He stroked her tenderly, and then buried his face in her hair, murmuring her name as if he couldn't get enough of her.

*

The shop was everything she'd dreamt it would be. The top floor was already spotless and gleaming with fresh paint, the empty rooms waiting for their furnishings. Mike wanted polished antique and Belle fancied pine, and in the end they compromised and bought a mixture of both. They agreed on the green brocade curtains and the scattering of rugs on the original floorboards.

In the shop downstairs Belle was given a completely free hand. With a team of workmen at her side she chose the same white paint and gold leaf she'd fancied in Kemp Town. She also had red plush curtains, and brass wall-lamps with pleated silk shades. The back room was furnished with a desk and a sewing-machine, and there was room for two curtained cubicles with gold-plated hooks for clothes, full-length mirrors, and comfortable chairs with delicate spindle legs. She left the Chinese vase in the window: it made a suitable setting for the silk-embroidered nightwear and the huge paper parasol that formed her first display. It certainly encouraged the public to stop and look.

NEEDLES AND PINS opened for business in the beginning of June. It was a good time to catch the first of the holiday trade, and Brighton was full of visitors with money in their pockets.

Belle already had a staff of twelve young women working from their homes. She'd advertised widely for experienced machinists and embroiderers, but even so each applicant had to come into the shop for a training session which Belle supplied in person. She particularly welcomed women with young children, and while the mothers learnt from Belle the babies slept contentedly in their carry-cots in the back room, lulled by the whirring of the machine.

Belle was glowing with achievement and pregnancy. She was happier than she'd ever been in her life, and her only worry was that everything seemed to be going too well. It was almost too good to be true.

She expected dedication and hard work from her staff and in return she treated them as equals, paid them well, and was always ready to listen to their problems. She hadn't forgotten what it was like to work for Mrs Watkins, and was anxious to do as well as that lady and – if possible – better.

One morning as she was trying to arrange a new window display and answer the telephone at the same time, she looked up to see a solid figure standing on the other side of the glass, watching her. The figure was severely dressed in navy and white, with hair neatly plaited and coiled around the ears, and flat lace-up shoes over hand-knitted stockings. It was a woman, and she looked familiar, but at first Belle didn't recognise her. But then the woman smiled. Of course, it was Joyce Binns: Lena Watkins's right-hand person, who had greeted the young Belle Kelly so kindly on her first day at the glove factory. The two women had always got on well despite the difference in their ages. Underneath Joyce's severe appearance she had a heart of gold.

'How are you?' They spoke at the same time, and then laughed.

Joyce stepped inside the open door and looked around curiously. 'You look as if you're doing well.'

'I am. Come and see.'

Belle was proud to have the opportunity to show off her shop, although she was constantly interrupted by customers and the telephone. Joyce seemed surprised to find a young woman in the back room bent over a sewing-machine, with a baby beside her asleep in a wicker basket. The girl looked up briefly and smiled, and then returned to her task of feeding the fine silk material under the needle.

'I can't imagine Mrs Watkins allowing that,' Joyce said indicating the baby.

'I'm not Lena Watkins,' Belle said emphatically. 'How is she anyway?'

'Planning to enter that craft exhibition. She thinks the prestige of winning will boost orders.'

'Is business bad then?' Belle asked.

'I think so. Are you going to enter?'

'I don't know anything about it.'

'I'll leave you a leaflet.' Joyce searched through her bag and handed Belle a piece of paper. 'It's all to do with a big conference by the Association of Fine Arts. The council and the hoteliers have got together and organised a competition. They're hoping to attract entries from local shops and craft groups, as well as art schools and colleges. Entries must have a local theme because they're going to call it 'Brighton Beautiful'.

Belle was studying the handbill, ideas already spinning through her head. To win a competition like this would be good for business. It would put NEEDLES AND PINS on the map, as well as getting newspaper publicity that could bring in trade from all over Sussex.

'You say Mrs Watkins is entering?'

'So I heard.' Belle looked up quickly; the other woman was looking uncomfortable, as if she had something on her mind. 'I don't work for her any more.'

'I don't believe it!' This news really was a surprise. She'd never imagined Joyce leaving Mrs Watkins of her own accord.

'What happened?'

'She got really difficult after you left. I know she was disappointed when you changed your mind about that partnership, we all were, but she didn't have to take it out on the rest of the staff.'

'So you gave in your notice?'

'Yes.'

Belle looked at Joyce and the same idea seemed to strike them at the same time, but Belle spoke first.

'Will you come and work for me? I need someone to keep the books in order and answer the telephone. I'll get you a typewriter – you can take care of things while I have the baby.'

Joyce laughed. 'I thought you were never going to ask.' She was so pleased that she threw her arms around Belle and hugged her. They calmed down enough to sort out the details but they were both delighted with the arrangement. 'And how's your husband?' Joyce asked when they'd at last exhausted their exchange of news.

'He's fine. This shop is all due to him.' Belle looked around proudly.

'And your little girl?'

'Lucy's very well. She had German measles a few months ago but she soon got over it.'

'What a good thing you didn't catch it – in your condition.' Joyce was busy gathering up her things.

Belle froze. 'What do you mean?'

'It's dangerous for a pregnant woman to catch German measles, didn't you know? I know I'm not an expert, but my next-door neighbour caught it and her baby was born deformed. Sometimes it affects the brain – oh dear! I mustn't talk about things like that: I'm upsetting you.'

Joyce quickly changed the subject but Belle didn't hear her. Her day was ruined and her joy dimmed. She felt the child in her womb stir as if it was trying to tell her something. A terrible fear threatened to overwhelm her.

30

The fear was so great that Belle could almost touch it. It was like a black dog, devouring her inside and dragging her thoughts down into a dark pit. But the worst thing of all was that she couldn't tell anyone, not even Mike. He wouldn't understand – how could he? Probably he'd just tell her it was her imagination and to cheer up.

Of course he knew there was something wrong. He didn't know what it was, but guessed it must have something to do with the feminine mystery of pregnancy.

Everything would be all right when the baby was born. He tried to be extra kind, extra caring; but nothing he could do, or say, could drive the horror away.

'Are you all right?' he asked a hundred times a day.

'I'm fine.'

'Why don't you go and rest. You look so pale.'

'No. I'm not tired.'

How could she rest when sleep brought bad dreams? Dreams of babies with twisted limbs, two heads, or missing fingers. The worst dreams were the ones about Peter. Such a pretty little baby he'd been as he nestled against Flora's shoulder, crushing his golden curls and sleepily rubbing his eyes with dimpled fists. In her dream he was asleep in his cradle and she was rocking him with her foot. He looked so peaceful: like the dream baby she'd always longed for. She held her breath, holding on to the precious moment, willing it to go on for ever. And then he opened his eyes. They were pretty eyes and such a delicate colour, but they rolled vacantly in their sockets while a dribble of saliva trickled from the corner of the rose-bud mouth. And then he put up his arms towards Belle and in his baby voice called her 'Mummy'.

She was afraid to sleep; afraid of the dreams; afraid of what she might see when her baby was born. She lost weight. The only thing about her that proclaimed her womanhood was her swollen belly, the rest of her was as thin and fragile as a pubescent girl. Her hair lost its rich colour and even her freckles faded.

Mike brought home presents to try to please her. A rocking-horse that only a healthy child could ride, toys that needed dextrous fingers, and tiny shoes and gloves designed to fit perfectly formed feet and hands. Belle smiled and hid them all away.

Mike was busy. He'd discovered a secret door under the stairs that wasn't mentioned in the deeds. After forcing it open with a crowbar he found, not the hoped for smugglers' passage, but a dry basement. It would be useful for a workshop or storeroom. Belle showed no interest in his find, she was too occupied trying to decide on a subject for her entry to the competition.

'What about something to do with the history of gloves?' Joyce suggested.

'But it's got to have a local connection.'

'How about buckskin with Sussex scenes embroidered on the backs?'

'No. I've always fancied trying something ecclesiastical,' Belle said thoughtfully, images of her church-attending days running through her mind. 'You know: copes or mitres, or a stole with doves of peace on it.'

'Would that be considered local?' Joyce asked doubtfully.

'It might, if we could get the Brighton clergy interested. Or we could make a mural.'

'That's a painting, isn't it – on a wall?'

'A collage then.' Belle grabbed a sheet of paper and began to sketch in an outline. 'A wall hanging, depicting a Brighton scene. What is the first thing that comes into your mind when you think about Brighton, Joyce?'

'The Pavilion,' Joyce said quickly.

'Exactly – the Royal Pavilion. What a wonderful idea. The details could be based on bonded appliqué or quilting, on a felt background, the palace picked out with machine embroidery with famous figures in the foreground – you know, the Prince Regent getting out of his carriage . . .'

'And Maria Fitzherbert?'

'Of course.'

'The figures would have to be worked by hand, to give a three-dimensional effect.'

'With lots of gold thread to give the impression of sunlight,' Belle added.

'How long have you got, Belle?'

'Three months.'

'You'll never do it.'

'Not me, Joyce – us. NEEDLES & PINS – it'll be a firm's entry. Everyone will work on a separate piece, like a giant patchwork quilt, and then we'll sew the whole thing together and I'll add the finishing touches by hand. The figures and so on. The horses can have real manes . . .'

'And Mrs Fitzherbert pearls in her ears.'

'And feathers and ribbons in her bonnet.'

Belle held out the sheet of paper with its rough drawing. Her blue eyes were sparkling: for the first time in weeks she'd forgotten the forthcoming baby.

No sooner said than done. A meeting was called and the work allotted. Everyone was keen to take part in the project but Belle chose only the very best workers. Every panel had to be perfect, every stitch a work of art. If it was the last thing she did Belle intended winning the competition.

One day Joyce came into the shop with a big grin on her face.

'Sorry I'm late,' she said to Belle who was busy folding monogrammed handkerchiefs into a flat cardboard box. It was part of an order for an important customer, and for a final touch she slipped a sprig of lavender under the lid to scent the linen. 'I met Jane Simmonds who works for Mrs Watkins. So of course I had to stop and ask her about their entry for the competition.'

The collage was coming on apace. The finished hanging would be at least ten feet wide and seven high. It was going to be the finest work Belle had ever executed and even if it didn't win them the fifty pounds prize money she knew they would have the satisfaction of knowing they'd done their best. Even so she was only human, and couldn't help being curious about the other competitors.

'Did Jane tell you anything?' Belle remembered Miss Simmonds for being a bit of a gossip. She guessed it hadn't been too difficult to pick her brains.

'Yes. She said Mrs Watkins had got them all working on an Indian costume.'

Belle looked up from the ribbon she was tying around the handkerchief box. 'Indian! What's that got to do with Brighton?'

'It's supposed to be a reproduction of the costume worn by Sake Deen Mahomed.'

'Who on earth's he?'

'That's what I asked. I'd never heard of him either.' Joyce

settled down in the chair behind her typewriter, ready for a good chat. 'It appears that he was the proprietor of the first Indian baths in Brighton, when George the Fourth was staying here. He was given the title of Shampooing Surgeon, and was in and out of Brighton Pavilion dressed in his ceremonial robes – you know: silk trousers, turban, the lot. Mrs Watkins found a picture in the library and she's copying it.'

'Not a bad idea,' Belle said. 'How is she going to display it? On one of those shop-window models, I suppose.'

'No.' Joyce put her hand over her mouth to hide a grin. 'She's going to wear it herself.'

'You mean she's going to dress up as this Mahomed fellow!'

'Yes.'

Belle joined in Joyce's laughter. For the rest of the day she kept trying to picture Lena Watkins dressed as an Indian and bursting into giggles. She hadn't laughed so much for ages and it did her good.

The weeks passed quickly. There was so much to do: completing orders, working on the mural, and getting everything ready for her confinement. She'd given birth to Lucy in the hospital, but this time she'd settled on having the baby at home.

The flat over the shop wasn't really suitable. There were too many stairs and it was noisy. Mike was worried that Belle would be disturbed by the customers coming in and out of the shop, and Joyce would keep running up and down asking advice and not leaving her in peace. She needed a chance to build up her strength for the ordeal ahead.

George and Maud came to the rescue as they had so many times before. They were shocked by Belle's appearance: her thin, drawn face and panic-stricken eyes. With Mike's permission they carried her off to Duke's Road. She was tucked up in the same huge bed where Bess had given birth to Belle and Charlie nearly thirty years before.

Maud was in her element having someone to look after. She liked to feel needed and missed Lucy. Never having had children of her own, she directed her maternal feelings on to her ready-made family. She sang cheerfully as she carried up cups of hot milk doctored with a dash of stout to give strength. She boiled marrow-bones for nourishing broth, and rice and honey to tempt Belle's sweet tooth. She was full of patience and endless kindness. Belle felt guilty. The black dog was still on her shoulder and nothing would shift him.

At last, in despair, they called in Doctor West. The baby wasn't due for another ten days, but he arrived promptly thinking the mother had gone into premature labour. He was surprised to find her resting in bed with no indication of discomfort. His spectacles polished and poised on his nose he stared at Belle, tapping his fingers together thoughtfully.

'What's this then?' he asked gently after taking her pulse. 'Last time I saw you you were blooming, and now you look as if you have all the worries in the world on your shoulders. What's the problem?'

'The baby's dead.' Belle spoke carefully, as if she'd been rehearsing this information.

'What makes you think that?'

'It doesn't move. I haven't felt it for days. I know it's dead.'

'I shouldn't think there's much room to move about in there.' Doctor West was looking at the tight swelling under Belle's gown. 'You're as tight as a pod full of peas. Let me examine you.'

Belle lay back dutifully; she didn't really care what Doctor West did to her. It was true that she hadn't felt the baby move, but she didn't believe it was dead. That would be too good to be true. Better dead than the monster she thought she was carrying.

The doctor removed his glasses and surveyed the patient. 'Well,' he said. 'Everything appears to be fine. When are you due?'

'Six days. The midwife worked it out for me.'

'The excellent Mrs Douglas! She's usually right; but I think she's a few days out this time.' Belle waited to hear his prediction. He felt her stomach again, leisurely, as if there was all the time in the world. 'The head's engaged; it's in the right position. Nothing wrong there. I'll tell Mrs Douglas to stand by.'

'Do you think it'll come earlier, Doctor?'

'I would say within the next two days, Mrs Walker. So I hope you've got everything ready.' He looked around the room, as if surprised that there was no lace-trimmed crib in sight. Then he glanced again at the tired woman in bed. 'Cheer up,' he instructed in his professional voice. 'It'll soon be over.'

'It'll soon be over,' Belle whispered as he left the room for a consultation with Maud. 'At least when it's over I'll know the worst.'

When Belle woke the next morning she felt different: unexpectedly cheerful, as if a cloud had lifted. Even when memory came flooding back she found she was feeling better than she had for a long time. Restless and hungry she swung her legs over the edge of the bed. The baby suddenly moved strongly as if it were trying to tell her something.

Maud looked up as she appeared in the kitchen doorway. Her hand was on her side as if to protect her stomach, and there was a dreamy expression on her face.

'You all right, Belle?' Maud asked, getting up quickly and pulling out a chair.

Belle sat down carefully, pushing the loose curls away from her face. 'I'm hungry.'

'I'll get you something. What would you like – eggs and bacon, sausages? You name it.'

Belle laughed. How kind Maud was. How anxious to please. 'Just toast,' she said. 'And there's no hurry.'

But she was wrong. She never did get the toast because, at that moment, the first contraction gripped her. It wasn't exactly pain, it was more a plunging sensation in the small of her back, sending waves and ripples up her spine and around her stomach, alerting her muscles and making them tingle. She put one hand to her side and leant over the table, supporting herself on the other.

'What is it?' Maud's plump face was full of concern.

Belle had no time to answer. The next contraction gripped her, nearly knocking her sideways.

'I think the baby's in a hurry,' she whispered.

Maud shouted for George to go for the doctor and midwife, and then helped Belle back up the stairs. George Kelly was in the backyard planting out seedlings, but he dropped everything at the urgency in his wife's voice.

Mrs Douglas, the midwife, had been warned by the doctor to expect a call. She came on her bicycle, weaving in and out of the traffic, to arrive in Duke's Road smart in her regulation uniform with not a hair out of place. She took one look at Belle, summed up the situation, and gave Maud instructions in a quiet professional manner.

'Hot water, plenty of clean towels, and I'd like a cup of tea, Mrs Kelly, when you've got time.'

Maud plodded down the stairs on her flat feet to obey the commands. Mrs Douglas closed the bedroom door firmly and turned her attentions on the patient.

The confinement was different from when Belle had given birth to Lucy. The contractions were stronger right from the start, as if both the mother and the baby were anxious to get it over with. Belle lost all sense of time and place. She drifted in a world of pain and hard work, obeying the gentle instructions of the midwife, whose quietly confident mood passed on to Belle. She became aware of Doctor West bending over her, his glasses twinkling in the light.

'Soon be over, Mrs Walker,' he said as if everything were going according to plan. 'You can push down now.'

Belle pushed with all her might, and at the same time she prayed a silent prayer. 'If the baby's all right, God, I'll start going to mass again.' Bargaining with the Almighty, Father Joe would have called it.

No miracle happened, but someone must have heard her because she was suddenly bathed in a feeling of peace. No more pain, no more work, just a wonderful feeling of ease and quietness. God Himself must have felt like this, Belle pondered, when He'd finished creating the world and rested on the last day. She lay with closed eyes, while all around her was bustle and activity.

'Would you like to see your baby?'

Belle opened her eyes. Mrs Douglas was standing by the bed with a big smile on her face, and in her arms a shawl-wrapped bundle. Was the smile meant to indicate congratulations, or sympathy?

Then Doctor West came forward. 'Never seen such a quick and easy birth, my dear,' he said. 'Only cats and rabbits give birth that easily.'

'Is it all right?' The question was urgent.

'All right!' The doctor laughed. 'Do you mean, has it got the right number of arms and legs? The answer's yes. Don't you want to see your son?'

'Son!' Belle struggled to sit up but the midwife stopped her. Instead she bent over the bed to place the bundle in Belle's arms. Such a pretty little face she saw peeping out of the shawl; already losing the purple tinge of the new-born and becoming as pink and white as apple-blossom. Long fair lashes lay on the smooth cheek, and a hint of rusty gold fluff haloed the tiny head.

'He's going to be a redhead just like you, Mrs Walker,' Mrs Douglas said. 'He's got the beginning of it already – and your fair skin. I bet he'll have freckles as well.'

All at once Belle knew how her mother had felt about Charlie – and why. The special relationships that only mothers can have with their sons. Daughters were different: just as special, but different.

And then the baby opened his eyes, and they were large and blue. They looked up at Belle, full of intelligence, as if trying to tell her that her worries were over – he was fine. Even so she had to unwrap him to make sure he was all in one piece; to count his toes and fingers. When she found everything as it should be she cried with relief, and no one seemed to mind. Mrs Douglas patted her hand and turned away until she'd controlled herself.

Doctor West had to leave then: he had other patients to visit. Mrs Douglas tidied the room and made sure the mother and baby were comfortable; then she told Belle that she had a visitor.

'You are feeling up to it, aren't you, dear?' she asked.

Belle assured her that she was, guessing that her first visitor would be Mike. It was. He stood just inside the doorway, looking slightly overcome, until Belle stretched out her hand. As he let her draw him down to sit beside her on the bed he saw that she was the old Belle again. The frightened, tortured Belle, of the last few months had gone away. The woman on the bed, cradling her newborn son so tenderly in her arms, was the same flame-headed girl he'd fallen in love with. The dark smudges had already faded from under her eyes and her hair had regained its life and lustre. There was such happiness and love in her face that he had to hug her.

'Mind . . .' she laughed. 'Don't crush us.'

'My son!' Mike said proudly. 'What are we going to call him?'

'I'd like to call him Charlie after my brother. Because he's got ginger hair and blue eyes.'

'Charles Walker,' Mike said, trying out the name. 'I like it, but I shall call him Chas.' So it was decided as quickly as that. 'Lucy's outside,' he suddenly remembered. 'I'll fetch her in.'

Lucy was looking rather indignant after being made to wait on the landing while all the exciting things were happening behind the closed door. Her frown soon turned to a smile when she saw her new brother. She inspected him carefully, nodded her head in approval, and then headed for the door again.

'Where are you going?' Mike called after her.

She turned briefly in the doorway, balancing on one leg. 'I've got to go and tell Alan,' she informed them importantly. 'He hasn't got a baby brother – Ben's a boy now.'

They were sorry to see her go, but it did give them a chance to put their arms around each other. Their kisses were as passionate as young lovers finding each other for the first time.

Belle recovered her zest for life quickly. She was full of energy and couldn't wait to get back to work. Mike and Joyce Binns had managed things very well during her absence, but she was ready to take up the reins again. It was the height of summer, the town was full of visitors – all potential customers. Her order book was nearly full, but there was still work to do on the mural for the competition. The conference and exhibition was to take place in the Corn

Exchange and it was barely a month away.

Belle was still hoping to win. The fifty pounds prize money would be welcome, but the Certificate of Merit awarded to the winning entry would give NEEDLES & PINS added prestige in the town. She could already see it hanging on the wall in the gilt frame, in a prominent position in the shop for all to see. All the winning entries, and runners up, were going to be presented with tickets for the celebratory ball which was to take place in the banqueting hall of the Royal Pavilion.

She put down her needle with a sigh of satisfaction: the collage was finished. The women she'd allotted the work to had delivered the completed background showing the façade of the splendid palace with its arched porticoes and minarets. Belle had sewn the whole thing together and placed the figures in the foreground: the men in their tight trousers and high collars, with tall hats made of black felt. But the central figures were the Prince of Wales and Mrs Fitzherbert. The prince was just alighting from his carriage. His breeches were made of blue satin and he had a leather belt with a minute gilt buckle. Maria had real curls and ribbons in her bonnet, and her skirt was embroidered with a pattern of rosebuds.

'Well, it's the best we can do,' Belle said.

Mike started to roll the hanging carefully. 'I'll take it down to the hall for you,' he said. 'It's too heavy for you to carry. Perhaps Joyce will give me a hand if you can spare her.'

It seemed an anti-climax when they'd left with the precious parcel and Belle was alone in the shop. Chas was fast asleep upstairs, but there was plenty of work to do.

She unrolled a length of fine white linen on to the counter, and placing a pattern on to it she began to cut out a panel, biting her lip in concentration. She was so occupied that she didn't notice that she wasn't alone. A woman had entered the shop and was standing in front of a glass show-case studying a new line in underwear made from lace and cotton. She was in her thirties; tall and very smartly dressed. Her pale linen suit was beautifully cut, and on the side of her tastefully arranged hair was perched a small white hat with a blue feather.

Seeing the woman's obvious interest in the display and hoping for a customer, Belle put down her scissors and stepped forward.

'Can I help you, madam?'

'These are beautiful. Did you make them?'

'I'm the designer, and then my staff make the garments,' Belle said proudly. 'I also do most of the hand-embroidery myself.'

'Do you make blouses?' The woman was looking at the simple smocked blouse Belle was wearing, with its fluted edge and design of daisies.

'I made this myself, to my own pattern,' Belle admitted. She opened a shallow drawer and laid out some other blouses for inspection. 'I can make anything to order.'

'Quite beautiful,' the woman said again, looking pleased. 'Thank you for showing me.' She didn't place an order, just walked out of the door and disappeared in the direction of the sea-front.

'Time-wasters!' Belle muttered, but she wasn't cross. Queries often turned to orders when people were drawn back for a second look.

Mike and Joyce returned from the Corn Exchange full of their morning's work.

'The collage looks splendid,' Joyce said excitedly. 'They've given us a good position facing the main door and catching the full light. You were right about the gold thread: it makes the carriage lamps look real.'

'What about the other entries?' Belle asked. 'How good are they?'

'There are some lovely things,' Mike said. 'Paintings, and a carpet with the town's crest on it, and a fishing boat made entirely from matchsticks.'

'And a model of the Chain Pier,' Joyce reminded him.

'What about Mrs Watkins's entry?'

'It's very good,' Joyce admitted. 'There's a short-sleeved green and gold embroidered jacket to wear over the silk robe; baggy scarlet trousers and a turban, all laid out in a glass case. But I heard someone saying that she still intends to wear them when the judges come round.'

They all laughed. They still didn't believe that Lena Watkins would be bold enough to dress up as Sake Deen Mahomed, even for the sake of a competition.

On the day of the judging they closed the shop early. Maud was looking after little Chas, but Lucy had insisted on coming to the Corn Exchange with them. Belle agreed because the child seemed interested, and was also now old enough to behave herself. She had a new red dress to wear, covered in white polka-dots of which she was proud.

When they arrived they found the huge hall, which was built to stable the prince's horses, a hive of activity. Viewers and exhibitors alike milled about, passing their own opinions. Then the mayor arrived, and was led up to his seat in the gallery, his heavy gold chain of office circling his broad chest. The judges from the Association of Fine Arts started their rounds. They paused for a long time in front of Belle's collage, and made a few comments among themselves, before passing on to the next exhibit.

'They liked it, Mummy,' Lucy said in a loud voice. 'They were smiling – I'm sure we're going to win.'

'Sh!' Belle said, wishing she could be as sure.

'Look,' Mike said, touching her arm. 'There's Mrs Watkins.'

Belle couldn't help staring because Lena Watkins looked wonderful. The Indian costume suited her tiny figure so beautifully embroidered with coloured silks. The result was exquisite. The skin of her face and hands was darkened, and her grey hair tucked well away under the head-dress. On her shoulder, as perky as a bird half his age, sat Warlock the parrot, his beady eye inspecting the crowds, a happy squawk occasionally erupting from his scrawny throat.

'Good for her,' Mike said. He couldn't keep the note of admiration for the old woman out of his voice. He thought she deserved to win for her audacity alone, but he didn't say so because he didn't want to upset Belle.

Then the judges disappeared discreetly to come to their decision. Everyone wandered about aimlessly, pretending they didn't care. When they reappeared they were carrying three gilt-edged cards to attach to the winning entries. The mayor himself, in his ceremonial robes, had the job of handing out the cards.

The winner was Lena Watkins for her Sake Deen Mahomed outfit. When the announcement was made Warlock got so excited he stood on one leg and almost lost his balance. Mrs Watkins had to put up her hand to steady him and stop him falling off her shoulder. The mayor was in danger of being pecked when he tried to hand her the winning card. They all took it in good part, particularly when the crowd applauded.

The second prize went to the man who'd made the replica of the Chain Pier. The third prize was awarded to NEEDLES & PINS for their collage of the Royal Pavilion.

Belle was disappointed, but she did her best to hide it. She congratulated Mrs Watkins and kissed her on the cheek, so that Warlock hopped up and down shrieking excitedly.

Lucy sulked and was close to tears, although her mother told her there'd be other competitions, and next time they'd be sure to win. They were given their free tickets for the ball and hurried home to change. The evening was going to end with a firework display in the palace gardens so there was plenty to look forward to.

The banqueting hall at the Pavilion had been cleared for the occasion. Everything glittered with gold and silver, from the twinkling chandeliers to the statues and portraits of famous people staring down from the walls. An orchestra had been hired for the occasion, and soft music greeted them as Belle entered the room on Mike's arm. They were shown to a glass-topped table set in one of the long windows overlooking the lawns. A waiter in full dress came forward with a tray of wine-glasses.

Couples started to circle round the floor, the women's dresses as colourful as exotic butterflies. When Mike heard the strains of the *Merry Widow* waltz he led Belle out on to the floor. He was so proud and she looked so beautiful in her green voile gown, with its skirt like a sea mist floating around her shapely figure. She'd put on some of the weight she'd lost, but she was still as slender as a young girl although she was nearer thirty than twenty. Her hair hung in shining red curls to her shoulders, caught back with a silver comb, and on the bodice of her dress she wore a brooch in the likeness of a silver cat.

'I ordered champagne,' Mike said, as he led Belle back to her chair.

'But we didn't win.'

'We'll think of something else to celebrate.'

A woman was approaching their table: a tall woman wearing a beautifully cut grey evening-gown. When she smiled Belle recognised her as the woman who'd visited the shop and shown an interest in the blouses, but left without buying anything.

'I'm pleased to see you again,' she said.

Belle introduced her to Mike and he asked her to join them, but she shook her head.

'I represent a shop in London,' she said, and she named an exclusive shop in Mayfair. 'We were given your name by one of our customers. We only buy from the best fashion houses, because our clients expect first-class workmanship and materials, and are prepared to pay for them. We like to work with firms all over the country who can come up to our standards. I wondered if you'd be interested in our adding your name to our list?'

Would they indeed! Belle was too excited to reply so Mike had to speak for her.

'I know we can do business together,' the woman continued placing a card on the table. 'I'll be in touch,' and with a friendly nod she disappeared into the crowd.

Mike reached out and took Belle's hand across the table. He looked deep into her blue eyes and saw the disappointment had gone. She was sparkling with excitement. 'I think it's time to have that champagne,' he said.

While they waited for their drinks to arrive Belle picked up the card from the table. 'Look at this,' she said, holding it out with trembling hands. There was a familiar name printed in large letters – and in the corner a crest, and underneath the words:

'By appointment to Her Majesty the Queen.'

Other bestselling Warner titles available by mail:

The prices shown above are correct at time of going to press. However, the publishers reserve the right to increase prices on covers from those previously advertised without prior notice.

W

WARNER BOOKS

WARNER BOOKS
Cash Sales Department, P.O. Box 11, Falmouth, Cornwall, TR10 9EN
Tel: +44 (0) 1326 372400, Fax: +44 (0) 1326 374888
Email: books@barni.avel.co.uk.

POST AND PACKING:
Payments can be made as follows: cheque, postal order (payable to Warner Books) or by credit cards. Do not send cash or currency.

All U.K. Orders	**FREE OF CHARGE**
E.E.C. & Overseas	25% of order value

Name (Block Letters) _____

Address_____

Post/zip code:_____

☐ Please keep me in touch with future Warner publications

☐ I enclose my remittance £_____

☐ I wish to pay by Visa/Access/Mastercard/Eurocard

Card Expiry Date

_____